"I'll allow you to g

Relieved that he had believed her and unaware of his train of thought, Devon answered quickly, "Anything."

Hunter suppressed a groan. This girl didn't realize how enticing her offer was to a man whose blood sizzled through his veins. Unable to completely resist the temptation before him, he gave Devon his most charming smile: a smile that was meant to melt the coldest of hearts. "Your freedom will cost you a kiss and a promise that I'll not find you here again."

The room seemed to brighten as Devon returned Hunter's smile and raised her right hand. "A bargain, sir. You have my word."

"Then forfeit your kiss and be gone before I demand a higher price than you might be willing to pay for your freedom," Hunter murmured.

Capturing Devon in his arms, he molded her against him and lowered his lips to hers. . . .

DEVON

Cordia Byers

FAWCETT GOLD MEDAL • NEW YORK

A Fawcett Gold Medal Book
Published by Ballantine Books
Copyright © 1992 by Cordia Byers

All rights reserved under International and Pan-American Copyright Conventions. Published in the United States by Ballantine Books, a division of Random House, Inc., New York, and simultaneously in Canada by Random House of Canada Limited, Toronto.

Library of Congress Catalog Card Number: 92-90596

ISBN 0-449-14725-8

Manufactured in the United States of America

First Edition: November 1992

To Piper, my beautiful granddaughter
Love, Granny Byers.

Chapter 1

England, 1769

Golden rays of sunlight spilled through the high windows, slashing the blue haze enveloping the kitchen from the smoky fireplace. The cheerful sunbeams splashed down across the table where Cook had set out the precious oranges for her ladyship's breakfast tray. Shipped from the islands in the West Indies, the expensive bowl of fruit sat next to the silver tray that contained Queen's Ware china by Wedgwood. Presented to her ladyship on her sixtieth birthday by Josiah Wedgwood himself, her ladyship insisted she be served on nothing else. Beside the china a Belgian crystal vase containing a single scarlet rosebud from her ladyship's garden caught the sun's warm rays and splintered them into a rainbow of dazzling color. The prism added an unaccustomed display of brightness to the kitchen's otherwise gloomy atmosphere.

Those who worked at their daily tasks took no time to appreciate the momentary exhibit of beauty. They kept themselves busy, afraid of the hefty woman who ruled the kitchen much like the Queen of England herself. The strict disciplinarian was busily preparing an omelet of fresh eggs and ham that her ladyship demanded each morning promptly at nine o'clock. Cook beat the yellow eggs until they were fluffy, while keeping an eye on everything that went on in the kitchen. She was fully aware of her au-

thority. No servant in her charge would dally if they wanted
to keep their position at Mackinsey Hall.

A constant drone of noise filled the soot-blackened
chamber as her minions worked on the preparations for
dinner. The scent of burned feathers rose sickeningly in
the air as one scullion singed off the remnants of down
left on the fat hen being readied to bake. Bonnie, Cook's
helper, her cheeks rosy from the heat of the fire, stirred a
rich sugary sauce she'd been caramelizing for the custard
already in the oven. A scullery maid busied herself scrub-
bing pots and pans while Winkler, the servant boy, dawdled over a broom and a small pile of scraps that had fallen
to the floor while her ladyship's meal was being prepared.

At the servants' dining table, Higgins, the butler, sat
reading her ladyship's discarded paper and sipping a cup
of strong, dark tea. He was doing his best to keep himself
detached from the hustle and bustle surrounding him. Next
to the steward, he possessed more authority at Mackinsey
Hall than any other servant in Lady Mackinsey's employ,
but the butler was wise enough to leave the running of the
kitchen to Cook. This was her domain. She ran it like a
sergeant at arms and woe be unto anyone who tread upon
her authority. Higgins, having no taste for combat, minded
his own business when he came to the kitchen for his
morning tea.

The rattle of metal drew Higgins's attention away from
the latest London gossip. He glanced toward the doorway
that led to the coal cellar to see the tiny waif called Devon.
His gaze swept over the gaunt-featured child who lugged
a coal bucket half her size. Higgins pressed his lips into a
thin line of disgust and turned his attention back to his
paper. The child was another area where he kept his opinions to himself. He felt sorry for the little mite. Her clothes
were so big on her thin body, she looked as if she'd been
thrown into a coal bin and then wrapped in a horse blanket. Higgins shrugged off the uncomfortable feeling the

thought aroused. He knew there was nothing he could do to better the bastard child's lot in life. From the moment she had been found upon the manor doorstep, she had been relegated to the kitchens, neither lady nor servant in her father's household.

Keeping his expression guarded, Higgins glanced over the edge of his paper to the little girl struggling to maneuver the heavy bucket across the kitchen without mishap. He didn't doubt the child's parentage. The tavern wench who had given birth to Devon ten years ago had sworn her babe had been sired by Lord Mackinsey. And when the wench had been offered marriage by a farmer who refused to feed another man's bastard, she'd had no second thoughts on leaving the babe on its father's doorstep. Lord Colin Mackinsey, already possessing a well-bred wife and a mannered legitimate daughter, had given one look at the product of his liaison and immediately denied his paternity. Pretending a concern for those less fortunate than himself and proclaiming he didn't have the heart to send the child to a foundling home, he'd sent his illegitimate daughter to the kitchens to be reared by the servants.

Until his death Lord Mackinsey had refused to recognize the child as his own, but it took only one look at Devon to know who had sired her. She possessed the finely sculpted features of the Scottish Mackinseys. Like her ancestors, she, too, had eyes the color of a forest at dusk and hair so deep and dark and red it looked like aged mahogany, until sunlight made it burst into flame.

Higgins drew in a long breath and turned his attention back to the paper. He'd mentioned the child to her ladyship after Lord Mackinsey's death and he'd not be foolish enough to broach the subject again. Her ladyship, her pale, grief-stricken features pinched with age, had turned upon him, her glassy eyes riveting him to the floor like hot bits of metal. She had reprimanded him for daring to dishonor her son's memory by mentioning his past indiscretions.

She had also threatened him with immediate dismissal should he overstep himself again. No, Higgins mused as his gaze rested on the list of winners at Ascot, he'd done what he could for the child and that was that.

A loud clatter and screech jerked Higgins's attention away from his newspaper to the commotion erupting in the middle of the kitchen. Winkler, the servant boy, his freckled face alight with mischief, sidled out of Cook's path as she bore down upon Devon. Wide-eyed and skin paling beneath the sooty smudges, Devon stood her ground as Cook swooped down and grabbed her fiercely by the ear. "Ye little brat. Now look wha' ye've done! Ye've gone and spilled coal all over my clean floor."

"I didn't mean to—Ouch, let me go," Devon squealed, visibly cringing from pain. "Yer 'urting me!"

"I'll do more than hurt ye, ye little by-blow. Now get this mess cleaned up or ye'll not eat today." Cook shoved the child away in disgust. She dusted her hands together. "Her Ladyship's breakfast is awaiting to be taken up, Molly. Now be about it before Mrs. Henry comes down to see what's keeping ye from yer duties." Cook glanced once more toward the wide-eyed child. "Get this mess cleaned up or I'll have ye whipped for the luggard ye are."

Eyes shimmering like emerald glass, Devon wiped her nose on the rough woolen sleeve of her coat, leaving a slug's trail along the worn fabric. She cast an accusing glance toward the thin figure lingering in the shadowy doorway and saw Winkler grin before he disappeared from sight. Devon pressed her lips together and bent without a word to clean up the coal scattered across the floor. Swain Winkler would regret getting her in trouble again with Cook. This time she was going to make him pay for tripping her with the broom.

A half hour later and one final swipe of the rag mop, Devon cleaned up the last streak of coal soot and turned to leave. Her stomach rumbled beneath her ribs and she glanced longingly toward the warm brown loaves of bread fresh from the oven. It was still several hours before she'd be allowed to eat. She'd been late to take the slops to the pigsty and had missed the servants' breakfast, which was served promptly at six.

Again Devon's stomach gave an angry growl, and her eyes slid past the large-boned cook to the table where the bowl of oranges sat invitingly displayed. There never seemed to be enough food for her at Mackinsey Hall. Hunger was the only constant thing in her life. It lived with her day in and day out. Devon's glance slid past the bowl of fruit to the cook. During the past years she had learned early how to survive. It was wrong to steal, but to appease the ache beneath her ribs, she took a few extra morsels of food while Cook wasn't watching. A biscuit or a bit of meat snatched at the right moment helped relieve her hunger.

Devon's gaze flickered over the scullery maid wiping the large dough table free of flour, on past Bonnie, still busy at the fire, and back to the broad back of the cook. Throat dry, Devon snaked out a small shaking hand. It closed over one of the precious oranges. In less than a blink it was safely tucked into the pocket of her tattered coat. A triumphant glimmer entered Devon's eyes. As usual there was a certain thrill of excitement—as well as a niggling of guilt—that accompanied her thievery. She pushed both emotions aside and turned to leave the kitchen with her ill-gotten treasure.

"Ye little thief. Ye'll not steal in my kitchen and get by with it," Cook yelled, clamping a red, work-roughened hand down on Devon's thin shoulder and spinning her around. She glared down at the child, her heavy features mottling with fury. "I've suspected it was you who's been stealing from my pantry, but I didn't have proof until now."

Devon swallowed uneasily. Even at ten years of age she

knew the price thieves paid for their crimes. She'd seen their vulture-picked bodies hanging from the tree at the fork in the road near the village.

Cook swiveled her head toward Higgins. "I want the sheriff called immediately. I'll not have a thief in my kitchen."

Higgins slowly came to his feet and cleared his throat. "Now, Cook. Surely you don't mean to call the sheriff because the child took an orange?"

"I most surely do. The brat has been thieving for some time. I've missed cheese and bread as well as pieces of meat. And now she's taken one of Her Ladyship's oranges." Cook reached into Devon's pocket and retrieved the fruit. She shook it in front of Devon's nose.

Higgins cut in, "Cook, be reasonable. She's only a child."

Cook, her eyes red and bulging with fury, looked down at Devon. "A thief is a thief, no matter what the age. Better to let the sheriff see justice done than to have this little bastard stealing until she's grown. It's an orange now. Next it'll be the silver if I don't put a stop to it. Us poor, honest, hard-working souls deserve better than to have a thief among us."

Higgins drew in a long breath, suppressing the urge to remind Cook exactly who the child was. Devon was stealing her own food. She was a Mackinsey.

"No matter what you say, I'll not turn over a child to be hanged because of an orange without first speaking with Lady Mackinsey. Since Lord Colin's death, she is the one responsible for Mackinsey Hall . . . as well as those who reside within it." Higgins looked down at Devon. "Go on now. Get out of here."

Devon glanced uncertainly from the butler to the cook and quickly decided it was in her own best interest to take his advice. For the moment she had a reprieve. Pulling free of the restraining hand on her shoulder, she dashed out of the kitchen. She ran toward the stables and the dark little haven she'd found in the hayloft. Casting a quick glance about, she scurried up the ladder and over the bales of sweet-smelling hay. She slid back the planks that hid the small boxed space and scrambled inside. She tugged the boards back into place, shutting out the harsh world beyond the cozy warmth of her hiding place. Curling herself into a tight little ball, Devon hugged her bony legs to her chest and pressed her eyes against the rough material covering her knees. At last she released the first sign of emotion in a shaky half sob. Her chest burned with the need to cry, but no tears came to release her pent-up fears. She'd learned years ago that tears did no good. They only gave strength to those who wielded the power. Tears were a visible sign of weakness that an enemy used against you.

Devon shuddered. Soon the sheriff would be summoned and she'd be hanged. Devon raised her head and wiped her nose on her sleeve. She had little hope of being saved by 'er ladyship. It would be beneath Lady Mackinsey to interfere with Cook's decision.

A mutinous light entered Devon's forest green eyes and she thrust her small chin out at a pugnacious angle. The thought of ''her betters'' upstairs always made her hackles rise. The memory of the first time she'd heard the rumor of her parentage was still as fresh and as painful as if it had happened only yesterday. She'd been six when she began to understand the taunts made about her by the other servants. Instead of being hurt with the realization that her father was Lord Mackinsey, she'd been so thrilled she'd sneaked into his study one sunny afternoon to meet the man. She'd never forget the look he'd given her when she burst out from behind the door and grabbed him about the legs, calling him Papa. Horrified, Lord Mackinsey shoved her away like any minor annoyance and ordered her back to the kitchen. Undeterred by his reaction, she'd tried to make him understand that she was his daughter.

With nostrils narrowing as if a foul odor were present, lips thinning into a flat line of derision, Lord Mackinsey had looked contemptuously down at her. He spared no thought to her six-year-old heart as he told her, in no uncertain terms, that there was no place in his life for the product of one night's indiscretion. He had finished by reminding her that he owed her nothing more than she was already receiving. He told her that she should be grateful that he'd not sent her away, but if she persisted in embarrassing him by claiming a kinship, he'd be forced to send her to a foundling home.

The meeting with her father had been brutal and heartbreaking. It had also brought home the stark reality of what she had already learned from living in her father's household. She could depend upon no one but herself to survive. It had been a hard lesson at a young age, but it had held her in good stead since that day. It was the only thing she could say her father had ever given her.

"And Higg'ns thinks 'er Ladyship will stop Cook from calling the sheriff. Umph!" Devon muttered in disgust, her cynicism far older than her ten years of age. "I'll be meeting me maker in a blink if it's left up to 'er Ladyship." A resolute expression settled over Devon's features. "But before I go, Swain Winkler is goin' to pay for the trouble he's given me. 'e'll wear a black eye to me 'angin'."

Sliding back the board, Devon crawled from her hiding place, straightened her ragged coat, pushed up her sleeves, swiped an unruly curl from her soot-smudged brow, and squared her shoulders. She marched to the ladder and climbed down. Winkler would be hiding out, like the rat he was, near the granary.

A lazy whistle alerted Devon to Winkler's presence before she saw him. Quietly she edged along the rough stone wall of the storehouse and peered around the corner. Winkler lay with shoulders propped against the wall, one leg casually draped over a knee, one thick-soled clog dangling from a stockinged foot. He twirled a twig of grass between his grubby fingers, content with the day.

Devon stepped around the corner, hands on hips, face set, legs spread. "Ye ain't getting away with it this time, Winkler."

Winkler jumped with a start. Spying his adversary, he scrambled to his feet and took a step backward. He was two years older than Devon and a head taller, but there was something about the small girl that sent a chill down his spine. He enjoyed playing tricks on people and watching them get into trouble, but at heart he had no taste for confrontation of any kind. A coward, Winkler swallowed nervously and licked his lips. "I was just teasing, Devon."

"And I'm goin' to be just teasing when I put my fist down yer throat," Devon ground out between clenched teeth. She took a menacing step forward.

His stomach sinking, Winkler blustered, "Ye can't whip me. 'm bigger than ye, runt."

Before the words were completely out of his mouth, Devon launched herself at Winkler, her fist catching him squarely in the jaw. He screamed and turned—and ran toward the safety of the manor house. Devon gave chase. She caught him just as Winkler scurried over the fence behind the stables. They tumbled into a pile of manure the stable boys had shoveled out of the stalls earlier that morning. Winkler fell facedown into the stench as Devon clambered onto his back, hitting him and pulling his hair. Winkler cowered. Covering his head with his arms and kicking his feet helplessly, he screamed for mercy. None was forthcoming. Devon didn't relent from her revenge until a hand at the nape of her neck jerked her away from the servant boy.

"Sweet Jesus! Look at you! Can't you stay out of trouble?" Higgins asked, exasperated. The corners of his mouth drawn downward in distaste, his nostrils pinched from the odor, he held Devon away from his own immaculate attire.

Devon pulled free of Higgins's hand and straightened her coat. Ignoring the stench rising from her own clothing, she flashed a mutinous look at the butler before turning her attention back to the sobbing Winkler. The boy struggled to his feet and stood watching Devon warily. " 'e's the reason I'm in trouble, and I'm goin' to see 'e pays before I 'ang."

"My God, child. You're not going to hang for stealing an orange."

"Then the magistrates 'ill send me to prison, but I intend to see 'e knows what it's like to suffer before I go."

Higgins shook his head. "You're not going to prison, either. I've talked with Lady Mackinsey and she wants to see you before she makes any decision on what to do."

Devon's head snapped up and she looked at Higgins, unable to believe what he'd just said. " 'er ladyship wants to see me?"

"She does," Higgins said, repressing his own apprehension about the coming meeting. Lady Mackinsey had said she would decide the fate of the child who had set Cook off on a tangent to call the sheriff. What worried Higgins was his own position at Mackinsey Hall when her ladyship realized the child was her granddaughter. Higgins knew he was risking his career and pension to help the little waif. The prospect of dismissal wasn't heartening to a man of his age, and it was taking every ounce of courage he possessed to follow through with his plan to bring Devon and her grandmother together.

"I don't want to see 'er," Devon muttered, setting her small jaw at a stubborn angle. Her meeting with her father had taught her she'd receive no mercy from the Mackinseys at Mackinsey Hall. It would be less painful to be sent directly to the sheriff instead of having to face 'er ladyship and see the scorn in her eyes as she denied leniency.

"Don't talk foolish, child. Now come along and get yourself cleaned up. I'll not take you in to see Lady Mackinsey covered in dung."

Devon remained still. "I said I don't want to see 'er."

Higgins's patience snapped. He had already risked too much to allow Devon's streak of Mackinsey stubbornness to thwart him now. "It was not a request but an order. Now go and get yourself cleaned up. You will meet with Lady Mackinsey within the hour or I'll have you whipped myself."

Not waiting for Devon's response, Higgins turned and marched back toward the manor house, his back straight, his head high, and a frown of concern creasing his brow.

Devon watched him go. She glanced toward the boy, who still stood regarding her warily. "I'm not goin' to 'urt ye again, Winkler." She shook her small head. "Ye deserve everythin' I gave ye and more, but it's over now." Devon glanced once more toward the manor house. "Everythin's over now."

"Sorry, Devon. I didn't know I'd be gettin' ye into such trouble with me pranks. I just wanted to 'ave a little fun. I meant no 'arm." Winkler sniffled. "I don't want to see ye 'anged. Yer me friend."

Devon blinked at the older boy, wondering at his use of the term *friend*. If the way Winkler treated her was a sign of friendship, she could well do without it. Devon didn't voice her feelings. The woebegone, guilty expression on Winkler's face stopped any remark. It wasn't his fault now that she would hang. "Ye've played many a prank on me, but yer not the cause if I 'ang. I stole an orange."

Winkler's face lit with new respect for the younger girl. "Ye really snatched one of 'er Ladyship's precious oranges?"

Devon nodded. "I was hungry."

"Gawd, Devon, ye do have a nerve. And it's proud I

am to call ye me friend.'' He stuck out his grubby hand.
''No more tricks, Devon. Ye 'ave me word on it.''

Expecting another trick at any moment, Devon hesi-
tantly accepted Winkler's hand. He smiled at her and then
clapped her on the back. ''They'll not 'ang ye, Dev. We
won't let that 'appen.''

A half hour later Devon stood nervously before Higgins,
her small face framed by damp tendrils of rich mahogany
silk. She'd scrubbed the soot and manure off in a tub of
cold water in the laundry room and changed into the only
other set of clothing she possessed, a ragged shirt and
patched skirt.

Higgins inspected her from head to toe and nodded his
approval. ''You'll do. Now come along. Lady Mackinsey
is awaiting us in the drawing room.''

Mouth dry and eyes wide with mounting trepidation,
Devon followed the butler along the carpeted hallway to
the wide double doors that led into her ladyship's exclusive
domain. She swallowed with difficulty as Higgins rapped
lightly against the polished walnut panel. Her breath froze
in her throat at the sound of the soft voice that bade them
enter.

The door swung open and Devon looked upon her
grandmother. She strained against the hand Higgins placed
between her bony shoulders to urge her forward. She didn't
want to enter the dimly lit chamber where the regal old
woman sat in a pool of golden light provided by the oil
lamp on the table beside her chair. Thick burgundy velvet
drapes covered the tall leaded windows overlooking the
rose garden, effectively shutting out the sunlight. Gray
head bowed, Devon couldn't see the dowager's features.

''My lady. I've brought the child,'' Higgins announced,
shoving the reluctant Devon into the room ahead of him.

Lady Mackinsey glanced up as Higgins and Devon
paused near her chair. It took an effort to collect her

thoughts from the morose gloom that had shrouded her mind since her son's death. Day after day she sat in the darkened sanctum of the drawing room, praying for death to come and take her as it had taken her beloved son and his family. Regrettably God had not seen fit to answer her prayers.

Squinting at the butler, she cleared her throat. "My lorgnette, Higgins. I want to take a look at him before I decide his fate."

Higgins retrieved the eyeglasses from the table and placed them in Lady Mackinsey's blue-veined hand. He smiled to himself as she raised it and peered down her long, thin nose at the child who stood before her. Her imperious mannerisms, as innate as the color of her eyes, reminded him of the woman he'd served before the accident claimed her son's life. Since that time he'd seen little of the Lady Mackinsey he'd known for nearly twenty-five years. Grief had waged a successful campaign upon the seventy-year-old woman. Her body had weakened until she was little more than a shrunken shell of her former robust self. It was only at times such as this that her grief was set aside and she once more became the grand dame of Mackinsey Hall.

Lady Mackinsey studied Devon thoughtfully for a long, tense moment and then turned her puzzled gaze up toward Higgins. "This child is female, Higgins."

"Aye, my lady," Higgins answered, focusing his attention on the far wall in an effort to repress a smile.

Lady Mackinsey's frown deepened the creases about her mouth as she turned her dark gaze back upon Devon. She clicked her tongue in disgust. "What is this world coming to? Now the females are turning to thievery."

"Yes, my lady. Cook feels the same. She wants this culprit sent to the sheriff to hang."

"Perhaps I should heed her wishes," Lady Mackinsey said, her eyes never leaving Devon's thin, pale features.

Higgins flashed a startled glance toward Lady Mackinsey. "My lady, she is only a child of ten years of age. Surely you can't mean to see her hanged?"

Lady Mackinsey flashed Higgins a silencing look and a glimmer of a smile touched her lips for the first time since her son's death. She gave an imperceptible shake of her graying head. "I'll decide her fate once I hear why she stole one of my oranges."

Higgins glanced down at Devon and ordered: "Tell Lady Mackinsey why you took the orange."

Her eyes glued to the lush carpet at her feet, Devon remained still, unable to look at or speak to her grandmother.

"Child, you have nothing to fear from me if you tell me the truth. I have always been fair in my dealing with servants," Lady Mackinsey said. "Now tell me why you took the orange."

Devon moistened her dry lips, flashed Higgins an anguished glance before she slowly raised her head to look at the woman who sat in judgment upon her. Her eyes wide, anxious pools the color of the forest at twilight, she cleared her throat and said, "I was hungry."

Lady Mackinsey opened her mouth to say that none of her servants ever went hungry at Mackinsey Hall. The words died in her throat as she looked fully into the child's face for the first time. She saw her son looking back at her through the thick-lashed green eyes. Lady Mackinsey allowed herself a moment to take in the rich mahogany hair, fair, flawless skin, and the sweetly shaped lips, but her gaze was drawn back to the child's eyes. Within them Colin still lived. Lady Mackinsey felt her heart skip a beat before beginning a rapid tattoo against her ribs. She clutched at the suddenly tight black bombazine covering her chest and gasped for breath as her eyes snapped to the man standing beside the child.

"This was your plan all along, wasn't it?" Her accusation seemed to shatter the stillness that had invaded the chamber.

"My lady?" Higgins said, feigning ignorance.

"You've concocted this entire scheme about stealing oranges to get her into my presence."

"My lady, I don't know what you mean. Cook wants this child sent immediately to the sheriff. I only wanted your opinion before I carried out her wishes."

"Don't lie to me, Higgins. I know you too well—"

"He's not lying, yer ladyship," Devon interrupted. "I did steal the orange."

Lady Mackinsey flashed Devon a contemptuous look. "Do you expect me to believe you stole an orange because you were hungry? Ridiculous! There is plenty of food at Mackinsey Hall so no servant would have to resort to stealing. I have always prided myself on seeing that my servants are well treated. There is no need to try to protect Higgins. I know this was all a scheme to get me to see you. But it's not going to do any good."

Devon thrust out her small chin, her lower lip trembling. Her green eyes sparkled with the light of battle as she looked up at the old woman. She knew from the experience with her father that she'd receive no mercy at the hands of her relatives. Lady Mackinsey would summon the sheriff, and she'd be hanged for her crimes. Old for her years, Devon accepted her fate, but she couldn't allow the woman to blame Higgins. He was the only person at Mackinsey Hall who had ever had a kind word for her and he'd not be here now had he not tried to help her. "Me lady, send me to hang, but don't blame 'iggins for me crimes. He's a good man."

"*My* lady," Lady Mackinsey corrected automatically, feeling the first stirrings of admiration for the small girl. She stood brave and defiant, fully accepting her guilt, but ready to defend the butler. "And why should I not blame Higgins? He is the one responsible for bringing you here."

"My lady," Devon said, her tongue sliding uneasily over the correct pronunciation, "I'm not asking ye to save me from 'anging, but ye can't blame 'iggins for having a tender heart. He didn't mean to upset ye. 'e was only trying to 'elp me. 'e's a good man, my lady."

Lady Mackinsey took in the resolute tilt of Devon's chin and her flashing eyes. The child had inherited much of the Mackinsey spirit. With that thought, a chill rippled down the dowager's spine.

Lady Mackinsey shifted her gaze away from the child. Colin, my dear, beloved Colin, she mused silently as her crooked, aged fingers picked absently at the dark material of her skirt. Until this moment she had been able to look upon Colin's life-style with a blind eye. He was her son, and that was all that had mattered to her. She had loved him more than anything else on earth.

Lady Mackinsey expelled a long, sad breath and looked back at the child her son had sired. She had known the truth the moment she'd looked into Devon's eyes, but to recognize her as a Mackinsey was to recognize Colin as what he was—a spoiled, irresponsible man who had lived as he had seen fit, without a care for anyone else in the world. A man cruel enough to sentence his own offspring to a life of drudgery.

Her hand trembled as she reached out and cupped Devon's small chin in her palm. She stared down into the eyes so much like her son's and acknowledged her own guilt. Her blindness toward her son's actions had denied this child even food to put into her mouth and had forced her to resort to stealing. Lady Mackinsey glanced away from Devon to the tall, slender butler who stood tense and anxious, awaiting her decision upon both their fates. A weak smile touched her wrinkled lips. "I should have known long before now."

Higgins breathed a sigh of relief. He understood the torment laced in her words and nodded. "There is no crime in making a mistake, my lady. The crime comes only when you know the truth and then don't try to change things.''

Lady Mackinsey nodded her comprehension. "Thank you, Higgins. I won't forget what you have done.''

"It has been my pleasure, my lady,'' Higgins answered, and smiled his satisfaction.

Confused, Devon listened to the exchange between the butler and Lady Mackinsey. Suddenly Lady Mackinsey was acting as if Higgins were an old friend who had done her a great favor. She looked from one face to the other, trying to puzzle out the situation.

Lady Mackinsey turned her attention back to Devon and her lined features cracked with a wide smile. "Devon, you will not be sent to the sheriff, but you are to be sent away.''

Devon shot an anxious glance at Higgins and rapidly shook her head. "I won't steal anythin' else. I promise. Please don't send me to a foundling home.''

"You're not being sent to a foundling home. You're to go to a very exclusive school. Only young ladies of quality are sent to Mistress Cameron's Academy for Young Ladies.''

Devon looked at Lady Mackinsey as if she'd suddenly lost her wits. "I ain't no lady of quality.''

"You soon will be. Once you learn all Mistress Cameron can teach you, you will return to Mackinsey Hall to take your rightful place as my granddaughter.''

Knowing the dowager had surely lost her mind, Devon took a step back and cast Higgins a dubious look that spoke more loudly than words. He smiled smugly down at her. "It's true, Devon. You are Lady Mackinsey's granddaughter.''

"I know that,'' Devon answered, her tone implying that everyone knew of her relationship with the lady of Mackinsey Hall.

"Then you understand why you must go to Mistress

Cameron's Academy. My heir must not live and work in the kitchens, nor must she talk and act like a scullery wench. She must be a lady in all respects.''

Lady Mackinsey turned her attention once more to Higgins and began to give orders. She instructed him to have Devon's belongings moved to the room down the hall from her own chambers in the east wing. Then he was to summon her seamstress from London while she wrote to Mistress Cameron to inform her that her granddaughter would be arriving shortly and that she expected the best attention money could buy for the child.

God had seen fit to give her another granddaughter and she intended to make sure Devon filled the place in society vacated by her beautiful Eunice. Devon could never take Eunice's place in her heart, but she could help ease the loneliness left by the other girl's death.

Bewildered, Devon drifted along on the wave of excitement Lady Mackinsey had set into motion. She didn't know what to feel or how to react to the sudden turn of events. She had come here expecting to be sent to her death. Now she was being sent to a school for young ladies—to be groomed to take her rightful place as the Mackinsey heir. It was too much for her ten-year-old mind to comprehend. All Devon knew was that her life was being turned upside down by the woman who had, until a few moments ago, chosen to ignore her very existence.

Chapter 2

London, England, 1777

The muted light of the streetlamp managed to penetrate only a few feet through the thick fog swirling in from the river. A giant octopus of misty vapor wrapped its tentacles around London, enclosing it within its chilling embrace. The damp, murky night encapsulated anyone brave or foolhardy enough to venture out on foot from their homes. It obscured their vision and made their senses less acute, leaving them vulnerable to those who thrived in the darkness of the night.

The sound of hurried footsteps echoed eerily along the cobbled street before a shadowy figure emerged from the darkness. Dressed in black from head to toe, his features hidden by the black tricorne he wore, he paused in the circle of dim light. He cast a furtive glance about as he retrieved a watch from the inside pocket of his waistcoat. The gold metal gleamed against the black leather of his gloved hand as he checked the time and then snapped it shut. He tipped his head to one side, listening intently for anyone who might have followed him. Satisfied his passage had gone unnoted, he merged once more with the darkness beyond the streetlamp.

He made no sound, moving with the stealth and grace of his namesake. The phantom, who had become known to his victims as the Shadow, traveled along the damp streets, toward his destination on St. James Square. Spying the three-storied mansion he'd come to rob, he gripped the thick-vined ivy covering the brick wall and bounded up and over.

The Shadow landed lightly on the other side, the damp earth muffling the sound of his footsteps. He paused, drew out a black mask, and tied it about his features before he moved toward the home of the wealthy Lord Trevor Montmain.

The luxurious town house was only one among many in the exclusive section of St. James Square. Built of bricks, with tiled roofs and glazed windows, the elegant mansions housed the cream of Britain's society during London's social season. Every night along the square, sumptuous balls were given to display the wealth of their owners. Diamonds, emeralds, and rubies glittered in the light of a thousand candles as London's elite swirled beneath crystal chandeliers to the soft music of Bach and the latest genius in the world of music: Mozart. The cost of one extravagant gown a lady wore would feed several of London's poor families for a year.

The thought helped lessen the guilt that lay in the Shadow's stomach like tainted meat. By telling himself that men like Lord Montmain could well afford the loss of a few baubles and coins, the Shadow could deal with the prick of conscience that accompanied each burglary. Drawing in a resolute breath, the Shadow gazed up at the window on the second floor. If his information were correct, he'd find his prize in Lord Montmain's dressing room, behind the thick velvet drapes.

The Shadow scanned the house. His informant had said Lord Montmain would be out for the evening, enjoying himself at Lord and Lady Fitzroy's ball, but he didn't want to risk running into any of the servants. Seeing no light coming from any of the high leaded windows, the Shadow smiled his satisfaction. Like most employees of the rich, Lord Montmain's staff was using his absence to retire early.

The Shadow once more used the lush green ivy growing up the brick wall as a ladder to reach his destination. He eased open the window sash and agilely slipped inside. He quickly realized his mistake about all being dark when he eased back the burgundy velvet drapes drawn over the window. The thick fabric had served to prevent any light from escaping the house. Peering between the heavy folds of cut velvet, the Shadow glanced uneasily at the slice of light coming from the bedchamber beyond the door. Heart pounding, he listened for any sound to indicate a presence in the adjoining room. Hearing nothing, he released a long, slow breath and moved from his hiding place. Spying his treasure on the dressing table, he moved swiftly toward the pile of gold coins and diamond stickpin. The carpet silenced his passage.

A confident smile touched his lips as he reached for the gleaming reward of his night's work. The coins would make things easier for a few more days. His fingers were only inches away from the booty when the sound of movements in the next room made his hand freeze in midair.

"Trevor, oh, Trevor! That feels wonderful," a husky female voice said. "Do it again."

A deep, throaty chuckle emanated and then was followed by the sound of movement on slick, satin sheets. Again a soft female moan broke the silence.

"You like that, don't you, Cecily?"

"Yes, love," Cecily panted.

Frozen to the spot, the Shadow swallowed uncomfortably as he realized what was taking place in the adjoining room.

"Open to my lips and tongue," Trevor whispered, his voice husky with passion.

The Shadow shifted uneasily and glanced once more toward the glittering gem lying on the dressing table.

"Oh, Trevor-r-r! John never pleases me this way. Take me now, love. I need you!" was Cecily's breathless plea.

Hand shaking from the close proximity to those in the adjoining room—as well as to their activity—the Shadow reached for the coins and pin. He wanted to put as much distance between Lord Montmain and his ladyfriend as quickly as possible. Haste making him careless, his hand brushed against the crystal candlestick as his fingers closed about his prize. It clinked against the mirror, the sound dangerously loud in the Shadow's ears.

All sound ceased in the bedchamber.

"What was that?" Lord Montmain grumbled, his voice hoarse from the strain of interrupted pleasure.

"What was what?" asked Cecily, her voice little more than a pant.

"I thought I heard something in the dressing room."

"It's probably only your valet," Cecily murmured. The bed squeaked.

"My servants know they are forbidden to come up here when I have guests."

"Oh, bother the servants and everything else, Trevor." Again the bed squeaked.

A deep chuckle came from the bedchamber. "You just can't keep that hot little ass still, can you?"

"Not when I want something," Cecily purred. The bed squeaked several times in succession. Lord Montmain's moan of pleasure filtered into the dressing room.

"God, you're a ripe one. John must be a fool to let such a woman as you out of his sight," Montmain breathed as the bed's rope springs began a steady rhythm.

The Shadow released the breath frozen in his throat and pocketed the coins and diamond stickpin. Casting one last uneasy glance toward the bedchamber, he quietly made his way back to the open window and slipped out into the mist-shrouded night.

The phantom figure moved swiftly away from St. James

Square. He didn't breathe a sigh of relief until he reached the dark alley where his informant awaited. Tonight had been too close for comfort. He had broken one of his own strict rules. He had assumed Montmain wasn't at home without making sure that he was at Lord and Lady Fitzroy's ball.

The Shadow slipped off the black leather gloves and untied the black mask. Tucking them into the pocket of his black superfine coat, he climbed into the coach, where his bowlegged companion awaited.

"What did ye get tonight?"

The Shadow dropped the diamond stickpin into the calloused hand. His companion lifted it and turned it about in the light from the coach lantern. He gauged its value. "It'll bring a few shilling, but it 'on't be enough to pay fer all ye need. Couldn't ye have gotten something a little bit more valuable?"

"I might have, had Lord Montmain not been home this evening."

"At 'ome? Sweet Jesus! 'e didn't see ye, did 'e?"

"Fortunately not. He was otherwise occupied," the Shadow answered, and looked away from the curious brown eyes.

"Ye don't mean what I think ye mean, do ye?"

The Shadow nodded uncomfortably. "If you're asking if Lord Montmain was in bed with a woman, yes, that's exactly what I'm saying." The Shadow flashed a guilty glance at the man at his side. "I'm afraid when I realized I wasn't alone, I didn't take the time to search for anything of more value."

A calloused hand came to rest on the Shadow's shoulder. "Let's get 'ome before a thief decides to take it into 'is mind to rob us."

The Shadow chuckled, relieved to let the subject drop. "The way my luck is going tonight, it wouldn't surprise me."

"There'll be other nights."

The Shadow leaned back against the aged leather seat and nodded, resigned to the fact that there must be other nights like this one. There would be more robberies and more danger to be faced. It had been that way for more years than the Shadow cared to remember. He glanced out of the foggy coach window and wondered when it was ever going to stop.

Devon opened the door to the darkened bedchamber. Quietly she crossed the thick carpet and set the bed tray down on the side table before pulling open the thick drapes. The morning sun streamed in through the leaded panes, chasing away the gloom that clung tenaciously to the corners of the room. The warm rays bathed the shrunken figure on the bed in soft light and disturbed her restless slumber. Thin, stubby lashes fluttered open and the old woman stared vaguely at her surroundings.

Unable to breathe while lying flat, Lady Mackinsey lay propped up against the fat down-filled pillows. It took a moment to orient herself and focus her gaze enough to recognize her granddaughter. A semblance of a smile touched her bloodless lips before she drew in an agonized breath and closed her eyes once more.

Her heart constricting, Devon plastered a smile on her own lips as she lifted the tray and crossed to a high four-poster bed. "Good morning, Grandmama. I've brought a surprise with your breakfast: fresh oranges."

With an effort Lady Mackinsey slowly opened her eyes and looked up at her granddaughter from a face deeply lined from time and illness. It took every ounce of willpower she possessed to force her throat to work. "I'm not hungry."

Devon's cheery smile wobbled as she bent over to adjust the bedclothing. She couldn't allow her concern for her grandmother's health to be seen. "I'm sure once you have tasted the orange your appetite will return. After you've eaten I have a treat for you. Lady Agatha allowed me to borrow her copy of Goldsmith's *The Vicar of Wakefield*. She felt you would enjoy it.''

''I'm not hungry, child. You enjoy the orange,'' Lady Mackinsey whispered.

An uneasy sensation tingled up Devon's spine and she glanced about the room. She felt the black angel's ominous presence hovering nearby, just waiting to reach out and take her grandmother into his cold embrace. Devon absently rubbed at her arms. The specter of death watched and waited, and there was nothing she could do to stop him from claiming her grandmother's fragile life.

''I brought the orange for you to eat, Grandmama. You have to eat to keep up your strength.''

Lady Mackinsey's face mirrored the strain as she raised one crooked finger to caress Devon's rose-tinted cheek. ''Had it not been for an orange I would have missed out on all these years with you.''

Devon pressed a kiss against the translucent skin and held the fingers within her own. She nodded. ''You've given me so much, Grandmama. During the past eight years my life has been wonderful; I'll always be grateful.''

''I've given you only what was rightfully yours.'' Lady Mackinsey's voice faltered and she struggled to draw in a wheezing breath before she could continue. ''You filled a place in my heart after Eunice's and Colin's deaths, and I'm the one who should be grateful to you.''

Tenderly Devon placed Lady Mackinsey's hand back on the satin comforter. Even after all this time she didn't like to talk about her father and her half-sister. She knew she would still be working in the kitchen at Mackinsey Hall had they lived. Devon pushed the thought from her mind. It was ungrateful of her to even think in such a way. Her grandmother had publicly recognized her by legal adoption, making her the heir to the Mackinsey estate. She had given her the best education money could buy, molding her into a lady who could proudly hold up her head in society. She owed her grandmother more than she could ever repay.

"Grandmama, we have talked enough. It's time for you to eat. You must keep up your health so you'll be well enough to attend my wedding when the time comes."

Lady Mackinsey's crooked fingers fidgeted with the satin comforter. Her watery gaze anxiously searched Devon's lovely features. She knew she didn't have much time left and agonized over the thought of leaving Devon alone in the world. If she could see her married, she would be willing to leave this decrepit, pain-ridden body behind for the comfort of death. "Have you had an offer?"

Devon shifted her attention to peeling and quartering the expensive orange. "No. Not as yet. But I soon expect one from Lord Sumner."

"Lord Sumner?" Lady Mackinsey whispered, fighting to keep a ragged cough at bay. "I don't believe I know him."

Devon busied herself spreading the napkin across the front of Lady Mackinsey's linen gown. "I'm sure you have made his acquaintance, but have only forgotten. Lord Sumner is well known to Lady Agatha."

Lady Mackinsey gave a feeble nod. "I'm sure you are right. Of late it's hard to recall all of the names of the prominent families, much less their offspring."

"When you're feeling better, I'll introduce Lord Sumner to you," Devon said as she settled herself on the side of the bed and attempted to feed Lady Mackinsey the orange that had cost more than it would take to feed the entire household for the day. Devon didn't begrudge her grandmother her fondness for the fruit. She wanted to keep everything as normal as possible. Lady Mackinsey must never suspect the dire financial straits they were in. She feared the worry would snuff out the tiny cinder of life that remained in her grandmother's fragile body.

Lady Mackinsey made a valiant effort to eat. She managed a few bites before the exertion became too much. Breathing heavily, she lay her grizzled head back against the satin pillows and closed her eyes. In less than a moment she slipped into an exhausted sleep.

Devon released a long breath. Tiny lines of worry creased her brow as she set the tray aside and wiped the sticky orange juice from her fingers. Her grandmother's health deteriorated further every day. Devon closed her eyes. She felt so helpless. There was nothing she could do to stop her grandmother from slipping away. Time and age were against her. All she could do was make her grandmother's last days as comfortable as possible.

Devon tucked the sheets about the old woman and placed a kiss on the withered brow. She'd not allow the financial situation facing her family to harm this kind woman. It was a situation created during the years when Devon had been a servant in her own father's house. A situation that had grown worse after Lord Mackinsey's death. Her grandmother had been reared as a lady, not an estate manager. She had left Mackinsey Hall's affairs in the hands of an unscrupulous steward and he, knowing his employer knew nothing of business, had made himself rich by pocketing the profits.

Devon had learned of the situation soon after returning from school. The debts had gone unpaid for so long that the creditors were threatening to foreclose on Mackinsey Hall, leaving her family and their retainers without even a roof over their heads.

Quietly Devon left her grandmother's room and made her way down the back stairs to the kitchen. Taking the apron from the hook, she tied it about her slender waist and then crossed to the fireplace, where a pot of watery broth simmered. Tipping the lid, she nodded her satisfaction. When she added the vegetables, it would become oxtail soup.

Devon covered the pot and turned to the scarred worktable, where she'd left the carrots and potatoes before taking up her grandmother's breakfast tray. The few small, round pieces of oxtail had been all the meat she could afford to purchase after buying the orange for her grandmother. Resigned to the fact that she, Higgins, and Winkler, the only servants who had remained with her, would have to pull in their belts again tonight, she set about peeling the carrots and potatoes.

"How's Her Ladyship this morning?" Higgins asked as he closed the kitchen door behind him and slipped off his rain-drenched cloak. He shook the beads of moisture from it and draped it about a chair to dry.

Devon looked up at her friend. Her fathomless green eyes were anxious as she replied, "She's growing weaker by the day."

Higgins crossed to the fireplace and lifted the lid of the pot simmering over the flames. "Soup again?"

Devon nodded. "Hopefully there'll be more tomorrow. I've sent Winkler to pay the rent and the seamstress's bill, so we don't have to worry about those again until next month."

Higgins settled his arthritic frame in a straight-backed chair across from Devon. His frown was the only visible sign of the pain his movements created. Inflamed by the cool, damp weather, his joints were so swollen that it took an effort to move. He could barely clasp his hands in front of him on the table. Pushing aside his own discomfort, he turned his attention to Devon, who was preparing the vegetables for the soup. His thin face, age-lined and hollow-cheeked, showed his mounting concern for his young friend. "How much longer do you think you can go on like this, Devon?"

Without looking up, Devon conceded, "As long as I

have to. You know it would kill Grandmother should we lose Mackinsey Hall to the creditors.''

"But it's not your fault. You shouldn't have to sacrifice your own happiness to keep that heap of stones. It's not right.''

"As you already know, the jewelry and everything else of value was sold long ago. I'm the only thing I have left to sell now. If finding a husband will save Mackinsey Hall, then I must do it. I owe Grandmother that much, Higgins. She went into debt to educate me to be a lady.''

"Humph! Look how far that fancy education has gotten you, Your Ladyship. You're still a servant in the kitchen, even though you are now the Mackinsey heir. You don't have a lady's maid to even help you dress to go out to the fancy balls, and it's taking every pence you possess to even buy the gowns to wear. You can't afford to entertain any of the high-and-mighty lords you meet because oxtail soup is all you have in the house to eat.''

Devon chopped down sharply on one thick carrot, sending the two pieces in different directions. Her green eyes snapped with annoyance as she looked at her friend. "That's enough. The welfare of the family is now my responsibility since Grandmother is no longer able to continue as head of the household. I'm doing what I think is right. Once I marry, everything will be fine. My husband will see the creditors are paid and that Mackinsey Hall is safe.''

"Devon, listen to me. Let it go. Lady Mackinsey can't live much longer, and there is no reason to tie yourself to a man you don't love because of the debts she and your father incurred over the years by their extravagant lifestyles.'' Seeing the mutinous light that flickered in Devon's eyes, Higgins raised a hand to stay her protest. "I know you feel you owe Lady Mackinsey a great deal, but you don't owe Her Ladyship your happiness. Your responsibility to her ends at her death. You have to think of your own future.''

"I have been thinking of my own future," Devon said, her voice tinged with a note of desperation. "And I know that when Grandmother dies and Mackinsey Hall is lost to the creditors, I'll have nothing. I'll be back where I was eight years ago, without family or a home to call my own. I deplore the thought of marrying for financial security, but what other choice do I have?''

Higgins released a long, resigned breath. Devon was right. She deserved to be loved for the wonderful, sensitive woman that she had become—not just because of the blood that flowed in her veins.

Higgins lowered his gaze to the graceful hands now slicing the potatoes. When Lady Mackinsey had finally seen fit to recognize Devon as her granddaughter, the child had been so starved for affection she had put the fact that she had been ignored by her own family out of her mind. She had set about molding herself into the lady Lady Mackinsey expected of her heir. During the past eight years she had done everything within her power to prove her worth to the old woman upstairs.

Like a silkworm, Devon had gone into the chrysalis of Mistress Cameron's Academy and had come out years later a beautiful butterfly who possessed a quiet, gentle strength woven from the years of adversity. Looking at her now, no one would ever suspect that she had once brawled with Winkler in a pile of manure.

Higgins suspected Devon's determination to save Mackinsey Hall was only another effort of the little urchin to prove that she was just as good as any Mackinsey born on the right side of the blanket. She wanted everyone to see that she wasn't less of a person because she had been chosen to fill the void created in Lady Mackinsey's life by Eunice's death. Higgins feared Devon's resolve had become an obsession. She didn't even realize that there were far deeper reasons behind her efforts to save Mackinsey Hall. She could say what she was doing was for her grandmother, but Mackinsey Hall had become a symbol to Devon of her right to carry the Mackinsey name.

It saddened Higgins to think that subconsciously Devon still felt she had only temporarily been granted a reprieve from the kitchens—and should she not do the right thing, she would be sent back into the world from which she had come. Higgins knew there was nothing he could say or do to change the way she felt. Devon's insecurities were too deeply rooted from the years spent at the beck and call of those with more power. It would not be easy for her to overcome them.

Someday, Higgins prayed, she would see her own worth as he did. A time when she would realize she was an intelligent, courageous, and desirable woman whom any man would be proud to call his own. However, he feared she'd never be given the opportunity to come to terms with herself if she continued on the course she had mapped out. Her determination to save Mackinsey Hall at all costs could be her downfall.

Knowing there was no use to continue to harangue Devon, Higgins changed the subject to the more immediate future. "Do you plan to go out tonight?"

"You know I must."

"I know, but that doesn't mean I have to like it any better now than when you came up with this scheme. Do you plan to see Lord Sumner again?"

Devon ignored the reproach she heard in Higgins's voice. "Lady Heath is giving a ball in honor of Lord Barclay's nephew, who's visiting from the colonies. Lady Agatha says that anyone who is anyone must be present tonight."

"Then you intend to wangle an introduction to Lord Barclay's nephew?" Higgins said, silently praying she'd set her sights on any man besides the fair-haired Lord Sumner.

Devon shook her head. "I'm not interested in Lord Barclay's nephew."

Higgins released a resigned breath. "Then it is Lord Sumner Lady Agatha is still encouraging you to pursue?"

"Lord Sumner is an eligible bachelor. And Lady Agatha assures me he is also one of the wealthiest men in all of England."

"What does Lady Agatha have to say about how the wealthy Lord Sumner feels about young women without large dowries?" Higgins inquired, his voice filled with irritation for the woman whom Devon had hired to help in her quest for a husband. The dowager was pushing Devon toward a man with a reputation for debauchery. He was known to enjoy women and then toss them away without a thought to their soiled reputations or broken hearts. As far as he could glean, Lord Sumner's only true love was adventure. That was why he left the running of his estate in the hands of his steward while he remained in the army.

"I'm sure a man of Lord Sumner's wealth will not expect a large dowry," Devon answered evasively.

"Even if he accepted a small dowry, that is far more than you possess at present." Higgins's exasperation mounted by the minute.

"But no one else is aware of my financial situation." Devon felt her stomach churn as a hard knot of guilt settled once more in the pit of her belly. She had become an expert liar of late, but that didn't stop her from feeling contrite over her actions. It wasn't easy for her to lead a double life. She went from ball to ball, acting as though she didn't have a worry in the world, yet deep inside she expected at any moment to be exposed as the fraud she really was. She could envision the shock—and then the scorn—of those who had accepted her as their equal. It wasn't a pleasant image.

"What do you think Lady Agatha would do should she learn the truth?"

Devon shrugged and kept her attention on the task at hand. "Should Lady Agatha or anyone else learn the true state of my affairs, it would end my association with my chaperon. She doesn't escort me out of the goodness of her heart."

Devon sliced through another potato. To speak of Lady Agatha in such a way sounded cruel, but she'd spoken only the truth. The prim and proper Lady Agatha would be aghast to learn of the Mackinsey penury. Like everyone else, she had assumed when Devon came to acquire her services that the Mackinsey wealth was still intact.

Lady Agatha, a widow of an impoverished lord, didn't possess the wealth or the prestige it took to be a member of the inner circles of London's society. However, through the years she had used her intelligence to gain entrance to their closely knit community. By watching and listening, she had gleaned information that had proven useful in her quest up the social ladder. And she knew just the right moment to drop the right tidbit into the right ear to gain the invitation she desired.

A shrewd businesswoman, she had seen the advantages of using such invitations to earn her livelihood by chaperoning young women like Devon to events such as Lady Heath's ball. She had only two requirements to attain her services: her charges had to possess a good family name—*and* have the money to pay her healthy fee.

Though not openly spoken of, Devon was aware that Lady Agatha would also expect to receive a large bonus should any of the invitations she arranged lead to marriage. To further that purpose Lady Agatha kept her eyes and ears open for information that might aid that conclusion.

Devon knew many viewed Lady Agatha's activities through jaundiced eyes. In their opinion she was little more than a blackmailer. Others looked upon her chaperon as only a matchmaker. However, none ever sought to take her name from their guest lists.

In her present situation Devon didn't look upon Lady Agatha's actions as any different than the mothers and grandmothers who rushed their offspring to London each season to find husbands. Perhaps Lady Agatha's methods were a little more unscrupulous, but as far as Devon could learn, the woman had truly never done any actual harm to anyone.

Devon looked up from the task at hand. "I couldn't blame her. There's no profit to be made from a pauper."

Higgins gave a snort of disgust. "Aye. From what that woman is charging you, she's probably richer than King Croesus himself."

"I don't begrudge her the few shillings she requires. With Grandmother ill, I have no other choice. A proper young lady must have a proper chaperon with the right connections, even if she has to hire one."

"Does she ever wonder why you never stay to dance away the night like most young women?"

Devon collected the potatoes and carrots and dumped them into the simmering broth. She wiped her hands on her apron as she turned once more to her friend. "She believes it's my concern for Grandmama that makes me return home early."

"Then she doesn't suspect anything else?"

"No. In fact, Lady Agatha seems impressed that I'm a reasonable young woman who chooses to retire before dawn."

"Just be careful, Devon. From what you've told me, Lady Agatha is a keen old woman. She's made her living by keeping the secrets of others."

"I can only hope that soon this will all come to an end and we can return to Mackinsey Hall. I'm tired of London, and I'm tired of living two lives." Devon swiped a shimmering mahogany curl from her brow.

"Then let it go before it's too late."

Devon ignored her friend's plea as if he'd not spoken. "Lord Sumner is the perfect choice for my husband. His army career will allow me to continue to live at Mackinsey Hall. Of course, when he returns to England on leave, I will visit his estate in Kent."

"It would seem you've already made up your mind. You've got everything mapped out. All you lack is getting the bridegroom to propose." Higgins's heart constricted. Devon was so sure Lord Sumner's attentions meant marriage, but he wasn't at all convinced of it. The man was a rake of the first degree.

Devon's expression grew serious and she nodded. "As I've said before, I have no other choice. Time is running out. The creditors are growing more impatient by the day. I must get enough money to pay them off or they'll take Mackinsey Hall."

Devon sank down into the chair across the table from Higgins. Her slender shoulders sagged as she looked at her longtime friend. The anxiety in her eyes reflected her need for his understanding and support. Higgins had always been a solid anchor in her stormy life. Even before she had become the Mackinsey heir, he had been there for her, and she needed him now more than ever. "I know you don't approve of what I've done in the past months. And I know you don't like the thought of my marrying Lord Sumner because of his reputation. But I must think of Grandmama."

"I understand your reasons, Devon. That's why I've been foolish enough to go along with your scheme. So far you've been lucky, but I'm afraid you're starting to tread in very dangerous waters. Men like Lord Sumner are sharks that just wait to tear an innocent like you to pieces."

Devon reached across the table and squeezed Higgins's

hand. A gentle smile curved her sweetly shaped mouth. "Thank you for caring, Higgins. It means a great deal to me that you've always given me your support, but you must stop worrying. I find Lord Sumner a very nice man. He's young and handsome, and he possesses the wealth to help my family."

"Devon, you're like a daughter to me. I've watched you grow into a lovely young woman . . . and I can't help but worry when you think you're capable of dealing with a man like Sumner. He's not the knight in shining armor his fair looks lead you to believe. He's rich and powerful. A man of his ilk eats young girls like you for breakfast without a thought. I fear when he learns the truth, he'll show no mercy. He has a reputation for never forgetting an offense."

Devon's smile deepened at the thought of the handsome army captain and his pursuit of her. Higgins worried far too much. A man in love would understand and forgive her for her duplicity. And she didn't doubt Lord Sumner was falling in love with her. She had seen the heated look in his eyes when they danced, and she expected him to propose in the very near future. Then, hopefully, their troubles would soon be over.

Chapter 3

A steady drizzle chilled the night. The coachman's breath fogged about his head in a gray cloud and he shivered beneath his damp cape as he drew the team to a clattering halt along the dark, deserted street. Taking a quick survey of his surroundings, he gave a grunt of satisfaction and leaped down from the driver's seat to the rain-slick cobbles. In such foul weather no one would be traveling through the park at this late hour. Even lovers who meant to keep a tryst wouldn't be foolish enough to do so outdoors. A full moon or a cozy fire made Cupid's work much easier. The driver clicked his tongue and chuckled. "A night such as this makes the little devil's arrow go astray of its target."

Hunching his shoulders against the night, he cast a furtive glance toward the street beyond the row of ancient oaks with bowed limbs that gracefully draped the soggy earth. Seeing no one, he opened the coach door and peered inside. Lantern light splashed across his face, revealing the features of a man in his early twenties. A frown of worry creased his broad forehead as he looked anxiously from beneath his heavy brows at his passenger. His deepset eyes reflected specks of light as well as concern for the shadowy figure cloaked in black.

"This ain't right, I'm a telling ye. I feel it in me bones. It's too dangerous for ye to go in when ye don't know nothing about the nob but that he's rich. He could be at 'ome—and even if 'e's not, ye don't even know where he keep 'is valuables.''

Features hidden by the brim of the black tricorne, the passenger pulled on soft black gloves and smiled at his driver's concern. He grasped the coach's leather hand strap and agilely stepped down to the cobbled pavement. "There's no need to worry. Lord Barclay is enjoying himself tonight at Lady Foxworth's. It will be hours yet before he leaves the entertainment. I have plenty of time to search his study as well as his quarters for his strongbox.''

"Humph! That's what ye also thought about Lord Montmain. But 'e fooled us all.''

"I don't think we have anything to fear from Lord Barclay in that area. His age should deter him from such sport,'' the Shadow answered matter-of-factly, jerking up the collar of his cloak to ward off the chilly night air.

"I wouldn't be so sure if I was ye. Old men ain't no different from us young'uns. They like women even if it takes 'em longer to get into the race. A good-looking filly can make an old stallion's blood run so 'ot and fast that 'e'll jump the pasture fence.''

The Shadow chuckled at the comparison of Lord Barclay to an old stallion set out to pasture. His imagination seized upon the image. It sprang to life and he could see an old gray horse with Lord Barclay's features racing wildly across an open field toward the fence, just as a young lady happened by. Laughter threatened, but the Shadow staunchly held it back. He had no time to enjoy his mirth. The night was flying by on swift black wings and he must attend to the business at hand.

The Shadow glanced toward the three-storied mansion across the street and then up at the black sky. He drew in a breath of the crisp, damp air to steady the queasy tremor that settled in his belly. Every time it was the same. The tension, anticipation, and the excitement of each robbery played havoc with his nerves.

It seemed worse tonight because he needed far more than the few coins and baubles he usually stole to keep his creditors at bay. Tonight he intended to come away from Lord Barclay's with enough booty to live for more than a fortnight without worry. He was tired of risking his neck for only a pittance.

Resigning himself to the task at hand, he touched his fingers to his hat in a jaunty salute to the coachman and set off down the dark street toward Lord Barclay's town house.

The coachman watched his friend disappear into the darkness and muttered, "I'm telling ye, I don't like this. The few baubles ye've taken to keep us going these last months weren't enough to get ye hanged. But what ye've set yer sights on tonight will change all that." The driver shook his head and climbed inside the dry coach. He huddled uneasily in the pool of lantern light that spread across the aged leather seats.

The Shadow cast a furtive glance up and down the street before he slipped, with catlike grace, through the thick privet hedge that grew in front of the spiked wrought-iron fence. He frowned up at the menacing obstacle. The fence surrounded Lord Barclay's property on all sides. It would be difficult in fair weather to get enough leverage to maneuver over the deadly iron spikes without impaling himself, much less managing the feat when the iron bars were slick with rain.

Seeking an easier way inside the grounds, the Shadow stealthily crept along the iron bars until he found a small, narrow gate. Seeking the rusty latch through his experienced fingers, he smiled. It would take only a few jiggles with the tip of his dirk to open the ancient lock. The gate creaked as it swung open. The sound grated on the Shadow's taut nerves and made a shiver of apprehension race up his spine. Yet he didn't retreat. He entered the dark garden and, with pantherlike strides, quick and silent, he

approached the town house. He swiftly made his way up
to the balustraded portico and crossed to the wide, multipaned doors. A warm glow of firelight filtered out into
the damp night as he rubbed a circle on the misty glass
and peered inside.

The Shadow could have laughed aloud at his good fortune. He had happened upon the very chamber he sought:
Lord Barclay's study. The Shadow took in the lavish masculine chamber, noting each object in his path to the large
mahogany desk. Bathed in ebony and scarlet, the study
revealed much of the man the Shadow had heard so much
about. Well known in London as an avid sportsman, Lord
Barclay's study reflected his taste. The oak-paneled walls
were hung with paintings of his favorite hunters and racing
horses. A large gun cabinet held prized muskets and pistols; while silver cups and ribbons from races won lined
the oak mantle. Two large leather chairs sat at angles in
front of the fireplace to allow Lord Barclay a clear view
of his triumphs as he relaxed before the fire. A side table
held the sustenance required of a sportsman: a crystal decanter of brandy and a pipe stand to smoke the sweet Virginian tobacco imported from the colonies.

Not wanting to know more about the victim of this
night's work, the Shadow ran a gloved hand over the brass
latch and slid the blade of his dirk between the crack in
the wood. A little pressure, combined with a twist of the
wrist, opened the door easily. Again a triumphant smile
tugged up the corners of the Shadow's shapely lips and he
slipped unseen into the study.

Sparing only a glance at the rest of the chamber, he
swiftly crossed to the desk littered with papers and led-
gers. Intent upon his purpose, he flipped open one heavy
volume and briefly scanned the rows of figures. He gave
an inaudible whistle at the money Lord Barclay spent and
earned in only one month. He could well understand why
the man was one of England's wealthiest citizens.

The Shadow shook his head in disgust and envy as he turned his attention to the desk drawers. He searched each one, hoping to find where Lord Barclay kept his strongbox. Like his other victims, he hoped the gentleman kept himself a ready supply of gold on hand to pay his gaming debts and other out-of-pocket expenses that gentlemen incurred on their social rounds.

The last desk drawer gave up nothing of value. Straightening, the Shadow stood surveying the chamber, looking for any clue that might lead to Lord Barclay's hiding place. His examination was abruptly cut short a moment later when the click of the door latch and the murmur of voices alerted him to the fact that he was no longer alone. Bolting beneath the desk, he crouched in a ball and listened as the heavy footsteps approached. A golden pool of light spilled over the desk and the Shadow tensed for discovery.

"Mordecai, I didn't expect you tonight, though it's damn good to see you after so many months. How have you been, man? Barclay Grove isn't the same without you."

"It's good to hear it, Hunter. I miss the place. England makes my old bones ache with all this Godforsaken rain. I sorely yearn for the clean air and open space of Virginia after months in this smoky town. Every breath you take is filled with soot."

"Cecilia and Elsbeth will have my head if you don't sail home with me when I leave."

"Then there's nothing left for me to do but to return to Barclay Grove." Mordecai chuckled. "I wouldn't wish those tempers upon my worst enemy, much less my best friend."

The Shadow heard the clink of glass and realized the two men were enjoying Lord Barclay's brandy.

"How's your uncle, Hunter?"

"I only saw him for a few moments tonight, but as far as I can judge, he's as fit as a fiddle."

"That's good to hear. I don't wish the man any bad luck, no matter how much I disagree with his politics."

"Speaking of politics . . . I know you didn't come out on a night like this—and pull me out of my bed—just to taste my uncle's brandy and to see my pretty face, Mordecai."

"Damn me. The ladies all seem to think you're a damned fine-looking gent, but I don't see it myself. However, your looks—no matter how pretty or ugly—wouldn't get me to come out on a night like this. It's urgent, Hunter."

"You wound me, old friend. Now what news do you bring?"

"It's Lord Gilbert. He's getting nervous. It's taken all my persuasive powers to keep him from backing out on the deal until you arrived. You need to see him immediately."

"I'll go and talk with him the first thing in the morning. We need his support. He's far too valuable—and knows far too much—for us to allow him an easy way out. Should his information reach the wrong ears, there would be hell to pay from here to Virginia. Starting with our hides."

"Have the shipments of weapons and ammunition arrived at St. Eustatius as planned?"

"I checked on them when we made port in the islands. Several shipments are stored in the warehouses and are just waiting for the navy ships to arrive."

"That's good. At least I don't feel like my time here has been wasted."

"Mordecai, the Congress is deeply indebted to you for all of your work. You've risked life and limb for the cause of freedom."

The Shadow's eyes widened in shock. They talked treason. The Shadow swallowed convulsively at his precarious position. Should the two men find him eavesdropping on their conversation, they could not allow him to leave alive. It could mean their death.

"I'm not the only one who has risked his life for freedom. You've done your share, and I for one owe you more than I can ever repay."

"You've repaid me twofold, Mordecai. I was the fortunate one the day I found you on that British Navy frigate. Few men are lucky enough to have such a loyal friend. Now," Hunter said, and cleared his throat, "it's time for us to quit talking like two sentimental old women. I need to get some rest if I'm to see Lord Gilbert in the morning. It was one hell of a voyage from St. Eustatius and I'm worn out."

The Shadow breathed a sigh of relief as the two men said good night and the sound of footsteps faded as they left the study. Thinking only of making good his escape, he waited until the murmur of voices died away and all grew quiet once more. Confident that he was alone in the study, he crawled from his hiding place and stood.

An audible gasp escaped as he glanced toward the door and looked directly into a pair of dark eyes fringed in thick black lashes. Like a rabbit mesmerized by a cobra, the Shadow stared back into penetrating eyes as the man came forward. The Shadow's heart froze and he swallowed at the uncomfortable lump of terror lodged in his throat. One way or the other—as thief or eavesdropper—he knew he'd not survive this encounter.

The Shadow's mind whirled as he frantically sought an avenue of escape. A glance told him he could never overpower his captor. The man dwarfed him in size. He exuded strength from his large body with every breath he expelled. Though dressed in an elegant velvet dressing gown, he looked anything but the gentleman. The deep V opening exposed a wide chest furred in crisp, dark hair. His slightest movement made the thick muscles banding his rib cage ripple beneath his tanned flesh. His shoulders, seemingly as wide as a mountain, strained against the expensive material covering them.

A foreboding chill cascaded down the Shadow's spine. Bathed in scarlet firelight, the man looked like Satan. The thought broke through the trance that held the Shadow immobile. Darting a quick glance at the glass doors, he eased away from the desk.

"I wouldn't try it if I were you," Hunter Barclay warned, his voice reverberating like a deep rumble of thunder in the quiet study.

A lump of fear wedged in the Shadow's throat and a cold sweat broke out across his upper lip. He suddenly understood how a caged animal felt. The man blocked escape through the french doors. Uneasily the Shadow glanced toward the only other route—a door to the interior of the house—that might lead to freedom. It was his only option.

The Shadow tensed to flee. He knew it would be highly unlikely for him to escape in that direction, but he had to try. Anxiety pressed down on his chest, making it difficult to breathe as he bolted toward the hall door. In a flash he sprinted down the hallway toward the dimly lit foyer and the wide double doors. He fumbled with the latch, but his hand froze against the gleaming brass as another rumble came from behind him.

"You little bastard. You're not going to get away." A hand clamped down on the Shadow's narrow shoulder, spinning him around. Reacting on instinct, the Shadow brought up both hands and shoved with all his strength against the man's wide chest.

Unprepared for the sudden attack, Hunter staggered backward. The soft leather of his slippers found no purchase on the shining black and white marble tiles. He fought to maintain his balance but failed. He crashed to the floor with a thud and a roar of fury.

Giving no thought to his pursuer's welfare, the Shadow turned to flee. Before he could make good his escape, a long-fingered hand shot out and grasped the material of his cape. Inexorably and with what seemed effortless ease, Hunter dragged him backward.

Choking from the pressure of the ties about his throat, the Shadow struggled. Frantically he tore at the cloak's braided cords and, when at last they gave way, he didn't look back. He clamped a hand down on his tricorne to keep it in place and dashed toward the stairs, leaving the man holding the garment. Taking the stairs two at a time, the Shadow sought any means of escape. Heavy footsteps close upon his heels, he sprinted through an open door and across the chamber toward the windows. Panting from the exertion, the Shadow fought to raise the sash. It would not budge. For one brief, despairing moment, the Shadow rested his brow against the cool glass. He had failed.

The bedchamber door seemed to rock the very foundation of the house as it slammed with a bang behind him. The Shadow spun about to face his pursuer. Backed against the heavy drapes he stood his ground and watched the man approach, his expression grim.

The Shadow drew in a long breath and thrust his chin out at a pugnacious angle. He accepted his fate. He had known since the beginning that one day this could happen and he would face it bravely.

"You little thief. You're lucky I don't have my pistol or I'd blow your head off and save the authorities the trouble of hanging you," Hunter Barclay growled as he eyed the small man cowering against the drapes. He was in no mood to catch thieves. His voyage from Virginia had been filled with one disaster after another. Storms and sickness had plagued the ship since leaving the islands. Exhausted they had made port a week late. And he'd arrived at his uncle's intent upon taking a well-deserved rest when his uncle had informed him that he was to have dinner at Lady Foxworth's. Too tired to even make an appearance at the Foxworths', he'd poured himself a relaxing brandy and had gone up to bed.

He had been dozing when the valet had awakened him with the news that Mordecai Bradley awaited him downstairs. Knowing his friend would not have come this late at night without it being urgent, he'd gone down to meet with him. After seeing Mordecai out, he'd returned to the study to put out the light and had found, to his amazement, that during the few short minutes it had taken to show Mordecai out, the thief had entered to do his dirty work. He'd just started to rifle through his uncle's desk when Hunter had found him.

"Do you have nothing to say for yourself?" Hunter challenged as he assessed the thief through narrowed lids, taking note of the man's slender build and small stature. The tricorne hid his features from Hunter's view.

Hunter strode purposely toward his quarry, determined to wring the little man's neck if he put up any more resistance when he tried to take him back downstairs to summon the authorities. However the moment he was at arm's length, the thief bolted.

The dressing table to one side, the bed on the other, and Hunter Barclay blocking the clear course to the door, the Shadow bounded for the bed, taking the path of least resistance and doing everything within his power to outmaneuver the large man. A hand captured the Shadow's small ankle as he scrambled toward the opposite side of the huge four-poster. Futilely the Shadow gripped the satin counterpane, trying desperately to find a handhold of resistance. Instead the satin slithered beneath him like something alive, aiding his pursuer in his efforts as he drew the Shadow back across the bed.

The Shadow dug his fingers into the down mattress and let out a screech of frustration as he struggled against Hunter's efforts to turn him onto his back. He failed. Hunter flipped him over, the motion sending the black tricorne toppling over the side of the bed to the carpeted floor. Long, gleaming strands of mahogany hair spilled across the white counterpane, spreading like a cloud of dark red silk about the Shadow.

Intent upon subduing the intruder, Hunter failed to note the evolution taking place. Grasping both of the thief's wrists, he slammed them down against the bed, pinning them to the mattress at the same time he pressed a knee into his captive's middle to thwart any further attempt to flee. Breathing heavily, his muscular chest rising and falling from the exertion, Hunter finally looked down at his hostage. The soft light from the lone candle burning on the bedside table illuminated the mass of thick curls as well as the sculpted features that the tricorne had hidden from his view. Hunter's eyes widened with shock. The small man had transformed into a beautiful woman.

Hunter stared down at his captive, unable to believe what he was seeing. His thickly lashed, slate blue eyes reflected bewilderment as Devon squared her chin and stared haughtily back up at him.

"What in the hell is going on here? Is this some kind of game? Does my uncle have a penchant for his mistress to play out certain roles? And why in hell didn't you tell me if that's the case? I'm too damned tired to go chasing after my uncle's doxy."

Devon remained mute.

"Damn it. I asked you a question . . . and I mean to have some answers before I send for the authorities," Hunter ground out. "Now tell me who you are and what you are doing here!"

Devon lowered her thick lashes to hide the uncertainty his questions aroused. She couldn't tell this man her true identity. She couldn't bring such disgrace down upon her grandmother. News that her granddaughter was awaiting a noose at Tyburn would kill Lady Mackinsey. It would be far better for all concerned were she to just disappear without anyone ever learning her fate.

"I ain't yer uncle's doxy, gov'ner. Now ye can get off me. Yer squeezing me guts out with yer knee," Devon said, falling back into the dialect of the first ten years of her life. She couldn't speak as a lady if she wanted to keep her identity a secret.

"I'm not moving an inch until I know what kind of game you're playing. Why are you dressed like a man, and why have you broken into my uncle's house?"

"Why do ye think, gov'ner?" Devon said, looking up at Hunter. "It shouldn't be too hard for even a fine gent like yerself to figure it out. I certainly wasn't out taking the air for me health on a night like this."

"So you came to rob my uncle?"

Devon nodded. "I got a family that's hungry, and I figured 'is nibs could spare a few coins, being 'e's so rich and all."

Hunter stared down at Devon, puzzled. She spoke like a guttersnipe, but that was where the resemblance dissipated. Her skin, her hair, and even the haughty way she held her chin belied her words. "Then I suppose there's nothing left for me to do but to call the authorities and have you taken to Newgate."

"Ye could be a good sort and let me go," Devon offered. She caught her lower lip between even white teeth and held her breath as she awaited his reaction to her request.

Hunter's enigmatic smile didn't reach his eyes, nor did he loosen his grip on Devon's wrists. "So you think I should just let you go?"

Devon nodded quickly. "I didn't steal anything, gov'ner."

"God, you're a brazen wench. You enter my uncle's home intent upon thievery and then, when you're caught before you can steal his valuables, you think I should just let you go on about your merry way.''

Devon nodded again. ''It sounds logical to me.''

Hunter chuckled in spite of himself and shook his head at her incredulous suggestion. ''Perhaps I should also give you a few coins for your trouble.''

''It'd be much appreciated, gov'ner. Me family hasn't 'ad a decent meal in more than a month. Me poor old pa died last year of the flux and me ma is blind and withering away from grief. And I 'ave six younger sisters who depend upon me to keep them fed.'' Hoping to gain the man's sympathy, Devon elaborated in a small voice. ''And they be crippled.''

''All six are cripples?'' Hunter asked, suppressing a smile at the young woman's ridiculous story. However, he had to admire her ingenuity. It was the first time, to his knowledge, that a thief had tried to escape by using emotional blackmail.

''Aye, they all be cripples and like to die if I'm sent to Newgate. I'm the only one they have to look after them. Should something 'appen to me, I don't know who'd put a few morsels of bread into their poor, hungry bellies.''

''I'm sure your blind mother and crippled sisters can manage well enough without you. In their situation, they can make more begging than you can by stealing. A man would have to have a heart of stone to refuse a coin to such needy souls.'' Hunter shook his head, feigning dismay. ''Six cripples and a blind woman. 'Tis heart wrenching.''

''Then ye'll let me go, gov'ner?'' Devon asked eagerly.

''I didn't say that.'' Hunter smiled down at her. ''I said it was heart wrenching about your poor blind mother and six crippled sisters.''

Hearing the mockery in his voice, Devon stiffened. The man had been toying with her. He had no intention of releasing her. Anger flushing her pale cheeks to a becoming rose, she turned her head away and valiantly sought to keep her temper in check. She stared blindly at the intricately crafted headboard, where the artist had carved the images of two lovers hidden in a bower of trees. Above them cupids watched from the clouds.

"Then ye'll not let me go?" Devon ground out through clenched teeth.

"Not unless you tell me the truth. I'm not a man who can be easily duped, my dear. You can create a host of crippled and sick relatives for the rest of the night, but you'll not make me believe it."

Defeat welled within Devon. "Can you spare no mercy?"

Hunter freed Devon's wrists and levered himself off the bed. He straightened his dressing gown and retied the belt about his trim waist, once again enclosing the wide expanse of muscled chest in velvet. A grim frown knit his dark brows over the bridge of his narrow nose as he looked down at her. "Before I can answer that question, I must first have answers of my own."

Devon struggled upright and sat regarding Hunter from beneath the shield of her thick, feathery lashes. She rubbed absently at her wrists. There were no answers she could give unless she wanted the world to know that Lady Devon Mackinsey had turned to thieving to survive. Devon shuddered at the thought.

"Are you cold?" Hunter asked, noting the involuntary shiver that passed over the young woman on the bed.

Devon shook her head.

"All right, that's settled. You're not cold, and I suspect you're not the guttersnipe that you pretend, so exactly what are you? And exactly how long were you in my uncle's study? It's time to start talking. I should like to have this settled before my uncle returns home."

Devon nervously ran her tongue over her lower lip. She couldn't tell him she'd overheard his conversation with the man he'd called Mordecai. Such a rash move could jeopardize her life. Devon's mind spun in a dozen different directions as she frantically sought a plausible story to convince her captor that she had not overheard his treasonous conversation and he didn't need to call the authorities and have her taken to Newgate.

Devon could find only one. She cleared her throat and looked Hunter directly in the eyes. Curious slate blue met apprehensive forest green. "My lord, I would beg you on bended knee for your mercy. I was only in the study a moment before you found me, and I plead with you to believe I do not lie when I say there are those who depend upon me."

"More crippled sisters and blind mothers? Or is it now starving brothers and fathers?"

"Perhaps I don't have six crippled sisters and a blind mother to care for, but I do have one old woman already near death. I steal to keep her from starving."

Hunter frowned. Something in the girl's words rang true. He searched her face for the lie, but could find none. Thoughtfully he ran his long fingers through his tousled hair. "Damn me, if I don't believe you this time."

Devon felt her spirits rise and asked eagerly, "Then you'll let me go?"

For the first time since their encounter, Hunter allowed his gaze to move slowly over Devon. The sight of her shapely legs encased in black stockings and breeches made the blood stir restlessly in his veins. He felt the old familiar heat settle in his loins. It had been far too long since he'd had a woman.

Hunter's gaze traveled upward, taking in the woman's soft shape that he'd failed to note during the chase. This woman was a beauty in face and form and would do very well to appease his needs with the right persuasion.

Hunter pushed the thought aside. Damn! He was worse off than he even realized if he could consider the thought of blackmail to force a woman into his bed. He cleared his throat. "I'll allow you to go for a price."

Relieved that he had believed her and unaware of his train of thought, Devon answered eagerly, "Anything."

Hunter suppressed a groan. The girl didn't realize how enticing her offer was to a man whose blood sizzled through his veins. Unable to completely resist the temptation before him, he smiled down at Devon. "A kiss for your freedom— and a promise I'll not find you here again."

The room seemed to brighten as Devon smiled up at Hunter and raised her right hand. "A bargain, sir. You have my word."

"Then forfeit your kiss, my lady, and then be gone before I demand a much higher price for your freedom," Hunter murmured, capturing Devon in his arms. Molding her against him, he lowered his lips to hers and felt his body betray all his good intentions at the taste of her luscious mouth. Damning himself for every kind of a fool, he set Devon away from him and strode across the room. It was best to put as much distance between them as possible.

With his back to Devon, Hunter stared down into the dying embers of the fireplace. Sharpened by the desire searing through him, he snapped, "It's time for you to leave. And I warn you, don't let me catch you again, my lady. I won't bargain with you again."

Slightly dazed by what had just transpired, Devon swallowed with difficulty as she looked at the wide back turned toward her. The man's kiss had shaken her to the very core. Her heart felt like a caged bird trying to get free as it thumped wildly against her ribs. She'd been kissed in the past, but never had a kiss made her forget everything except the explosion of sensation that had rocked her as his lips devoured hers. She moistened her lips and drew in a steadying breath as a sense of relief and humiliation mingled as one. However, Hunter didn't have to repeat himself. She'd not wait to understand her rioting emotions. In a flash, she swept up her hat and was gone.

Devon again took the stairs two at a time as she descended. She left Lord Barclay's town house by the path she had entered it; however, everything seemed changed as she fled into the night. She paused at the small gate and looked back at the town house. Something odd had happened to her tonight, but she couldn't put her finger on it. All she knew was that when Hunter Barclay took her into his arms to collect the toll for her freedom, she'd forgotten she was kissing a stranger and a traitor to England. All she knew was that she never wanted the kiss to end. It had drugged her senses . . . until he had abruptly sent her away from him in disgust.

Devon's cheeks flushed at the memory. She'd allowed the man's seductive kiss to obliterate all common sense. She knew she should be grateful that he'd not found her to his liking, but to her dismay, she found herself piqued that the kiss had not affected him as much as it had her.

The gate squeaked loudly as Devon closed it behind her and stepped out into the puddled street. She had gained little tonight beyond experience. That meant her coffers were still bare of the coin she needed to pay the creditors. Devon crossed the street and made her way back down the narrow lane to where Winkler awaited with the coach. She wouldn't go home empty-handed. Nor would she allow her encounter with Hunter Barclay to frighten her into forgetting about returning to Mackinsey Hall. Devon glanced up at the black sky. There were still a few hours left before dawn.

Chapter 4

"Yer looking good tonight, Yer Ladyship," Winkler said, giving Lady Agatha a mischievous grin as he assisted her into the Mackinsey coach.

"Well, I never!" Lady Agatha spluttered, offended by the coachman's audacity to speak to her, much less compliment her on her appearance. It was outrageous behavior for a servant. Settling herself huffily back against the worn leather seat, she looked at her charge and shook her head. The gesture made the gathered silk of the black caleche covering her powdered coiffure bob slightly and slip to one side. She sniffed her disdain at Winkler's familiarity as she straightened the whaleboned headpiece that always reminded Devon of a carriage hood that could be lowered and raised at will.

"Your coachman leaves much to be desired in a good servant, Devon. He should be told it is far too forward to compliment his betters on their appearance."

"I'm sorry, Lady Agatha," Devon said, relieved that the shadows hid her smile. Winkler would never change. Even as a grown man he couldn't stop getting himself in trouble. "Winkler meant no harm. He's a good servant, but I fear he wasn't trained for the position in which he now serves. He is temporarily acting as my coachman since Sims was unable to come to London with us." Devon didn't add that the Mackinsey coachman had left her service several months earlier to find an employer who could afford to pay his wages on a regular basis.

"Being a loyal servant should count for something, I would guess," Lady Agatha snipped. Devon's lack of chagrin over the servant's boldness annoyed the older woman. It touched a raw nerve. She had worked too hard, for too many years, to attain her current position in society and she'd allow no one to detract from it by word or deed. "However, it is your responsibility to see that he doesn't do it again, Devon. He is your servant, and one must never allow them to become too familiar or they'll take advantage. You must remember that, my dear."

"I will speak with Winkler, and I'm sure he'll not insult you again, Lady Agatha." Devon lowered her eyes to her gloved hands to hide the flash of irritation that swept over her. She could feel her hackles rise at Lady Agatha's haughty attitude. The woman had no right to feel so superior with her reputation. In the eyes of many she was little more than a servant herself.

Winkler might still fill the position in her household as a servant, but since the day she had trounced him in the manure pile, he'd become her friend. She considered Winkler and Higgins part of her family. They had remained when others had abandoned their posts after learning of her financial situation. And they had served her faithfully with their friendship, acting when needed as coachman, butler, footman, and serving maid. Thanks to their support, no one suspected that the young woman, dressed in exquisite gowns made of the finest of fabrics—fabrics found in her grandmother's trunks in the attic—possessed only a few pence to her name.

Devon glanced out into the rain-drenched night. God! How she hated all the deception she'd woven about herself of late. Hopefully Lord Sumner would propose soon and she could quit parading herself beneath the glittering chandeliers like a prize heifer at a country fair. And with her marriage she could also stop her nightly excursions into crime.

"I do wish this weather would let up," Lady Agatha said, jerking Devon's mind away from her morose thoughts. "It's ruining the entire season. We can't have any outdoor soirees, nor can there be any dancing in the gardens." She gave Devon a calculating look and smiled. "I've found gardens are wonderfully romantic places to set about obtaining a husband. I always tell my young ladies that many a staunch bachelor has succumbed to the allure of a moonlit night perfumed by roses. An atmosphere such as that can weave a spell of enchantment about a man and, before he knows what has hit him, he's on his knees proposing to his lady."

"I fear tonight will not be such a night," Devon replied as she peered out into the fog-shrouded evening. She couldn't stop herself from wondering if Lord Sumner was merely waiting for the perfect night to ask for her hand in marriage. Nor could she stop herself from remembering the conversation she'd had with Higgins about Lord Sumner. Was he the type of man her friend believed him to be? Devon didn't have the answer. Nor did she have the experience to judge a man's character. She had only Lady Agatha's word to rely upon.

Lady Agatha gave an exaggerated shiver and snapped the curtain shut over the window. She cast a surreptitious glance about the small enclosure, as if to make sure they were alone, before leaning forward. A note of awe filled her voice as she asked, "Did you hear the latest gossip about the Shadow?" Lady Agatha lowered her voice another degree. "Lady Pope told me this morning that he had the audacity to enter Lord Montmain's house two nights ago while the man was in bed in the adjoining room." Lady Agatha gave another exaggerated shiver and leaned back against the leather seat. "I don't know what on earth this world is coming to. A body is not safe even in his own house. Criminals are free to come and go and take anything they please while we sleep."

Devon once more shifted her gaze to the gloved hands she had tightly clasped in her lap. The folds of her black velvet cape contrasted starkly with the white silk. "Do they have any inkling of the man's identity?"

"Not to my knowledge. Lady Pope said the authorities believe he has connections who tell him the whereabouts of his victims because he always seems to know when they're away from home. Had Lord Montmain not taken ill at Lady Fitzroy's party, he wouldn't have known what had transpired until the next morning when he went into his dressing room and found his valuables gone. Fortunately for Lord Montmain, the thief didn't have time to find the jewels and money that he keeps in his dressing table." Lady Agatha sniffed and raised her chin haughtily in the air. She gave Devon a meaningful look. "I told Lady Pope it was probably a disgruntled servant who helped the scoundrel. But she wouldn't believe me. She said it would be nearly impossible for one servant to learn so much about so many people."

Devon breathed a sigh of relief. Hunter Barclay had not told anyone of his encounter with her. And from what she had gleaned from her eavesdropping, he had not been in London long enough to hear the gossip about the Shadow's crime spree. That was fortunate for her. Had he suspected that she had been robbing his uncle's friends, he might not have been so lenient. Devon shivered at the thought. She would now probably be sitting in a cell in Newgate Prison awaiting her hanging at Tyburn.

Misconstruing Devon's reaction, Lady Agatha leaned forward and gave her hand a motherly pat. "I didn't mean for the news to frighten you, my dear. I'm sure we have nothing to fear. It seems the scoundrel only robs very rich men. He has yet to enter any of the ladies' boudoirs." She smiled reassuringly. "He's like the Robin Hood of old, though I'm not at all certain that he gives his ill-begotten gains to the poor.'' Lady Agatha chuckled at her small jest and gave Devon's hand another pat before settling back against the seat. "But it's not anything for you to be concerned about. You must put all thoughts of the Shadow out of your mind and concentrate on your future. Hopefully tonight will be the night Lord Sumner puts an end to all these cat-and-mouse games he's been playing and propose to you. Now pinch your cheeks, we've arrived at Lady Heath's.''

A long line of sleek coaches wound through the circular drive in front of Lord and Lady Heath's magnificent three-storied town house. Candlelight and music spilled out into the foggy night, banishing the gloomy atmosphere created by the dreary weather. The misty evening became magical as England's society, bejeweled and bedecked in their finery, alighted from their coaches to enjoy Lord and Lady Heath's hospitality. Winkler maneuvered the coach along the cobbled drive and drew it to a halt at the flagged walk, where liveried footmen awaited to assist the ladies down. Torches lighting their way, Devon and Lady Agatha allowed the footmen to escort them up the fanned marble steps to the wide double doors encased in an intricately scrolled marble entablature.

They crossed the threshold into a foyer tiled in black and white Italian marble. Ablaze with light from the crystal chandelier suspended from the vaulted ceiling by a chain of velvet and brass, the entrance was done in the rococo design recently imported from France. Elaborate carved columns, ornamented with scrollwork similar to the design over the double doors, supported the archway leading to the corridor beyond. Family portraits overlooked the entrance from the balcony overhead while liveried servants, their expressions as staid as the marble busts of the Heath ancestors displayed on pedestals along the walls, took their wraps and led them up a winding mahogany staircase inlaid with polished strips of brass.

The ballroom, its walls hung with shimmering gold silk and shining mirrors to reflect the brilliant images of the guests, claimed the entire second floor of the mansion. Gleaming chandeliers, alight with a thousand candles, cast an air of enchantment over the lords and ladies swirling to the soft strands of music filtering through the velvet drapes that hid the minstrels' gallery from view.

Matrons and dowagers who preferred not to take part in the dancing sat regally ensconced in silk damask-covered chairs, chatting with their contemporaries while keeping a keen eye on the younger set. They were the hierarchy of London's social elite. They made certain that society's rules were obeyed by everyone. Not even members of Parliament or the royal household possessed the courage to set themselves up against England's grand dames.

With a glance Devon took in the glittering array and felt the old familiar knot settle in her stomach. Valiantly she swallowed back the nervous lump that rose in her throat and raised her head regally in the air. It was the same each night. At the beginning of the evening she always had the eerie sensation that when she was announced everyone would look at her and suddenly see her as the impostor she was.

Devon pasted a pleasant smile upon her lips and stiffened her spine as the footman announced her and Lady Agatha. Heads turned, and for a fleeting moment in time the two women were the center of attention. A second later another couple's name was called out to gain them their moment in the sun before they, too, were forgotten for someone more interesting.

"Come, Devon," Lady Agatha ordered briskly. "We must pay our respects to our hostess before you can be introduced to any of her guests." In one sweeping glance Lady Agatha took in the assembly, mentally categorizing each by importance of rank and wealth. She smiled at the sight of the gray-haired man standing near the refreshment table sipping a glass of champagne. "I see Lord Barclay has already arrived. I wonder which young man is his nephew?"

Devon cast a fleeting glance at Lord Barclay and then scanned the assembly. She was relieved to see no sign of the man's handsome nephew. Pushing aside the thought of Hunter Barclay, she allowed her gaze to wander to the man she had set all her hopes upon. Lord Neal Sumner stood with head bowed as he listened intently to a golden-haired beauty Devon recognized as Amy Ferguson.

A mixture of emotions swept over Devon. Jealousy and apprehension mingled as she watched Lord Sumner smile at the girl. An eerie chill of foreboding tingled down Devon's spine. She'd seen the look on Neal's face often in the past weeks. The only difference now was that he was bestowing it upon Amy Ferguson. Shaken by the knowledge that her hold upon Lord Sumner wasn't as firm as she had believed, Devon didn't realize Lady Heath had spoken to her until Lady Agatha gave the back of her arm a furtive pinch.

"Devon, where are your manners? Lady Heath is greeting you," Lady Agatha scolded, though her tone remained polite and friendly.

"I'm . . . I'm sorry," Devon stammered, jerking her thoughts away from Lord Sumner. "I'm afraid my mind was on other things. Please forgive me, Lady Heath."

Lady Heath smiled knowingly. She wasn't so old that she had forgotten what it was like to be young and in love. She'd seen Devon's obvious attraction to the handsome rogue, Neal Sumner, and hoped it would not end with the girl's heart broken. Linnett Heath knew Lord Sumner by reputation and on a far more personal basis. She'd enjoyed a few afternoons in his bed several years ago herself. "You're forgiven, my dear. It isn't easy for a young woman to keep her mind on such trivial matters as polite conversation when her heart urges her otherwise.''

Devon's cheeks heated with a blush. "My lady, I fear there is no excuse for my bad manners, though you are kind to forgive them. And I want to thank you for your invitation tonight. I'm honored.''

"You're always welcome, my dear. I've known and liked your grandmother since I was a girl. I'm just sorry she's too ill to join us tonight," Lady Heath said, pointedly ignoring Lady Agatha with the remark. "I'm also sorry to say that Lord Barclay's nephew may not be able to join us tonight. He's had some sort of urgent business that he must attend before he can enjoy himself.''

"I'm sorry to hear that," Devon said, her relief magnifying by the moment.

"My dear, you are not the only one. Everyone here was expecting to meet Lord Barclay's heir.''

"Lord Barclay's heir?" Lady Agatha asked, her mind pouncing instantly upon the advantages for herself. "Is the young man married?''

Reading Lady Agatha like a book, Lady Heath sniffed. "I'm certain I don't know the young man's marital status. Perhaps you could ask Lord Barclay. I'm sure he would be more than glad to tell you where to go for your information, Lady Agatha." With that pleasant, parting barb, Lady Heath snapped open her mother-of-pearl-and-satin fan, gave a disdainful flick of her satin and lace skirts, and strolled haughtily toward the newest arrivals.

Taking the insult as intended, Lady Agatha raised her chin in the air and softly prophesied, "That woman will live to regret such rudeness.''

Oblivious to the undercurrent of hostility between her hostess and her chaperon, Devon's attention centered once more upon Lord Sumner and the young woman who seemed fascinated by each word he spoke. Sadly, he seemed equally engrossed with Amy. Devon's heart summersaulted sickeningly against her ribs. It was quite evident from the look on his face that her plans for a future with Lord Sumner were premature.

Disheartened, Devon forced herself to look away from the golden couple. As Winkler would say, she had put all her eggs in one basket—and now it looked as if none of them would hatch! She had spent her time and money unwisely in trying to woo Neal Sumner, and now everything she had worked to achieve was in jeopardy. Unfortunately she didn't have the time or the finances to launch a new effort to capture a husband. Disaster would be only a few days away when her creditors learned Lord Neal Sumner had lost interest.

Devon drew in a deep breath. She wouldn't allow these people to see the devastation she felt. She had to pretend that she saw nothing out of the ordinary about Neal and Amy cozily chatting the night away. Her pretense would keep her from becoming a total laughingstock when everyone realized she no longer held Lord Sumner's eye.

"Devon, I want you to meet Lord Barclay," Lady Agatha said. Taking hold of Devon's arm, she began to subtly drag her across the room—toward the gray-haired man Devon had attempted to rob the previous night. Lady Agatha whispered, "If Lord Barclay's nephew is unmarried, then he might do very well as a husband for you."

Devon's head snapped about and she came to an abrupt halt. She looked at her chaperon as if Lady Agatha had suddenly lost her mind. "I have no intention of marrying a colonial," Devon blurted out before she realized no one had mentioned Hunter Barclay was a colonial.

"My poor, misguided child. Did you not hear what Lady Heath said?" Lady Agatha pasted a false smile on her lips as they paused. She fluttered her fan back and forth, nodding greetings to passersby as if nothing out of the ordinary were taking place between herself and her ward. "Lord Barclay's nephew may be a colonial, but he is also heir to one of the largest estates in all of England. That, my dear, is an alliance you can't sniff your nose at. Lord Barclay's wealth makes Lord Sumner look like a pauper. His family is one of the oldest and most respected in England. His ancestors fought alongside William at the Battle of Hastings.''

And his nephew is fighting now against England, Devon thought acidly, but said, "I'm sorry, Lady Agatha. I understand you mean only to help me, but I have no desire to leave England—no matter who the man's ancestors may be.''

"Don't be a fool, Devon. You might have to live in the colonies for a few years, but Lord Barclay is an old man. When he dies, his nephew will have to return to England to accept the title and his inheritance.'' Lady Agatha watched Devon's gaze wander back to where Lord Sumner stood with Amy Ferguson. She released a disgusted breath and her voice filled with disappointment as she spoke. "I thought you far wiser than this, Devon. Because of the man's reputation I assumed that you had the intelligence to woo Lord Sumner without allowing your own heart to become involved. I would never have encouraged the suit had I thought otherwise.'' Lady Agatha shook her head sadly. "Lord Sumner is considered a good catch for any young woman, but I must warn you he's as wily as a fox in a henhouse. He's escaped the bonds of matrimony many a time. But it's not too late to set your sights on Lord Barclay's nephew . . . or any of the other eligible bachelors—''

"Lady Devon, we have been looking for you,'' Sir Christopher Grant said as he and his friend, Sir Reginald Halstead, stopped in front of the two ladies, neatly cutting short Lady Agatha's tirade about Lord Barclay's nephew. "We both insist that you reserve us a dance. It's unfair that old Sumner does his best to keep every beauty away from us when he's home. I know he's a captain in the king's army and that makes him irritably daring in your eyes, but 'tis unjust that we poor devils have to suffer being ignored.''

Christopher's banter brought a smile to Devon's lips even as his last words added to her dilemma over Lord Sumner. She'd met both Christopher and Reginald at her first ball and had grown to like them during the ensuing weeks. They had given her their friendship without question, and it was a shame that neither one fit the one requirement she needed in a husband. Both were nice young men from good families, but neither possessed the wealth it would take to save Mackinsey Hall for her grandmother.

After a few moments of conversation several other young people joined their group. Feeling excluded by her age and status, and knowing it was futile to continue to try to convince Devon of the mistake she was making by not considering Lord Barclay's nephew, Lady Agatha moved out of the group. She found a seat several chairs away from the ruling hierarchy of matrons and dowagers. She wouldn't press her company upon them. She knew exactly how they felt about her and had long ago resigned herself to ignore such treatment. She had managed to enter their world, but she was wise enough not to intrude upon those who ruled within it. Even she didn't possess that much bravado. She could avenge her hurt pride upon those lesser mortals like Lady Heath.

Relieved by the momentary reprieve, Devon forced herself not to think of the man on the other side of the ballroom—or the problems his disaffection would create in her life. During the past months she had been accepted by the younger set and she intended to enjoy their company as long as possible. She had known few people of her own age even at the expensive boarding school she'd attended during the past eight years of her life. And she'd made even fewer friends. At Mistress Cameron's Academy she'd been looked upon as an outsider. Her ignorance of the social graces had set her completely apart from the other girls. After several vain attempts to fit in, and being spurned for her efforts, Devon had learned to keep to herself. She'd find isolation far less painful than the punishment she'd received after attempting to trounce one of the girls who had ridiculed her. She had turned her attention to her lessons, absorbing everything her mentors could teach, determined to show everyone that she had a right to exist—to be a Mackinsey.

The lessons learned at the academy had held her in good stead these past months. London's younger set hadn't guessed that she had once been little more than a scullery maid. They included her in their group and made her laugh with their droll comments. From criticizing their elders for their decrepit ideas on how the young should behave, to talking exuberantly about the next race at Ascot, or a dozen other trivial matters, their witty conversation made Devon forget for a short time that her life was far more complicated than the young people's who had befriended her.

However, reality always returned once she left the balls and glamour behind. Sitting beside her grandmother's sickbed, she had to put aside the fantasy created beneath the glittering chandeliers. She was not one of the wealthy young women who flocked to the balls in search of a husband. She was Devon Mackinsey, bastard of Lord Colin Mackinsey and heir to a paupered estate. Her quest was also for a husband, but her responsibilities made it necessary to survive. She had to make an advantageous marriage to renew her family's fortunes. She couldn't afford to waste the time and the few resources she possessed in innocent flirtation.

While Christopher launched into another amusing tale, Devon glanced once more toward Lord Sumner and saw him smile in greeting. She returned the gesture with a provocative one of her own and haughtily turned her attention back to Christopher Grant's humorous repartee. She'd be damned if she'd allow Neal Sumner to suspect how desperate she was.

A few moments later she felt Lord Sumner's presence behind her before he took her hand and drew her away from the group. His cinnamon-colored eyes smiled possessively down at her. "My lady, I believe you promised me this dance."

A streak of rebellion stiffened Devon's resolve. She needed a rich husband, but she'd not let him fawn all over Amy Ferguson and then march over to claim her attentions as if it were his due. She couldn't force herself to grovel. She'd done many things in the past months that made her cringe with mortification, but she hadn't completely lost all of her pride. Perversely she withdrew her hand from his. "My lord, I fear there has been a mistake. I have promised the next dance to Sir Christopher."

"I fear Sir Christopher is unable to keep the dance, my lady. It seems he's too caught up in one of his ridiculous stories." Lord Sumner flashed Christopher Grant a quelling look, daring him to protest.

Christopher's taut expression reflected his resentment at Lord Sumner's pretentious behavior, but he made no objections. He knew well the older man's reputation with sword and pistol and he didn't want to risk being called out over such a minor thing as a dance. Christopher's eyes begged Devon's understanding as he looked at her and lifted one shoulder in an inconspicuous shrug of defeat.

Devon shot Christopher a piqued glance before she accepted Lord Sumner's hand. "It would seem, my lord, I am the one who made the mistake."

Too arrogant to understand her double meaning, Neal Sumner's teeth gleamed white against his sun-bronzed skin as he bestowed one of his most charming smiles upon Devon and led her onto the dance floor. As he took her in his arms, he whispered, "You are forgiven, my sweet."

Devon nearly groaned her vexation aloud. Her temples throbbed from the blood coursing through her veins. The gall of the man! He had the audacity to grant his forgiveness . . . when in truth he should ask her clemency! In that moment it took all of Devon's willpower to keep from walking off the dance floor. Swallowing back a few well-spiced words about him and his ancestry, she plastered a sweet smile on her lips, pointedly glanced in Amy Ferguson's direction, and responded glibly, "My lord, how benevolent you are to forgive my transgressions."

Noting the direction of Devon's look, Lord Sumner cajoled, his voice low and seductive, "Ah, sweet Devon. Surely you aren't angry with me for amusing myself with poor Amy until you arrived?" He smoothly maneuvered Devon toward the doors which opened out onto a balcony overlooking the misty torch-lit gardens.

"I have no right to be angry, my lord. You are free to amuse yourself with whomever you choose, as am I," Devon said, breaking their embrace as they passed through the tall multipaned doors. She stepped away from Neal and turned her back to him. She absently rubbed her arms against the chill in the damp evening air and strove to get a grip on her mounting temper.

Lord Sumner's warm hands came to rest on Devon's shoulders, drawing her back against his lean body. Vanity in his appearance, as well as his years in the army, kept him hard and trim. "Ah, Devon, you know you are the only one who holds my heart."

"Surely you jest, my lord," Devon boldly stated. The time had come to put an end to the games. She had to know Lord Sumner's intentions. "I have as yet to hear you say you love me."

Lord Sumner brushed his lips lightly against the side of Devon's neck. His touch sent an involuntary tremor down her spine.

"Surely you already know my feelings. You know I want

you. You are one of the most beautiful women I've ever seen.''

''Are you then asking for my hand in marriage, my lord?'' Devon held her breath, waiting for Neal to make a liar out of Higgins. She felt his hands tense on her shoulders and sensed his withdrawal before she heard him expel a long breath. Devon closed her eyes. She had the answer to her question before he spoke.

''Devon, don't ruin what we have together by putting strings on it. Let us enjoy the time we have before I'm sent to fight the colonials.''

Lord Sumner's subtle reminder of the precarious life he led as a soldier missed its target. Devon was too preoccupied with her own problems for it to work on her—as it had done on so many other naive young women in Neal Sumner's past. ''Then you have no intention of offering for me?''

Lord Sumner let his hands fall to his side. ''Devon, you are one of the most desirable women I've ever encountered, but even that isn't enough to make me want to marry you. If that is what you've been working to achieve, I fear you've failed.''

Devon spun around to face Lord Sumner. Her forest green eyes blazed with dark fire. ''Then you have only been toying with my affections during the past weeks? Your pursuit has meant nothing?''

Lord Sumner shrugged and grinned sardonically, the gesture lifting one side of his shapely mouth. ''I wouldn't call it toying, my dear. You've been hot after me since the first night we met. If anything, I would say you're the one who has been pursuing me instead of the other way round.''

''Sir, no gentleman would say such a thing to a lady,'' Devon ground out. She held her fists balled at her sides and struggled valiantly to suppress the urge to slug the man in his hard, flat middle.

''I beg to differ with you, my lady. Had I not been a

gentleman I would have already tossed up your skirts and given you exactly what you've been begging for all these weeks."

"How dare you speak to me in such a way!" Devon spluttered indignantly.

Lord Sumner's brown eyes sparkled with annoyance. He took a step closer and his voice came low and steely. "I dare because I am Lord Neal Sumner and you are nothing but a kitchen maid decked out like a lady."

Devon gasped. His words struck her like a physical blow. Mortification burned her cheeks, yet she didn't cower. "If that is the way you have felt, then why have you wasted your time with me?"

Lord Sumner's hand shot out and grasped Devon by the arm, dragging her once more against him. He peered down into her lovely face and sneered. "As I've already told you, you are one of the most desirable women I've ever encountered. Being Lord Mackinsey's bastard doesn't dampen my craving for you. Between the sheets all women are alike, be they ladies or whores or even bastards. The difference is made when it comes time to breed them for an heir. Then only a woman worthy of my name shall possess it."

Devon's hand shot out before she had time to reconsider her actions. She slapped Lord Sumner's cheek with a loud, resounding crack. The force of the blow staggered his senses long enough for Devon to escape his bruising grip. She backed away from him and regally raised her head in the air. She drew upon every lesson she'd ever learned at Mistress Cameron's and confronted Lord Sumner. "Don't you ever touch me again. I may not have been born a legitimate Mackinsey, but I am one now, legally. And I will not be insulted again. I will bid you good night, Lord Sumner. May our paths never cross again."

Lord Sumner rubbed at his stinging cheek. His narrowed eyes glittered with malice as he watched Devon stalk away with back stiff and head held high. One way or the other he vowed to make the haughty bitch pay dearly for striking him. And before he was through with her, she'd be in his bed—as he had planned since the first night he'd seen her stroll gracefully into the ballroom at Lord Sedgewick's less than two months ago.

Shaken from her encounter with Lord Sumner—and in a rush to put as much distance as possible between herself and the hateful man—Devon wasn't watching where she was going. She bumped into a hard, lean figure near the refreshment table. Strong, long-fingered hands came out to steady her. She glanced up at the man and opened her mouth to apologize for her clumsiness. The words died on her lips and her heart froze. Her eyes widened in horror and shock as she recognized Hunter Barclay.

Hunter's grip tightened about Devon's arms as he stared down at her, his own eyes mirroring her shock. "Well, I'll be damned if it isn't my little thief."

Afraid someone might have overheard Hunter, Devon glanced anxiously from side to side. She breathed a sigh of relief when she realized no one had been close enough to hear his damning remark. Her relief, however, was short-lived as she looked back at her captor. She swallowed uneasily at his stony expression and her heart began to beat furiously against her ribs.

Thinking fast, Devon tried to convince him that he'd mistaken her for someone else. "Sir, I'm afraid I don't know what you are talking about. I've never seen you before in my life, nor am I the person you seem to believe." Devon bluffed and silently sent a prayer toward heaven for divine intervention.

Hunter's brow furrowed as his gaze swept over each of Devon's finely sculpted features. He never forgot a name or a face. That talent was one of the reasons he had been chosen to come to England by General Washington. Once he saw something, it was imprinted upon his memory as if carved in stone. He knew he wasn't mistaken about this girl. Only once before had he ever seen eyes the color of hers—and that was last night at his uncle's house! "Mistress, you must truly think me a fool to try to convince me I've made a mistake."

"Sir, I don't know you well enough to think anything of you. Now if you would please release me, I would like to make my excuses to our hostess and leave. I have the beginnings of a splitting headache."

"You're not going anywhere until I have some answers, mistress. You have managed to insinuate yourself among Lady Heath's guests, but I'll not stand by and allow you to line your pockets with their coin and jewels. I warned you last night that my benevolent nature would not last should you cross my path again."

Devon felt a sinking sensation in the pit of her belly as she looked up into his flinty blue eyes. This night had been a disaster from beginning to end. Her hopes of making a good marriage had evaporated in the heat of the ballroom, and now she faced Newgate if this man chose to expose her as the Shadow. Devon closed her eyes and sought to draw the protective chrysalis around her once more. She needed its protection now as much as she had all those years ago when she'd worked in the kitchen at Mackinsey Hall. Her days as a society butterfly had abruptly come to an end. Now she was nothing more than a moth to be squashed under the heel of Hunter Barclay's boot.

"Devon, my dear. I was just looking for you. I wanted you to meet Lord Barclay's nephew, but I see I'm already too late," Lady Agatha gushed. She gave Hunter an ingratiating smile and glanced knowingly at the hand resting upon Devon's arm. Things were going well between the two young people if Devon allowed him to touch her after such a short time. Devon had kept even Neal Sumner at arm's length for several weeks after their first meeting.

"I'm afraid we have as yet to be introduced, my lady.

Would you do the honors?'' Hunter asked, his eyes never
leaving Devon's stricken face.

Too elated to question why Hunter should touch Devon
so intimately before being properly introduced, Lady Agatha glanced from one young face to the other. ''Of course.
Sir, I would like to present Lady Devon Mackinsey. If my
memory serves me correctly, I believe her grandmother
and yours were girlhood friends.''

Only a slightly arched brow revealed Hunter's surprise
to find his thief had a well-connected family. However,
that changed nothing in his eyes. He smiled coolly down
at Devon and her name rolled like fine wine over his
tongue. ''Devon, how nice to finally make your acquaintance. I feel we've known each other far longer than just
a few minutes. Would you allow me this dance?''

Devon shot Lady Agatha an agonized look and raised
an unsteady hand to her brow. ''I'm sorry. I suddenly don't
feel well. It must be the heat. The muggy weather makes
it stifling in here. If you will excuse me, I'll go and sit
down.''

Hunter hid his smile. He expected no less from the little
baggage, and she didn't disappoint him by trying to use
any ruse to escape. ''My lady, I'm so sorry to hear it. I'm
sure a few moments of fresh air would do wonders for
your health.'' Without waiting for Devon's answer or an
apology to Lady Agatha, who stood with mouth open in
astonishment at Hunter's rudeness, he firmly led Devon
out onto the balcony.

Wanting no further interruptions, Hunter closed the glass
doors securely behind them before turning to look at
Devon. She stood with back braced against the marble
balustrade and arms folded belligerently over her ripe
bosom. She regarded him warily as he approached.

Hunter paused within arm's length of Devon. He couldn't
stop himself from admiring her boldness. Knowing the
game was up by this time, many a man would have been

groveling at his feet for mercy. Not Lady Devon Mackinsey. She eyed him as if daring him to do his worst and be damned.

Hunter felt his blood stir. What was it about this one woman that set him on fire with just a mere glance from her forest green eyes? He had met women who were far more voluptuous and in ways far more beautiful, yet this girl had something about her that got under his skin and made him itch to take her to his bed. Itch, Hunter thought, and smiled to himself. That wasn't exactly the proper term to use for the way she made his body react.

Hunter drew in a deep breath. "Now Lady Devon Mackinsey, I think it's time that you explained yourself without dredging up a dozen imaginary cripples and blind mothers."

Devon couldn't stop the smile that twitched her lips at the memory of her far-fetched story. She had to admit it was the most absurd lie anyone could have concocted.

"You may laugh all you want, my lady. But before this night is over, I promise you, you'll regret making a fool of me."

Abruptly sobered by his harsh tone and knowing there was no need for further denial, Devon looked at Hunter. "At the time I wasn't trying to make a fool of you. I was only trying to keep you from sending me to Newgate. I would have said or done anything last night to avoid that fate."

Unable to stop himself, Hunter only half listened to Devon's excuse. Caught in the snare of her forest green eyes, he felt himself drowning in their expressive depths. His heart began to pump wildly within his chest as his body instinctively reacted to the alluring creature standing before him. He swelled against the tight fabric of his black velvet breeches as his gaze drifted down to Devon's luscious mouth. His mind seized upon the memory of the previous night and he could nearly taste her lips again. Drawn by the memory, he leaned forward, so close that his velvet jacket and the ruffles of his intricately tied cravat brushed Devon's folded arms. He raised a hand to her cheek and lightly traced its delicate line. His voice was soft and husky as he asked, "What would you do tonight to keep me from exposing your secret, Lady Devon?"

Devon nervously moistened her lips. She recognized her danger, but knew she was powerless to deny him. He held her life—as well as her grandmother's—in his strong hands. Devon swallowed and lowered her lashes. "Anything you ask."

"Ah, sweet Devon. You make it too easy for a man who hasn't had a woman in his bed for several long weeks," Hunter said, pushing back the guilt stabbing at his conscience for taking advantage of the lovely girl in such a way. After all, he rationalized, she was only a common little thief who, for all her expensive gowns and haughty title, was little better than the guttersnipe she had pretended to be the previous night. From what he had seen of Devon Mackinsey, she had few morals. And he doubted she'd object to sharing his bed to earn her freedom. She did owe him something for not turning her over to the authorities.

Great tears of fright brimmed in Devon's eyes and she blinked rapidly to stay them as she repeated hoarsely, "I will do anything you ask of me if you will give me your word not to tell anyone of what you have learned. I ask not for myself, but for those I love."

Hunter lowered his mouth to her trembling lips. His arms came about her, crushing her to his urgent body. Devon felt the hard swelling through the thick layers of her gown. She felt repulsed, but forced herself to remain still, allowing him to have his way. She cringed as his tongue slid between her teeth and then plunged into her mouth. She knew he expected a response, but she could not give it. It took every ounce of willpower she possessed to keep from flailing at his chest with her fists. He only kissed her, but she felt raped, both physically and mentally.

Hunter lifted his head and peered down at Devon. He frowned. Skin ashen, her eyes pressed tightly closed, she wore a martyred expression. Her rose-tinted lips were held in a mutinous line. Damn her, Hunter thought, as a streak of perversity shot through him. His temper snapped. If any other woman showed such disgust at his touch, he would have turned his back and walked away. But this little hussy played too many games for him to trust the look on her face now—any more than he could trust her stories. He'd be damned if he'd fall prey to them again. "It won't work, Devon. I'm not going to let you off the hook that easy. You've agreed to do anything I ask and I intend to take you up on the offer. I'll give you a few hours reprieve tonight, but tomorrow evening I will expect you no later than eight o'clock at my uncle's house."

Devon's eyes shot open and she stared up at him, unable to speak.

Hunter smiled, but there was no warmth in the gesture as he looked at her. "I know you know the way, my dear, so I'll not give you directions. However this time, come in by the front door. It will be much more convenient than coming through the garden gate."

Hunter released Devon and turned to leave her.

"What will you do if I don't obey your wishes?" Devon's question was little more than a desperate whisper.

Hunter didn't turn. "I think you already know the answer. Nor do I think I will have to contact the authorities and tell them of our little secret, do you? I know who you are now, Devon, and I can always find you. I'm not a man to be trifled with. So don't even think of going back on our bargain."

Hunter opened the doors and stepped inside, leaving Devon trembling on the balcony. She closed her eyes and leaned her head back to draw in a steadying breath of the damp night air. Defeat welled within her breast. She had less than twenty-four hours before she had to pay Hunter Barclay's price to keep her secret.

Devon gave herself a sharp mental shake and grasped the marble balustrade firmly with both hands. Her chin set determinedly and her eyes glittered with spite as she stared out into the torch-lit garden. She wouldn't accept defeat until the moment she had to surrender. She had been given time to find a way to avoid Hunter Barclay's demands and she'd not stop until she found it.

Devon heard a giggle below and looked to see Neal Sumner leading Amy Ferguson into the damp garden for a lover's tryst. Her eyes narrowed thoughtfully as she watched the couple stroll down the path and into the shadows.

Devon considered her options and realized there was only one sure way to avoid Hunter Barclay's demands. She had to find a place to hide until Hunter left England. She would go to Mackinsey Hall. But before she could leave London, she had to pay off her creditors.

Devon's gaze wandered back to the spot where Lord Sumner and Amy Ferguson had disappeared into the darkness. She smiled. Her hopes of solving her financial problems with her marriage to Neal Sumner had come to an end this evening. However, Lord Sumner could still help her save her home. She'd once overheard Neal bragging to one of his friends that out of consideration for his banker's feelings, he always kept a ready supply of money on hand to pay his gaming debts. It kept him from disturbing his banker's sleep when he ran low on funds and allowed Neal to enjoy himself without leaving any personal markers behind to worry about collecting later. At the time Devon had thought him wise and kind for his thoughtfulness of the banker's feeling. Now that she'd seen the real Neal Sumner, she knew he had no consideration for anyone's feelings beyond his own. And after the weeks he'd led her to believe he loved her, she felt he owed her some recompense.

Devon's smile deepened. For once in her checkered career as a burglar, she'd feel no remorse about taking the gold she needed to pay her debts and free her from Hunter Barclay's demands.

"I'm going home," Devon murmured softly, her voice mirroring her longing to be back at Mackinsey Hall.

Devon held her head high as she left Lady Heath's without a backward glance. She didn't notify Lady Agatha of her departure. She had paid the woman a healthy sum for her help and now had no further need of her assistance since she had decided to put London's society behind her. She was gathering her family and going back to Mackinsey Hall, where they all belonged.

"Take me back to the town house to change, Winkler," Devon said as he assisted her into the coach. "We have work to do tonight."

Chapter 5

Preoccupied with her plans to return to Mackinsey Hall, Devon wasn't aware of the gentleman who followed her from Lady Heath's. Nor did she note the sleek, black coach that stayed close behind her vehicle until she reached home. It drew to a halt only a few feet away from the iron gates in front of the town house.

Anxious to put this night behind her, Devon didn't glance up as she stepped down from the coach and hurried along the flagged walk that led to the gate. She wanted to see how her grandmother fared before she set out to repay Neal Sumner for his insult. While he used his wiles to seduce another unwitting young woman, Devon would be filling her pockets with his coins.

Heedless of the vehicle at the curb, Devon jerked off her gloves as she went. She came to an abrupt halt as a black-cloaked figure leapt down from the coach into her path. A gasp of surprise escaped her and her eyes widened in dismay at the unexpected and sudden appearance of Hunter Barclay. She had hoped never to see the man again.

"Good evening, my lady," Hunter said, with a gracefully polite nod of his dark head.

"What are you doing here?" Devon asked uneasily.

"My lady, I've decided we don't need to wait to complete our bargain," Hunter said, and proffered his hand to Devon. "From my previous experience with you, I doubt you'll be within a hundred miles of London by eight o'clock tomorrow night.''

Devon's cheeks flushed with guilt at his accurate assumption. She stepped out of the lantern light spilling from within the coach. Hopefully the deeper shadows would effectively hide the look of contrition that she knew crossed her face at being caught in her deception. Feigning a bravado she didn't feel, she glanced haughtily at Hunter's extended hand, but made no move to take it. She raised her chin proudly in the air. ''You may doubt my word, sir, but that changes nothing. Nor does your decision not to wait. We made an agreement . . . and I haven't changed my mind. It still stands.''

''I've made the decision for both of us,'' Hunter said. He closed the space between them and took Devon by the elbow, turning her toward his coach. After leaving her on the balcony, Hunter, still intrigued, had positioned himself so that he could observe her without her notice. He had seen her expression when she entered the ballroom and knew instantly some plan was afoot in her devious little mind. And so he had followed her.

''What in the devil do ye think yer a doing, me fine bloke?'' Winkler growled, leaping nimbly from the driver's seat to the sidewalk and hurrying toward Devon. ''I'd take me hands off the lady if I was ye, or I'll take 'em off fer ye. Starting at yer shoulders.''

''Tell your man to leave us, Devon. This is between you and me.'' Perturbed by his own erratic behavior, Hunter was in no mood to argue the point with Devon or her servant.

Devon flashed Winkler a beseeching look. ''Winkler, it's all right.''

''It don't look all right to me. This bloke ain't got no right to come and manhandle a lady like yerself. And I won't mind giving 'im a good thrashing to teach 'im better manners.''

"Winkler, please. Go inside and tell Higgins I'll be along shortly. Mr. Barclay and I have some things we need to discuss." Seeing the rebellious expression that crossed her friend's face as he eyed Hunter suspiciously, Devon shook her head. "I'll be all right. Now go and wait for me inside."

"I ain't a liking this one little bit, Devon. Nor will 'iggins like it when I tell 'im what's 'appened," Winkler muttered as he turned away. He paused at the fanned steps that led up to the front door of the town house, glanced back at Devon, and then shook his head. "Ain't right. No matter what ye say. The bloke deserves a good trouncing."

Devon breathed a sigh of relief as Winkler closed the door behind him. She looked back at Hunter, her temper flaring. "Are you satisfied? Must the world know what you're forcing me to do? Can't you just leave me alone? I agreed to meet you tomorrow night."

"Come, Devon," Hunter said, undaunted by her explosion. "I've arranged for us to have a late dinner in a private room at the Cock and Crow. We can discuss this there."

Devon jerked free of Hunter's hand. She lost the rein she'd held on her temper and it loosed her wayward tongue. Before she could draw them back the words spilled out, revealing far more than she'd intended. "I'm not going anywhere with you, nor am I going to meet you tomorrow night. I'm a thief—not a whore to service you while you're in London. Send for the authorities if that is your want, but be aware that they might be far more interested to know the true reason you've come to London than they are to catch the Shadow. Treason, like stealing, is a hanging offense."

Hunter stiffened. She had heard his conversation with Mordecai. He'd been a fool not to have realized that she had been in the study all along.

Hunter looked down into Devon's beautiful shadowed face. The knowledge she now possessed could jeopardize the people who provided the finances—as well as the information the colonies needed to secure arms. It would be a disaster should anyone learn of it. The Dutch rulers would stop the supplies because they couldn't risk creating more tension between their country and Britain. At present they had already put an embargo on naval supplies and ammunition. Fortunately for the patriots, they had also turned a blind eye to the smugglers who continued the shipments of contraband stores. However, should Devon tell what she knew, everything would be ruined.

Hunter's face turned to stone. His eyes glittered with a dangerous light as he looked down at Devon and his voice was velvet-coated steel when he spoke. "So, my lady, we are at an impasse. In my hand I hold the secret that could put a noose about your lovely throat . . . and in your hands you also tie the knot for mine."

Devon's breasts rose and fell rapidly as she breathed. She had stupidly allowed her temper to get out of control and had placed her life in jeopardy. Silently vowing to cut out her unruly tongue, Devon knew she couldn't back down now. Nothing she could say or do would alter the fact that Hunter Barclay knew she had overheard his conversation. The only thing left her was to brazen it out.

Devon looked into Hunter's stony face. "I agree, sir. And I think we can come to a mutual understanding. I see no need to reveal what I overheard as long as you keep my secret."

Though he might want to wrap his hands about her silky throat and strangle the life from her, Hunter couldn't stop the flicker of admiration Devon's courage roused. The girl was no fool. She saw the benefits for herself and bargained like a man instead of simpering and whining for mercy. In a no-nonsense manner, she cut through the fluff and got to the heart of the matter. Should either reveal what they knew of the other, both would end up on the gibbet.

"But can I trust you? If I recall, you have a penchant to lie and break agreements. Can you deny you had no intention of keeping our bargain tomorrow night?"

Devon shook her head. "No. I won't deny it. What you proposed was indecent and degrading. I have done many things in my life of which I'm not proud, as I suspect have you. But I'm no man's whore."

One corner of Hunter's mouth lifted in a cynical little grin. "You expect me to believe you are all innocent virtue when I found you trying to rob my uncle? And when nearly every word you've uttered since our unfortunate meeting has been a lie?"

"I don't expect you to believe anything of me. I just want you to leave me alone. I'm leaving London tomorrow morning, so you have no need to fear that I will tell anyone of your exploits here in England. I have no quarrel with you or your colonies. I have far too many other things to give my attention."

Hunter arched a skeptical brow but didn't argue. The point was moot. Either he had to accept her word and go his own way—or silence her before she could put a noose about his neck. Hunter drew in a deep breath. For the first time in his life he was torn with indecision. Here he faced one of the most dangerous situations in his life and he couldn't decide what should be done . . . because of a pair of unforgettable forest green eyes and a mouth meant to give a man pleasure.

Exasperated, Hunter snaked out a hand and captured Devon by the arm, drawing her close. He peered down into her lovely face. "My lady. Let me caution you. I have many friends in England. Betray me and neither you nor those you love will live to watch me hang."

Devon swallowed the lump in her dry throat. It went down slowly, making it difficult to speak. "I, too, have friends, Hunter Barclay. Live up to our agreement and you will live to fight in your Revolution. And I suggest you pray for my safety. Should anything untoward happen to me, or should someone perhaps learn of the Shadow's identity once you leave England, your friends' lives will rest in your hands. Can you live with that thought?''

Hunter's fingers tightened on Devon's arm until she could deny the pain no longer. She cringed. ''Don't threaten too much, my dear. Remember, you have as yet to tell anyone of what you heard. But I do have you now. I could easily snap your neck and no one would ever be the wiser.''

''Winkler saw you here.''

Hunter's smile was cold and deadly. ''Yes, but who will the authorities believe? Lord Barclay's heir or the coachman of a thief. Or better yet, I could also have poor Winkler silenced. It would be much simpler.'' Even as the words left his mouth, Hunter knew it was an empty threat, but he hoped Devon would believe it enough to keep her beautiful, intoxicating lips closed about his meeting with Mordecai.

''Please, just leave me. I won't jeopardize my friends or family to save my own life.''

Hunter's fingers relaxed, but he didn't release Devon. He stared down at her, bewildered. He believed her. Hunter gave himself a mental kick. He'd also believed her last night. Shrugging the doubts aside, a rueful grin tugged up the corners of his shapely mouth. ''Then let us seal our deal with a kiss, Lady Mackinsey. For it will be the last time that we meet.''

Before Devon could protest, Hunter's arms came about her and his mouth claimed hers in a searing, soul-shattering kiss. His lips seemed to drain the resistance from her, leaving her only aware of the tingling new sensations forming in the very depths of her being. They rippled in tiny, ever widening circles, and like a tidal wave they grew stronger until they washed every reasonable thought from her mind. Devon unconsciously relaxed, molding herself against Hunter's sinewy length, fitting there as if finding her other half.

Man's world came to a jolting halt in the few moments Hunter's mouth demanded a response from hers. Gone into the misty night were the verbal sparring, the lies, the threats. There was no thought of the morrow or of the past. All that existed were the feelings sweeping over them. The moment, the sensation, the pull of pure animal magnetism so strong that it could no longer be refuted laid claim to them as they stood bound on equal ground by their passions.

Lost in the pleasures she had denied herself from his kisses before, Devon stared mutely up at Hunter when he abruptly set her away from him. He gazed down into her eyes for a long moment and then shook his head as if to clear it. "Good-bye, Lady Mackinsey. I wish you a safe journey on the morrow."

Hunter didn't look back. He walked to his coach and climbed once more into the driver's seat. He picked up the whip and snapped it across the horses' backs, setting them abruptly into motion. He didn't allow himself to think of the beautiful thief he'd left standing on the sidewalk or the feelings she'd aroused in him. He had to concentrate on the job he'd been sent here to do. His homeland was under siege from George III and he'd fight to his dying breath to see it free.

Staggered by Hunter's kiss and then his abrupt departure, Devon watched the coach until it rounded the corner and moved out of sight. She touched her lips and felt hot tears sting the backs of her eyelids. She suddenly felt a keen sense of loss.

"Stop this, you silly twit. You're lucky you're not in Newgate," Devon muttered softly to herself, and turned toward the flagged walk. She had work to do tonight if she wanted to return to Mackinsey Hall. Devon paused with her hand on the latch and glanced once more toward the silent street. "Good-bye, Hunter Barclay. May the angels keep you out of harm's way. May no one else learn your secret." Devon opened the door and stepped inside.

After tonight her secret would be put to rest, Devon reasoned as she tossed her black velvet cape aside and glanced up the winding stairs. She would not mourn the Shadow's demise, but she would her grandmother's. Drawing in a deep, bracing breath, she started up the stairs.

Higgins rose from the chair outside her grandmother's room. "She's resting, Devon. I just looked in on her."

"Thank you, Higgins," Devon said, relieved to know that her grandmother had survived a few more hours. "I know I'm asking much of you, but will you stay a short while longer. I have another errand I need to attend to tonight."

Higgins closed his eyes and shook his head. "Devon, this has to stop."

Devon reached out and placed her hand on his sleeve. She could feel his bony arm through the worn fabric. "This is the last, Higgins. Have Winkler pack our things while I'm gone. We are going back to Mackinsey Hall early tomorrow. Grandmother needs to be at home."

"You need Winkler to be with you," Higgins said. "I won't hear of you going by yourself."

"I don't need Winkler tonight. Lord Sumner lives only a few streets away. Should my coach be seen there, someone might suspect the true identity of the Shadow."

"My God, Devon. Have you gone mad?" Higgins gasped.

"No. I've finally come to my senses, thanks to you, old friend. You warned me about the man, but I refused to listen. Now I know him for exactly the scoundrel he is and I intend to see that he pays for leading me to believe he loved me. Now I won't hear any more arguments. The hour is growing late and I must hurry before he returns from Lady Heath's.''

Higgins watched Devon walk briskly down the hall to her chamber. He felt as if he'd aged ten years in the last few days. For a while everything seemed to go in Devon's favor, but the moon had changed the tide. She had nearly been caught at Lord Montmain's and, though she hadn't told him exactly what had transpired last night at Lord Barclay's, he knew something had gone wrong with her plans. Now, tonight she planned on robbing Lord Sumner. Should the man catch her, he would see her hanged out of pure meanness of spirit.

Higgins slumped down in the chair and buried his head in his swollen-jointed hands. God! How he wished he could convince her to let things be. But he knew Devon far too well. She was too stubborn for her own good.

Devon held the candle above the open chest and gave a low, astonished whistle. She'd found Neal's strongbox easily. However, she'd never expected to find such booty. Unable to restrain the impulse, Devon dipped one hand down into the shining mass and lifted it into the air. The coins filtered through her fingers in a cascade of gleaming gold.

"My God, there's enough here to pay off Mackinsey Hall and to buy a new herd of sheep," Devon murmured softly. Lost in her visions for the future, she didn't hear the click of the door latch behind her or the soft tread of footsteps on the thick carpet.

The prick between her shoulders from the point of a rapier's sharp blade made Devon stiffen in alarm. A foreboding chill tingled down her spine when a soft, menacing male voice warned, "Make no swift moves or you're a dead man."

Instantly recognizing the voice of her captor, Devon nodded her assent and balled her fists in impotent fury at her sides. It took all her willpower to suppress the urge to scream her vexation at herself. God! She had allowed herself to become so engrossed with her plans for Neal's gold that she'd let down her guard. Now she found herself caught again. However, this time she doubted she'd find the mercy from Neal Sumner that she'd found with Hunter Barclay. Devon could already hear the prison gates slam closed behind her.

"Have I managed to catch the great, elusive Shadow?" Neal asked, prodding an answer from Devon with added pressure on the rapier. She nodded even as she felt the blade sink through the material of her jacket to prick her skin.

Neal laughed in triumph. "Damn me. I've heard a great deal about you. Turn round and let me get a good look at the face of the man who has all London talking about how cunning he is."

As Devon slowly turned to face her captor, Neal continued. "You know you've become something of a legend. But like all things, legends have a way of coming to an end when someone reveals the—the myth . . ." Neal stuttered to a halt. His eyes widened momentarily in surprise as he recognized the finely sculpted features of the woman who had slapped him at Lady Heath's a few hours earlier. Eyes narrowing, his expression filling with icy rancor, he absently rubbed his fingers over the jaw Devon had struck.

"My, my," Neal growled contemptuously. "It seems fate has once more seen fit to cast us together, dear Devon." Neal lowered his rapier and eyed his captive insolently from head to toe.

Devon didn't cower under his hostile glare. She looked him directly in the eyes and strove to squelch the tremor of fear that quaked her insides. "What do you intend to do with me?" she asked.

A cruel grin lifted one corner of Neal's mouth as his gaze once more slid insultingly over Devon. "I'm sure the authorities will be more than happy to deal with you since you've made it so very difficult for them during the past weeks, my dear. I doubt they will have much sympathy for the Shadow once they get you into their hands.''

"Then what are you waiting for? Call the authorities and be done with it," Devon said, her stomach churning.

Neal took a step closer, backing Devon against the desk that held the strongbox. Her heart began to pound against her ribs as she looked into his eyes. They seemed to gleam with pinpoints of fire. Devon swallowed nervously as she suddenly realized Neal had no intention of turning her over to the authorities until he had taken his own revenge.

"Dear, foolish, Devon," Neal scolded softly, as if speaking to a misguided child. "You must truly believe me an idiot if you think I'm going to allow you to be sent to Newgate before I extract payment for the blow you gave me tonight."

Devon's back felt as if it would snap as she leaned farther away from Neal. Her voice was only a shaky whisper as she asked, "What do you intend to do?"

Neal grinned. "I intend to have you, my dear. As I had planned from the first moment I laid eyes on you."

"I won't let you." Devon's insides trembled at the smile her words brought to Neal's lips.

"You won't have any choice." Neal brought his hand up to caress Devon's ashen cheek. His voice suddenly became dreamy. "It's been a long while since I've had a woman against her will. You know, that's the one thing I've always liked about being a soldier. After a hard-fought battle there are always the women who resist surrendering to the victors. I like the fight they put up in their attempts to save their virtue. It heightens my pleasure to see them squirm in pain as I thrust into their tight, unwilling bodies. There is nothing better than dipping my sword into my enemies' blood and my prick into their women."

A look of horror crossed Devon's face. "You're disgusting."

Neal's fingers tightened on Devon's skin and his mouth thinned into a snarl. "You'll change your mind after I've had you. You'll beg me not to send for the authorities, but it'll do you no good, bitch."

The threat giving impetus to her effort to escape, Devon brought up both hands and shoved at Neal's chest with all her might. Caught off-guard by her sudden attack, he staggered backward, but didn't lose his balance. He reached out and grabbed her as she made a dash for the door. He fought to subdue her, wrapping both arms about her squirming body. Twisting and turning, Devon struggled to free herself from the iron bands encircling her. Her hat slipped from her head and her hair tumbled in a mass of gleaming mahogany about them. With a squeal of fury, she brought her foot down on Neal's instep. A cry of pained surprise escaped him and he momentarily lessened his hold upon Devon, giving her the advantage she sought. Turning in his arms, a mass of bared claws, she went for his eyes.

Accurately assessing his perilous situation, Neal caught Devon's hands before she could do him lasting damage. Vainly he tried to subdue the wild thing clawing and biting at him. He wrestled her about the study, twisting and banging into furniture. Chairs toppled and books crashed to the floor in the fury of their wake.

At last Devon struggled free of Neal's hold and once more turned to flee. A growl of outrage rumbled from deep within Neal's chest as he launched himself into her path. Catching his movement from the corner of her eye, Devon danced to one side and pushed at him with all her might. Neal staggered again, his own momentum making him lose his balance. He stumbled toward the fireplace, where red coals glowed hot and bright. Seeing his danger, he threw out his hands in time to prevent himself from falling face first into the fiery embers. Neal's left hand sank into the blazing inferno. The sleeve of his velvet jacket burst into flames as he screamed in agony and rolled across the carpet, withering from the fire licking greedily up his arm.

Reacting solely on instinct, Devon jerked off her cape and threw it about him, beating at the flames until they were extinguished and Neal lay panting for breath on the floor.

"I will get help," Devon said, hurrying to her feet. She turned to the door and found Neal's entire staff gaping at her. "Send for a doctor. Can't you see your master has been hurt?"

A tall gray-haired man, who Devon assumed was the butler, nodded at a young footman who stood scratching his blond head and looking slightly bewildered by all the excitement surrounding him. After a moment and several elbows in his ribs from the young maid standing next to him, he realized he'd been given an order and hurried to obey.

"He needs assistance to bed," Devon said, taking charge. The room filled with servants eager to help as Devon knelt and lifted her cape away from Neal's smoldering arm.

Neal groaned and scooted away from her, shaking his head. "Stay away from me, bitch."

"Neal, I only want to help. The doctor is on his way and you need to be put to bed so he can see to your arm."

"I don't want anything from you," Neal growled as he pushed himself into a sitting position. The scent of burned flesh filled the room as he held his charred arm cradled against his chest. His eyes seemed to reflect the flames that had eaten at his arm as he looked up at the gray-haired man. "Stevens, have Raymond and Mathison take this bitch to Newgate. Tell the constable we have captured the Shadow for them and I will gladly testify against her."

"My lord, there is time for that later. Let us get you up to bed. You're in a state of shock from your wounds."

"Damn you, Stevens!" Neal growled. "I am a soldier and won't collapse from pain. This bitch is responsible for my injury and I'll not rest until she is deep in the bowels of Newgate. I want her hanged."

Realizing the mistake of staying to help Neal, Devon eased toward the door with the hope of escaping while the butler argued with his master. She had nearly reached the exit when Stevens pointed a long finger in her direction. "You heard Lord Sumner. Seize her. She's to be taken to Newgate and charged with thievery . . . as well as attempting to murder Lord Sumner."

Strong hands clamped down on each of Devon's arms, halting her retreat. She glanced up into the ruddy faces of her captors and knew it would be useless to put up any resistance. Such action would be swiftly rewarded with violence.

Neal's threats filled the night air as they dragged her from the study. "I'll see you rot in hell, Devon Mackinsey. Mark my words. You'll never steal again."

The misty night had turned into a steady drizzle by the time the two footmen led Devon down Holborn Street to the prison. She shivered from fear as well as from the cold, soggy clothing clinging to her slender body as her guards rang the bell for Newgate's gatekeeper. A moment later a small grate slid open in the thick iron-bound portal and a pair of bulging eyes peered out into the darkness from beneath thick, bushy brows. "What in hell do ye want at this time of night?"

"Our master, Lord Sumner, said to tell ye this here is the Shadow."

The bulging eyes peered down at the small figure standing with head bowed between the two burly men. "Don't look much like the Shadow to me. Now be off with ye. It's too late in the night fer yer jests."

"Ain't no jest, gatekeep. So ye'd best open up if ye knows what's good fer ye. This woman tried to rob me master and then tried to burn him alive when he caught her.''

The grating of keys against metal locks and the scrape of bars against wood sounded eerily out of place in the still, dark hours of the morning. A dim ray of light permeated the shroud of night as the gate swung open. The gatekeeper, a fat man, his scarred face blackened by beard stubble, his heavy, jowled mouth revealing yellowed, broken teeth, eyed the three dubiously. He scratched at his hairy, bulging belly and ran his thumb beneath the waist of his breeches and hitched them up. ''She don't look so vicious to me.''

''That just goes to show what ye know. Me master said this wench was the Shadow, and if I was ye, I'd not question Lord Sumner's word. He don't fancy anyone doubting him.''

''I ain't a doubting yer master's word, ye fool. But she just looks like any other woman to me.'' The gatekeeper smacked his lips together and cleared his throat. He spat on the stones at Devon's feet. His bulbous eyes ran over her insultingly. ''Newgate's full of whores and another 'un don't mean nothing.''

''This ain't a whore from down at the docks. This here is the Shadow,'' Devon's guard pronounced proudly.

''Humph!'' the gatekeeper said. ''If ye say so.''

''Are ye going to stand around here blabbing all night or are ye going to take her off our hands? I'm sure Lord Sumner will be most upset if ye don't do as he's ordered,'' the second footman said.

The gatekeeper called for a guard's assistance. He would take no chances that something might go wrong and the girl would escape. If what the footmen said was true—which he seriously doubted—then he had a real prize. The Shadow had been the talk of all London of late. He looked back at the girl standing between the two men. From the looks of her, she didn't seem big enough to do all the things that had been laid at her door. And for that matter, he didn't see how a woman could be the Shadow in the first place. Who had ever heard of a woman burglar? Thievery was a man's profession. The gatekeeper scratched at his bearded jaw and stepped aside to let the guard lead the woman up to the third floor, where all female felons were kept in the second ward. He had learned long ago not to question his betters. If Lord Sumner said this girl was the Shadow, then she was the Shadow to him, even if she'd never stolen anything in her life.

Devon felt the world close in about her as the guard led her to the lodge and fettered her in irons. The cold metal bit into her ankles as she struggled up the narrow flight of stairs to the women's ward. The stench of human refuse permeated the air, making it difficult to breathe. Devon's stomach churned sickeningly from the foul odor and she gagged as the guard swung open the thick door to her prison. He gave her a shove, and she stumbled inside as he slammed the door closed behind her.

A scream of terror built in the back of Devon's throat at the heavy, sinister silence surrounding her. Standing with her heart pounding in her ears, breath held, and muscles taut with tension, she knew she was not alone.

A high-pitched chuckle sounded behind her. Forgetting her fetters, Devon spun about, ready to defend herself. She stumbled over her chains and would have fallen had a rough, calloused hand not steadied her. "There ye go, me deary. Can't have ye falling in me lap—not with me babe only a few days away from birthing."

"Ye bloody bitch, quit yer blathering. O'm trying to get me beauty rest."

"Beauty rest?" Devon's rescuer spat. "Ye trying to grow another wart, toady?"

"Ye fat pig. I'll slice out yer heart and eat it fer breakfast if ye don't shut yer bloody trap."

"Oh, bloody hell! Alma . . . Moselle . . . Both shut

yer mouths or I'll shut them fer ye," a low, angry female voice said from the darkness.

"Ain't trying to start no trouble with ye, Big Nan. But this bitch is asking fer a killing," Alma said. "I was just trying to be friendly to our new arrival when Moselle has to stick her big, ugly nose into it."

"I don't give a bloody damn what either of ye were trying to do. I want to get some rest." Several other prisoners muttered their agreement.

Cold droplets of sweat beaded Devon's upper lip and brow as she listened to the exchange. She couldn't stop the tremor of fear that started at the bottom of her feet and worked its way to the top of her head. The scream edged closer to the back of her throat and her jaw muscles ached to release it. She balled her hands into fists and felt her nails bite into the tender flesh of her palms. The flicker of pain brought a momentary reprieve from her mounting fear. Devon drew in an unsteady breath. She had to get a grip on herself. She couldn't allow herself to fall to pieces if she wanted to survive in this hellhole.

"Come on, deary. 'ere's a place by me to rest," a deep feminine voice offered, patting Devon on the leg. "Just settle right down here and let old Aggie take care of ye. O'll not let Alma or Moselle bother ye. Ye'll be safe with Aggie. Yes sir'ee."

"Aggie, leave the chit alone," Big Nan growled from the darkness. "Give 'er time to settle in. Then if she wants to entertain ye, yer welcome to 'er."

Devon inched her way toward the door. Her fetters rattled eerily with each movement, making her destination obvious to the other occupants.

"Ain't no use, deary. The guards won't hear ye if ye call, and even if they did, they'd not come. Ye might as well get use to it here with the rest of us," Moselle said from her spot on the filthy floor.

Slowly Devon sank to her knees. She sat huddled with

arms wrapped protectively about her legs. Futilely she stared into the ebony darkness in an attempt to see the other prisoners. It was too dark to make out even an outline. Only the sound of breathing and an occasional curse, snore, or moan muttered in a dream told her she wasn't alone.

Near dawn, exhaustion claimed Devon and her head drooped against her arms. Her last thought before she succumbed to sleep was of her grandmother and Higgins and Winkler: her family. She would never see them again. As she slept, several wayward tears seeped slowly down Devon's cheeks and dropped onto her breeched leg. Like her hopes for the future, they vanished into the dark fabric.

Face pinched and ashen, Winkler faced Higgins. He ran a shaky hand through his tousled hair and his voice quivered as he tried to explain what he had witnessed. "They took 'er to Newgate, 'iggins. And I couldn't do a thing about it."

Higgins slumped down into the straight-backed chair. His haggard expression reflected his worry as he looked at the younger man. "I told her this would happen, but she wouldn't listen. I tried to get her to let you go along tonight to help, but no, Devon had to have things her way." Higgins lay his graying head back and fought to suppress the tears burning the backs of his lids. He balled his hands impotently in his lap. "And there's nothing we can do for her now. We don't have the resources it would take to even bribe our way into the prison, much less get Devon out."

"I doubt all the gold in England could free Devon now. From what I overheard Lord Sumner's lackeys tell the gatekeeper at the prison, me fine lord is determined to see our Devon hanged. They know she's the Shadow, and they've accused her of attempting to murder Lord Sumner."

Higgins pressed two fingers against the bridge of his

long nose to forestall a new rush of moisture. He swallowed against the lump of emotion that had lodged in his throat when Winkler had told him Devon had been thrown into Newgate. He looked once more at Winkler. Futilely he searched the younger man's features for any sign of hope for the young woman they both loved. He found none.

Drawing in a deep breath, Higgins glanced toward Lady Mackinsey's bedroom door. There would be more than one death in the Mackinsey family from this affair. When the old woman learned Devon's fate—and that she had lost the power to save her granddaughter from the gibbet at Tyburn—the end would come swiftly. Lady Mackinsey couldn't endure such stress. Her heart would burst from the grief of losing Devon.

"Ain't there something we can do fer her, 'iggins. We just can't let 'er rot in Newgate without at least trying to help."

Higgins shook his head sadly. "I wish to God there was, but the power the Mackinseys once possessed is long gone. All they have now is the name, and that won't buy a drink of water in Newgate."

"Well, I'm goin' to find a way to help Devon. She did what she did fer us just as much as it was fer herself and that old lady in there."

"There's nothing you can do but get yourself hanged alongside of her, Winkler. Go near that prison and they'll accuse you of being her accomplice . . . like you were." Seeing Winkler's belligerent expression, Higgins knew he hadn't gotten through to the younger man. Winkler would do exactly as he pleased, just like Devon. And they would both end up at the end of a rope at Tyburn Hill.

"I'll find a way, just you wait and see. Devon's like me sister, and no matter what you say, I won't leave things be."

"Then go ahead. You've never thought twice before you

rushed headfirst into trouble. So why should you change now?'' Higgins said, exasperated.

"Ain't no reason that I can see,'' Winkler said, and gave Higgins one of the wicked grins that always predicted trouble to come.

Devon opened her eyes to the nightmare. Hands came at her from all directions, ripping at her clothes, her hair, her shoes, and stockings. She screamed and fought, but could not wake from the terrible throes of her hellish dream. A sharp kick in the ribs sent her reeling in pain and brought her to the stunning realization that she wasn't asleep. The filthy, haggard faces looming over her; the hands, their nails broken and black with dirt, belonged to her fellow prisoners.

"Let me go!" Devon demanded, and kicked out in self-defense. She struggled as several pairs of hands grabbed her arms and pinned them behind her. A grimy face, deeply lined from age and excess, peered down at her. A semblance of a smile touched the hag's mouth as she bent close to inspect Devon. She nodded. "Yer a pretty piece, me girl. Very pretty indeed. Do ye have any money?''

Devon rapidly shook her head.

The hag shrugged. "It's a bloody shame. Without money, O'll just have to give ye to Aggie. She's made me a good offer.''

Devon blinked up at the woman, confused. "You can't give me to Aggie. I don't belong to you or anyone else.''

Big Nan threw back her head and laughed, revealing black stumps of teeth. " 'ho the bloody 'ell do ye think ye are. The queen herself? In here, me dear, the strong rule. And O'm the strong.'' Big Nan swept the other prisoners with a withering gaze and they seemed to cringe away, though they didn't move. "And there's not a soul here 'ho'd dispute me word. I'm king, queen, and Parliament." She gave Devon a piercing look. "And God fer as long as I keep me neck."

"I'll report you to the guards. They won't allow you to harm me."

Again Big Nan threw her head back and her laughter shook her heavy frame. "Deary, the guards don't give a bloody damn 'hat goes on in here as long as we're willing to service them whenever and however they want."

Big Nan clamped a brutal hand down on Devon's breast and squeezed. "You've got nice tits, deary. I'm sure Aggie'll enjoy 'em." Again Big Nan chuckled at the look of bewilderment that flickered over Devon's face. She cocked her head to one side and winked broadly at Alma. "I believe we've got ourselves a real innocent here. Reckon she's a virgin?"

"Ain't likely, Big Nan. She's over ten, and ye know no gel past the age of seven can keep her cherry if she's from the streets of London," another prisoner chimed in.

"Aye, but this'un don't talk like she comes from the streets. She nearly sounds like a real ledy," Big Nan said, her eyes narrowing thoughtfully upon Devon. She rubbed a coarse hand over her straggly-haired chin. "Come to think on it, she even *looks* like a ledy, though she's dressed like a gent."

"Ledies don't wear men's breeches," Moselle said, shouldering her way into the circle surrounding Devon and her captors. "I bet she's just a whore like old Alma."

"I'm not a whore," Devon said. "Nor am I a piece of meat to be bartered away at your whim."

"Then who exactly are ye, Miss High and Mighty?" Big Nan asked, sensing from Devon's speech and demeanor that she wasn't the ordinary pickpocket or prostitute. If she was a lady, as Big Nan surmised, there might be more profit to be made by befriending the girl.

Devon opened her mouth to answer and then snapped it shut. Revealing her identity served no purpose here. She was doomed to hang and she'd not disgrace her family name with these people. She was the Shadow, and that was how she would be known. Devon drew in a long breath. "I am known as the Shadow."

Big Nan shook her head dubiously. "Ye seriously don't expect us to believe yer the famous Shadow, do ye?"

"I don't expect you to believe anything. You asked me a question and I told you who I am. If that doesn't satisfy you, then I'm sorry."

"Yer a smart-mouthed bitch if there ever was one," Big Nan said, frowning. If the wench wasn't careful, she was going to find herself on the wrong side of Nan's temper, be she lady or whore.

"O'll cure 'er of 'er smart mouth, Big Nan," Aggie said, pressing close to the ward ruler. "Just give 'er to me, and O'll see to 'er manners. She'll learn right quick to keep 'er mouth shut to her betters."

Devon jerked free of the hands holding her arms and quickly got to her feet. She suppressed the urge to turn and flee. There was nowhere to go, nowhere to hide, and like chickens in the hen coop at Mackinsey Hall, these women would attack at the first sign of weakness. Eyeing the ward ruler, Devon squared her shoulders, cockily tossed her hair back, and braced her hands on her hips. "If either of you touch me, I'll tear out your throat with my bare hands. I haven't survived this long as the Shadow by being afraid of the likes of you."

The prisoners' shocked gasps rippled through the chamber before a deathly quiet settled over the ward. The women awaited Big Nan's reaction to the new girl's remark. To their surprise, Big Nan grinned. "Ye got spirit, bitch. But make no mistake 'ho rules the roost here. Fer now, and ledy that I am, I'll look over yer threat to do me bodily harm. Just beware not to tempt yer fate too much, deary. Or I'll make sure they won't have to hang ye at

Tyburn. They'll find yer innerds smeared all over the walls one morning.''

A sigh of relief passed through the audience and they began to drift back to the places they claimed as their territory on the filthy floor. Food, feces, and urine matted what had once been rushes into a stagnant odorous mass that worked with vermin of every description.

Realizing Big Nan had called a truce between them, Devon nodded. She had managed to bluff her way through the situation and she'd not tempt the fate Nan had mentioned. It was enough for now to be left alone. Nan smiled, and Devon returned the gesture before the other woman turned away. Each knew exactly where the other stood.

"Well, I'll be damned and in hell. Yer the first I've seen make Big Nan back down," Alma said, and chuckled.

Devon glanced at the pregnant woman who stood behind her, back braced against the stone wall, her hands resting on her large, extended abdomen. "She didn't back down. She merely postponed the confrontation."

Alma pursed her lips and nodded in agreement. "Ye best hope ye hang before Big Nan decides it's time fer ye to pay the piper. 'hat she does to a person ain't pretty. If she don't kill ye, ye'll wish ye were dead when ye see yer face again.''

Devon didn't doubt Alma's word, but she couldn't worry about what Big Nan might or might not do to her. She doubted she'd be in Newgate long enough to have to deal with Big Nan again. Neal Sumner would use all of his influence to see her brought to trial as soon as possible, so he could see her hanged.

Devon smiled wryly to herself. Big Nan was the least of her troubles.

Chapter 6

"Lord Sumner, do you see the person who attempted to murder you in this chamber?" the barrister asked in his best orator's voice. The deep, resonant timbre didn't suit the little man who looked much like a skinny sheepdog in the long, curly wig that proclaimed his position in England's judiciary system.

"I do," Neal said, and pointed an accusing finger at Devon sitting in the prisoner's box.

"And is this woman the same who boldly confessed to being the infamous thief known as the Shadow?"

"She is."

All heads in the courtroom turned to look at the young woman who claimed to be the famous thief. A low murmur rose among the spectators as arguments broke out over her guilt and innocence. "She couldn't be," as well as "She's guilty as sin," could be heard spouted back and forth—before a loud bang from the jurist's gavel and a firm, "The chamber will be cleared if we don't have silence immediately," quieted the crowd. The spectators, much like unruly children, straightened in their seats and clamped their lips shut.

"And did you catch her in the act of stealing?"

"I did," Neal volunteered, without hesitation. His eyes never left Devon's ashen features as he absently touched his bandaged arm. A look of revulsion crossed his handsome features. Sitting in the prisoner's box, with head bowed and greasy strands of lank hair falling into her face, Neal wondered what he had seen in the girl in the first place. She looked like what she had been born, a slut's bastard. Stripped of all her lady's finery, the real Devon Mackinsey had been revealed to the world. Neal smiled to himself. Revenge was sweet.

The barrister waved one black-robed arm in Devon's direction and turned to the three jurists presiding over her trial. "Your Honors, this woman's guilt is obvious. My witness caught her in the very act of thievery and then, when he attempted to bring her to justice, she assaulted him. And we, as loyal citizens to the crown and England, may have lost the services of this brave soldier because of this woman's vile act. Her attempt to murder Lord Sumner may prevent him from going to fight for England against the revolutionaries in the colonies. His arm was so badly burned he may be crippled for life. Such a heinous crime demands justice. Lord Sumner demands justice from you. Look at him, a fine, brave soldier—one of England's finest—and tell me that this woman's crime doesn't demand the harshest penalty you can give. I ask your verdict to be death by hanging."

Devon flinched, but made no other visible sign that she heard anything the barrister said. From the moment she'd been led into Newgate she'd known she'd pay with her life for her crimes. And during the proceedings of the last few days, the jurists' expressions hadn't altered her expectations of the outcome. Each berobed, bewigged judge had found her guilty even before they heard the evidence against her. She had betrayed her class and her sex in their opinions, and she should receive no mercy from them for her brazen behavior.

Standing at the rear of the chamber, Hunter Barclay couldn't take his eyes off the young woman in the prisoner's box. It was hard to recognize her as the elegantly gowned young lady he'd left standing on the street in front of her town house only a few short weeks ago. When she'd been led to the box and locked inside, he'd thought he'd made a mistake. It wasn't until Devon looked up as Neal Sumner was called to the witness box that Hunter knew for certain that the girl was truly Devon Mackinsey.

Hunter's gaze moved over the unkempt girl. She had lost weight, and beneath the grime that coated her flawless skin, there was no sign of the spirited young woman he'd come to admire in their two brief encounters. Hunter glanced down at the man standing at his side and wondered again, for the hundredth time, why on earth he'd even allowed Winkler to involve him in the girl's troubles. She was nothing to him except a threat to the success of his own mission in England. She knew his secret.

Hunter turned his thoughtful gaze once more toward the prisoner's box. He studied Devon's ashen features for a long, reflective moment and wondered why she had not revealed what she knew of him to better her own condition. From what Winkler had told him, she had been imprisoned in the women's felon ward in Newgate for more than three weeks. And from what he'd learned of the place, that in itself was enough to drive a sane person mad. The ward was considered one of the worst. The female inmates, most the very dregs of society, lived in their own filth, sleeping on the floor and fighting like dogs for the few morsels of food they were given twice a day.

Hunter felt his heart constrict for the vibrant young woman he'd verbally sparred with at Lady Heath's ball. She had kept their agreement, even when it could have bought her a private cell and a few extra morsels of food. That alone merited Hunter's attempt to save her from the gibbet.

Hunter couldn't deny this entire situation had also roused his curiosity about the girl who had become a thief to gain enough money to capture a rich husband. Oddly that was all Hunter had been able to learn about Devon Mackinsey from her bandy-legged friend. When Hunter probed into Devon's past, the little man clammed up. He'd only say it wasn't his place to talk about his mistress's business. Hunter suspected Winkler's own involvement in the Shadow's nefarious schemes was the reason that kept him from divulging too much information about Devon. Hunter hadn't pressed the issue. He, himself, didn't want his own motives for coming to Devon's aid revealed.

"Have ye seen enough? Are ye goin' to help 'er or not? Or are ye going to let 'em send her to Tyburn without so much as raising a 'and to stop 'em?"

Hunter glanced down at the anxious man at his side. He understood Winkler's concern, but he couldn't stop the proceedings at this point. He would have to wait until Devon was sentenced. Hopefully the jurists would spare her life. It would make his work far easier when he attempted to have her set free. He said as much to Winkler.

Winkler's bushy brows lowered. "I don't like it one little bit. Ye said ye'd help, and now yer a goin' to let them 'ang her."

Hunter's temper snapped. A head taller than Winkler, he grabbed the smaller man by the scruff of the neck and dragged him out of the courtroom. He slammed him against the wall. Hunter's blue eyes shot fiery sparks as he glared down at Winkler.

"I told you exactly what I intend to do. If you will recall, you are the one who came and asked for my help. At this point, I'm not at all certain that even my uncle's influence can gain her freedom, or save her neck, for that matter. Nor am I sure that I want to be associated with any of this. I've only met the girl twice, and then not under very pleasant circumstances. But there is one thing that I do know. I'll be damned if I'll listen to any more of your criticism. If you can do any better, then I suggest you do it!"

The bluster went out of Winkler and he seemed to wither

before Hunter's eyes. "She's like a sister to me. We've growed up together, and me and 'iggins is all she has left since old Lady Mackinsey died last week." Winkler jerked his coat straight and swallowed with difficulty. "Devon don't even know 'er gran's done gone on. The old lady be long buried, but they didn't have enough heart to let me or 'iggins visit Devon in the jail to tell her. It's goin' to kill Devon when she 'ears about her gran."

Hunter dropped a hand on Winkler's shoulder. "I understand your feelings, but you must also understand mine."

Winkler nodded. "I'm sorry, and I'm grateful that ye agreed to even try to 'elp me Devon. All the other nobs wouldn't even see me when I went to ask fer 'elp. They act as if they've never known 'er."

"That's understandable. She did play them for fools," Hunter said frankly.

Winkler shrugged. "She had 'er reasons. She didn't mean no 'arm to anyone."

"Perhaps. But your Devon made many enemies. If we do manage to get her set free, it would be in her best interest to leave London."

"She was planning on leaving London before she was sent to Newgate. But now with the old lady dead and 'er home gone, she ain't got nowhere to go."

"That's not my problem. And it may not be her problem if the jurists don't see fit to lessen her sentence," Hunter said, glancing back at the tall double doors leading into the courtroom. He dreaded what he would hear on the other side. The evidence was already stacked against Devon and the outcome didn't look promising.

The low murmur of spectator voices ceased as the three jurists filed back into the chamber and took their seats behind the high podium. A bang of the gavel set the proceedings into motion again. The jurist handed a piece of paper to a bewigged clerk who then ordered Devon to stand and accept the verdict from the jurists.

Devon came to her feet and stood with back straight and head held high. Her emotions wrapped once more in the protective chrysalis that she had used as a child to guard herself against hurt, she stared blindly out at the gaping faces filling the crowded courtroom. She didn't see Hunter or Winkler as they stood, tense and anxious, for the jurists' verdict to be read.

The clerk drew in a deep breath and glanced smugly about the courtroom. His importance to the proceedings grew in his own mind as he began to read. "Under the power invested in our office, we find the defendant, Devon Mackinsey, guilty of the crimes of attempted murder and thievery. Her sentence is to be death by hanging. On the twelfth day of this month, the sentence is to be carried out. She is to be taken to Tyburn and hanged by the neck until dead."

Devon felt her world tremble as the verdict was read. She had thought herself prepared to face the worst, until she heard the words read aloud. The courtroom began to spin, the faces staring back at her whirled rapidly, until they became a blur before her eyes. The clerk's pronouncement, death by hanging, echoed round and round in her mind. Devon's eyes rolled back and she slumped to the floor of the prisoner's box in a dead faint.

"Here, now. Back with ye," the guards ordered as Hunter and Winkler forced their way through the crowd toward the prisoner's box. "The prisoner ain't allowed to talk with nobody."

"Can't you see she needs a physician?" Hunter demanded, exasperated by his own inability to help Devon as her guards dragged her limp, unconscious body from the prisoner's box and carried her away.

"She'll come round after a while. Ain't many who can keep standing once they've been sentenced to death. It makes 'em weak in the knees," the guard answered. Undeterred from his duty he blocked Hunter's path until Devon was out of sight.

Winkler opened his mouth to protest but Hunter silenced him with a shake of his head. It would do them no good to cause a disturbance here. He had less than twenty-four hours to find a way to save Devon from hanging and he didn't want to risk landing himself in jail.

Winkler gave Hunter a bullish look but didn't argue. He didn't ask any questions until they were both safely in Hunter's coach. "Devon's to 'ang tomorrow."

"And I've much work to do if we're to stop it," Hunter said as he leaned back against the soft velvet seat and wearily ran a long-fingered hand through his dark hair. At the present moment he didn't have the foggiest idea of how he was going to prevent Devon's execution. Had her sentence been imprisonment, he was certain he could rescue her by purchasing her indenture papers, but now he wasn't at all sure even his uncle's influence could help the girl. He looked at the man sitting across from him. "It may take a miracle to find a way out of this coil, Winkler. Devon has powerful enemies."

Devon stood in the faint light coming through the ward's lone window. She felt a hand come to rest on her shoulder and looked to see Big Nan. During the past weeks the wary truce that had begun between them had continued, with each avoiding the other to save a confrontation. Now Big Nan had sought her out, and Devon tensed, wondering if the time had come to pay the piper for the peace of the past weeks.

"We heard ye'll be leaving us soon."

Devon nodded mutely. The chrysalis she had woven about herself was now ripped and torn from the horror of the day. No matter how well she had thought to prepare herself for her conviction, she realized she hadn't really accepted the possibility that she would have to face death. And she wanted desperately to live.

The thought brought tears to Devon's eyes. Vision blurred, she looked away from the ward queen and felt Big Nan give her shoulder a compassionate squeeze. Devon turned her puzzled, glassy gaze back to the older woman and simply stated her feeling. "I don't understand."

"Aye. O'm not sure I understand meself. Ye don't mean nothing to me, but when I look at ye, yer youth, yer looks, I see something that's going to be wasted at Tyburn. Ye weren't meant to be here like the rest of us. Though ye've put up a good bluff to keep me and the other bitches at bay, ye ain't hard. Ye just a poor mite who's done her best to survive."

Devon swallowed at the sudden lump of emotion that clogged her throat. She felt like throwing herself into Big Nan's arms and crying out her misery. She needed the comfort of another human being. She needed a mother's arms about her now more than at any other time in her life. Before she could succumb to her needs and embarrass Big Nan with an emotional display, Devon gave the older woman's hand a squeeze and turned away. She moved into the shadows, hiding her face against the rough stone wall. The tears she'd suppressed came burning their way to the surface as she allowed herself to cry for the first time in years.

Big Nan glanced toward the window and knew it was time. Soon the guards would come for the girl. Nan glanced at the small figure quietly standing alone in the corner. She touched the string that held a precious vial of laudanum hidden between her large breasts. Something akin to sympathy moved her across the ward to Devon's side. Casting a surreptitious glance about the chamber, she tugged the vial free and slipped the string over her head. Another glance about and she pressed the small bottle into

Devon's hand. "Drink this, gel. It'll help ye get through the next few hours."

Devon looked down at the small bottle. She prayed Nan had given her an easier death than hanging.

Sensing Devon's train of thought, Big Nan shook her head in denial. "It's only laudanum, gel. I use it when I need something to numb me senses for a time. It helps make me forget where I am and why I'm here."

Devon uncorked the vial and raised it to her lips. She prayed the burning liquid would make her too numb to feel the fear that tied her insides into knots each time she thought of her hanging.

Her stomach empty, exhaustion from the long night's deathwatch taking its toll, Devon felt the effects of the opium-laced alcohol immediately. Her forest green eyes grew vague and glassy as she looked at the older woman. "I wish it had been poison," she murmured, before leaning weakly against the cold, damp wall.

"Sweet Jesus, gel. You've got to be strong. Don't ye be giving the bastards the pleasure of seeing ye beg for mercy. It will do ye no good, and only the crowd will gain anything from it."

Devon blinked at Big Nan and gave her a lopsided smile. "I'll do my best not to let you down, Big Nan. You've been a friend."

"Damn me, but the laudanum has effected ye worst than I thought if ye think we're friends. No one here is anyone's friend, chit," Big Nan blustered.

"No matter," Devon murmured. "It's too late for friendships now."

At the sound of the key rattling in the rusty lock an eerie, watchful stillness settled over the ward. The inmates stood suspended in something akin to mutual grief over the fate of the young woman destined for the gibbet on Tyburn Hill. Few had even spoken to her during her stay in Newgate, but every woman present momentarily exchanged places with the girl as the guards trooped in and grabbed her by the arms. All sensed that in time they, too, might have to walk down the narrow flight of stairs to the oxcart awaiting outside. From there it was only a short distance to the gallows. Alma's pathetic weeping was the only sound to break the stillness as Devon was led away.

"Show 'em what yer made of, gel," Big Nan called out as the guard swung the thick door closed. "Don't give 'em the pleasure of seeing you beg for mercy."

The last of Big Nan's advice was only a vague murmur in Devon's ears as she numbly followed the guard outside. She glanced dreamily up at the blue sky. Her head felt as light and fluffy as the cotton clouds that scudded overhead. She smiled. It was a lovely day. The ordinary and the minister, who had the duty to accompany the accused to her execution, looked at each other and sadly shook their heads. Newgate had once again claimed the sanity of its prisoner.

It's a lovely day kept echoing through Devon's mind as the guard forced her into the cart and tied her hands to the side board to prevent an attempt to escape. In her opium daze, she didn't hear the jeers or the bawdy comments directed at her as the lumbering cart jolted down the cobbled street toward its destination. It was too lovely a day to be concerned about the jostling crowd that followed.

People flocked to any execution, rich and poor alike. It was fine entertainment to watch the convicted's last moments on earth. Many addressed the crowds with great verbosity, beginning with their childhoods and giving an account of their life, dwelling on their sins, their family, and how they had come to such a pass. Some left the world with the crowd weeping at their demise while others roused the spectators to cheers. No one ever knew exactly what to expect at an execution.

The crowd grew as they neared the end of Marylebone Lane. Tall elms shaded the spectators as they watched the convicted led to the gallows. Wheeled carts were rented out for a shilling, giving a better view of the proceedings to those who could afford such luxuries. But Devon paid no heed to the staring throngs as she hummed quietly to herself.

"Damn me, but she's lost her wits," one guard said as he untied Devon's hands and hauled her from the cart. "She acts as if she's only going out for a morning stroll."

"It's such a lovely day," Devon murmured, smiling up at him.

"A lovely day to hang," the guard muttered, taking Devon roughly by the arm and pulling her toward the gallows.

"Hang?" Devon questioned, suddenly digging her heels into the dirt.

"Aye, bitch. What did ye think we'd come here to do? Take the morning air?"

Devon blinked up at the man, vaguely aware that something was terribly wrong. She shook her head to clear it of the swirling fumes that seemed to block any coherent thought. Her actions only served to make her head spin and dark shadows dance before her eyes. She reached out and clung to the thick-muscled arm of her guard for support.

"Come on, bitch. I ain't got all day to stand around here lollygagging with ye. I've got a job to do," he growled, jerking her toward the steps. Numbly Devon followed. She gazed out at the flock of peering faces, wondering why so many people had been invited to Mackinsey Hall. She looked at the black-hooded figure, standing with arms braced across his chest, and she smiled. Of course, her grandmother had planned a masked ball. Groggily she closed her eyes and tried to remember what costume she had planned for the entertainment.

Devon stood swaying like a sapling in the breeze as the black-hooded executioner placed the noose about her neck.

* * *

"What in the hell do you mean that she's already been taken to Tyburn? She's not supposed to be executed until two o'clock." Hunter glared down at Newgate's warden and fought to keep from throttling the man for his incompetence.

"What difference does one minute or one hour make?" the warden answered with a shrug. "She was going to hang whether it be one or two o'clock, and she was only taking up the space I need for other prisoners."

"Damn you, *this* makes the difference." Hunter tossed a paper down in front of the man. "You fool. You had best pray that I reach her in time or you'll live to regret your haste." Before the man could say a word, Hunter stormed from the chamber.

Unperturbed by the man's threats, the warden picked up the paper and perused it. His expression altered dramatically as his gaze came to rest on the signature at the bottom of the page. His eyes widened and he swallowed uneasily. The king himself had signed the girl's indenture papers. Her death sentence had been commuted to indenture for life and she was to be transported to the colony of Virginia in the custody of one Hunter Barclay. The warden wiped at the beads of sweat that formed on his brow and upper lip. He ran a finger beneath the edge of his collar and swallowed uncomfortably. His position as Newgate warden could well be in jeopardy if the girl hanged before Hunter Barclay reached her. . . .

Hunter swung himself into the saddle and spurred his mount into a gallop. He urged the animal into a race through the streets, scattering pedestrians in all directions as they dived for safety out of the black stallion's path. Sparing no thought to the cursing Londoners he left in his wake, Hunter forged ahead, the stallion's iron-shod hooves sparking against the cobbled street. The milling crowd parted like butter beneath a hot knife as he neared Tyburn.

Hunter's heart froze at the sight of the small figure sway-ing beneath the weight of the heavy hemp rope about her neck. The distance separating them seemed like miles. Should the executioner release the latch to the trapdoor, it would be too late to save Devon. Hunter cringed at the thought. He could nearly hear her slender neck bones snap as she fell.

"Out of my path," Hunter shouted as he drew his dress sword and kicked his mount in the side. The stallion reared and leapt forward. Startled by the screams of the unlucky spectators who stood too close to the stallion's hooves, the executioner paused with his hand on the latch to the trap-door. Hunter swooped down on him before the black-hooded figure fully realized his intentions. With a swift slash from the razor-sharp blade of his sword, the thick hemp rope fell limply about Devon's neck. The hangman and the guards scrambled out of Hunter's path as he swung his mount back around and forced the stallion to take the steps up the gibbet. He lifted Devon onto the saddle in front of him and urged his horse forward. The animal obeyed. In a swift bunching of powerful muscles the stal-lion leapt to the ground, running at full speed.

Cries of "Halt in the name of the king," and "The prisoner's escaping," followed Hunter down the cobbled street toward the road that led out of London. He held his limp passenger in his arms as he urged his horse east-ward along the hard-packed lane. It followed the Thames to where his ship and crew awaited him. Mordecai had been instructed to weigh anchor the moment they were aboard.

Hunter glanced down at Devon and found her sleeping peacefully against his chest. Thick lashes shadowed her mysterious green eyes and she held one graceful hand curled beneath her cheek. She looked as innocent as a young child. Hunter shook his head in dismay. The girl acted as if she didn't have a care in the world. Again

Hunter shook his head. How could she sleep at a time like this? Hunter chanced a glance over his shoulder and was relieved to find no one followed. His plans for this visit had suddenly gone awry when he'd agreed to try to save Devon's life.

Fortunately he had completed his mission before Devon had been sentenced to death. The transactions had taken place to ensure the continued support of the colonists with arms and money. He had hoped to remain in London for another week—to enjoy himself for the first time in more years than he cared to remember.

A cynical little grin curled up one corner of Hunter's shapely mouth. It seemed life didn't intend to give him a moment of respite from other people's troubles.

Since his parents' deaths when he was sixteen, it seemed every time he thought to set aside time for himself, something or someone needed him. There'd been little time for anything beyond caring for his sister, Cecilia, and seeing to the running of Barclay Grove. And during the past year, since her father's death, he'd also taken on the added responsibility of overseeing Whitman Place for Elsbeth.

Hunter didn't begrudge his responsibilities. He'd known little else since even before the death of his parents. His father had been determined to see that everything he'd worked to build wouldn't be destroyed by his son. He'd made certain that Hunter didn't grow up to be a wastrel like many of his friends' sons. He'd started teaching Hunter about Barclay Grove when he was five, and by the time of his parents' deaths Hunter knew every aspect about the plantation and the rest of the Barclay enterprises in America. His father's determination to ensure the survival of Barclay Grove had also taken away most of Hunter's childhood and adolescence leaving him little time to enjoy himself.

Hunter glanced down at Devon curled peacefully in his

arms. He certainly didn't need any new responsibilities in his life. Hunter's features hardened unconsciously with resentment. Women, Hunter thought with exasperation. Sometimes he wondered if they were worth all the havoc that seemed to surround them. His sister, Cecilia, was more than a handful. Her wild shenanigans kept him on his toes, and it took every ounce of patience he possessed to cope with the beautiful sixteen-year-old. He admitted he was partly responsible for making her so headstrong. She'd been only a baby when their parents were killed, and he'd spoiled her rotten ever since in an effort to make sure she felt loved.

Hunter's thoughts drifted to the other woman in his life. Unlike his sister, Elsbeth didn't possess a demanding bone in her body. Yet her quiet acceptance of the world, and of him, made Hunter feel even more obligated to her. Since they were children everyone had paired them together, expecting them to marry. And he assumed they would eventually. He was at an age to settle down and start a family to inherit Barclay Grove. Marrying Elsbeth would also be a wise business move. By merging Barclay Grove and the adjoining Whitman Place, he would own the largest plantation in Virginia. When the colonies won their independence from Britain and trade resumed, he'd make a fortune from his tobacco crop.

Hunter's gaze rested once more on Devon's dirt-smudged features. At least he didn't owe this one anything beyond what he'd already given her. She was only a temporary inconvenience. When they reached Barclay Grove, she'd work for her living like all the rest of his indentured servants. And that would be the end of the strange relationship that had developed between them. She had kept his secret, and he had given her her life in return. He owed her nothing more.

Hunter's face lightened and he smiled as he gently brushed his knuckles against the smooth line of Devon's cheek. Mistress Devon Mackinsey might be a welcome inconvenience after all. She could make the long voyage home much more pleasant if she were willing to show her gratitude for his timely rescue. Hunter's smile deepened. He was sure she would—once she learned he held her papers and her life in his hands.

Hunter felt a prick of guilt but ignored it. Devon Mackinsey belonged to him to do with as he pleased, he rationalized. She was the one woman in his life who couldn't demand anything of him. A wave of excitement roiled through him at the thought. Oddly he suddenly felt free to feel, free to live. Unconsciously Hunter tightened his arms about Devon. He didn't belong to her, but she belonged to him.

Chapter 7

Roused from her drugged slumber by a beam of golden sunlight filtering through the porthole, Devon peered up at the lantern swaying overhead. Squinting against the bright light, she watched it move back and forth through the thick veil of her lashes. A moment later a pained expression crossed her face and she paled. Eyes flying wide in distress, she bolted upright and clamped a hand over her mouth. She gave the room a swift, agonized survey and then scrambled from the bunk toward the porcelain chamber pot she'd spied in the corner. Taking no time to note anything more of her surroundings, Devon emptied her heaving stomach.

Sweat beaded her brow as she turned and made her way back to the tousled bunk. Wretched and wanting nothing more at that moment than to die, she plunged facedown into the mattress. Her long, shapely legs and feet extended over the side of the bunk as she gulped in air to quell her nausea. Her churning stomach ceased its violent rampage long enough for her to realize she had another agony to confront. Her head suddenly felt as if a demon had crept inside and was trying to find a way out through her temples. His pick and sledgehammer were doing an adequate job of pounding through her skull. The pain throbbed sickeningly against her brain as another wave of nausea sent her scrambling once more toward the chamber pot.

Gagging, Devon stared numbly at her surroundings

through tear-misted eyes. Too miserable to think or wonder about her whereabouts, she managed to retrace her wobbly path back to the bunk. She crawled in and pulled the covers over her aching head. She tried to recall anything that might give her a clue as to why she was so miserable, but for the life of her she couldn't. She remembered only drinking Big Nan's laudanum and, after that, her memory failed her completely. However, from the way she felt, she suspected her hanging must have taken place at Tyburn as scheduled. She had to be in purgatory atoning for her sins.

Lost in the throes of her suffering, Devon failed to hear the click of the well-oiled latch or the quiet swish of air as the cabin door opened. She wasn't aware of another presence in the cabin until the sound of a masculine voice ricocheted off her aching brain like molten pellets of lead. She cringed.

"Don't you think it's about time you woke up and faced the world, mistress?"

A jagged edge of pain raced across her skull and Devon clamped a hand down over her ear in an effort to block out all sound. Yet even under the attack of this new torment she couldn't stop herself from finding something very familiar about the voice on the other side of her shadowy haven. Slowly Devon eased back the blanket and peeped up at the man standing by the bed. Hunter Barclay stared down at her, his face revealing not an ounce of sympathy for her plight.

Devon squeezed her eyes tightly shut and prayed that when she opened them again she'd find that Hunter Barclay had only been a figment of her imagination. Swallowing against another sickening wave of nausea and dread, she once more peeped through the thick veil of her lashes to find her fears realized. Hunter stood with arms folded across his wide chest and long legs splayed for balance. Devon released a weary breath. She had been wrong when she had thought she was in purgatory. She knew now that she had not been so fortunate. She had been condemned directly to hell, and Hunter Barclay now proved what she had begun to think of him in London: he was the Devil incarnate.

Devon's gaze swept over the man whose very presence unsettled her far more than she cared to admit. As she had acknowledged upon their first encounter, Hunter Barclay was a handsome man. However, the dignified gentleman of London had disappeared. In his place stood a rogue dressed casually in a loose-fitting white lawn shirt with long, flowing sleeves. The garment's deep V neckline lay open, exposing his corded throat and a glimpse of the smooth, hard muscles beneath the crisp mat of hair that downed his chest. A wide black belt with a gold buckle emphasized his lean waist and the nankeen breeches he wore hugged his slender hips and muscular thighs, drawing attention to his long, strong legs. Strangely he wore no shoes. Devon drew her eyes away from Hunter's bare feet and looked up to find him smiling rakishly down at her.

"Do you approve of what you see, Mistress Mackinsey?"

In no mood to banter with the arrogant man, and feeling far worse mentally than when she'd first awakened, Devon turned her back to him and covered her head as she muttered, "Just leave me alone."

Her attempt to block out Hunter didn't work. A moment later he jerked the covers off her and tossed them to the floor. "Mistress, I think it's time for you to be up and about. You've been a slugabed far too long as is." With that he reached out and grasped Devon by the ankle, slowly pulling her from the bunk.

"Unhand me, you beast!" Devon squealed as she clung to the down mattress and kicked out at Hunter with her free foot. To her consternation, Hunter captured it as well and easily drew her—and the down mattress that she gripped fiercely—from the bunk. She fell to her belly on the floor. The man's shirt that she wore slipped up to reveal her shapely thighs as she sprawled facedown at Hunter's feet.

Unaware of the tempting display presented to Hunter's view, and forgetting the misery in her stomach and head, Devon twisted about and came to her feet. She stood glaring at Hunter in the beam of sunlight. The morning sun's rays caught her long mahogany hair and made it into flames of silken fire that haloed her to below the waist. Her breasts rose and fell rapidly with her breathing, bringing Hunter's attention to the hardened nipples pressing enticingly against the shirt fabric.

Hunter drew in a sharp breath as a searing heat coiled like a serpent in his belly and sent fire rushing through his blood. His gaze swept over the beautiful, furious deity standing before him and his mouth went dry with desire. Devon tempted him greatly.

Hunter gave himself a sharp mental shake. It would be so easy to succumb to the primitive, untamed side of man's nature that civilization has as yet to breed out, but Hunter wouldn't allow it to dominate him. He had too much pride to take Devon in such a way. He was no animal. Fighting the warring elements within him, Hunter turned toward the door. If he thought to win this battle, it would be best to put as much distance between himself and Devon as possible. It had been too many months since he'd had a woman, and no matter how civilized he prided himself on being, there was just so much any man could take.

"Where are you going?" Devon demanded, her fury unabated. Hunter paused with his hand on the latch and looked back at her. "And what am I doing here?" Devon encompassed the cabin with a wave of one graceful hand. "And for that matter . . . where am I?"

"Mistress, I suggest you clothe yourself and then we shall discuss matters."

The door closed behind Hunter before Devon had time to form another question. She looked at the door for a long moment and then slowly looked down at herself. Her fury died a quick death as she flushed with embarrassment. She had stood before Hunter Barclay clad only in a thin lawn shirt to cover her nakedness. A moment later her mortification intensified as she realized that at sometime and someplace, someone had taken off her clothes, bathed her, and then put her to bed wearing the man's shirt. In prison she had worn the clothing she'd had on since the night of her arrest. They had allowed her no other clothes or a way to bathe herself.

Devon closed her eyes and rubbed her hands over her face, trying to find a small thread of reason in all of the confusion. But nothing made any sense. She could remember nothing beyond her last minutes in Newgate.

Devon shook her head and let her hands fall to her side. Her gaze swept over her surroundings and, for the first time, she truly looked at them. It took only a few seconds for her to comprehend that she was on board a ship. She could feel the roil of the ocean beneath her bare feet and she could see the waves beyond the porthole. Devon pressed a hand to her stomach. It had been the motion of the ship that had been at the root of her strange illness. She was merely suffering from seasickness.

Devon crossed to the porthole and opened it. She drew the fresh sea air into her lungs and welcomed the brief moment of relief it gave her from the demon pounding against her temples.

Staring out across the white-capped waves, she tried to understand how she had come to be on board a ship with Hunter Barclay. By rights she should now be moldering in a common thief's grave near Tyburn Hill. But somehow Hunter had managed to save her life. For what reason, she didn't have the slightest inkling, but she was grateful that he had seen fit to rescue her, and she would thank him when he returned.

Drawing in another deep breath, Devon turned away from the porthole. Hunter had told her to clothe herself, but she was bewildered as to how she would obey his order. She didn't even know what had happened to the pants and shirt she had worn in Newgate. Spying a trunk at the end of the bunk and hoping to find something to wear in it, she crossed the cabin and opened the lid.

Devon's wide-eyed expression reflected her surprise as she stared down at the contents of the trunk. Inside lay her gowns and underclothes, as well as several pairs of shoes. Devon blinked down at the clothing. How had Hunter gotten her here . . . and why had he gone to so much trouble for her? Devon shook her head, unable to find an answer. The questions boiled to the surface, but like all the other hows and whys, only Hunter Barclay could answer them.

The brush Devon had been holding clattered to the floor at the sound of Hunter's knock. He didn't wait for her to bid him enter, but strolled in with the air of a man assured of his dominion. His gaze swept approvingly over Devon. The green gown she wore emphasized the color of her thick-lashed eyes. It made them even more alluring. The dark, fathomless depths seemed to hold all the secrets to the mysteries of the world.

Hunter smiled his appreciation. For all her sins, Devon Mackinsey was still the most beautiful woman he'd ever encountered. "You look much better than you did yesterday. The satin ribbon about your throat suits you far better than the hemp you wore then."

Devon felt her cheeks flush rose and quickly glanced away from Hunter. The look in his eyes belied his light banter. She recognized the expression within his velvety gaze as it swept over her. She'd seen the same look of desire in Neal Sumner's eyes. Devon swallowed uneasily, not knowing what to expect—nor what Hunter Barclay expected of her. She cleared her throat. "I'm afraid I don't remember anything of yesterday's happenings beyond waiting for the guards to come and escort me to Tyburn. But I assume from my being here that you rescued me from hanging, and I want to thank you for saving my life."

"You should thank Winkler. He's the one who came to me for help."

Devon's face brightened. "Winkler's here?"

Hunter shook his head. "No. Winkler's still in London with Higgins."

Devon smiled. "Of course. Winkler and Higgins wouldn't leave Grandmama alone."

Hunter drew a chair from the table and settled his lean frame in it. "Mistress, I'm afraid Winkler and Higgins aren't with your grandmother."

Devon's brow puckered. "Of course they are. Winkler and Higgins are like family to me. They'd not leave my service. Nor would they allow anyone else to watch over Grandmama."

Hunter drew in a long breath. He had come to the moment he had been dreading. It wasn't easy to tell anyone of a death in the family, much less a girl like Devon. "I'm afraid I have some bad news, mistress."

Sensing what Hunter was about to tell her, Devon shook her head. "No. I don't want to hear it." Her lower lip began to tremble yet her eyes remained dry.

"I'm sorry, but your grandmother died three weeks ago," Hunter said. The pinched, constricted look on Devon's face made Hunter want to reach out and take her into his arms, as he'd often done when Cecilia was upset. However, he suppressed the urge. This woman was an indentured servant, not a relative. He had to remember her position in his household or it would make the situation untenable when he returned home. He couldn't expect Elsbeth to accept Devon into her household if she thought there was more between them than master and slave.

"I don't believe you. What kind of sick joke are you trying to play on me. I want you to take me back to London. Or just let me off this ship at the nearest port and I'll make my own way back," Devon said, her voice cracking with emotion.

"I'm afraid I can't do that, mistress. We are at sea, and the nearest port is the West Indies, on the island of St. Eustatius."

Devon came to her feet, her eyes shimmering with emerald fire. "How dare you kidnap me? I'm grateful for your rescue, but you had no right to take me away from my home and family. I demand that you turn this vessel around and take me back to England."

A cynical little smile curled up the corner of Hunter's mouth as he shook his head, yet his features mirrored no regret. "Mistress, you have no right to demand anything of me. You are now my property—to do with as I see fit."

"I—I don't believe I heard you right," Devon stuttered indignantly. "I belong to no one but myself. And I must return to England. I must try to regain Mackinsey Hall from the creditors."

"I fear you are mistaken. When the king signed the writ to save you from hanging, he also added the provision that you were to be transported to the colony of Virginia—to serve as my bond slave for life. As for Mackinsey Hall, it has already been sold for the debts owed. It brought only a farthing of what the creditors demanded."

Devon stared at Hunter as if he were a stranger speaking a foreign language. After a few long, tense moments she turned away from him. Only the weary angle of her slender shoulders revealed any sign of her feelings. She crossed to the porthole and, without looking back at Hunter, asked quietly, "My lord, may I have your permission to grieve for my grandmother in private?"

Hunter slowly came to his feet. The misery he heard in Devon's voice made him remember how he had felt at the loss of his own parents. He could understand her need to be alone, yet he knew she needed comfort in this hour of her grief. When his parents died he would have given all his wealth to have had someone to comfort him. Yet there had been no one. He'd had to ignore his own pain and turn his attention to his sister's welfare, as well as ensuring everything continued as usual at Barclay Grove and the shipyards. Ignoring his earlier decision, Hunter crossed to Devon and lay a comforting hand on her shoulder. He didn't speak but let his nearness convey his sympathy. He felt Devon draw in a shuddering breath and then withdraw from his touch. Hunter felt Devon's rejection and gave a mental shrug. He had done his best to give her comfort, even against his own better judgment. Hunter turned toward the door. "I'll leave you to your privacy, mistress."

Devon waited for the door to close behind Hunter before surrendering to her grief. Her eyes burned with the need to cry but no tears would come to relieve the constriction growing in her throat. Grief, anger, self-pity, and hurt united and she let out a low curse as she brought up her fist and slammed it against the smooth planking of the cabin wall. The force of the impact broke the skin across her knuckles and they bled. Devon made no move to stop the bleeding. She stared down at the red essence of her life beading on her white skin and wondered what she had done to be denied what every human being craved—love. During the past few years with Lady Mackinsey she had been given a glimpse of what others had . . . and now it had been taken away as abruptly as it had been given. The Lord giveth and the Lord taketh away.

"But why?" Devon muttered angrily, staring at the blue horizon in the distance. "Why didn't you just let me stay in the kitchens where I didn't have any hope. But, no, you let me have a taste of what it was like to be loved, to be in a family, to have someone to care about me. I know I was only a substitute for my sister, but I could accept that to have Grandmama's love. Why, God? Why did you take her away from me? What have I done so wrong that I have to be punished?''

Devon pressed her brow against the wall, hiding her anguished expression from the world. "I wanted nothing more than a family. Is that so wrong?''

Devon curbed the curse that rose to her lips against God. She could blame Him for taking her grandmother, yet in her heart Devon knew that in His beneficence He had eased her grandmother's suffering by allowing her to die. However that knowledge didn't stop the impotent fury that welled within her against the man who had sired her. Because of his extravagant life-style, she had been forced into the life of a thief to survive. No, she couldn't blame God. It was Lord Colin Mackinsey who was responsible for the tragedy in her life. Her anger simmered against her father and his kind, as well as for the country that left only the option of marriage open for women if they wanted to live a decent life. It had also been England's laws that imprisoned her as her grandmother lay dying. England's laws that had denied her even the right to bid farewell to the woman who had given her so much during the past years.

To God and England. The words to the salutation echoed through Devon's head and her expression hardened. She rubbed at her burning eyes as she buried her grief beneath the layers of anger welling within her. She muttered a low curse, yet her voice broke as she said, "Be damned to England and her laws. She will never have my loyalty again.''

Devon tossed back her head and stared at the roiling waves of the sea. A brittle smile touched her lips. If what

Hunter Barclay had said was true, it truly didn't matter what she felt about England. She would never see it again. She was on her way to the colony of Virginia as Hunter Barclay's bond slave.

The ship sailed southward toward the West Indies. The night crept stealthily through the porthole, across the bare plank floor and over the bunk to gradually wrap the ship's cabin in its velvety embrace. Only the pinpoint reflection of starlight in the sea broke through the obsidian shroud encompassing the world.

Devon sat alone in the darkness, calmly listening to the waves lapping against the hull of the ship. Through the long day she had pondered the fate that awaited her once she reached Virginia. It was not easy to accept the fact that she was now Hunter Barclay's servant. But she had managed to come to terms with the idea. The resilient spirit that had always given her the strength to face adversity had once more come to her aid. Her life had never been easy but she had survived—and she would survive again to find her freedom.

Absorbed with her thoughts, Devon jumped with a start and came to her feet at the sound of a heavy knock. The door seemed to tremble from the force of the blow. Before she could utter "enter," another loud knock reverberated through the cabin and the door swung open to reveal a giant ox of a man. He filled the doorway as he ducked his salt-and-pepper head and raised the lantern high. Bushy eyebrows hid his eyes as he searched the cabin until he saw Devon. Something akin to a smile touched his lips. "Mistress, I'm Mordecai Bradley. The captain has asked me to escort ye to his cabin for dinner."

"Please tell Lord Barclay I'm not hungry," Devon said, having no desire to see Hunter. She had managed to accept her fate, but she couldn't force herself to act as if she liked it by dining with the man who was to be her master.

"Mistress, the captain expected such an answer and told me to bring you, no matter what you said. Will you come calmly of your own accord . . . or shall I carry you?" Mordecai asked, noting the angry flush that heightened Devon's color at his ultimatum.

"I will come on my own," she muttered, and swept past him as he stepped out of the doorway. She took only a few steps before she stopped and turned back to Mordecai. She flashed him an exasperated look. "Where is the captain's cabin?"

Mordecai couldn't suppress his smile at Devon's expression. From the few things Hunter had said about her, he knew the girl had endured much in the past, but from the glint in her eyes he suspected adversity hadn't broken her spirit. And from the jut of her jaw, he also guessed she possessed a stubborn streak in her a mile wide. It was going to be interesting to watch what happened between Mistress Mackinsey and his friend. She wasn't some weak-kneed miss who Hunter could easily dominate. "It's down the hall to your left, mistress."

Devon lifted the hem of her muslin gown, raised her head in the air, and squared her shoulders. She'd meet Hunter Barclay in the captain's cabin but if he thought to make her jump to his tune then he had to think again. She might be his servant but he'd not see her grovel at his feet, no matter what he did to her. She was Devon Mackinsey, of the Scottish Mackinseys. Her ancestry went back to the Bruces of Scotland. She might be a pauper, a felon, and an indentured servant, but she still possessed her pride. And damn the man, Hunter Barclay would soon know it.

Mordecai's knock also trembled the door of the captain's cabin before he opened it and allowed Devon to step inside. He lightly touched his brow with two fingers in a salute to his friend before leaving Devon and Hunter alone.

Devon stood stiff and silent, making no move to ease

the palpable tension mounting in the cabin. She'd give this man no quarter. She had obeyed his commands as a good servant must, but she'd do no more.

Hunter stood watching Devon. He thoughtfully tapped his chin with one long finger and lifted one dark brow in question. When Devon didn't respond, he smiled grimly. "Mistress, it seems we are going to have to come to an understanding if we are to have any kind of relationship. I don't enjoy constant battle."

"My lord, you have already made it clear as to my standing . . . and I accept my relationship to you as your servant. I admit I dislike my position, but I've found myself in far worse situations in the past and have managed to cope. Now, my lord, if that is all you require of me, I will retire for the night." Devon turned toward the door.

"Mistress, I have not given you permission to retire. And as you well know, a good servant always awaits her master's desires."

Devon closed her eyes and drew in a deep breath to stop herself from telling him exactly what her master could do with his desires. He could shove them where they'd never see sunlight again. However, when she turned once more to Hunter, her lovely face revealed none of her rebellious thoughts. "As you wish, my lord."

Hunter felt a surge of annoyance. He had saved this woman's life little more than twenty-four hours ago and now she stood before him, stiff and unyielding and silently implying that in some way he was at fault. Hunter's irritation mounted and he clenched his teeth. The pleasant expression he'd worn when Devon entered the cabin faded into oblivion.

"Mistress, I had not planned for your duties to begin until we reached Virginia. However since you seem determined to play out your role as my servant, I see no need to waste your talents." Hunter strolled across the cabin and casually seated himself at the table. He flashed

Devon a taunting look before reaching across the table and calmly turning the extra place setting upside down. "You may now serve me," Hunter said.

Devon thought she would choke on the fury that burst within her like a match to a powder keg. The arrogance of the beast! He was enjoying himself! Nostrils flaring she crossed the cabin to the small table that held several covered dishes. Her hands shook with anger, making the dishes rattle against each other as she crossed back to the table and set the first course down in front of Hunter. She had already begun to turn away when Hunter captured her hand, drawing her back to face him. He gazed up at her, his indigo gaze gleaming with an expression she couldn't read.

"Devon, a good servant makes little sound as she goes about her duties. Since I know you are new to your position, I will overlook your mistakes for a while. However, I suggest you practice your duties so that you can become adept at performing the tasks assigned to you."

His lecture broke the slender control that Devon held upon her temper. The man had saved her life and she owed him her gratitude, but she wouldn't lick his boots. He could just send her back to England to hang. With a squeal, she jerked her wrist free of his hand and, before Hunter realized her intent, she dumped his plate into his lap. Gravy ran down one leg of his nankeen breeches, while the dumplings landed in a grotesque lump at his crotch.

"My lord, I suggest you get yourself another maid if you don't like the way I do things," Devon replied sweetly before she turned and stamped to the door. She opened it, but paused upon the threshold to look back at the man who still sat with hands upraised in surprise, his eyes wide with shock as he looked at the mess in his lap. "Shall I come and serve your breakfast in the morning, master?"

Hunter's burning gaze flashed to Devon, but before he could form a furious answer, she smiled and was gone.

Devon nearly skipped back to her own cabin. That would teach Mr. High and Mighty to treat her like a menial.

Her moment of triumph lasted until she closed the cabin door behind her. She leaned against the thin wooden portal and wondered what demon had possessed her. She had just insulted the man who owned her for the rest of her life. He had the power of life and death over her.

Devon drew in an unsteady breath. Before today she'd had only two encounters with Hunter Barclay, but she already knew him well enough to know he'd not let the insult or her disobedience pass.

"What on earth have I done?" Devon muttered. A moment later she knew. The entire ship seemed to rock from the force of Hunter slamming his cabin door behind him. Devon recoiled and slowly backed away from her own door as she heard the heavy, furious tread of footsteps coming down the passageway. Hunter did not knock, but kicked the door open. He stood framed in the doorway, the lamp behind him leaving his features in shadow to further intimidate his quarry as he glared at Devon.

"I've had it up to here with your shrewish behavior!" Hunter ran a finger across his throat. "I've tried to deal fairly with you, and in exchange all I've received is a lap full of dumplings. I'll have no more of it. You are here to serve me, and I think it is time that you realized that fact. I own your life lock, stock, and barrel, and I can do with you as I please, mistress." His temper still driving him, Hunter crossed the cabin in less than three strides. His large frame blocked any avenue of escape as he grasped Devon by the shoulders and drew her, slowly but inexorably, toward him.

Seeing the hot, furious light in Hunter's eyes, Devon rapidly shook her head. She strained against the strong hands holding her captive. "No. I am your servant; not your whore." Her voice broke and she trembled. "God! Please don't do this. I'll not disobey you again."

The defeated plea broke through the haze of rage that had possessed Hunter after Devon left his cabin. In a swoosh, all anger seemed to leave him. Drained, he stared down at her. He raised a hand and gently traced the outline of her quivering lips. "I'm sorry, Devon. I shouldn't have allowed my temper to get away from me. I know you're still upset and I can't blame you. I shouldn't expect you to act as if nothing has happened. You need time to grieve and to come to terms with your situation."

Devon swallowed against the lump that filled her throat at Hunter's compassion. It was so unexpected—and so needed—that it was hard to remember that only a moment before she had feared he would rape her. His tenderness was her undoing. She gulped in a shuddering breath and her eyes glistened with moisture, but no tears spilled down her ashen cheeks. In all of her eighteen years she had never asked for another human's touch, yet at that moment she felt she needed Hunter's arms about her more than she needed air to breathe. Succumbing to her need before she realized her own intentions, she whispered, "Hold me, please."

His own heart torn by the look of despair on her lovely face, Hunter took Devon into his arms and held her close. At that moment she reminded him of Cecilia. The girl in his arms was only a few years older than his sister, yet her life had been far different. From what little information he had managed to worm out of Winkler about Devon, he knew the girl was guilty of the crimes she'd been accused. She was no innocent by far, but Hunter also knew she was young and alone and needed the comfort that he could give.

Gently Hunter raised a hand and stroked Devon's mahogany tresses. As fine and soft as skeins of gleaming silk, they curled about his fingers as he brushed his lips against her brow and soothed, "It will be all right, Devon."

Devon pressed her face against his chest and shut her

burning eyes. "Nothing will ever be right again. Everything is gone."

Tenderly Hunter tipped up Devon's chin and gazed down into her misty eyes. "I wish I had the words to ease the pain of your loss, but man has as yet to create words that have that power. I can give you comfort and understanding, but only time's healing hands will succor the pain."

"Thank you," were the only words that Devon could force past the constriction in her throat. Her lower lip trembled again as she drew in another shuddering breath and fought to regain control over her emotions.

The appeal of that sweetly curved mouth was too much for Hunter to resist. Eyes locked with Devon's and heart pounding against the hard, muscular wall of his chest, he lowered his head and tasted the sweetness of her soft, pliant lips.

Devon didn't resist. The touch of his mouth tantalized her senses and she sought the sensations that made her forget for the moment the harsh realities of life. Unbidden, she instinctively molded herself to his lean frame, curving her softness to the hard planes of his masculine body. She wound her arms about his neck, clinging to him to savor the current of lightning that seemed to flow between them as their kiss deepened. Hunter symbolized life, strong and sure. He was the creator, molding the thunder and lightning into a universe filled with light and wonder. It shimmered about her, its fiery aura rainbow-tinted. It claimed every inch of her body, heating her flesh and igniting the very core of her being. Her belly quivered as she pressed herself against Hunter's desire-hardened body.

Hunter tore his mouth free of Devon's and struggled to bring his raging blood under control. He had told himself that he had meant the kiss only to give comfort, but as soon as he tasted her lips, he knew he'd lied to himself. Like a cannonball, his desire for Devon exploded into a molten current that raced through his body like an uncon-

trollable wildfire blazing through a dry forest. He burned
to sink into her soft body and quench the ache she aroused.
He throbbed with his need for her.

Drawing in a deep, agonized breath, he stared down
into Devon's glorious eyes. Lit by passion, they reminded
him of rich green velvet, so soft that he could nearly feel
their caress upon his skin as she looked up at him. Hunter
cleared his throat and struggled to speak of the desire that
made his mouth dry. "Devon, you know I want you. I
ache for the comfort your body can give mine."

Devon stared up at Hunter, too shaken by her own feelings to speak of the wonder his kiss had aroused.

"Tell me now," Hunter whispered hoarsely, "if you
don't want the same thing. I'll not force myself upon you."

Devon raised her hand to tenderly stroke Hunter's cheek.
She, too, needed the comfort this man could give. She
was alone and faced with a life of servitude that would
have little joy within it. She needed to forget, to lose herself in the sensations that Hunter brought to life within
her. Devon instinctively knew from the quivering ache in
her belly that Hunter could ease her pain for a short while.
He could make her forget. Slowly she raised her lips to Hunter's, yielding herself to his passion.

Hunter again tasted the sweetness of her mouth and surrendered to his own needs. There was no more thought of
right or wrong, of acceptance and denial, of guilt or innocence. He was a man and she was a woman. That was
enough. With a moan of satisfaction he wrapped her tightly
in his arms, pressing her lithe body against his hard length.
He savored the taste of her mouth before slowly exploring
a trail along her cheek to the soft skin beneath her ear. He
flicked it with the tip of his tongue and felt Devon shiver
with pleasure as her arms came up about his neck to draw
him close. Her head fell back, giving him access to the
slender column of her throat, and he tasted her skin with
his tongue, slowly tracing a path downward. Devon's fin-

gers curled into his dark hair as he dipped his head and lightly kissed the tops of the soft mounds exposed above the neckline of her gown. Again she shuddered with pleasure.

Tantalized by the sweet smell of her, he dipped his tongue enticingly into the shadowy valley between her breasts, and she arched instinctively toward the warm breath that bathed her through the thin material separating her flesh from Hunter's caress. She didn't protest as Hunter's fingers worked loose the lacing of her gown and then slowly slid it downward to pool at her feet. His hands returned to her shoulders and his strong, warm fingers gently slipped off her chemise, gliding it downward over her breasts and hips to fall atop the green muslin.

In the same instant the moon crept over the horizon, spilling over the ship and ocean, its icy light shimmering through the porthole to bathe Devon's naked body in silver. Hunter's breath caught in his throat. Devon was fire and silver, and he had never seen anything more beautiful. He tore his gaze away from the beckoning coral-tipped mounds of her breasts and looked once more into her captivating eyes. There was no shame or regret in their mysterious depths, only an answering call to the need that throbbed hotly in his own loins. He lifted a hand and stroked his thumb against her lips, bringing a tender smile from her as she caught his hand and brought it up against her cheek. Like a sultry kitten she rubbed her cheek against his hand, her eyes and body calling to him, though she remained silent.

Hunter captured the back of her neck, burying his fingers in her thick, silken tresses as he pulled her against him and took her slightly parted lips in a long, slow, hot kiss that left nothing unsaid and no sense untouched. In one swift movement, Hunter bent and lifted Devon into his arms. He crossed to the bunk and lay her down, but didn't join her there. He stood for a long moment gazing down at her body before he reached for the hem of his shirt and jerked it over his head. He tossed it carelessly aside. A slow smile touched his shapely mouth as he stripped off the stained nankeen breeches and dropped them on the floor beside the bunk.

Devon's breath caught at the beauty of the man who stood naked in the moonlight. He reminded her of a god turned mortal. Made of hard, lean, masculine flesh, his virile body was perfection with its wide shoulders and chest, its flat belly banded by hard muscle, its narrow hips emphasizing the strong, corded thighs of his long legs. And in the dark glen at the apex of his thighs, his sex rose proud and sure with its need for her.

Devon drew in a shaky breath and moistened her dry lips as she slowly raised her eyes back to Hunter's. He was watching her reaction to him. The look in his eyes made liquid heat spiral through her and her body responded to it, dampening her as it settled achingly in the very core of her being. She wanted Hunter badly. He made her feel things she'd never felt before.

A prick of uncertainty challenged Devon as Hunter stood towering above her, his body hard with desire. Devon pushed it aside. After tonight she would face the reality of life, but for now she would forget everything but this man and the way he made her feel. Slowly Devon lifted her arms, beckoning Hunter to her.

Hunter claimed her lips again and everything else vanished into the night except the sensations his touch aroused. Her senses centered upon the man who began an exploration of her body, tantalizing her as he touched and tasted his way down the length of her. She moaned her pleasure when he captured a beaded nipple in his mouth and lavished it with his tongue before suckling. The sensations shot through Devon, tingling through her skin to center at the peak of her breast. She pressed herself against Hunter, her hips instinctively arching toward his swollen sex.

Devon experienced a fleeting moment of bereavement as he took his attention away from her breasts and slowly began to inch down her body, toward the downy triangle. Her muscles quivered with anticipation as his tongue teased . . . flicking, tasting, nuzzling. She opened to him and felt no shock at his intimate caress. Wave after wave of sensation rippled upward as he explored the satin depths, taking her breath as she gasped out Hunter's name, her unspoken plea as ancient as time, as ancient as the mating ritual of man and woman. Her fingers dug into the mattress and she tossed her head from side to side as she lifted her hips to him, offering all of herself. A moan of despair and need escaped her bitten lips as the fiery current of desire burned through her. Driven only by the need to quench the fire incinerating every inch of her flesh, she wantonly begged, "Hunter, love me, please."

Hunter needed no further invitation. He spread her legs, lifted her hips, and drove deeply into the soft, moist sheath. Devon jerked and stiffened. Her wide, pain-filled eyes reflected the end of her innocence as Hunter stared down at her, his own face mirroring shock. He couldn't believe what he'd just found. This woman, so voluptuously sensual, so responsive to his caresses, so wantonly pleading for his lovemaking, had been a virgin.

Hunter shook his head as if to clear it. What his body and mind told him was impossible. No woman with Devon's past could have remained innocent. She had stolen to live. She would have done anything for money.

I may be a thief, but I'm not a whore. Devon's words flashed agonizingly through Hunter's mind. He hadn't believed her. He had thought she had only been acting the incensed innocent.

"Damn . . ." Hunter swore softly, even as his body called to him to finish what he had begun. Her tight, hot warmth hugged him and, with each breath she took, her lithe muscles caressed his length. The sensations were nearly too much for him. They pushed aside his guilt. It was too late now to make amends . . . and he could deny himself satisfaction no longer. Gently he caressed Devon's cheeks and stared down into her bright eyes. "I've given you pain, now let me give you pleasure."

He captured her lips again, devouring their sweetness. He began to move his hips slowly to allow her to adjust to him. He felt her relax and then began to respond. Hunter's blood roared in his ears as his senses soared. He felt like an eagle, swooping and then ascending toward the heavens with his mate. They glided upward on the hot currents of their passion, each thrust of hip and pelvis taking them higher into the realm where their spirits met and joined to savor the blessing bestowed to lovers by the gods. Around them floated shimmering stardust and magic that dewed their bodies with diamonds. They danced in unison, playing out the primeval ritual that begat life from the beginning of man. Their bodies pulsed together, striving amid the intoxicating sensations to reach the summit of pleasure.

Hunter drove himself deep within Devon's welcoming body and heard her cry of pleasured fulfillment as he arched his back and spilled his seed within her. Face taut and head thrown back, he felt her throbbing ecstasy as his own. Breathing heavily, his heart pounding against his ribs, he collapsed over her, taking his weight on his elbows as he lay his head against her damp breasts.

She cradled him there and tenderly brushed the dark tendrils of hair from his sweaty brow as her own heart slowed to normal and reality crept back into the cabin, pushing its way into Devon's mind. She didn't want to face the truth. It was too soon. She wanted to cling for only a short while longer to the enchantment of having Hunter in her arms. She wanted to pretend that she lived in a world where Hunter Barclay could come to love her as she loved him. She wanted to keep him at her side for the rest of her life. Yet as the night air cooled and dried her love-flushed body, she knew it was impossible. Reality wore heavy boots that stamped out idle dreams. To the man in her arms she could never be more than a piece of property that he owned.

Devon tightened her arms about Hunter. He now owned far more than her body. During the last hour he had also laid claim to her heart. The thought was not reassuring. She was forever doomed to live on the outskirts of this man's life. As his servant she would never be given the chance to be loved, to be his wife, or to be the mother to his children. She would have only the time they spent together here in this cabin. Once they reached his home in Virginia, she would be relegated back to a bond slave.

"Then I'll make the most of the time I have," Devon whispered into the night, and caressed Hunter's cheek. She would savor their moments together during the weeks it took them to reach America . . . and she would store up enough memories to last her the rest of her life.

Chapter 8

Hunter felt his blood quicken at the sight of Devon standing at the rail. The sea breeze molded her gown against her lithe body and fanned her hair. The afternoon sunlight caught her windswept tresses and flamed the rich mahogany into shining copper. Standing there, with her beautiful face raised to the wind, Devon reminded him of the mythical goddess Aphrodite. Risen from the sea that had given her life, she stood regally surveying her domain.

"What are your plans for the girl once we reach Virginia?" Mordecai asked from where he stood at the wheel.

Hunter drew his eyes away from Devon and turned to look at his friend. From Mordecai's expression he knew there was more to the question than his friend had asked. "I haven't given it much thought."

"I suspected as much," Mordecai said, turning his attention back to the open sea. Fine lines feathered his pale blue eyes as he squinted against the reflection of the bright sunlight against the green waters. He used both blunt-fingered hands to hold the rudder steady and keep the ship on course. He didn't look at Hunter as he asked, "How do you think Elsbeth will feel when you arrive with Devon?"

"Elsbeth will understand that Devon is my bond slave."

A wry grin twitched at one corner of Mordecai's mouth and he gave Hunter a dubious look. "After Elsbeth sees

140

Devon, do you seriously think she will believe that's all there is between the two of you?''

"Why shouldn't she? It's the truth," Hunter said, and glanced once more toward the topic of their conversation. "Devon and I have an understanding. She knows her place in my life."

"Does she now?" Mordecai arched one bushy brow. "Devon Mackinsey must truly be a rare young woman to understand that she's only sharing your bed until you get back to Virginia . . . to the woman you intend to marry. Most young women of my acquaintance have hopes of sharing their future with the man who shares their bed."

"Then maybe you should find a young woman like Devon. She's known from the beginning that nothing can come from our relationship. I didn't force my attention upon her, Mordecai."

Bushy brows lowering to shade his pale eyes, Mordecai frowned. "Had I thought that of you, even our friendship wouldn't have kept me quiet. I wouldn't see the girl hurt, no matter what she's done in the past. I know she's made mistakes and can't claim to be one of those uppity English ladies, but there's something special about her. In ways she reminds me of Elsbeth.''

Hunter gave Mordecai a puzzled look. "How in the world can you even compare the two? Elsbeth is quiet and reserved, while Devon's temperament can border on shrewish at times. There's not a reticent bone in her beautiful body. Devon is fire, while Elsbeth is gentle warmth."

"Aye, Elsbeth is gentle warmth," Mordecai said. His face held a look of longing as he stared out across the open stretch of water and clamped his jaws tightly together. He drew in a long breath of the tangy sea air and expelled it slowly. The blue water separated him physically from the woman he'd come to love during the past years but there was far more that separated them than just the expanse of sea. Elsbeth Whitman loved his best friend,

Hunter Barclay. A realist, Mordecai accepted the fact. No matter how he felt about Elsbeth, he never expected her to return his feelings. Elsbeth and Hunter had been destined for each other since childhood. He knew as long as Hunter didn't do anything to hurt Elsbeth, her feelings for him would never change. She idolized him.

Mordecai glanced back to the girl at the rail and asked, "Have you told her about Elsbeth?"

Hunter looked away and shook his head. He'd meant to explain to Devon about his intentions to marry Elsbeth when they returned to Virginia. But the past weeks with Devon had been so glorious he hadn't wanted to ruin their time together by speaking of the future. For the first time in his life he'd felt young and carefree. His time with Devon had managed to push all thought of the war and his responsibilities to the back of his mind. Her uninhibited sensuality had enthralled him so deeply that he'd thought of little else as the ship sailed toward the Windward Islands.

Hunter glanced back to the woman of his thoughts. Devon was the only person in his life who made no demands upon him. She had accepted him without question, as if sensing his need to experience a moment of freedom. He didn't understand her. She was different from any woman he had ever met, and he regretted the fact that he would have only this time with her. Once they reached Virginia she could be nothing more to him than his bond slave—and to ensure his resolve didn't weaken, he'd decided to marry Elsbeth as soon as possible. No matter how Devon stirred his senses, there was no future for them together. She was his servant—*and* a convicted felon. With her past, she could never make a proper mistress for Barclay Grove or a proper mother for his children. However, Hunter was honest enough with himself to admit that since tasting Devon's sweet sensuality, he had more than one reason for hurrying his marriage to Elsbeth. Unless he married, he knew he wouldn't be strong enough to keep away from Devon while she remained at Barclay Grove.

A heavy weight settled in the pit of Hunter's stomach at the thought of never touching Devon again, of never feeling her soft, velvet skin beneath his hands, of never tasting the sweetness of her luscious mouth, and of never feeling her warmth surrounding him as he spilled his seed into her. Even now his body was responding to his thoughts of their times together.

"Don't you think it's about time you told her you're getting married? We should make port in St. Eustatius by tomorrow. Once we load the cargo, then it's only a few days north to home," Mordecai said, breaking into Hunter's thoughts.

A muscle worked in Hunter's cheek and he flashed Mordecai an annoyed look. "I'll tell her when I think it's time."

"Why don't you just give the girl her freedom when we reach St. Eustatius, Hunter? That would solve all your problems. Devon can make a life for herself there—and Elsbeth wouldn't ever have to know anything about your time with the girl."

"No. It's out of the question. Devon is my responsibility. She has no one else to look out for her. She couldn't survive on the island alone."

Mordecai paused to retrieve his pipe. He packed the globe with tobacco grown on Hunter's plantation and then turned his back to the wind to light it from his box of flint and tender. The spark caught flame in the tobacco and he took several puffs of smoke before eyeing Hunter thoughtfully. "From the look of her, I doubt she'll be alone long. She'll have a new protector before the *Jade* is out of the harbor. But should that not happen, you should remember she managed well enough on her own before you came into her life."

"Humph! She managed enough to get herself hanged,"

Hunter muttered, and shook his head. "No. Devon will go with me to Barclay Grove—and she'll stay there until I'm satisfied that she can make her own way."

Mordecai eyed Hunter obstinately. "Damn it, Hunter. You're too involved with Devon. You're going to hurt Elsbeth if you don't get rid of the girl. Elsbeth loves you, and it's not right to flaunt your mistress in her face. She's a good, decent woman and she deserves better."

"When we return to Barclay Grove, Devon will be only my servant."

"I can see how it is between you and the girl, Hunter. You take her back to Barclay Grove and you'll not be able to stay away from her. I've watched you during the past weeks and you're just like the ocean to the moon. You don't have a choice. You're drawn to her. She's in your blood, and the only way you're going to get her out is to set her free."

"I've told you what I intend to do about the situation and I don't want to discuss it any further." Hunter turned and stalked away, ending their conversation and leaving Mordecai biting into his pipe stem.

A gentle breeze stirred the palms as the moon rose from the sea to sprinkle a trail of silver across the waves that lapped against the white beaches. From her vantage point on the balcony overlooking the inn's courtyard, Devon took in the beauty of the night. In all of her dreams, she'd never imagined anything as lovely as the island. When the helmsman had called "Land ho" that afternoon, St. Eustatius had appeared as only a small speck on the horizon. However, as the ship sailed into port, she bloomed into a verdant paradise, with white sand beaches skirted in green velvet palms. Blue and white herons, sandpipers, and other colorful birds dotted the beaches as a blaze of pink flamingos swooped overhead, their graceful, long necks rising toward the sky. Two dormant, rocky-coned volcanos gave evidence of the island's birth, and the sultry sea breeze carried the sweet, tantalizing aroma of pink and red oleander and other exotic flowers to tease the senses.

The crystal waters surrounding the island changed in hue, varying with depth from the palest aqua to a deep emerald green. Blue-gray porpoises frolicked in the clear waters, escorting ships into the harbor to Fort Oranje. They danced effortlessly through the waves, ignoring the native fishermen who plied their nets from their small boats to catch sea bass, crayfish, pompano, and red snapper.

Devon drew in the sweet-scented night air and released a small sigh of regret. Saint Eustatius was paradise, but it would soon be gone. Tomorrow or the day after they would sail away, taking only the memory of this tropical splendor with them. How she wished she could reach out and grasp time in her hand, to hold it still. She didn't want anything to change. Everything at the moment was perfect. She was in paradise with the man she loved. She could ask nothing more from life.

"Hunter," Devon whispered dreamily. He filled her senses and her dreams, as well as her every waking moment. She loved him far more than she could ever have imagined loving anyone. Hunter had never spoken of his feelings for her, but she knew that somewhere, deep in his heart, he also cared for her. It was this assurance that had allowed her to give herself freely each time Hunter took her into his arms. This assurance also made her secure enough to forget that she had only a short time with him.

Devon shifted restlessly, desperately trying to keep her thoughts on the beauty of the night and the man who would soon return from the docks. She didn't want to think of the time when they reached Virginia and she was relegated back into the shadows of Hunter's life as his servant. For now he belonged to her, and, against all logic, she secretly dreamed of a future in which Hunter realized he couldn't live without her and asked her to be his wife.

Without hearing him, Devon sensed Hunter's presence behind her before he slipped his arms about her waist and drew her back against his chest. Holding her wrapped in the security of his embrace, he rested his chin gently on the top of her head and peered out into the moon-drenched night.

"What are you thinking?" he asked, his voice as soft and sultry as the warm sea breeze.

"Nothing, really. I was just enjoying the night," Devon lied, unable to voice her thoughts out of fear that once the words were spoken aloud, the illusion they had woven about themselves during the past weeks would be shattered.

"St. Eustatius is lovely. It's a shame that we won't have enough time for me to show you the rain forest that grows inside the crater of the volcano. But the cargo is nearly loaded and we sail tomorrow."

Devon squeezed her eyes closed to shut out the future looming like a dark shadow over her happiness.

"Devon, after we sail it will be only a few days north to Virginia . . . and there are some things I need to tell you."

Devon turned in Hunter's arms and pressed her face against his wide chest. She hugged him tightly about the waist, as if he were her lifeline. "I don't want to talk about the future. Please, let us just enjoy tonight."

Relieved by this momentary reprieve, Hunter tenderly ran his fingers through Devon's long, silky hair. "All right. We'll speak no more of it for now. Our dinner should be awaiting us in the dining room. Afterward we can explore the island by moonlight."

"That sounds wonderful," Devon said. She forced away the prick of anxiety Hunter had roused and smiled up at him. Their time was growing short and she'd not waste it worrying about the future. As she had learned early in life, it would come whether you wanted it or not. And until it did, you couldn't change it, not with all the worry in the world.

Hunter stepped back from Devon and gave her a wicked grin as he bowed gracefully over her hand. "Will you allow me to escort you to dinner, my lady?"

Devon dropped Hunter a neat curtsey and her lips curled mischievously up at the corners as she flashed him a coquettish look. "I would be honored, my lord."

Hunter chuckled as he took Devon's hand and placed it in the crook of his arm to escort her to the door. Unable to deny himself the treat of a brief taste of her luscious mouth, he bent his head and brushed his lips against hers. A current of electricity shot through him and his voice reflected the surge of heat that made it grow husky. "Ah, sweet Devon. You make me forget about food and everything else."

Devon's stomach rumbled her answer, and Hunter quirked a dark brow at her. He grinned his surrender. His time would come later. "I suppose that means I don't have the same effect upon you, my lady."

"I think, my lord, that means I must eat to keep up my energy . . . in order to keep up with you." Devon laughed, unashamed of her effect on Hunter.

"All so true, my lady. But be warned. Once I've seen you well-fed, I also intend to see you well-bedded before this night is done." Hunter opened the door and winked at Devon as she passed into the hallway beyond. "Bon appétit, chère."

The inn's dining room was also a popular gathering place for the seamen who had come ashore with a thirst for rum and women. A hush fell over the night's revelry as Hunter and Devon came downstairs and made their way to the table Hunter had reserved earlier. The inn's patrons, seamen and islanders alike, made no apologies for the stares they directed in Devon's direction. They eyed her wistfully, each longing to be as lucky as the man at her side, each imagining how it would be to take her to his bed.

Yet they kept any risqué thoughts to themselves. They didn't want to offend the man who had staked his claim upon the young beauty. His expression and the evil-looking sword at his side made them wary of attempting to trespass upon his territory.

Devon glanced uneasily about and watched as several sailors hurriedly turned their attention back to their rum or the serving wenches. She looked back at Hunter and found him smiling at her. Her cheeks flushed becomingly with color and she lowered her eyes to her wineglass. She fidgeted with the pewter stem, feeling the smooth, cool texture of the metal as if thoroughly interested in its workmanship.

Hunter captured her hand, stilling it in his own, and bent forward. "They stare because you are so beautiful, Devon. There's not a man here who would not give his eyeteeth to be sitting in my place at this moment."

Devon's cheeks flushed a deeper hue at his compliment. Her gaze met Hunter's and in the dark depths of his eyes she saw the reflection of her own desire. She sought the right words to tell Hunter of the feelings he aroused in her, but before she could speak, she was rudely cut off.

"Damn me, cousin. I didn't expect to see you here. Are you here to see how we lesser mortals live?" a darkly tanned man said boisterously to Hunter. Uninvited, he swung one of the straight-backed chairs about and negligently propped a black-booted foot on the seat. He rested a white-sleeved arm across his knee as he bent forward to inspect Hunter's companion. He eyed Devon with interest, boldly assessing her merits as had every other man in the room. After a long moment his full, shapely lips spread into a devastating smile that revealed his white, straight teeth. They contrasted starkly with his sun-bronzed skin as did the gold earring that he wore in his ear. It gleamed in the lantern light as he cocked his head to one side and said, "Ah, sweet beauty. How is it you come to be with my dear, boring cousin? I'm sure you could find several men here who would appreciate your charms far more than Hunter.''

Before Devon could make a comment, Hunter came to his feet and stood glaring at the other man who stood of an equal height to him. Their resemblance didn't end with their height and build. Each man possessed dark hair, and eyes so blue and deep in color they now gleamed like onyx.

"That's enough, Roarke. You've had your fun. Now I think it's time you rejoined your friends—or should I say acquaintances—because I seriously doubt you have any true friends.''

"Tisk, tisk, cousin. Where are your manners? It's been over a year since we last encountered each other and I would think you would introduce me to the lady—and perhaps ask me to stay and have a drink with you for old times' sake.''

"There're no old times between us as you well know. I don't have anything to do with men who sell their souls for a pence.''

"My feelings exactly, cousin,'' Roarke said acrimoniously. "I also don't like men who give their loyalty to the highest bidder—to protect themselves while others suffer.''

"At least I have some loyalty, Roarke, whereas you have none. You work for anyone who has the money to pay you.''

Roarke shrugged laconically. "It's a living, cousin. I wasn't fortunate to have been born with a silver spoon in my mouth. As you enjoy reminding me, the O'Connors come from the wrong side of the blanket. We can't inherit from Lord Barclay and all your rich and influential relatives in England.''

The jab hit its intended target. Hunter had tried to help Roarke when they were younger, but the man had had too much pride to take anything from him. Where the old adage about biting the hand that feeds you fit many people, Roarke O'Connor was a man who didn't just bite, he tried to chew your arm off to the shoulder if you offered help. He had been determined to show the world that he was just as good as his wealthy, legitimate cousins at Barclay Grove. And he had turned to the seas, making his living by any means and calling himself a privateer. "I make no excuses for the things that have happened in the past. Nor do I intend to apologize for my own actions to a man who is little more than a pirate."

Roarke arched a dark brow at Hunter. "My, aren't we the righteous one? You tar me with the brush of pirate and then act the saint for your loyalty to King George. But I fear you're no saint, dear cousin, but a liar. You're here enjoying yourself with this beauty . . . while poor Elsbeth is back at Whitman Place pining away for her intended's return. I may be many things, but at least I'm honest with my women. They don't expect undying love from me— because I haven't lied to them. And I'm certain poor Elsbeth wouldn't continue to look upon you as a saint should she learn of this little tryst."

"That's enough, Roarke. Leave Devon and Elsbeth out of this. My private affairs are my own," Hunter growled, his hands clenching into fists of fury at his sides. He wanted to throttle Roarke, but repressed the urge. He didn't have time to think of vengeance at the moment. He had to consider the woman sitting at the table. He sensed Devon's pain without even looking at her. He dreaded seeing the accusation he knew would be in her eyes.

Sensing that he had finally pierced his cousin's aloof armor, Roarke smiled. Hunter Barclay needed to be brought down a peg or two. He needed to realize that the world didn't revolve around him and his kind. "Oh, ho! So you haven't seen fit to tell the young lady that you are engaged to be married when you return to Virginia!"

"Damn you, Roarke. No man has any say about his birth, but he does about his life. You don't have to be a bastard because you're born illegitimate. But you're proud of what you are." Hunter looked down at Devon. "Devon, I wanted to tell you, but the time was never right."

Dreams crushed beneath the knowledge of Hunter's plans to marry a woman called Elsbeth, Devon glanced up at the two men and slowly came to her feet. The future had come as she had feared. She didn't say a word but turned and walked through the forest of legs and tables and out of the inn.

Hunter watched her walk away with head held high. He had seen that same haughty stance when she'd left the ball at Lady Heath's, and he knew her well enough to recognize the signs of brewing rebellion. He glanced back at Roarke. "You bastard. I'll see that you pay for this!" he swore before he followed in Devon's wake.

"I tremble from fear." Roarke laughed, eyeing Hunter defiantly.

"Don't doubt my word," Hunter said, and strode out into the night.

Roarke O'Connor watched his cousin until he blended into the darkness beyond the inn door. His expression grew thoughtful. There had been something different about Hunter tonight. Something that he just couldn't put his finger on. He seemed to have mellowed since their last meeting. In the past, had Roarke provoked him as he'd done tonight, Hunter would have done his damndest to throttle him.

Roarke gave a mental shrug and set the matter from his mind. What difference did it make if Hunter had mellowed? His feelings for Roarke certainly hadn't. Roarke released a breath and returned to the table where his friends were enjoying their rum. He drew in a deep draught of the sweet brew. Who gave a damn about cousins and their feelings? He was making a good living and enjoying himself, and that was all that mattered.

Hunter found Devon on an isolated section of the beach. Drenched in silver moonlight, with the sands shimmering like crystals at her feet, she looked like a statue made of ice. Frozen in place and time, she didn't move as he approached, but remained staring out at the dark, glistening waters of the bay.

Devon hugged her arms about her to ward off the chill of the night breeze—as well as the icy feeling of debasement that had crept over her as she listened to Hunter and the man called Roarke speak. Hurt and anger warred for supremacy within her, yet Devon remained silent as Hunter paused at her side.

He didn't touch her. He stood so close that Devon could feel the heat of his body as he turned to look out at the water. His words came quietly, as soft as the foam upon the beach. "I tried to tell you earlier tonight that things between us would have to change once we reached Virginia."

In the distance a ship's bell rang, echoing eerily across the waters. To Devon it sounded like the death knell for all her hopes and dreams. She could no longer hide from the truth. Like the rough hemp of the hangman's noose it tightened about her throat, cutting off her air until she thought she would suffocate. She had allowed herself to be blinded by the pleasure Hunter gave her. She had then allowed her imagination to create a world that had never existed anywhere but in her own mind.

Hunter Barclay owned her as he had once told her: lock, stock, and barrel. He had used his property to his own enjoyment. Yet she had no one to blame except herself. He had not forced her into his bed. Devon's cheeks burned with shame at the thought of her reaction to him. She had given herself freely, even eagerly. Like a poor, beaten puppy begging for a tender touch from its master, she had come to him, breathless for his caresses.

Devon's eyes were bright with unshed tears as she turned her head and looked at Hunter. The moon highlighted his wide brow, high cheekbones, and straight nose, but the expression in his eyes lay hidden in the shadows. Devon yearned to reach out and touch the cheek she'd often caressed though she kept her arms tightly wrapped about herself. Never again would she be so weak where this man was concerned. She had already touched fire and had learned her lesson. The burn she'd received went all the way to her heart and she doubted that even time's healing hands would be able to soothe the pain. However, Hunter would never know of her feelings. Her pride would not let her grovel at his feet for a morsel of his affections.

Drawing in a deep, steadying breath, Devon forced a calmness into her voice that she was far from feeling. "I understand. You never promised me anything beyond the moment, nor did you force yourself upon me. However I would ask one last favor of you."

"Anything within my power," Hunter said. Devon's calm acceptance suddenly made him feel as if someone had kicked him in the stomach.

"Will you leave me here? I would cause you no more trouble, and I can start a new life for myself."

An emotion Hunter refused to recognize tightened his chest and he shook his head. "No, Devon. I can't leave you here. The king made you my bond servant for life."

Devon's anger rippled to the surface, shattering the cloak of calm that she had wrapped about herself. Her green eyes snapped with silver moonlit sparks. "Are you so cold and unfeeling that you care nothing for the woman's feelings whom you are to marry? Leave me here, Hunter, please. I've provided you with entertainment throughout the voyage to the island; you need me no more."

"We've not reached Virginia yet," Hunter snapped. His

words were sharp-edged and cut to the quick. The glory of the past weeks seemed to evaporate into the night. A muscle in his jaw twitched and his eyes narrowed as he looked down into the stubborn little face thrust up at him. "You're mine for life, Devon, unless I decide to return you to England to hang. As for my relationship with Elsbeth, that is my concern. So don't worry your beautiful head about it."

"You're a bastard, Hunter Barclay," Devon ground out between clenched teeth. Before Hunter had time to realize her intentions, she drew back her hand and slapped him with all her might.

Hunter captured Devon's wrist in his steely grasp before she could withdraw it. He jerked her against him. His face looked like sculpted granite as he imprisoned her against his hard body.

"I'll show you what a bastard I truly am," he growled as he lowered his head and took her mouth in a fierce kiss. His tongue forced her lips apart, triumphantly reclaiming the sweet cavern as his own. He ran a hand down the slender curve of her back to the soft swell of her hips. Possessively he spread his fingers wide and brought her up against his swollen sex.

Devon squirmed in protest and beat at his back with her fists, but Hunter didn't retreat from the battle he had launched. He would conquer this foe, this hellcat, once and for all. She would know he was her master, the man who owned her. She belonged to him, and he would never let her go. Hunter deepened the kiss. No, he would never allow her to leave him.

Devon stilled in his arms. His kiss called out to her bruised heart to remember the love she had so valiantly tried to ignore since learning of Elsbeth. It brought all the emotions churning to the surface and thoroughly shattered her resolve to keep Hunter at bay. Against her will, her arms came up and encircled his neck and beckoned by an unseen force, her body molded itself to his lean frame. She sighed. She had come home once more. Her breath trembled upon her lips as she clung to Hunter, all logic crushed beneath the sensations he aroused.

The battle Hunter had intended to be violent and victorious subtly changed. The punishing kiss altered into a caress as Devon's warmth pressed against him and her arms held him tightly to her. The urge to dominate, to hurt, evaporated under the sweet current of desire that spilled into his bloodstream and began to simmer his passion. The heat of it settled in his loins, and all conscious thought left Hunter as instinct took over. He needed this woman. He needed the feel of her warm flesh beneath him. He needed the taste of her silken skin upon his tongue. He needed the fragrance of her femininity to fill his senses. He needed to bury himself deep within her, to spill his own essence into her womb. God, he needed all of her. She was as addictive as the opiate that seamen brought back from the Orient and, deny it as much as he liked, he couldn't get enough of her.

They sank to the glistening sand, their quarrel forgotten under an avalanche of emotion. Eager to experience again the rapture they had shared so many nights on board the *Jade*, they soon lay naked upon their clothing. Moonlight bathed the two figures merging as one; their lithe bodies glistening silver as they moved to the rhythm of love. The roar of the surf matched the swirling, roiling current carrying them toward fulfillment. Hunter's sleek body shadowed Devon's soft form as he moved over her, the muscles in his hard buttocks flexing as he thrust into the warm, moist depths that sheathed him. Her nectar bathed him as she rose to meet him as an equal, her mouth clinging to his, her fingers digging into the smooth, tanned flesh of his wide back. He pulsed inside of her, and she answered, tightening her muscles to give pleasure as well as receive it. Hunter jerked his mouth free of Devon's. His face reflected his ecstasy as he arched his back and spilled his seed. A shattering wave swept over Devon as she brought her hips up to receive him again. It began at the very core of her—and radiated outward in ever widening spirals of sensations that made her tremble from head to toe from the force of her release. Hunter captured her cry of ecstasy with his lips, savoring it as he felt her undulating climax.

Hunter held her close as the sea breeze dried their bodies and left its chill. They lay together, unspeaking, not truly knowing what to say to each other as the moon slowly crept across the sky and sank behind the palms to leave them in darkness.

The shadows had finally come to hide the joy they had found in each other and they slowly got to their feet and dressed. It was a quiet time, the early hours of the morning when the world seems at peace. Yet there was no peace between the two who walked back toward the inn. There could never be peace between them. The passion they shared forbade it.

Hunter paused at the edge of the beach and looked down at the woman who walked at his side. ''You know I can't let you go,'' he said quietly.

Devon nodded. ''And you know that after tonight I will try everything within my power to escape you.''

It was Hunter's time to nod. ''I expected no less of you, Devon. But you'll not succeed. The king gave you to me . . . and I intend to keep you.''

''I will leave you, Hunter. One way or the other, be it in life or death I will find a way to leave you. I won't live as your slave.'' Devon turned and left Hunter to ponder her words. The chill that rippled up his spine had nothing to do with the cool night air.

Chapter 9

To insure no arms and ammunition were smuggled into port to aid the revolutionaries, red-coated soldiers inspected the cargo as each crate and barrel reached the pier from the *Jade*'s hold. Stevedores, their work-hardened muscles straining under the weight of the cases, their skin glistening with sweat, made swift work of unloading the goods Hunter had brought back from the island. Kegs of rum, barrels of sugar, and fresh fruit lined the dockside, waiting to be taken to the Barclay warehouses where they would be sold to the merchants in Williamsburg.

Nervous nausea churned Devon's insides as she stood watching the activity from her place at the rail. The sight of the soldiers only added to the anxiety that had begun the previous night when Hunter had come to tell her they would be making port by midafternoon.

Devon hadn't looked forward to her arrival to the colony of Virginia. The past two weeks had been spent on board the *Jade* trying to find a way to be free of Hunter Barclay. However as they sailed north, each day bringing them closer to their destination, no plan emerged from the morass of jumbled emotions she had become.

She had worried herself sick. Since leaving Saint Eustatius the seasickness she'd experienced on their first days out of England had returned with a vengeance. She'd only been able to keep a few morsels of food in her stomach each day. She'd lost weight, and the hue of her skin matched the gray clouds overhead.

Devon swallowed against the sickening wave that rose again in her throat. Watching the soldiers check each crate for contraband stores did little to soothe her taut nerves. Should they ever suspect that the *Jade* had already delivered part of its cargo in the wee dark hours of the morning, Hunter would be arrested and tried for treason against the crown.

To assure no such calamity happened, Hunter had planned his mission well. In the middle of the night he had lowered the sails and skillfully maneuvered the *Jade* into one of the narrow estuaries down the coast. There he'd been met by several men with small boats. They had silently loaded the precious arms into their vessels and slipped quietly away, taking the inland waterways to deliver the goods to the men who desperately needed them to fight for freedom.

Devon glanced at the man standing on the quarterdeck, overseeing the unloading of his cargo. She couldn't stop herself from admiring his courage as well as his appearance. Hands clasped behind his back and legs splayed, he stood once more the proud English gentleman that she had first met in London. Dressed in dark serge coat and breeches, his white lawn shirt and intricately tied cravat making his sun-dusted skin seem even darker, he was nothing like the wicked rogue who had captured her heart as the *Jade* sailed from England toward the Windward Islands. Looking at Hunter now, no one would ever suspect that his loyalty lay with the men he called patriots.

Devon watched as he leaned toward the giant named Mordecai and spoke. Mordecai laughed and nodded in agreement, and then they both waved toward the docks. Devon glanced in the same direction and felt her heart sink. Two women stood waving back. One was slender and petite and possessed a riot of dark hair that tumbled to her waist in curls. There was a marked resemblance on her lovely young face to Hunter Barclay. The other was of the same height, but slightly plump and pleasant of face.

Like any animal sensing a rival for its territory, Devon instantly knew that she was looking at the woman whom Hunter intended to marry. Sizing up the competition in a glance, she felt herself equal to the challenge. Elsbeth Whitman was of no great physical beauty. A moment later, Devon felt a new stone added to the weight in her heart. When Elsbeth smiled up at Hunter, the gesture held so much warmth and kindness that it made the woman's face light with an inner beauty that left no doubts to her sweet nature. She would be a rival for any of Europe's great beauties.

A sudden chill swept over Devon and she pulled her shawl closer around her arms. Though the cloudy day was warm, the ice forming in her blood had nothing to do with the weather. She had dreaded this moment since learning of Hunter's plans to marry. Within Elsbeth Whitman's lovely face, Devon saw only the cold, lonely shadows of her own future. She would now be cast away from Hunter . . . to live on the fringes of his life as his servant.

Though there was a hive of activity surrounding her, Devon felt again as she had felt at ten years of age in her father's house: isolated. Past the tall ship's masts lay a new land filled with people. But the wood and brick buildings of the town of Williamsburg—that Hunter had told her lay eight miles inland—would even be worse than Mackinsey Hall while her father still lived. It would hold no one who cared for her. Here in America she was totally alone, without friends such as Higgins and Winkler.

Devon gripped the rail for support as another sickening wave of nausea rushed over her. How she missed those two stalwart friends. They had always stood with her during the most trying times of her life. Now she had no one. Her future held no promise of happiness, for Hunter's fu-

ture stood waving at him from the docks. He had made
his position painfully clear at Saint Eustatius. Devon was
nothing more to him than his bond slave, and he had vowed
never to release her.

The past two weeks on board the *Jade* hadn't been easy.
Hunter was so close that he could have come had she called
out to him, but the chasm that had opened after their lovemaking on the beach was far wider than feet or inches.
The knowledge that there was another woman in his life
had caused a rift that no amount of physical desire could
easily mend.

Hunter had come to her cabin only once during the voyage, but she had managed to remain aloof by keeping a
tight rein on her emotions. She had not allowed him to
penetrate the barriers she'd erected against him. Though
she had ached to be in his arms, she had kept her feelings
well hidden. He had been angered by her coolness, but he
had not forced himself upon her. He had slammed out of
the cabin and had left her to her own devices—until the
previous evening when he'd come to tell her they'd be making port today. He had also informed her of the *Jade*'s
early morning rendezvous with the patriots who awaited
them. Devon knew he hadn't done so to make her feel a
part of his life. He'd had no other choice if he wanted to
insure that neither sound nor light escaped into the night
to reveal their whereabouts to the British ships that pa-
trolled the coastline looking for arms smugglers.

Devon's gaze rested once more upon the red-coated soldiers. She knew she possessed the knowledge to buy her
freedom. All she had to do was to tell the authorities of
Hunter's activities for the patriots. On several occasions
during the past weeks, when Hunter had pricked her temper to the boiling point, she had thought of it, but as
quickly as the thought had come, she had pushed it away.
She could never betray Hunter. No matter what he had
done to her, no matter how much he had hurt her, she

loved him too much to put his life in jeopardy. It would be far easier to live on the fringes of his life than to know she was responsible for his death.

A hand at her elbow jerked Devon from her reveries. She looked up to find Hunter smiling down at her. "Devon, it's time for us to go ashore. The cargo's unloaded and Cecilia and Elsbeth are here to meet us."

Unable to get any words past the lump of cold dread in her throat, Devon nodded mutely. Only a few more feet and then she would be completely swallowed up by the shadows—shadows beyond the circle of light that was Hunter's life. Accepting the fact that she had no other alternative, she followed him across the deck and down the gangplank . . . to the dock where the two women awaited.

An agonizing pain banded Devon's heart as Hunter immediately forgot her existence under the exuberant welcome from his sister and fiancée. The three hugged, laughed, and talked, all at the same time. Standing quietly to one side, Devon looked away, too unhappy within herself to endure the sight of their joyful reunion. She scanned her surroundings, seeking anything to keep her attention away from Hunter and his family. Devon found herself staring at the man who stood at the top of the gangplank. Unaware that he was being observed, Mordecai Bradley watched the scene below, his weather-beaten features reflecting the emotions he thought he kept hidden from the world.

Struck by the stark look of longing on the giant's face, Devon slowly followed his gaze—to where it rested upon Elsbeth Whitman. Poor Mordecai, Devon thought, you know exactly how I feel because you're in love with the woman your best friend intends to marry. Her heart went out to the man in understanding and sympathy.

"Elsbeth, this is Devon Mackinsey, my new bond servant," Hunter said, jerking Devon's attention away from Mordecai.

"I'm pleased to meet you, Mistress Mackinsey. I hope you will be happy at Barclay Grove," Elsbeth said, and extended her hand to Devon. Possessing a geniality that many thought could charm the devil himself, Elsbeth's round face lit with a smile that few could resist.

Confused by the rush of warmth the other woman's gesture had created, Devon's face reflected her bewilderment as she took Elsbeth's hand. In England a lady of Elsbeth's standing would not have deigned to speak with a servant. Against her will, Devon found herself responding to Hunter's future bride.

"And this incorrigible minx is my sister, Cecilia," Hunter said, affectionately draping a strong arm about the young girl's shoulders.

Devon extended her hand to the younger girl as she'd done to Elsbeth. "I'm pleased to meet you, Cecilia."

Cecilia looked down at Devon's hand and sneered, "I'm Lady Cecilia to you. And I suggest you not forget it in the future."

"Yes, my lady," Devon said, and let her hand fall to her side.

Ignoring Devon, Cecilia looked up at her brother. "What did you bring me, Hunter? Did you get the silk I asked for in London?"

Hunter flashed Devon an apologetic look before he delved into his coat pocket and retrieved a small velvet box. He placed it in Cecilia's hand. "Maybe this will do for starters."

Cecilia's squeal of delight pierced the afternoon air as she opened the box and discovered a pair of sparkling diamond earrings. "Oh, Hunter, they are beautiful. I can wear them to Mary's coming-out ball next month and I'll be the envy of all my friends. They only possess a single strand of pearls because their mamas say they're still too young to wear diamonds."

"Then perhaps I should rethink my present, missy. I

don't want everyone gossiping about how spoiled you are because I allow you to get away with murder.'' Hunter reached for the box.

Summer lightning moved slower than Cecilia's hand as she hid the earring box behind her back. Her curls bounced about her shoulders as she vigorously shook her head. "Oh, no, big brother. You gave them to me and I will keep them. And I intend to flaunt them before everyone next week. Mary and Sarah won't speak to me for a month." Cecilia laughed at the thought of being the center of attention at Mary McDougal's coming-out ball.

"All right, imp. You may keep them if you behave yourself. Now will you allow us to go to our carriage? If you don't, the rest of your gifts will be at Barclay Grove long before we are."

"You mean there're more?" Cecilia said, her face lighting as she grasped his arm.

"Yes, miss. There is more. Now, let us go," Hunter said, feigning exasperation. He smiled at Elsbeth and proffered his other arm to her. He glanced over his shoulder at Devon. "You will travel with us, mistress. Mordecai will bring our boxes."

Physically ill, her emotions teetering precariously between anger, resentment, and hurt, Devon glared at Hunter's back. At that moment had a British soldier approached them, she'd have been more than happy to tell him Hunter smuggled arms to the patriots. And she would have gladly watched him and his sister both hang!

Devon glanced back, toward the man who remained standing at the top of the gangplank. She would have preferred to travel with Mordecai instead of being cooped up with Hunter and the two women in his life. She and Mordecai now had something in common: pain. They both had foolishly allowed themselves to fall in love with someone who could never return their feelings.

Hunter assisted Elsbeth and Cecilia into the carriage

before he offered Devon his hand. She ignored it and managed the narrow steps alone. Huddled tightly in the corner of the seat, she stared out at the passing landscape while Hunter entertained Elsbeth and Cecilia with the latest gossip from London. By the time the gates of Barclay Grove came into view, Devon knew she was going to be sick. There was no way around it. Hunter's stories, combined with the jolting of the carriage over the bumpy, sandy road, were serving the same purpose as the sea. Devon flashed Hunter a stricken look and mumbled, "Please stop the carriage. I'm going to be sick."

The thought of the consequences of ignoring Devon's order shot Hunter into action. He banged on the roof and ordered the driver to stop. The carriage had barely swayed to a rocking halt when Devon clamped a hand over her mouth and stumbled toward the door. Fortunately she made it down the steps and to the side before her stomach revolted.

A strong arm circled her waist to give her support and a cool hand held her head as her stomach heaved and convulsed. When at last nothing was left to come up, Hunter wiped the perspiration from her brow and lifted her gently into his arms. He deposited her back in the carriage without comment and climbed in beside her. A moment later the carriage jolted into motion. Devon lay her head back and closed her eyes. She had no wish to face the people who had witnessed her humiliating display.

Elsbeth was the first to speak. "Is there anything I can do for you, Mistress Mackinsey?"

Devon shook her head. "I'll be fine. It's only a touch of seasickness."

"You're no longer at sea, mistress," Cecilia snapped peevishly. "Are you certain you aren't coming down with some dread disease? We certainly don't need anyone contagious at Barclay Grove."

"That's enough, Cecilia," Hunter said protectively.

''Mistress Mackinsey has explained her illness. Now we will speak no more of it. Once she's got her land legs back, she'll feel fine.''

''I just wanted to make certain, Hunter. You never know what kind of disease a servant can bring when we don't know where she's from or where she's been. She could have caught anything before you purchased her papers.''

''I didn't purchase her papers. The king gave them to me. Now, if you know what is good for you, young lady, you will keep your snide remarks to yourself and act like a lady instead of a shrew.''

''I was only thinking of you and Barclay Grove,'' Cecilia muttered obstinately. She flashed Devon a look of loathing before turning up her nose and focusing her attention on the passing scenery.

Elsbeth gave Devon an apologetic look and cast her eyes down upon the hands she held tightly clasped in her lap. She didn't approve of Cecilia's outburst, though she understood it. Like herself, the girl sensed there was far more between Mistress Mackinsey and Hunter than papers of indenture. The moment she'd seen them together on board the *Jade*, when Hunter laid a proprietary hand upon the girl's arm to escort her ashore, Elsbeth had felt a foreboding chill run up her spine and a prick of insecurity. The girl was far too beautiful for any man not to be attracted to her. And Hunter had been at sea with her for nearly three months.

A dull ache formed about Elsbeth's heart as she remembered Hunter's tone only moments before. He had come to the girl's defense against the most important person in his life: his spoiled little sister. That in itself spoke far more loudly about his feelings than any words he could have voiced.

Through the fringe of lowered lashes, Elsbeth studied the woman she sensed could well be her rival. She sat like a wan queen, ashen-skinned, delicately shaped lips edged in white. Elsbeth drew in a deep breath. She prayed Mistress Mackinsey's illness was only a bout of seasickness.

Elsbeth sought to push the disturbing thought from her mind as she glanced at the man sitting across from her. Hunter Barclay had laid claim to her affections when they had been a few years out of nappies and she had loved him like family ever since. She would trust him with her life.

Elsbeth turned her gaze once more upon the woman at Hunter's side. She didn't truly believe anything had happened between the girl and Hunter. He was far too honorable a man to take advantage of the girl's situation. She would have to keep an eye on Mistress Mackinsey, but not because of any suspicions she might have about Hunter's relationship with her. The girl was in a new land, with no family or friends, and she might need Elsbeth's understanding and help should her sickness prove to be caused by other than the roil of the waves.

A lazy spiral of smoke rose from the washhouse chimney as Devon stepped out into the morning sunlight and weakly sank down on the bench beside the door. Perspiration beaded her pale brow as she leaned forward and put her head between her knees in an effort to counter the faintness that had threatened to overcome her as she'd rung out the bed linens. The oppressive heat of the wash fire, combined with that of the Virginia summer, made the washhouse an inferno. Damp stains darkened the material beneath her arms and down the back of her gown. Her skin burned from her own perspiration where it touched the red heat rash that banded her middle from the tight fit of her dress.

Devon drew great gulps of air into her lungs. She had to get hold of herself. It would never do for Cecilia to find her in such a state. Since her first day at Barclay Grove, the girl had seemed determined to do everything within her power to make Devon's life miserable. She hadn't forgotten Hunter's reprimand and did nothing in front of him that would make it seem that her mission in life was to torment Devon. However, when her brother was overseeing the work in the fields or was away on business, she saw to it that Devon was put to work on the worst chores.

Devon brushed a damp tendril of hair from her brow and leaned back against the brick wall. The sight of her ugly red, work-roughened hands caught her eye and she stared down at her broken fingernails and chapped skin. She shook her head at the irony of her situation. The pendulum had swung completely around. Fate had never intended for her to be free of her origins. History was repeating itself. Like her mother, she had fallen in love with a man who thought her beneath him. Devon squeezed her eyes closed and drew in a shuddering breath. And, like her mother, she would bear his child.

Devon placed her hands over her rounding belly. Each day her condition was becoming more evident. Fortunately no one as yet suspected her pregnancy. For the past few weeks she had tried to deny it by ignoring all of the signs. She had told herself that her nausea had been caused from her new environment, or the food, or the tension, or anything else that came to mind to use as an excuse. However, she'd now missed her third monthly and she could deny it no longer. She carried Hunter Barclay's child.

Devon worried her lower lip with the edge of her teeth as she stared out across the wide green lawns that led down to the creek that wound its way through the marshes to feed into the James River. The tall marsh grasses that bordered Barclay Grove to the southeast swayed in the morning breeze moving in waves like a green ocean. Soon she would have to find a way to leave Barclay Grove if she wanted to keep her child a secret. How she would accomplish that feat she didn't know. She had no friends here in

America, or any money to secure passage on coach or ship.

Devon spread her fingers protectively over her belly. She'd not allow history to repeat itself in one way. She wouldn't be like her mother. She'd never give up her child. She intended to keep her baby and no one, not even its father, would have a say in the matter. She had never known the love of her mother, and she was determined that her child would never know the aching void that Devon still felt from having been abandoned. She would fight to the death to keep her babe. "You're mine, little one. And no one will ever harm you or take you away from me."

"So, it's as I feared," Elsbeth said resignedly from where she stood in the shadows of the washhouse. She'd ridden over to Barclay Grove to have lunch with Hunter and Cecilia. She had taken the shortcut through the woods and had seen Devon stumble from the washhouse and sink down on the bench. The girl had looked deathly ill, and Elsbeth had quickly come to give aid. She had been about to make her presence known when Devon placed her hands on her rounding middle. From the swelling beneath her chapped hands it was apparent to Elsbeth that the girl's earlier illness had not been caused by the sea. The girl had been pregnant when she arrived at Barclay Grove. Once more the thought of Hunter being involved with Devon flickered through Elsbeth's mind, but she quickly denied it. It was just impossible. She and Hunter were going to be married.

Devon snapped around, her already pale features draining of all color. She pushed herself to her feet. "I don't know what you're talking about."

"Mistress, I'm no fool. I know you're with child. How long did you think you could keep it a secret?"

Devon remained mute. She had no answer. She couldn't tell Elsbeth that she'd planned to keep it a secret until she managed to flee from Barclay Grove.

"Do you know who the father is?" Elsbeth asked softly. Her voice held no accusation or criticism, only concern.

Stricken, Devon looked away from the soft brown eyes searching her face for answers. The words tumbled to her tongue, but she refused to release them. She couldn't tell the woman that the man Elsbeth intended to marry was the father of her child.

"You must tell me, Devon. I need to know so I can do something about it before it's too late. A woman in your condition is not looked upon kindly. You could be taken before the church and sentenced to the whipping block as punishment for your sins."

The world went out of focus, whirling, contorting into bizarre images of blue and green. Devon sank back down on the bench and lowered her head between her knees once more. Heart beating furiously, she gulped in deep breaths of air and tried to think coherently. She couldn't allow herself to dissolve into a trembling mass of hysteria.

"Take in long, slow breaths," Elsbeth urged, dipping her handkerchief into the barrel of rainwater that sat beneath the drain spout from the roof of the washhouse. She pressed the damp cloth against Devon's brow as she once more leaned back against the wall. "Devon, I want to be your friend. If you'll tell me who fathered your child, perhaps I can persuade him to do the right thing and give your child a name."

Devon pushed Elsbeth's hand away and shook her head. "I thank you for your concern, but this is my problem. I never want the man who sired my child to know of my condition."

"Surely the man would marry you if he knew?"

Again Devon shook her head. "No. I'm afraid he wouldn't. Now, please, I beg of you. Don't say anything to anyone about what you've learned."

"You can't mean to try and keep this a secret? In time everyone at Barclay Grove is going to realize that you're not just getting fatter. In less than nine months you're going to have a baby, mistress. And you can't hide that fact. Hunter must be made aware of your condition. You can't be expected to continue to do such hard chores. It's not good for you in your state.''

"I don't mean to try and hide my condition, but I want to be the one to tell Lord Barclay. Please, my lady, allow me this,'' Devon lied. She had to convince Elsbeth to keep silent.

Elsbeth looked uncertain. "I won't lie should I be asked, but I won't volunteer the information unless I feel it is for your own good.''

Devon breathed a sigh of relief. She had a momentary reprieve. Hopefully by the time Elsbeth revealed what she knew, Devon would be far from Barclay Grove. "Thank you, my lady. I'm grateful for your kindness.''

"Just remember, Mistress Mackinsey, you must think of your child's well-being. Life will not be easy for you without a husband. A woman with a bastard child is condemned to lead a life on the edge of society. It will be a very hard life. Should you change your mind about telling the father, I will help you in any way I can to see that he does the right thing.''

"I understand what you are trying to tell me, but there's little I can do to remedy my situation. 'Tis too late now to change my mind. I made the mistake, and I will bear the burden for it as best I may. And I will do everything within my power to see that my child does not suffer for my mistake.''

Elsbeth smiled and gave Devon's shoulder a comforting squeeze. "You are a brave woman, Devon Mackinsey. In some ways I envy you. You have far more courage than I could ever claim to possess.''

Devon watched Elsbeth stride up the path to the two-storied, red brick manor house that she would be mistress of one day. She doubted Elsbeth would have been so generous with her had she realized the child Devon carried belonged to Hunter Barclay.

Devon glanced back to her rounding stomach and sadly realized her time had run out. Now that Elsbeth knew of her baby, Devon had to find a way to flee Barclay Grove before anyone else learned of her condition.

The sound of soft whistling drew her attention to the stables, where Mordecai Bradley worked, currying down Hunter's black stallion. Mordecai Bradley was her only hope of getting away from Hunter. She knew he alone would understand her feelings. They were in much the same situation, only the proof of her love for Hunter now rested beneath her heart.

Devon pushed herself to her feet and rearranged her apron to hide the slight bulge of her stomach. The time had come to seek Mordecai out and ask his help.

For a long moment Devon stood quietly watching the giant man work. Though his hands were so large that they nearly hid the currying brush, they moved swiftly and expertly over the animal with a certain gentleness that seemed slightly foreign for a man of his size. A gentle giant, Devon thought as Mordecai glanced up and saw her. He paused in his work. The lines about his pale eyes deepened as he smiled.

"Now what brings you to the stables, mistress?"

Devon slowly moved around the stallion, patting the animal's sleek back. She stroked its muscular neck as she looked up at Mordecai. "You're a man of many talents, Mordecai. You seem as much at home on land as at sea. Most men either love the land or sea, but it seems few enjoy both."

Mordecai chuckled and ran a calloused hand over the back of his neck, wiping away the perspiration from his exertions. "I was born to work the land, and would have been satisfied to live my life on my family's small farm had I not been pressed into the English Navy."

"You didn't choose to go to sea?"

Mordecai shook his head, a wry smile curling his lips. "Nay. I'm a farmer at heart, but a man does what he must to survive."

Devon's expression sobered and she looked directly into Mordecai's eyes. "We all do things to survive."

Sensing that Devon hadn't sought him out to learn of his past, Mordecai nodded. He laid the currying brush aside and took the stallion's bridle to lead him into the barn. "Is there something on your mind, mistress?"

Devon stepped aside to allow the horse to pass and then followed Mordecai through the wide double doors. "I wanted to ask a favor of you."

Mordecai put the stallion into its stall and turned to look at Devon. "What kind of favor, mistress?"

Nervously Devon twisted her fingers together and swallowed uneasily. "I . . . I . . . came to ask . . . if you'd help me leave Barclay Grove."

Mordecai arched one bushy brow. "You don't ask little favors, do you, mistress?"

Desperate now that she had finally broached the subject, Devon pleaded, "Please, you're the only one who can help me. I must get away from here."

Mordecai drew in a deep breath and shook his head. "Mistress, Hunter Barclay is my best friend. I can't help one of his indentured servants run away."

Eyes feeling as if they would bulge from her head from the pressure of her disappointment, Devon spat, "I thought you would understand. You're the only one here who knows how I feel."

Mordecai gave a sad shake of his head. "I understand it's hard for you to be a servant after the life you lived in London, but mistress, 'tis not such a bad fate. Hunter isn't a cruel master."

Devon balled her fists at her side, her face flushing a dull red with vexation. "Don't try to act as if you don't know what I'm saying. I saw the way you looked at Elsbeth Whitman and I know how you feel . . . because I feel the same way about Hunter. Because of your feelings I thought you'd be willing to help me. You understand what it's like to love someone who is out of your reach.''

A chill ran down Mordecai's back before his face flushed a dull red with anger. ''Mistress, you're speaking of things that you know nothing about. Now, I think it's time you returned to your duties and allowed me to return to my work.''

''Mordecai, I'm not trying to hurt you. All I want is to leave Barclay Grove. I can't continue to live here. Soon Elsbeth will be Hunter's wife and she must never know about what transpired between he and I. She doesn't deserve to be hurt for my loving a man who can never return my feelings.''

''There's no reason for her to ever know if you don't tell her,'' Mordecai reasoned.

Devon drew in a long breath and closed her eyes. She didn't want to see Mordecai's expression when he learned the real reason behind her need to leave Barclay Grove. ''She already knows I'm carrying a child.''

''Is it Hunter's?'' was Mordecai's low question.

Devon's eyes snapped open, their green depths flickering with golden fire. ''How dare you ask such a thing!''

Mordecai shrugged. ''One can never be sure about a woman with your past, mistress. You wouldn't be the first woman who tried to better her position by telling the best prospect that he was the father.''

''I won't dignify your statement with an argument. All I want is your help to leave Barclay Grove. I'm asking for nothing more.''

''So the babe is Hunter's,'' Mordecai stated without doubt, Devon's reaction affirming it in his mind.

Devon struggled to hold on to her temper. ''The child I carry belongs to me.'' ·

"If he learns of it, he'll come after you."

Devon shook her head. "No. He won't. My child will mean nothing to him. Hunter will marry Elsbeth and she'll give him the heirs he needs for Barclay Grove."

"You're wrong, Devon. I know Hunter Barclay. Should he learn of the babe you carry, he'll move heaven and hell to get the child. It doesn't matter how he feels about you, he'll never let you take away his flesh and blood."

"Then you must help me get as far away from here as possible so he'll never know the truth."

"God, woman!" Mordecai swore and rubbed at the back of his neck in frustration. "I'm damned if I do and damned if I don't. Any way I go, I'm going to hurt someone I love. If I help you get away, Hunter will be hurt, and if you stay and Elsbeth learns who fathered your babe, then she will be the one to suffer."

"Think of Elsbeth, Mordecai. You love her. Don't let her be the one to be hurt because of my mistake."

Mordecai shook his head. "I just don't know. I'll have to think about it."

"Don't think too long, because I don't have that much time. Elsbeth already knows my secret, but she has promised not to reveal it until I've spoken with Hunter."

"All right, I'll let you know something by tonight. Come to the stables after I return from Williamsburg. But remember mistress: I make no promises one way or the other."

"I understand, Mordecai. I know I've placed you in a difficult situation and I'm sorry. But I have no other choice."

Hunter's fork clattered to his plate and he gaped at Elsbeth. He swallowed the cold piece of ham nearly whole and then gulped down the glass of rich, red burgundy before he managed a shallow, "What did you say?"

Elsbeth, her attention centered on cutting the pink slice

of ham on her plate, noticed none of his discomfort. "I promised I wouldn't reveal her secret, but now that I re-think it, I feel it's the only right thing to do. She can't be expected to have this child alone. The father needs to be notified. Hopefully we can persuade her to tell us who the man is so we can encourage him to marry Mistress Mackinsey and give the child a name."

"I don't believe I heard you right, Elsbeth. Did you say that Mistress Mackinsey is going to have a child?" Hunter said, still unable to believe his ears.

Elsbeth took a dainty bite of the ham and chewed. She nodded as she swallowed. "You heard me, Hunter. And it's our duty to help the girl as much as possible. If we can't convince her to tell us who the father is and get them married, I fear that Reverend Morgan will call her up to repent for her sins. She could be sentenced to the whipping post for punishment."

Hunter tossed his napkin to the table and leaned back in his chair. He felt light-headed. He was going to be a father. Devon carried his child; he had no doubt that it was his. He felt like laughing aloud and, at the same time, like weeping. What on earth had he gotten himself into? My God! What was he going to say to the lovely woman sitting at his side. She deserved far better than she was going to receive from him. Hunter rubbed his temples and released a long breath. He looked at Elsbeth. There was no reason to delay telling her the truth. "Elsbeth, are you certain Devon is with child?"

"Yes, Hunter. I'm certain. I confronted her at the wash-house less than an hour ago and she admitted it to me. She pleaded with me to let her be the one to tell you, but I feel it's best for you to be aware of the situation. Now you'll be able to deal with it."

Hunter drew in a deep, bracing breath. "Elsbeth, there's something I need to tell you."

Elsbeth stilled at Hunter's tone. The dread she'd felt on

the day of Devon's arrival at Barclay Grove reclaimed her. Its cold fingers dug into her spine. Her suspicions resurfaced. She shook her head in denial as a wobbly little smile touched her lips. Her eyes grew glassy with suppressed tears. "I don't think I want to hear what you're going to say. Please, Hunter, don't tell me."

Hunter reached across the lace-covered table and took Elsbeth's hand within his own strong brown one. A sad little smile touched his shapely lips. "You've known from the beginning, haven't you?"

Elsbeth blinked rapidly to avert the rush of moisture that threatened to spill over her lashes. "She's a beautiful woman. Far more beautiful than I can ever be."

Hunter squeezed Elsbeth's hand. "You're just as beautiful, Elsbeth, and you know I love you. I've loved you since we were children."

Elsbeth gave a weak nod. "But she carries your child?"

It was Hunter's time to nod. "Yes, she carries my child."

"And you intend to marry her?"

"The child is mine. I have no other choice."

"Then I wish you happiness, Hunter."

"How can you be so generous, Elsbeth? I have just broken our engagement and you've just learned how deeply I've betrayed you."

"As you said, we've loved each other from childhood. I can't wish you unhappiness. You're too good a man, Hunter Barclay. Though at the moment, I feel I could wring your neck."

Hunter chuckled and gave Elsbeth's hand a final squeeze. "Don't ever let anything come between our friendship, Elsbeth. I don't know what I'd do without you."

"It doesn't seem that you have any trouble filling my place," Elsbeth said more sharply than she'd intended.

The jab hit home and Hunter looked sheepishly away. "I didn't mean to hurt you." He ran a hand through his dark hair and stood. He pushed back his chair and crossed to the wide windows overlooking the gardens. He stared out into the bright midday heat so intense that the flowers wilted on the stem. "I truly don't know what has happened to me since the first time I set eyes on Devon Mackinsey. In some way that I can't explain, I've gotten myself tangled up in her life and can't seem to get myself untangled."

Quietly Elsbeth crossed to where Hunter stood. She paused at his side and looked up at him. Her lovely face held no anger or pique, only understanding and regret. She sensed that Hunter's confusion lay far deeper in his heart than he was willing to admit, but it was not for her to tell him that perhaps he had fallen in love with his beautiful bond slave. Time would be the courier for that message. Only then would he realize why Devon Mackinsey had turned his life upside down. Elsbeth placed a comforting hand on Hunter's arm. "Will you allow her to tell you of the child herself?"

Hunter nodded. "I will try. That is all I can promise."

Chapter 10

The moonless night was clear. Diamond pinpoints of light bedecked the velvet cape of the stygian sky. All was quiet and still. No breeze from the river rustled the tall marsh grasses or the thick leathery leaves of the magnolias. Nothing stirred as the night slipped slowly toward the west.

Hands thrust deep into his pockets and one wide shoulder braced against the white column of the veranda, Hunter stared blindly up at the midnight sky. He saw none of its loveliness. There was only one specter in his mind's eye: Devon.

Hunter shifted restlessly. The summer night's heat had been oppressive most of the evening, yet the heat wasn't responsible for Hunter's insomnia. Since learning of Devon's condition he had been able to think of little else.

Hunter knew he should be in his bed trying to rest. Tomorrow he had to ride into Williamsburg to meet Seth Fields. The man was to have Hunter's orders from General Washington. Things were beginning to draw to a critical point for the patriots in the area. Unlike the earlier campaigns, events seemed to be conspiring against the patriots, both North and South. Should Georgia and the Carolinas fail to ward off the renewed British assault, Virginia would be the next main target.

Hunter ran a hand through his already tousled hair. From the information he had gathered, Hunter knew the British hoped to choke Virginia into submission. Now was not the time to lose his wits because of a woman. He had to be clear-headed, his mind on business. It was vital that no one guess his ruse as a loyalist. The information he could glean was too important to Virginia's welfare.

Hunter drew in a deep breath. He could tell himself what he should do until he turned blue, but no matter how hard he tried he couldn't get Devon and the child she carried out of his mind. He had promised Elsbeth he'd wait for Devon to tell him of their child, but every instinct he possessed urged him to confront her immediately. Her reticence to reveal her pregnancy made Hunter wary of the motive behind Devon asking Elsbeth's silence.

Hunter's suspicions mounted by the moment. He doubted Devon had any intention of telling him of his child. Somehow, in that devious little mind of hers, she planned to try to keep him from learning the truth. How she thought to accomplish that feat he didn't have the slightest idea, but knowing Devon as he did, he knew she had some scheme afoot.

Hunter's expression hardened and he unconsciously ground his teeth together in frustration. He'd be damned if he'd allow her to try and keep his child from him. No child of his flesh would be branded a bastard. Roarke was living proof of what that did to a child. It didn't matter how Devon felt about him personally, she would marry him to give his child a name—even if he had to hog-tie her and drag her by the hair to the altar at Bruton Parish Church.

"I'll be damned if I don't!" Hunter muttered as he turned and stamped determinedly down the steps to the flagged walk. It was high time that he finally showed Mistress Devon Mackinsey who was master at Barclay Grove. In this matter she'd do exactly as he said.

Hunter rounded the corner of the house and came to an abrupt halt at the sight of a shadowy figure stealthily moving toward the stables. Ever vigilant to the danger his own illicit activities might bring upon his family, Hunter momentarily forgot about his intention to confront Devon. Though he could think of nothing that might have brought suspicion upon himself, Hunter wouldn't put it past the British commander to have sent a spy to report upon his activities just to ensure his loyalty. In this time of turmoil, no man was above suspicion on either side.

Hunter paused a few paces behind the intruder and watched as he opened the stable door. A slice of golden lamplight spilled out into the night, revealing the lovely features of a woman. Hunter breathed a sigh of relief as he recognized Devon. A moment later his suspicions were renewed as she cast a furtive, uneasy look around before slipping inside and closing the door behind her. Hunter's eyes narrowed. Devon was up to something that he knew he wouldn't like.

Hunter's expression grew grim. Perhaps there was more than one reason for Devon's silence about her pregnancy. An icy lump settled in the pit of Hunter's belly. He had not made love to her since Saint Eustatius. She could have easily found another lover to take his place.

A sickening sensation careened through Hunter's insides and for a moment he thought he would vomit. The insidious sword of his own suspicions impaled him, piercing him through his chest like icy steel. Hunter didn't understand what was happening to him. Of late he was hard put to explain his emotions. When Devon was involved they had a tendency to veer from one extreme to another with the least provocation. The only thing he did know for certain was that he'd never let Devon go, even if she carried another man's child.

"Because she belongs to me and no one else," was Hunter's possessive growl as he swung open the stable door. Anger seized control of him, searing him to his toes at the sight of Devon standing close to Mordecai Bradley. "What in the hell is going on here?"

Startled by Hunter's sudden appearance, the couple stared back at him as he growled again, "I asked you a damned question and I want some answers."

Devon flashed Mordecai a beseeching look, but knew by the resigned expression on his craggy face that he would not lie. Desperate to keep Hunter ignorant of her condition *and* her intentions to flee Barclay Grove, the lie was out before Devon had time to reconsider it. "Can lovers not have a few moments of time together without asking your permission, my lord?"

Hunter's face turned to granite. His livid blue gaze raked over Mordecai. "Mordecai, is what she says true?"

Devon stepped closer to Mordecai and silently prayed he'd not make a liar of her as she wrapped her arms about his waist. "Are you calling me a liar, my lord? Can you not see with your own eyes what is going on?"

His gaze imprisoning his friend like a cage of steel, Hunter growled, "I'm waiting for an answer from you, Mordecai."

Mordecai's big hands removed Devon's arms from about him and then set her aside. "No, Hunter. It's not true."

"Then what are you doing here at this time of night?" Hunter asked, his jealousy making him unable to allay his suspicions completely.

"Mordecai, please," Devon begged, but saw her hope to escape Barclay Grove evaporate with the negative shake of his head. She turned away, defeated.

"I planned to help Devon leave Barclay Grove tonight." Mordecai answered evenly and without remorse.

Bewildered, Hunter stared at Mordecai. "Why in hell would you do such a thing? You know you'd be breaking the law to help a bond slave escape."

"That's a question you'll have to ask Devon. It's between you and her now. I should never have gotten involved in the first place because you're my friend." Mordecai flashed Devon an apologetic look. "Perhaps this is for the best.'' He left Devon and Hunter staring at each other.

"What did he mean, Devon?"

Unable to surrender meekly, Devon raised her chin in the air and glared at Hunter. "I don't know what he was talking about."

In less than two strides Hunter closed the space between them. He snaked out a hand and captured Devon's wrist. His fingers bit into her flesh as he drew her close enough to see the tiny specks of golden lantern light that laced the forest green depths of her flashing eyes. She was ready to do battle and, damn it, so was he! "Lies, always lies. Can you not be honest with me at least once? Can you not tell me the truth instead of me having to drag it out of you? Why do you want to leave Barclay Grove, Devon? Didn't I tell you I'd never let you go?"

Devon glared defiantly back at Hunter. Her voice was dangerously low as she quietly said, "And didn't I tell you I would never stop until I was free of you?"

Hunter raised a hand and laced his fingers into the mass of shining mahogany silk that spilled down Devon's back. He had not touched her since the night on the beach at Saint Eustatius, but the memory rested so tantalizingly close to the surface of his mind that he could nearly taste the sweetness of her lips as his eyes came to rest on their mutinous pout. Slowly he drew his gaze away from her enticingly provocative mouth. He looked into her scorching eyes.

"God! How I have missed you," he murmured as he lowered his demanding mouth to hers.

Devon struggled against the arms that came about her and pressed her against Hunter's lean, hard body. She didn't want to surrender again to the heady sensations his touch aroused. She had to put a stop to it before her heart yielded once more to the love she felt for this man.

Devon managed to tear her mouth free of Hunter's.

Breathing heavily she pressed both palms against his wide chest and shook her head wildly from side to side. "Leave me be. I will not be your whore again. I serve you with my labor as the law decrees, but I will not service you like a mare studs a stallion."

His own breathing labored, Hunter wound his hands in Devon's hair to still her. He held her face captured between his palms and gazed down at her, searching her features. He saw nothing but anger in her flashing eyes. Swallowing back an unexpected wave of bitterness, he snarled, "But you will bear my bastard, won't you?"

Devon blanched. She stared at Hunter mutely, unable to deny or confirm his question.

An ugly grin curled up the corners of Hunter's lips and his eyes narrowed with resentment. Devon's stricken expression and her silence confirmed what Elsbeth had told him. Devon carried his child and, as he had feared, she hadn't meant for him to learn of its existence. Fortunately he had caught her before she convinced Mordecai to help her leave Barclay Grove. Hunter's irritation mounted. Slowly he shook his head. "You don't have to answer, because I already know the truth. However, you will not bear my bastard. My child will carry my name."

Seeing Devon's startled look, he continued smoothly, "Does that surprise you so much, sweet Devon? I would think you had this planned all along."

Devon jerked free of Hunter's hands and winced from pain as several long, shining strands of her hair remained tangled about his fingers. "The child I carry is mine, and I have no intention of marrying you."

Hunter's expression didn't soften. "But I have every intention of making you my wife, Devon. If the truth be known, isn't that why you told Elsbeth about the babe— to let me know of my obligation to you?"

"You have no obligation to me, you arrogant bastard! I had no intention of ever letting you know of my child. Nor have I ever planned to wed with you,'' Devon spat, feeling no remorse for the lie. She alone knew of the girlish dreams of love and marriage she'd woven for herself on board the *Jade*. That was before she had learned of Hunter's intention to marry Elsbeth Whitman.

"You don't truly expect me to believe that, do you?" Hunter asked sarcastically.

"I personally don't give a rip-roaring damn about what you believe. Just let me leave Barclay Grove and you'll hear nothing more from me.''

Hunter's icy expression seemed to chill the summer night. "The child belongs to me, and I would see you dead and in hell before I allowed you to take it away. There will be no time to have the banns read, so be ready for your wedding next week." Hunter turned away, but Devon's quiet, defiant words stopped him before he reached the door.

"Hunter, I won't marry you.''

Hunter glanced over his shoulder and smiled confidently at Devon. "Yes, you will—or you'll be turned over to the church. Our good pastor is a firm believer in punishing sinners for their sins. He'll have you stripped and flogged in front of the entire congregation of Bruton Parish Church. Then, when I tell him I'm still willing to marry you, though everyone knows of your disgrace, he'll say it is the best for everyone concerned, especially the innocent babe that you carry.''

Feeling as if she could once more hear the gate of Newgate clanging shut behind her, Devon shook her head. "You wouldn't do that.''

"Test me, Devon, and find out. I will go to any extreme to ensure that my child has the name he deserves. That means I'll see his mother whipped if that is what it takes to bring her to her senses. It's up to you. Now, mistress, I'll bid you good night." Hunter turned and stalked from the stable, leaving Devon standing alone in the pool of lantern light.

She gazed into the darkness beyond the door and saw her future. Had Hunter wanted to marry her, she would have been the happiest woman alive. But such happiness was not to be. Hunter didn't want her. He only wanted the child that she would bear him.

A shudder passed through Devon, an eerie sensation crept up her spine. Again history was repeating itself. In her life, she had never had anyone to want her for herself alone. A painful lump filled her throat and she swallowed with difficulty. Again she was second choice.

The coach rolled down the Duke of Gloucester Street, the crunching of its wheels against the shelled pavement seeming to shout to the world that its destination was Bruton Parish Church. Inside, Devon sat nervously watching the hands she held clasped tightly in her lap. She was too nervous to enjoy the rich feel of expensive fabric of the wedding gown Hunter had purchased for her. Made of creamy white satin embroidered in white silk flowers, its wide skirts were a froth of lace and ruffles about her feet. The low-cut bodice was also edged in delicate lace and accented by tiny satin bows at the square neckline that revealed the soft swell of her breasts. Nor could she look at the man who sat at her side, or the young woman who sat glaring with hatred from the opposite seat.

The day after Devon's confrontation with Hunter, Cecilia had been told that her brother was to marry Devon. The girl's squeal of outrage could have been heard to Williamsburg. She had lashed out at Devon, calling her every kind of vile creature that she could think of until Hunter had stepped in and silenced her with the threat of turning her over his knee. Cecilia had grudgingly obeyed her brother, but had done everything in her power to stop the nuptials from taking place. She had even called in Elsbeth with the hope that she could talk some sense into Hunter.

Devon swallowed against the painful memory. Hunter had moved her into the manor house after telling Cecilia about his marriage, and she had just come from her room when Elsbeth arrived at Barclay Grove. She hadn't meant to eavesdrop, but she had felt too uncomfortable about facing Elsbeth after everything that had transpired. Elsbeth had been kind to her, and Devon didn't feel any victory in ruining Elsbeth's own future with Hunter. She had paused, out of sight on the stair landing overlooking the foyer when a furious Cecilia met Elsbeth at the front door.

Unaware of her presence, Cecilia hadn't waited until they had privacy to expound upon her grievances. She immediately launched into her story of despair for her brother's sanity, telling Elsbeth that she alone had the power to bring Hunter to his senses and stop his disastrous marriage to Devon. Cecilia had reaffirmed what Devon had already feared when she told Elsbeth that Hunter still loved her and she alone could convince him of the mistake he was making by linking himself to his bond slave.

Devon had listened to the conversation with her heart in her throat, a heart that slowly withered as Elsbeth tried to make the younger woman understand that her brother had no other choice. He had to think of his child. Unaware of the agony she was inflicting upon Devon, she repeated what Hunter had said the day she'd told him of Devon's pregnancy. Elsbeth had comforted the girl by telling her that Cecilia would never lose her brother or Elsbeth's friendship. Elsbeth had held the girl in her arms and soothed her as she pleaded with Cecilia to accept Hunter's marriage for the sake of his child. Since that day, Cecilia hadn't been as vocal about her feelings, but Devon knew the girl still hated her.

There was nothing Devon could do to change Cecilia's feelings any more than she could Hunter's. She had resigned herself to that fact—and to her coming marriage. During the past few days she had come to accept Hunter's decision as the right one, though it brought no joy to either herself or him. It was the only reasonable thing to do. She knew now that her own resolve to keep Hunter's child away from him had been a decision rooted in pain. It had not been to benefit her babe. Had she succeeded, she would have condemned her child to the same life she had led. She would have denied him the very things she had been denied by her own father: a name and family. No matter how much it hurt her, she could not do that to her own flesh and blood. She would learn to live with her pain and, hopefully, in time she could find a way to deal with it.

Devon knew it would not be easy to live with Hunter and know that he loved another woman. But she could expect nothing more. He had never made any promises to her, or any vows of love. They had shared a passion that still made her pulse race when the memories of their moments together came crashing to the surface. The consequences of their unbridled passion now made it imperative for them to marry.

No, life had never been easy for Devon. But she knew she was a survivor. She also knew she now faced her biggest challenge: living with Hunter and never having his love. Since her earliest memories she'd had to fight to live and, oddly, nothing would be any different when she was Hunter's wife. She might never be hungry or dressed in rags again, but her emotional survival was in jeopardy. Her only consolation was the bond she would share with Hunter through their child. Hopefully she would find some peace—in giving their babe all the love she was denied giving its father.

Devon was jolted away from her reveries as the carriage rolled to a halt in front of the gate to the churchyard. The driver jumped down and swung the coach door open.

Hunter exited first and then assisted Cecilia down before helping Devon maneuver the two small steps to the ground. He didn't release his hold upon her as she hesitated at the church gate and looked up at the steepled brick building where she was to be wed.

Bruton Parish Church sat on the corner of Gloucester, at the foot of the Governor's Palace green. Designed in the shape of a cross in 1715, the church was surrounded on all sides by a bricked wall. Elms, red and sugar maples, and live oaks, their graceful limbs reaching toward the sky, shaded the peaceful glade of green lawn beneath. The tranquility of the churchyard soothed Devon's anxiety over the ceremony to come and she glanced up at the man at her side, searching his handsome features for some sign of reassurance. She gave him a trembly smile when he looked down at her.

Sensing her discomfort, Hunter gave her hand a comforting squeeze. "Everything will be all right, Devon. I promise you."

Devon nodded mutely. She prayed Hunter was right—and that with God's help she would have the courage to face the future now awaiting her as Lady Barclay.

News of Hunter's impending marriage had spread like wildfire through coastal Virginia and up the James River. The event brought even political enemies together in a silent truce as they shared the same church pews for the ceremony. Through the years the Barclay family had been too well respected to allow the recent turmoil to stop the local residents from packing Bruton Parish Church. Dressed in their finery and sweating profusely from the sweltering summer heat, they came to catch a glimpse of the woman who had snared the most eligible bachelor in coastal Virginia.

Even the new governor, Patrick Henry, chose not to miss the event. He sat in the canopied pew of his predecessors, feeling slightly uneasy by its ostentatiousness and staunchly trying to ignore the black looks he received from those who disliked his political views calling for liberty. Today, like many of the other guests, he'd set politics aside for a few brief hours in order to come to celebrate an old friend's marriage. He didn't agree with or understand Hunter's continued loyalty to the crown, but since they'd grown up together, he'd graciously offered the Governor's Palace for the reception following the nuptials.

Devon felt her heart still as the wide double doors swung open before her and all heads turned to get the first glimpse of Hunter's bride. She thought her knees would buckle beneath her at the sight of so many strange, staring faces. She had Hunter's comforting presence at her side, but it took every ounce of strength she possessed to put one foot in front of the other to walk down the aisle.

Dressed like a gentleman in dark breeches, jacket, and an immaculate white linen shirt, Mordecai Bradley gave Devon a reassuring smile as she passed the pew where he and Elsbeth sat. His friendly gesture went unnoted under the assault of nerves that took Devon in their grasp. Her heart pounding against her ribs, her breath coming in rapid little pants, a sense of unreality descended upon her as she approached the altar on Hunter's arm.

The ceremony passed in a blur, as did the reception that followed at the Governor's Palace. Thanks to Mistress Cameron's lessons, Devon automatically gave the correct replies to the well-wishers. She danced and laughed with Hunter's friends as if there were nothing out of the ordinary about her marriage to the prosperous Virginia planter. Oddly removed from her surroundings, she floated through the evening, acting her part as a newly wedded bride while wondering when she'd awake from the lovely dream. She dared not question the fantasy, fearing it would vanish and she would find herself once more on her narrow bed in the slave quarters at Barclay Grove.

The sultry evening embraced the land as Hunter reclaimed his bride and bid farewell to their friends. A rousing cheer shook the gleaming paneled walls when Hunter swept his wife up into his arms and strode from the ballroom. He carried her down the long entrance hallway, where elaborate arrangements of muskets, pistols, and swords had been displayed by the British governors to impress the colonials.

Hunter's shining boots crunched on the graveled path as he made his way down the walk to the open carriage awaiting them. He deposited Devon in the vehicle he'd had garlanded with honeysuckle, jasmine, daisies, and rosebuds. The sweet, tantalizing fragrance rose about them as Hunter gave those who had followed from the ballroom a jaunty salute before he took the reins himself and snapped them against the horses' backs. The vehicle set into motion, taking Hunter and Devon home.

Still cocooned in the aura of the day, Devon snuggled dreamily next to Hunter and looked around at the lover's bower. She plucked a delicate pink rosebud and raised it to her nose. She inhaled its fragrance, savoring the sweetness as she glanced up at the man at her side. Hunter's thoughtfulness was so unexpected. He had made their wedding day special. No matter the reason behind his actions, he had made her feel treasured.

"What are you thinking?" Hunter asked, slowing the horses to a gentle pace. He relaxed back against the seat.

Bemused, Devon answered honestly. "I was thinking of how wonderful today has been. Everything was so perfect . . . It all seems like a dream, and I'm afraid I'll soon awake to find it all gone."

Hunter grinned. "My lady, after all the dancing I would think your tired feet would be enough evidence for you to know you've been awake all day."

Devon cocked her head to one side. All the love she felt for Hunter was in her eyes as she asked softly, "Why did you do all this?"

"You are my wife now, Devon. You're Lady Barclay. And because of that there are certain things that are expected of me," Hunter said, without taking his eyes off the road.

The dreamy glow slowly ebbed away as reality pushed its way through the veil of happiness surrounding her. Hunter had put her in her place. The rosebud that had given such pleasure a moment before now lay forgotten against the white satin skirt of Devon's wedding gown. She shifted away from Hunter and turned to stare out at the dark shadows that cloaked the live oaks alongside the road. Valiantly Devon tried to hide the hurt rising within her breast. "I understand," she said in a small voice, and concentrated on the passing scenery.

Hearing the forlorn note in Devon's voice, Hunter reined the horses to a halt and turned to her. He suppressed the urge to reach out and take her into his arms. He craved the taste of her mouth, yet he refused to allow himself the pleasure of satisfying his own needs. He feared he'd already made too many mistakes by reacting upon his instincts. For once in his relationship with Devon, he would try to think of her instead of himself.

During the past week Devon had come to accept the fact that their marriage would be the best thing for their child, but he wasn't at all certain she felt the same for herself. In his effort to protect his unborn babe, he had proven to her that he was master of Barclay Grove, and he feared he'd also proven he was an arrogant ass.

"Devon, I don't really think you do understand," Hunter said quietly. He had attempted to make amends for his mistakes with the elaborate wedding, the carriage, and the special dinner awaiting their return to Barclay Grove.

Devon didn't look at Hunter. She couldn't. "I do understand, and I appreciate all the trouble you've gone to to try and make people believe we both want this marriage. It will be much easier for everyone concerned when your friends learn of my condition. It's best for your heir that no one ever know the truth. I would not have him hurt in the future because of other people's cruelty."

The muscles banding Hunter's chest constricted and he swallowed hard. This was their wedding night, and he had wanted Devon to at least have a few good memories. Now he realized he had failed miserably.

Unable to stop himself, Hunter reached out and touched the mahogany tresses curled against the side of Devon's throat. They dangled enticingly over her bare shoulders. "Devon, I know you didn't want this marriage, nor did I. But it's too late to change things now. We can't turn back the hands of time. We have to look toward our future . . . and the future of our child."

Devon nodded, but refused to turn and allow Hunter to see her pain. "I will do my best."

"That is all anyone could ask," Hunter said. "We can have a good life together if we try. It'll take work, but we will have our child. Our blood mingles within his veins, and that is a bond that can't easily be broken between two people." Hunter brushed his lips against Devon's shoulder. "I would have us live in harmony again, Devon."

Devon slowly turned and looked up into Hunter's handsome face. She couldn't read the expression in his night-shadowed eyes, but she knew she would find no lie to his words within the indigo depths. He was being honest with her. He didn't spout words of undying love to win her favor. He offered her peace—the peace she needed. He offered her a truce, a truce that would allow them to live amicably together for the sake of their child . . . and for the sake of her own bruised heart.

"I want to be a good wife," Devon whispered and felt a thrill shoot through her as Hunter slowly lowered his head. She wanted his kiss, she wanted to feel his arms around her. It didn't matter that he loved another woman. That was yesterday and tomorrow. Tonight was her wedding night and he belonged to her. Hunter was her husband and she needed him.

Hunter paused only inches from Devon's mouth and murmured, ''Be my wife in all ways, Devon.'' He claimed her lips, succumbing to the temptation of the sweet, provocative mouth turned up to him. With a groan he buried his fingers in the rich silk of her hair and held her captive while he devoured her mouth, thrusting his tongue deep within the moist cavern. His heart pounded against his ribs, pumping furiously as desire spread its tentacles over his strong limbs and down through his belly. A white-hot heat coiled in his loins and wrapped itself about him, hardening the muscles in his buttocks and thighs as he swelled with need for the woman in his arms.

Hunter smothered Devon's face with tiny kisses as he murmured, ''God, how I want you. Please don't deny me tonight, Devon, or I won't be responsible for my actions. I need you.''

Devon could no more have denied Hunter than she could have reached up and plucked a star from the sky. She wrapped her arms about his strong neck and molded herself against him. They stretched out in the carriage, white satin and dark velvet strewn heedlessly and shamelessly among the garlanded flowers as they came together, their young, sinewy bodies seeking fulfillment.

There was no thought of the shock a passerby might receive upon seeing the newlyweds making love in their carriage in the middle of the road. There was no thought to what had brought them to that moment and place. Their need to give and receive pleasure drove them. And the song of flesh against flesh, mouth against mouth, and hip against hip, filled the still night. Two moans of ecstasy wafted upon the gentle breeze from the river. It floated among the tall marsh grass to the creatures of the night, who stilled at the sound of the lovers' quest.

* * *

Cecilia brushed a tear from her cheek as she watched Hunter and Devon drive away. She'd done her best to try and stop Hunter from making the biggest mistake of his life, but had failed miserably. Nothing she'd said or done had changed his mind. He'd been set on marrying Devon Mackinsey come hell or high water.

Cecilia's full lips pursed in disgust as she turned toward the path that led to the garden. She was in no mood to return to the dancing and merriment within the ballroom. She wanted to get as far away from the church and Governor's Palace as possible and try to forget what Hunter had done to their family that day.

Cecilia kept to the shadows, hoping that no one would see her. She'd been infuriated when Hunter had told her that she was to stay with Elsbeth for a few days to give him time to be alone with his new wife. However, in her present mood, she was eager to go to Whitman Place. Hopefully she could find Elsbeth without having to brave the flock of nosy gossips who would pounce upon her the minute they saw her enter the ballroom. All would be filled with questions about Hunter's new bride and their sudden decision to marry.

Even in her fury, she was wise enough to know that it was best for her future relationship with her brother that she avoid venting her feelings on the subject. However, if pressed, she feared she'd not be able to control herself. In her present state of mind she'd probably tell them exactly how she felt and the reason behind Hunter's madness. She needed time to think—and reconcile herself to Devon Mackinsey now being a part of her family. The very thought rubbed Cecilia the wrong way.

Cecilia took the first marble step leading up to the portico when voices coming from the shadows of the box hedges made her pause. Hand on the marble balustrade, she glanced toward the sounds and frowned. There was something familiar about the voices.

Quietly she turned and made her way to the hedged alcove. She paused at the entrance, listening intently as the two continued to speak quietly together. Cecilia's eyes widened with recognition of Elsbeth's voice. Wondering who the man was that could persuade her friend into the shadowy garden; her curiosity winning out over good manners, Cecilia stood eavesdropping.

"It hasn't been easy for me. You know I've loved him for as long as I can remember," Elsbeth said, her voice tight with suppressed emotion. "Hunter is like my own flesh and blood."

"Aye, I feel the same. He's like a brother to me as well."

Perched tenuously upon tiptoes, Cecilia leaned closer to the hedge. Her wide blue eyes reflected her shock when she identified her friend's companion as Mordecai Bradley. She nearly choked with indignation that Elsbeth should be so overwrought by Hunter's betrayal that she'd have to confide her feelings to her brother's hired help. It wasn't proper. Elsbeth was a lady—far too good to associate with the likes of a bilge rat.

Cecilia's temper soared to new heights against the woman her brother had married. It was all Devon Mackinsey's fault.

"You know, until today I hadn't truly realized that was how I felt about Hunter. But seeing Devon walk down the aisle on his arm made me see that I wasn't the right woman for him. He needs someone like her. She has the same fire that has always driven Hunter."

"You also have fire, Elsbeth. But yours is the kind that warms a man to his soul. It's the kind that makes a man want to come home at night. It's the kind that eases the trials of a man's life and makes him feel whole . . . instead of burning him into cinders that blow in the wind like a useless pile of ashes. Any man worth his salt would be proud to call you his own, Elsbeth, because there are few women in this world who have a heart as big as yours.''

"And you're a man whose love any woman would be proud to possess, Mordecai. I'm so glad we've had this time together. I've always felt a bond between us, but I thought it was because we both loved Hunter."

There came a sound of movement beyond the hedges and Cecilia quickly jumped back into the deeper shadows.

"There's only one woman who possesses my love, Elsbeth." Mordecai's words came as soft and as sultry as the summer night's breeze.

Cecilia clamped a hand over her mouth to stifle her gasp. She couldn't believe what she was hearing. The world had suddenly gone berserk. Hunter had married his bond slave, and now a common seaman thought himself good enough to speak to a lady in such a manner.

"I envy her," Elsbeth whispered. "She is a lucky woman."

Unable to listen further, Cecilia burst through the opening in the hedges. "You don't know what you're saying, Elsbeth. Have you gone mad because of Hunter's defection? Surely you'd not stoop so low as to take Mordecai as your lover."

Cecilia's head snapped back as Elsbeth's hand contacted with her cheek. Shocked by Elsbeth's burst of violence, a reaction so out of character for the soft spoken woman, Cecilia clamped a hand to her burning cheek and backed away. Her blue eyes filled with tears as she watched Elsbeth turn on her.

"How dare you say such a thing? If you weren't such a spoiled little child, you'd realize it would be an honor to have such a good, decent man to love you." Elsbeth glanced at Mordecai, standing quietly at her side. In all of her twenty years she'd never come to anyone else's defense, especially so violently. Until now she'd never raised a hand against another human being. Unbidden tears brimmed in her eyes and her lower lip began to quiver. She swallowed against the sob rising in her throat when she realized her actions stemmed from the fact that she had never cared enough about anyone before now.

Seeing her anguish, but rejoicing in his heart at her words, Mordecai lifted his arms to her. Elsbeth went into them, eagerly snuggling against his wide chest as if she'd found her other half. And in a way she had. For no one could have loved her more at that moment than Mordecai Bradley.

Hurt and anger mingled as Cecilia spun on her heels and fled. She had never been struck before. Not even at her worst behavior had Hunter seen fit to punish her in such a manner. Her cheeks wet with tears, she sped out of the garden and down the path to the Duke of Gloucester Street. She didn't know where she was going. All she knew was she had to get away from the madness that had seized everyone.

Head down and paying no heed to her surroundings, Cecilia didn't realize she had wandered into the section of Williamsburg that housed the taverns frequented by the planters, patriots, and seamen, as well as British soldiers. Immersed in her own woes, she passed in front of the King's Arms Tavern at the same moment the tavern door opened and a uniformed officer stepped out onto the sidewalk. Cecilia collided with his hard, masculine form. Startled back to reality, she looked up into the handsomest face she'd ever seen and teetered precariously on the brink of falling at his feet. She sought to regain her balance and collect her wits as a strong hand steadied her.

"My pardon, my lady," the officer said as he looked down at the girl standing in the beam of golden light that spilled through the tavern window. In a quick, assessing glance, he knew the girl didn't belong in this part of town at this time of night. Her expensive clothing and young face told him she wasn't one of the prostitutes that frequented the taverns looking to make a few pence each night. Never a man to ignore even the smallest opportunity, Neal Sumner gave her one of his most charming smiles. "Please, forgive me."

Drowning in his dark brown gaze, her cheeks heating with a blush, her heart in her throat, and her stomach somersaulting beneath her ribs, Cecilia managed to sound calm. "I'm sorry. It's my fault. I wasn't looking where I was going."

Neal's smile deepened. "For that I'm grateful. Since my arrival last week, I've had little opportunity to meet any of Williamsburg's lovely ladies." With a casual gesture toward the high-collared red coat that he wore with such poise, he said, "I fear my presence here in Virginia is not welcomed by many of Williamsburg's residents."

Taking note of the gold-fringed epaulets that graced his wide shoulders and signified his rank, Cecilia smiled. Standing here, talking with a colonel in His Majesty's Army, made her feel far older than her sixteen years. "Perhaps by many, sir. But I can assure you that I and my family at Barclay Grove welcome you to Virginia. We do not accept the ideas of many of our radical neighbors, nor do we harbor any need to be free of England's rule. My uncle is in the House of Lords, as will be my brother when he inherits the title."

"Then allow me to properly introduce myself, my lady. I am Colonel Neal Sumner, of His Majesty's Army."

Cecilia regally extended her hand to Neal. "And I am Cecilia Barclay."

Neal's face lit as he bent gallantly over Cecilia's hand. "By chance, are you any relation to Hunter Barclay?" As Lord Barclay's heir and nephew, Hunter Barclay was well known for his loyalty to the crown. His knowledge of the area and the rebels would be of tremendous value to Neal.

"I am his sister," Cecilia murmured, too caught up in

the tingling sensation Neal's kiss had sent up her arm to wonder about his question.

"Then our meeting is even more fortunate for me. I have orders to meet with your brother as soon as possible."

The memory of the reason she'd been wandering through the streets of Williamsburg bringing her back down to earth, Cecilia's tone chilled the night as she snapped, "I hope your need to meet with my brother isn't urgent. He was married today, and he's made it quite clear that he intends to see no one for a few days."

"I can understand his reasons. I will make an appointment with him for next week." Neal smiled to himself. From the girl's tone it was obvious she didn't approve of her brother's marriage. But that was her affair. His mission to Williamsburg would be finished once he'd contacted Hunter Barclay and told him to marshal the loyalists in the area together. They would be needed for the upcoming battles. The plans he'd delivered today to Colonel Braggert would set into motion the end to the resistance in the Southern colonies. Once that was done, the British forces could concentrate on squelching the hotbed that had bred the rebellion: Virginia. It would be a fierce battle, but Neal was confident of England's victory. The British forces far outnumbered the colonials. He'd heard that the Washington fellow who had been appointed general-in-chief of the rebel army had less than sixteen thousand men in his entire force. Such a piddling number could never defeat the well-trained British troops. It was unreasonable to even think that they could. However since coming to Williamsburg, he'd learned there were quite a few residents who were unwise enough to believe such a farce could take place.

Neal held his left arm against his side. How he wished he could be in on the action. He was now a colonel in His Majesty's Army, but he'd fight no more battles on the field.

The bitch who had injured him had seen to that when she'd pushed him into the fire. He could no longer handle a weapon because his fingers had grown together in such a manner that his hand was little more than a useless club. Nor could he grip the reins of his horse enough to command the forces in the field. He was no better than a glorified errand boy.

Damn her! Devon Mackinsey had been let off too easy by hanging. She should have been tortured every day that he had to suffer. He would give ten years off his own life were she still alive—so he could get his good hand on her.

"Colonel Sumner? Is there something wrong?" Cecilia asked, the look on Neal's face made her suddenly uneasy. She glanced nervously about as if realizing for the first time where she was. "Oh, dear. I must get back to the Governor's Palace. My chaperon will be looking for me."

As if in answer to her prayers, the Whitman coach rumbled to a halt a few feet away. The door swung open and Mordecai Bradley stepped down. He gave the British officer a hard look before his gaze settled on the wayward Cecilia. "Mistress Cecilia, Lady Whitman is ready to go home."

Cecilia glanced from the stern-visaged Mordecai back to her handsome companion. She might want to jump up and down and pitch a tantrum out of sheer vexation at having to do as she was bid, but she'd act a lady in front of Colonel Sumner. She didn't want him to think her a child, though Mordecai was treating her as such. "Thank you for your concern, Colonel Sumner. I hope I have not been too much trouble."

Neal took her hand and once more brushed his lips against her soft skin. "It has been my pleasure, my lady. I hope we shall meet again soon."

"I'm sure we will," Cecilia said, feeling her heart soar out of her body and spiral toward the stars. She knew in that moment that she was in love. New emotions singing through her, Cecilia forgot why she'd run away from the Governor's Palace as Neal assisted her into the coach to join Mordecai and Elsbeth.

Dreamily she settled back against the velvet seat. She ignored the censure she saw on the faces of the two people sitting opposite her as she relived her meeting with the handsome British colonel. The day Cecilia had thought one of the worst in her life, had ended on a special note of wonder.

Elsbeth and Mordecai glanced at each other and silently agreed that for now nothing would be said about Cecilia's behavior this evening. She had come to no harm, and they saw no reason to add to the dissension between them. She was young and spoiled. She needed time to adjust to her brother's marriage and the changes that would take place within her own life because of it.

Nor did they see any reason to bring up what had transpired earlier. It was still too new for them to discuss with anyone. They wanted to savor it like a sweet and heady wine, gently sipping it to get its full flavor. They understood that the emotions that had come forth in the garden at the Governor's Palace would not go away if they didn't shout it to the entire world. It would be there to treasure each day . . . for the rest of their lives.

Chapter 11

*Half-awake, Devon stretched her hand out to reassure her-*self that Hunter was not a dream. Finding only empty space beside her, she searched the rumpled covers and pillows before finally opening her eyes to look for her husband.

Squinting against the bright glare of the morning sunlight streaming into the bedroom, she sat up and peered about for any sign of Hunter. Seeing only his dressing gown tossed carelessly over the back of a chair, Devon hid a lazy yawn behind a hand before throwing back the covers and sliding her bare feet to the floor. She crossed to the chair and picked up Hunter's robe. She rubbed the soft fabric against her cheek and inhaled the masculine scent that clung to Hunter's dressing gown. Her belly quivered with the memories its smell evoked. She could nearly feel Hunter's hands upon her body. His touch had the power to stir her passion so easily that she reacted like a wanton in Hunter's bed. Scolding herself for such thoughts so early in the morning, Devon slipped the robe over her nakedness and smiled at the irony of having to wear her husband's garment. She might now be the mistress of Barclay Grove, but she still didn't possess a robe of her own.

The smile still curved her shapely lips as she crossed to the dressing table and looked at her reflection in the mirror. With the sleeves of the robe hanging a foot below her fingertips, she looked more like a drooping bird than Hunter's wanton wife. Devon chuckled and rolled up the sleeves before settling herself on the padded stool in front of the table.

Her smile deepened as she considered her reflection in the oval mirror. She felt like a fat feline, content and happy after a warm, filling bowl of milk. Her contentment had come from being with her husband for the past two days. Holed away in the master suite, Hunter had allowed no one to intrude upon their time together. Their meals had been left outside the door and their baths had been prepared in the adjoining dressing room without even a rustle of cloth to disturb the two lovers.

Her appearance now, with her hair falling about her shoulders and down her back in a tousled, gleaming mass, her lips still swollen from their lovemaking earlier that morning, and her skin glowing from her happiness, were all the evidence anyone would need to know exactly what had been transpiring behind the locked door.

"I've a good excuse for looking the way I do," Devon murmured smugly to her reflection and smiled wickedly. No woman could look cool and aloof after spending two entire days and nights in bed with Hunter Barclay.

Since their wedding night, when Hunter had carried her upstairs to his master bedchamber, she had lived an erotic fantasy. He had loved every inch of her, allowing no area to go untouched or unkissed. They had released all the passion that had been pent up since their last encounter on the beach at Saint Eustatius.

Devon raised her chin proudly. She wasn't ashamed of the moments she'd spent with her husband. But the thought of what everyone else at Barclay Grove must be thinking of them unnerved her slightly. Hunter's dressing gown slipped off one bare shoulder as Devon shrugged. It didn't truly matter what anyone else thought. Hunter was the only person whose opinion counted, and at the present time he seemed very satisfied with her.

The sound of voices below broke into Devon's reflections. She crossed to the window and glimpsed her husband's dark head just before he entered the house. Eager to show Hunter that he'd have no regrets for marrying her, Devon hurried to get dressed. A short time later, wearing a light-sprigged muslin gown, her hair tied back with a yellow satin ribbon, she descended the stairs.

The soft murmur of masculine voices drew Devon down the hallway to the study. She paused upon the threshold to adjust her skirt and pat her hair. She didn't want a hair out of place at this momentous occasion: her first appearance as Lady Barclay and mistress of Barclay Grove. She wanted to make Hunter proud of her.

Confident that she didn't look like a frump, she lifted a hand to knock on the door and realized the portal already stood ajar. Devon moved to press the door open when Hunter's words made her hesitate. She leaned closer.

"Damn it, Mordecai. I honestly don't know how I'm going to get the maps. Last week I managed to get into the colonel's office, but they were nowhere to be found. The only other place that he might have them is at his home."

"Then that's where we'll have to look. Seth said General Washington needs those maps so he will know exactly where Cornwallis will strike next."

Fighting to stem his annoyance, Hunter ran his hand over his cleanly shaved jaw and glanced toward the ceiling. He couldn't stop himself from wondering if Devon had awakened yet. They had made love at dawn and she had drifted off to sleep soon after. Naked as the day she was born and as beautiful as the breaking day, she had slept on as he prepared himself for his meeting with Mordecai. He'd managed to ignore the outside world for two days, but he couldn't any longer. It had come to reclaim him with a vengeance.

God, how he wished he could put all of his responsibilities aside and lock himself away with Devon for two months instead of only two days. But events were conspiring to keep him away from his wife. His orders from Washington were exact. He had to get the British maps to give advance warning to the Continental troops about the route the British would take in the South.

Washington's forces needed every advantage they could get. Less than sixteen thousand strong, they couldn't match the British troops per man. Though they equaled or exceeded the loyalists in bravery and determination, those qualities did little good if the men who possessed them were outnumbered two to one. General Washington needed to know every move the British forces made, and it was Hunter's duty to see that he got that information.

Hunter looked at his friend as he leaned back against the heavy oak desk. He folded his arms over his wide chest and cocked his head to one side. His expression was grim as he asked, "Do you have any suggestions on exactly how I might manage such a feat. Colonel Braggert's house is like a fortress itself. He keeps guards posted at all times. Since the day he landed in Virginia he's not trusted anyone, claiming the colonies are populated with nothing but wild savages—be they red or white."

"He should be the one to talk about savages!" Mordecai ground out. "He's one of the men who set the Cherokees on the colonists—all the way from Virginia to Georgia—back in '76."

"I know, but that doesn't help us now. I need to find a way to search Braggert's study without drawing suspicion upon myself."

Mordecai tapped the wooden chair thoughtfully. "I don't have any answers. All I know is that Seth said General Washington is depending upon us."

"I can be of help," Devon said, pushing the door open on the two surprised men. She crossed the study to where Hunter stood glowering at her. Listening to Hunter and

Mordecai, she had seen her chance to become a part of Hunter's life. It hadn't been an easy decision after her earlier thoughts, but she'd set her trepidations aside. This might be her only opportunity to truly be Hunter's wife, an equal partner.

A black look marring his handsome face, Hunter growled, "Go back upstairs, Devon. This is none of your affair."

"You're wrong, Hunter. It *is* my affair if my husband is involved," Devon said firmly.

"Devon, please do as Hunter asks. This doesn't concern you," Mordecai said, coming to his feet.

Devon flashed Mordecai a bemused look. "You think I shouldn't be concerned when my husband is a spy for the patriots?" Devon smiled as surprise flickered across Mordecai's rugged features. "I've known since London that you and Hunter might act and talk like loyalists, but you were supporting the rebellion against the crown. I've said nothing, for it was none of my affair then. However that has all changed. If you have forgotten, I am now Hunter's wife and the mother of his child."

"And as such, you will do as I say. Now go back upstairs, Devon. I will speak with you in a short while."

Devon gave a mutinous shake of her head. "No, Hunter. I won't go back upstairs when I can be of help to you. Furthermore I am the only person who can get the papers you need without drawing suspicion."

"Exactly how do you propose to do that?" was Hunter's smug question.

"I plan to walk in and take them," Devon said, raising her chin haughtily in the air.

Both men burst out laughing at the simplicity of Devon's scheme. At last Hunter finally managed to speak. "Just like that?" He snapped his fingers. "You'll walk in and take them?"

Devon nodded. "And no one will ever be the wiser."

Hunter eyed Devon for a long, thoughtful moment and felt the hair rise at the nape of his neck. "Exactly what kind of scheme do you have brewing in that beautiful head? I won't allow you to go crawling through windows again. You are pregnant, and I'll not risk your life or our child's for all the maps in the world."

A warm feeling spread over Devon at Hunter's concern for her safety. She smiled at him. "I won't have to climb through any windows. As I said, I'll walk in and take the papers by invitation."

Hunter glanced at Mordecai, his face alight with wonder. "Damn me! Why didn't I think of that? No one would ever suspect one of Colonel Braggert's guests—because everyone knows he only invites those whom he's sure are loyal to England."

"You're right, Hunter," Mordecai said. A deep, satisfied chuckle rumbled from his massive chest. "And you received an invitation to meet one of the newly arrived officers just yesterday. Colonel Braggert is giving a dinner in his honor next week."

Hunter nodded confidently. "Then, of course, I will accept. I would hate to disappoint my dear friend, Colonel Braggert."

"Not *I*, but *we* will accept, Hunter," Devon interjected.

Hunter shook his head. "No, Devon. I forbid it. It's too dangerous."

Devon glanced from one stern countenance to the other, but didn't back down. She steadfastly held her ground. She was determined to be involved in Hunter's life one way or the other. She might not possess his love, but she could gain his respect.

"It will be far less dangerous for me than you. Should anyone notice my absence, no one will think anything of it once they learn of my condition. They'll merely believe I escaped for a moment of rest or a breath of air to calm my queasy stomach."

"What you say may be true, but I still won't risk it. You carry my heir, Devon, and I'll not jeopardize his life."

"And neither will I, whether it's now or in the future. I want to work with you, Hunter, so our child can have the freedom to be its own man or woman. I think that is something we both want."

"She has a point, Hunter," Mordecai said, his tone reflecting his approval.

"And damn it, so do I! Devon could be harmed," Hunter exploded. He ran his fingers through his hair in exasperation and turned back to the side table that held the brandy decanter. The glass clinked against the rim as he poured himself a dram. He downed it in a gulp and then turned to look at his wife, standing proud and determined. Hunter ground his teeth together. Be damned to freedom and everything else if it meant he might lose Devon and his child.

Something inside him trembled at the thought. He couldn't say he loved his wife, but since the moment she'd crossed his path in London, they'd had a penchant for stumbling over each other—and now they were bound as man and wife. Generations of future Barclays would carry their blood. It was a staggering thought. One that made him even more determined to not let Devon have her way.

"Hunter, I won't come to any harm. If you will recall, I have experience in such matters."

"I haven't forgotten one thing about you, Devon. I remember how we met, and that a short time later I had to save your pretty neck from being stretched on the gibbet at Tyburn. I don't want that to happen again here."

Devon closed the space separating them. She laid a hand upon his arm and her eyes pleaded for his understanding. "That is one of the reasons you must allow me to help you. I owe you my life, Hunter, and I would see the debt paid."

Immersed in the intriguing depths of her forest green eyes, Hunter forgot that they were not alone. He raised a hand and cupped Devon's cheek. His words came softly. "The debt is paid, Devon. You give my child life in return for the one I saved."

"I thank you for your generosity, but I also have another reason for what I do, Hunter. I have an account to settle with England and her laws. Because of them I could not even go to my grandmother's funeral. Because of the rules set by English society, I was forced to either make a good marriage or steal to survive. I had no choice but to leave the only people I loved behind. I'll never see Higgins and Winkler again. I never want to see anyone forced to make the same mistakes that I made just to survive. Please, don't deny me my chance to help. I believe very strongly in what you do. It's my future as well as yours."

The intense light in Devon's eyes made Hunter hesitate. He glanced up to find Mordecai watching him closely. When their eyes met, his friend nodded. Understanding the silent message, Hunter surrendered. "All right. You win. We shall send our acceptance to Colonel Braggert this afternoon."

Giving way to impulse, Devon threw her arms about Hunter's neck. "Thank you. I promise you'll not regret allowing me to help."

"I pray you are right," Hunter said as he wrapped her in his arms.

Sensing that his presence was no longer needed, Mordecai quietly left the study. Smiling broadly at how well things seemed to be going between the newlyweds, he strode down the hallway and out of the house. He paused on the veranda and drew in a deep breath of the warm summer breeze. He was grateful that Hunter had seen fit to marry Devon. That decision had freed him to tell Elsbeth of his love, and she had stunned him by accepting it.

Mordecai's gaze wandered past the tall magnolias and

oaks, toward the road that led in the direction of Whitman Place, and his smile faded. It had been only two days since he'd last seen Elsbeth, but it seemed like a century. The warm, wonderful moments they'd shared in the garden at the Governor's Palace had kept his spirits buoyed during the past days, but the longer they were away from each other, the less sure he became of everything that had transpired between them.

Riding her brown mare, the object of his thoughts came into the clearing and galloped up the drive. Elsbeth smiled and waved when she saw Mordecai standing on the veranda. She reined her mount to a halt and agilely slid to the ground before he had time to assist her. A moment later, she threw herself into his arms and planted a kiss upon his slightly parted lips. He didn't manage to wrap her in his embrace before she stepped out of his reach and looked up at him saucily. "I've been dreaming of that ever since you left me at Whitman Place two nights ago."

Mordecai grinned and shook his head as if to collect his reeling wits. "May I be so presumptuous as to ask if this is the same Elsbeth Whitman from Whitman Place as the one I've known for the past years?"

Elsbeth, feeling more vibrantly alive than she'd ever felt in her twenty years of life, cocked her head to one side and gave him an impudent grin. "You can ask, but you may not like the answer."

Puzzled, Mordecai sobered. A wedge of doubt lodged in his belly. It took all of his courage to ask, "How so, my lady?"

"The Elsbeth Whitman that you knew no longer exists. It seems she died two nights ago in the garden at the Governor's Palace," Elsbeth said, trying to explain the new sense of freedom that had come over her when Hunter married Devon. It was as if a part of her life ended . . . and she had been reborn a woman unashamed to express her feelings to those she cared about. The sudden change of her destiny made her realize that life was too short to be wasted. She no longer feared ridicule or what people would think of her actions. She was free, as free as America would be when they forced the British Army back across the ocean. She would fight for liberty for the colonies and for herself alongside the man she loved.

Understanding flickered over Mordecai's face and he smiled. "I think I like the new Elsbeth far better. The one I knew before would never have dared kiss me. She was far too timid."

"Timid or stupid," Elsbeth said, her gentle laughter tinkling through the morning air.

Needing to feel Elsbeth in his arms again, Mordecai closed the space between them. He drew her against him. "I'm grateful for the new Elsbeth. I've suffered the agonies of hell thinking these past days that you might have changed your mind about us. I doubt Cecilia has made it easy for you. I suspect she's done everything in her power to blacken me in your eyes. Has the little vixen tried to tell you that I eat babies yet?"

Elsbeth shook her head as she braced her hands on Mordecai's shoulders and looked up into his pale eyes. "Poor Cecilia. I doubt she's even thought of us since she met that British colonel."

"Aye. She seemed taken with him," Mordecai said, and frowned.

Elsbeth placed a comforting hand against his craggy, weather-beaten cheek. "It'll be all right. You and Hunter have nothing to fear. She's young, and she knows nothing of how either of you feel about the war. She believes what she is told . . . and what she wants to believe."

"For once I'll have to say that's for the best. The girl needs a strong hand, but Hunter has a soft spot where she's concerned. And Cecilia has a violent temper. I tremble to think what might happen should she learn of our subterfuge. She could ruin everything during one of her tantrums and get us all hanged.''

"For now, I think we're safe. Cecilia has her first case of love and I'm afraid it's severe. If she's not sitting and dreaming of her colonel, she's burning my ears off with questions of every sort about men and marriage." Elsbeth smiled and shook her head again. "I fear she's asking the wrong person there. I only know what I've been told myself."

Mordecai chuckled, pleased at her answer. When they married, he would be her first and, hopefully, if God allowed them a long life together, her last lover. "I would have thought that by now she would be throwing tantrums to come home. Knowing her feelings for Devon, I thought she'd want to be here to stir up trouble for the newlyweds."

Elsbeth glanced toward the house. "How are things going?"

"Everything's going so well that a few minutes ago I thought it very prudent of me to get out of the study as fast as possible . . . if I didn't want to be embarrassed."

Elsbeth's eyes rounded and her cheeks grew pink. "You don't mean—"

Mordecai nodded.

"Surely not in the study. And it's daytime."

Mordecai gave her a wicked grin and winked broadly. "As you'll learn in the near future, there's a time and place for everything. And when you're in love, it's *any*time and *any*place." He chuckled as Elsbeth's blush deepened and she buried her face against his shoulder.

Cecilia reined her mount to a halt at the edge of town. She absently worked at the button at the wrist of her glove and glanced nervously about, uncertain of her decision to come to Williamsburg without a chaperon or at least a groom to escort her. She knew it was improper, but at Whitman Place she'd rationalized her situation on the grounds of Elsbeth's absence. How could she ask permission with Elsbeth gone? She needed to pick up some new ribands at the milliner's shop and also go by the shoemaker's to order a new pair of slippers. Her visit to town was a necessity. She couldn't be expected to do without because her brother wouldn't leave Barclay Grove and his new wife, or because Elsbeth was off riding with Mordecai.

Cecilia raised her chin in the air and adjusted the ribbons of her riding hat. She was a woman of sixteen and not a child. She'd made the right decision. And in doing so, if she happened, by chance, to see the handsome Colonel Sumner, no one could reproach her if she spoke. He had come to meet with Hunter, and she was only being polite. A brisk nod to reestablish her previous rationale, Cecilia urged her mount into a gentle canter down the cobbled street.

Later, Cecilia peered through the shoemaker's window and felt her pulse jump at the sight of Neal Sumner striding across the street in the direction of the shop. She raised a hand to her throat and prayed that her heart would quit drumming in her ears long enough for her to hear should he speak.

Drawing in a deep breath to steady her quivering belly, she pretended to study a pair of boots on display. She didn't want the colonel to know that she'd seen him enter the shop across the street a few minutes after her arrival, or that she'd dawdled for nearly an hour waiting for him to leave the apothecary so she could just bump into him again.

Cecilia tensed and focused her entire attention on the boots when the bell over the door tinkled and Neal entered. She thought she could smell his scent before he crossed the few feet separating them. Her heart quickened and she held her breath as a floorboard squeaked behind her.

"My lady," was Neal's polite greeting as Cecilia turned to face him.

"Colonel Sumner. I hadn't thought to see you again so soon," Cecilia said, extending her hand to Neal. She didn't want to give the handsome colonel the wrong impression.

Neal smiled. He wasn't fooled by the girl's obvious inexperience. That made the game more appealing to Neal. She was the niece of one of England's wealthiest lords, and he had reached a time in his life when, no matter how he felt about it, he was going to have to settle down on his estates. It wouldn't hurt to have a young little wife with wealthy relatives in England and America. Neal's smile deepened. Nor would it hurt to have a girl innocent to sex. He could train her to please him. She could learn all the different little vices that made having sex an art form. Neal gave himself a mental shake. The middle of a bootmaker's shop was no place to have sexual fantasies.

"And I feared I might not see you. Since our meeting I've thought of little else."

Cecilia's cheeks tinted a deep becoming rose. "How kind of you to say that, but I know you're a busy man. I'm sure the king's business has kept you at matters of importance since your arrival." Cecilia breathed a sigh of relief. She had managed to gracefully accept his statement without letting out the foolish giggle that was tickling her throat.

"It's true. I have been busy, but I still have had time to think of you. Would you join me for a cup of tea?"

Cecilia quickly shook her head. She'd already overstepped propriety's boundaries this afternoon and couldn't risk Hunter learning of her having tea without a chaperon. Gossips would have the news back to Barclay Grove before nightfall. "Thank you for the invitation, but I must decline. I fear I'm already late. Elsbeth will be furious should she learn I've come to Williamsburg."

A stricken look flickered over Cecilia's face and she felt

she'd drop through the floor. She'd gone to all the trouble to convince Colonel Sumner that she was a mature woman and then she'd allowed her wayward tongue to reveal her mischief. She wanted to groan aloud but oppressed the urge. That would only prove her even more childish.

Neal smiled to himself at her slip of the tongue and gallantly pretended he'd not heard. "I'm sorry that you can't join me. Perhaps you would allow me to call upon you some afternoon when you're free."

"I would love that," Cecilia said in a rush, once more forgetting her dignified manner in her excitement. "I'm staying at Whitman Place. Please feel free to come out any afternoon."

"I would be honored, my lady. Now I will bid you good day," Neal said, and brushed his lips against Cecilia's hand. He didn't look back as he made his way across the street to where his mount was tethered.

Cecilia managed to suppress her glee until Neal rode out of sight. Then she let out a squeal of pure delight, drawing strange looks from the shoemaker's patrons as she danced out of the shop and mounted her own horse. Though physically sitting in the side saddle on her bay mare, she floated back to Whitman Place on dreams of her future with the man she loved, the daringly handsome Neal Sumner.

"Where have you been, young lady?" Hunter stormed as Cecilia entered the drawing room. "We have been searching Whitman Place and Barclay Grove for you."

Hunter's foul temper bringing her back to reality, Cecilia eyed her brother mutinously. "I didn't think you would have time to search for me, dear brother. I would think you'd be with your wife!"

"That's enough, Cecilia. I am not here to talk about my marriage, but about your unchaperoned absence from

Whitman Place when Elsbeth was away. Where were you?''

"I decided to ride into Williamsburg. I needed a few things and you've been too tied up with that . . . woman . . . to act as my chaperon so I decided to go alone."

"Don't you have a brain in that head of yours? It's too dangerous for a young woman to be out riding by herself at this time. If you haven't noticed, there is a war going on."

"Elsbeth rides alone and I see no reason why I can't do the same. I'm a grown woman and I'm old enough to take care of myself. As for the minor rebellion we've been hearing about, I seriously doubt there's any danger in this area. The British forces are nearby and those rogues are too cowardly to stay and fight like gentlemen," Cecilia said.

"You're all of sixteen years old," Hunter growled. "And far from grown. You haven't even had your coming-out ball."

Cecilia sashayed across the room and regally seated herself. She absently smoothed the fabric of her riding habit as she said, "I've been rethinking my coming-out ball. As you've said, the colonies are at war and I feel I'm too old to have a coming-out ball. I really see no need for it."

Hunter's dark look turned black and he glowered at his sister. "I thought you wanted to show everyone how many eligible young men you could wrap around your finger?"

Cecilia shrugged. "That's childish. I'm too old for such nonsense."

A flicker of understanding passed over Hunter's frowning countenance. "Who is he, Cecilia?"

Cecilia centered her attention on a streak of dirt that had soiled the dark fabric of her skirt. She moistened her lips and fought to keep from revealing her rioting emotions to her brother. "I don't know what you mean."

"There must be a man involved in your decision or you'd

not give up a chance to be the belle of a ball. You enjoy attention too much.''

Cecilia didn't look at her brother as she shook her head. ''There's no man involved in my decision. I'm just growing up . . . and away from childish games.''

''For your sake, you'd better not be telling me a lie, little sister. You're only sixteen years old, and any man who thinks to play with your affections will answer to me. And, I had better not hear of you seeing anyone behind my back. Is that understood?''

Cecilia flashed Hunter a lethal glance before she nodded.

''Good. Now collect your things. You're coming back to Barclay Grove with me, where I can keep an eye on you.''

Cecilia came to her feet. ''I don't want to go back and live in the same house with that woman! I hate her—and I hate you for marrying her!'' Cecilia stamped her foot in vexation. She didn't want to leave Whitman Place after Neal said he'd visit her.

''I'm sorry you feel that way. Devon is my wife now and you must accept her. She will bear my child and you will give her your respect if not your friendship. I demand that of you . . . or I'll tan your bottom so you'll not be able to sit down for a week. Is that understood?''

Cecilia's nostrils flared as she drew in an angry breath. ''I'll do as you say because I don't have any other choice. But you'll never make me like her—even if you beat me to death.'' Cecilia spun on her heels and fled up the stairs.

''You were too hard on her, Hunter,'' Elsbeth said from the doorway.

''The problem is that I've been too lenient on her in the past,'' Hunter said, and ran his long fingers through his thick, dark hair.

''She loves you, and she feels Devon has taken you away from her.''

"I understand that, but I can't allow her to treat Devon badly out of spite. Devon is my wife. She's my first obligation."

"But try to understand Cecilia, too. She's at an age when she feels and looks like a grown woman, but she's still child enough to remind you of her years."

"I'll do my best, Elsbeth. I love that little devil, no matter how angry she makes me."

"I know you do, Hunter. Hopefully time will make everything right between the two of you."

Hunter nodded and looked toward the stairs. Cecilia had always been a handful—and that was *before* she wanted to spite him for marrying a woman she hated. He couldn't stop himself from wondering what she'd do next. He prayed it wasn't what he suspected. If she had set her sights on a young man, he didn't know exactly how he'd handle the situation. He knew what young single men were like. He'd been one himself less than a week ago. And because of his knowledge of his own sex, he hated the thought of what could happen to his sister if she wasn't cautious.

Chapter 12

Cecilia watched Hunter ride down the drive and turn in the direction of Williamsburg. She had been awaiting this moment since the day he'd forced her to come back to Barclay Grove. Cecilia glanced at the porcelain clock sitting on the mantle. It was now twenty until two. She had less than twenty minutes to reach the landing on the James River.

Cecilia crossed to the dressing table and eyed her reflection. She adjusted her riding hat to a jaunty angle, patted a stray strand of hair into place, and pinched her cheeks to make them rosy. She smiled, satisfied with her appearance as well as her own cleverness in outwitting her brother. Hunter might think he could control her every move, but he was mistaken. Her subtle laughter filled the bedchamber as Cecilia lifted the soft gloves from the table and slipped them on. She picked up her riding crop and headed for the door. There was no time to waste if she wanted to meet Neal.

Cecilia's smile deepened at her own ingenuity. She'd managed to outsmart her brother even before she'd left Whitman Place. When she'd fled upstairs she had only one thought in mind: contacting Neal Sumner. As the maid packed her bags for her return to Barclay Grove she'd hurriedly scribbled a note to Neal. She'd sent it by one of Elsbeth's servants. She'd explained as briefly as possible that she'd returned to Barclay Grove and, since her brother was often overprotective toward her, Cecilia felt it would be best for Neal not to call upon her at the house until after his business with Hunter was concluded.

She hadn't lied when she'd written that Hunter was often overprotective toward her, but she'd used the excuse of not wanting to cause dissension between the two men and hoped Neal would understand her position. However, she had added, should Neal happen to be in the area of the Barclay landing on the James River at two today, she would also be there.

Cecilia didn't know what Neal had thought when he'd received her message, but she prayed he'd be at the landing. She desperately needed to see him and try to make him understand that she might be a grown woman, but her brother still treated her like a child. And until the time when Hunter accepted the fact of her womanhood, they would have to see each other secretly.

Cecilia's eyes glittered with annoyance as she sped down the stairs and out of the house. She knew she was behaving like a brazen hussy, but she had no other choice. Hunter had forced this situation upon her and she'd do whatever she must to see Neal. She didn't want to have to go behind her brother's back, but Hunter had left her no alternative. He hadn't listened to her when he married that woman, and she saw no reason now why she should listen to him!

The ride to the landing seemed to take forever, though it was less than fifteen minutes away from the manor house. Cecilia drew her mount to a halt at the clearing near the pier. A gentle breeze from the river rustled the tall marsh grass that grew alongside the cattails at the river's edge. The afternoon sun mottled the slow, dark green water with bright spots of golden light. It flashed and shimmered blindingly across the wide expanse as the James's current gurgled a low greeting against the pier's barnacled pillars.

Having seen the landing all of her life, Cecilia paid no heed to the beauty of her surroundings. She was interested in seeing only one thing: Neal Sumner. Her spirits plummeted as she scanned the clearing and pier and found no sign of him. He hadn't come.

Cecilia drew in a shaky breath and her shoulders sagged as she reached for the reins. There was no reason to remain any longer without Neal.

Before she turned her horse, Cecilia glimpsed the uniformed figure. She felt the blood sing through her veins as Neal came striding up the riverbank with tricorne hat in hand and a beautiful smile spreading his well-shaped lips. He waved to her as Cecilia urged her horse forward. A moment later she found herself slipping eagerly into Neal's arms as he assisted her down.

"I thought you hadn't come," Cecilia breathed, making no attempt to step out of Neal's embrace.

Neal smiled knowingly. The young chit was eager for him to bed her. "Nothing could have stopped me from coming once I learned you'd be here this afternoon. It seems like an eternity since I last saw you."

Cecilia's belly quivered with excitement as she looked up into his handsome face. So close now that she could nearly feel his breath against her skin, she found herself wanting to sink into the dark, warm pools of his eyes. Reluctantly her gaze moved down his straight nose to his mouth and she moistened her own lips—that had gone suddenly dry with expectation. She swallowed uneasily as her eyes once more met Neal's. She didn't resist as he lowered his head and his mouth claimed hers.

Cecilia's world reeled out of kilter. Her knees turned to jelly beneath her and she had to cling to Neal's wide shoulders for support as she tentatively allowed her lips to part beneath the pressure of his. She moaned her pleasure as his tongue boldly entered her mouth and caressed hers.

Instinctively she molded her young body against his hard, masculine form.

It was Neal who broke the kiss and stepped away from Cecilia—to give himself a moment to regain control over his wayward body. He hadn't meant to respond to Cecilia, but he hadn't had a woman since the whore on the docks before he left England.

Neal ran a hand through his hair and drew in a deep breath. He couldn't just toss up this girl's skirts and have his way, no matter how eager she was for it. She was Lord Barclay's niece, and he couldn't risk ruining her before there was a betrothal. Neal's cheeks puffed as he blew out a long breath and glanced at Cecilia. God! It would be so easy. Too damned easy!

Neal held out his good hand to Cecilia and she took it shyly. She didn't know what to think of her own reaction to her first kiss. Her cheeks flushed with embarrassment. What must Neal think of her? First, she brazenly invited him to a secret meeting—and then she responded like a trollop the moment he touched her! Afraid of what she would see in Neal's eyes if she looked at him, Cecilia lowered her gaze to the ground as she allowed Neal to draw her close. She swallowed uneasily, uncertain of what to say or do.

"Forgive me, Cecilia. I should not have kissed you. My behavior is inexcusable," Neal said softly, feigning a remorse he didn't feel.

Cecilia jerked her head up and stared at Neal in surprise. She had misbehaved, yet *he* was apologizing. "I am the one at fault. Had I not acted like a hussy, you would not have responded in such a manner. I should never have sent you the message telling you I'd be here this afternoon. It was forward of me, and I can't blame you for your actions."

"Sweet Cecilia, I can't allow you to feel any guilt for what has transpired between us. I've wanted to kiss you

since the first moment I set eyes on you outside the King's
Arms Tavern. But I am a gentleman, and I should have
remembered that you are a lady. To my great shame, in
my need to taste your sweet lips I took advantage of you.''
Neal gave Cecilia a look filled with remorse. ''I pray you'll
forgive me.''

Neal's apology bolstered Cecilia's flagging confidence.
She seemed to bloom as her assurance returned. She raised
her chin and squared her shoulders. She smiled, feeling
once more in control of the situation. ''I think, sir, we
both are at fault. Now, shall we forget what has taken
place and begin again?''

Neal nodded and his shapely lips curled charmingly up
at the corners as he proferred his arm. ''Very well, my
lady. Will you walk with me?''

Cecilia placed her hand on Neal's sleeve. ''I'd be de-
lighted, Colonel Sumner.''

Neal halted in his tracks and cocked a sandy brow.
''Perhaps we can allow ourselves to bend the rules slightly
by calling each other by our given names. Would that be
too improper, my lady?''

''Cecilia, Neal.''

Neal chuckled and placed his good hand over Cecilia's
as they strolled toward the pier. Things were going well
for him and, after tomorrow night, he'd be free to openly
court this wealthy young beauty. He'd meet with her
brother at Colonel Braggert's and deliver his orders. Once
that was done there would be nothing standing in his way
of securing Cecilia's hand in marriage.

Neal smiled to himself. He hadn't thought that anything
good could come out of being a glorified messenger boy,
but now it seemed that he had been wrong. Should he
succeed in marrying Cecilia Barclay he'd return to England as an associate of Lord Barclay's, Earl of Trent.
Wealthy in his own right, Neal didn't need Cecilia's dowry.
However her relatives would prove a great benefit to his

future in the House of Lords. They had the prestige of centuries—and the influence that came with it.

Neal patted the gloved hand on his arm, satisfied with the decision he'd made for his future. His army career was nearly at an end, and his marrying Cecilia would give him the only thing he lacked, power.

Face flushed and hair flowing in a wild disarray down her back after her gallop home, Cecilia sped up the stairs, hoping that no one had noted her absence. She ran down the hall and quickly shut herself into her room. Breathing heavily she let out a throaty, triumphant chuckle as she leaned back against the door to get her breath. She had succeeded.

Tossing her gloves and riding crop on the bed, she turned to the dressing table to remove her hat. She froze at the reflection that stared back at her. Slowly she turned to face her new sister-in-law. "What the devil are you doing in my room? You have no right to be here. Just like you have no right to be at Barclay Grove."

Devon stood. After watching Cecilia ride out, she'd waited anxiously downstairs until the servants had begun to note her pacing. She'd decided it would be more prudent to await Cecilia's return in her bedchamber. She knew it wouldn't be easy to talk with the girl. Her sister-in-law had made her feelings about Devon very clear, yet Devon couldn't stand by and watch Hunter's relationship with his sister disintegrate because of her. They would never be a family if the dissension continued to pry them apart.

"I came to speak with you," Devon said, ignoring Cecilia's barbed remark. "I thought if we talked things over, we might come to an understanding so you and Hunter wouldn't be at odds. I don't want your relationship with your brother destroyed because he married me."

"You certainly think a lot of yourself if you think our quarrel was over you," Cecilia snarled. She untied the

ribbons about her throat and tossed her riding hat on the
bed alongside her gloves and crop. She shook her hair free
and ran her fingers through the dark, tangled mass.

"I know you didn't want your brother to marry me, and
I don't ask that you like me. I only ask that we live amicably here under the same roof. I will bear your brother's
child, and I would have him live in a happy home."

"As long as you're here, Barclay Grove can never be a
happy place. You ruined everything when you came here.
Elsbeth is the woman my brother loves, yet, slut that you
are, you got yourself with child. When my brother bought
your indenture papers, you knew he was a decent man who
would be too honorable to allow a child of his to be born
a bastard. You used him to become a lady. But no matter
who calls you Lady Barclay, I'll never let you forget that
you came from the gutters of London."

"You're right, Cecilia. Hunter is a good man, but I
didn't force him to marry me. I know how he feels about
Elsbeth, and I never wanted to come between them. Hunter
forced me to marry him when he learned of my babe."

Cecilia gave an indignant toss of her head and snipped,
"You surely don't expect me to believe such a story? I
may be young, but I'm not stupid. A woman in your position would do anything to better herself." Cecilia raked
Devon with an accusing look. "I doubt the child even
belongs to Hunter. I've heard women like you sell themselves to the highest bidder."

Devon clinched her hands at her side. Her palm itched
to slap Cecilia's angry face but she restrained herself with
great difficulty. She had come here to try to make peace
with Hunter's sister; not to give her a good trouncing as
retribution for the insult.

Devon forced her voice to remain even. "Hunter is the
father of my child. Should you have further doubts, I would
suggest you take your suspicions to him. I'm sure he will
explain things to you."

"Hunter's a fool to believe a word you say. You may have bewitched him for now, but after the babe is born, he'll know what you really are and he'll toss you out on your ear. Then Elsbeth will be the lady of Barclay Grove. That's where she should be now. Were it not for your scheming, she'd never have looked at that bilge rat."

Confused by Cecilia's train of thought, Devon tried to return to the subject at hand. "Cecilia, I came here to try to make peace between you and Hunter. Your brother loves you deeply."

Cecilia's lower lip began a nearly imperceptible tremble and her eyes brimmed with moisture. She blinked rapidly to stay the wayward tears. She didn't want this woman to think she was weak, but she missed Hunter. He had been mother and father—as well as brother—to her for as long as she could remember. She didn't like the feeling of abandonment created by his absence in her life. She had found a new love, but she still needed the comfort of the old.

Cecilia slumped down in the window seat and turned her back on Devon. She brushed at her eyes with the back of her hand. "Just go away and leave me alone. My relationship with my brother is none of your affair. Brothers and sisters often fight, but they understand each other because they are family. You're nothing here but an outsider. We all could be happy if you weren't here."

Cecilia's words burned painfully through Devon. Her face flushed a dull red and her eyes felt as if they would bulge from her head from the pressure of her own emotions. Cecilia was right. She and Hunter were a family into which Devon had only been admitted because she carried Hunter's heir. Elsbeth Whitman held his heart.

Devon swallowed at the lump that fixed itself achingly in her throat. She knew if she were a good and kind person she would try to offer comfort to the younger woman. But at that moment her own suffering made it impossible for her to be that generous. Like Cecilia, she hurt. But unlike her sister-in-law, Devon would never have Hunter's love.

Devon turned toward the door. She paused with her hand upon the latch and looked back at the girl who sat staring forlornly out of the window. Her voice was hoarse with emotion as she whispered, "Think about what I've said, Cecilia. No matter what you think, Hunter loves you."

Needing time to recoup her battered defenses before having to face Hunter at dinner, Devon made her way downstairs and out of the house. She sped toward the haven of the forest, beyond the lawns manicured so neatly by the slaves' sickles and shears.

The cooling shade of the trees soothed her heated skin as she made her way along the narrow path to the glade sheltered by tall live oaks draped in mists of gray-green moss. Through the leafy carpet of the glade floor, ferns unfurled their feathery leaves and reached toward the sky that could be seen through the canopy of thick, shiny leaves overhead.

Devon breathed deeply, savoring the cool, quiet glade. She'd found this spot only a few days ago when she'd needed to escape the tension-filled atmosphere created by Hunter and his sister every time they encountered each other. She had fled the manor house with the hope that her absence would give them time to settle the dissension that her presence at Barclay Grove had created.

The stillness of the surrounding woods, the shadows that kept out the heat of the day, and the gentle gurgle of the small stream that flowed nearby, reminded Devon of the cubbyhole in the stable at Mackinsey Hall. Like the dark, warm nook where she'd hidden as a child, this place was a balm to her battered spirits. Here she could think; here she could allow her emotions free rein without fearing the world would see her weakness.

Devon settled herself down on a tufted patch of grass beneath a large oak. The rough bark of the bole bit into her skin as she leaned back and raised her face to the sky. She closed her eyes and tried to force Cecilia's hurtful words from her mind. Unconsciously she lay a protective hand against her rounding middle. How she wished she could wave a magic wand to make everything right. But there were no fairy godmothers like those in Samber's *Mother Goose Tales* that she'd read for entertainment while at Mistress Cameron's Academy. Cecilia was right. She didn't belong at Barclay Grove. She was an outsider, and the only reason she was there as Hunter's wife lay beneath her hand.

Until Cecilia's hateful reminder, Devon had thought she'd managed to accept her position at Barclay Grove. Hunter's acceptance of her offer to help him steal the maps from Colonel Braggert had made her feel a part of his life. But she wanted more from her relationship with her husband. Her feelings for Hunter hadn't changed. If anything, they had deepened since her marriage.

Unfortunately she also realized that his feelings toward her were the same. He had said nothing, but Devon knew he still loved Elsbeth and, were it not for the child Devon carried, he'd have no use for her.

Devon swallowed back the painful lump of tears that lodged in her throat. She wouldn't allow herself to cry. Tears were useless. They would not change Hunter's feelings, nor would they make him love her.

Devon drew in a shaky breath and sought to regroup her wayward emotions. She couldn't allow herself to dwell upon things that would never be. She had known from the beginning how Hunter felt and had made a pact with herself that she would be satisfied as long as she could have any small part of Hunter's life. She wasn't the first woman who had married a man who did not love her, nor would she be the last. The thought didn't ease her pain, but it helped reinforce her desire to be a good wife. She couldn't allow Cecilia's vicious reminders to destroy the fragile bond that had begun to form between herself and her husband.

Consumed with her own thoughts, Devon felt only a gentle breath of air brush her skin before firm lips descended against hers. Her eyes flew wide with shock and she instinctively sought to defend herself. Even as recognition set in, her hand crashed against the side of his head with a resounding smack.

Hunter jerked back, clasping a hand to his battered ear. Brows lowered ominously, he eyed his wife as if she'd suddenly gone mad. "What the hell! Can't I even steal a kiss without you trying to crush my skull?"

Eyes wide with shock, Devon looked up at her husband and stuttered, "I—I—I mean—you frightened me. I thought I was alone." A tiny smile tugged at the corners of her lips as she watched Hunter rub the side of his still smarting head. "That should teach you not to sneak up on a person."

A wry grin touched Hunter's shapely mouth. "At least I know not to worry about you when you're alone. With a swing like that, you can take care of yourself."

"Hunter, I'm sorry," Devon said, coming to her knees in front of her husband. She suppressed another urge to laugh as Hunter winced when she placed a comforting hand against his aching head. "I didn't mean to hurt you," she continued softly, caressing his thick, dark hair. "I reacted before I had time to think."

His headache was soon forgotten as Hunter reached for his wife. He drew her unresisting body against him and he captured her soft lips with his own. No matter how many times he made love to Devon, Hunter couldn't get enough of her. It took only a glance from her provocative green eyes to set his blood aflame with desire.

Hunter plunged his tongue into her warm, sweet mouth and forgot everything else. Nothing existed in that moment except the fiery current searing him to the depths of his soul. He feasted upon her luscious lips as his experienced fingers worked loose the laces at the back of her gown and then slipped the bodice down. He lay her back upon the thick bed of green grass. For a long moment Hunter made no move to cover her. Awed, he looked down at the beauty displayed before him, savoring it like a fine piece of art before gently placing a hand against the sunlight-dappled peaks of her swollen breasts. His breath caught in his throat as he felt the sensitive coral buds harden with expectation to his touch.

Beckoned like a bee to a flower, he could deny himself no longer. He lowered his head to the tempting mounds that would one day give nourishment to the child growing within her swelling belly.

A thrill rushed over Hunter at the thought. Sensations that he couldn't explain raised every hair on his body and made him tremble. The God of man and the devil of mankind confronted each other as his spiritual and erotic sides clashed and then joined—to become fire and ice rushing through his veins in an explosion of feeling that went off in his brain like a cannonball. It shook Hunter physically from head to toe.

He raised his head to look down at the woman who carried his child within her. He smiled. "In the near future, I fear my son may grow jealous of my attention to his mother."

Devon shook her head and gave Hunter a wicked grin as she raised her arms to him. "He will just have to get used to it."

Hunter arched a dark brow as a frown of concern etched a path across his smooth forehead. He had made love to Devon since the day of their marriage, but now looking down at her rounding belly, he felt a chill of fear overshadow his desire. "Perhaps it would be best if I left you now. I might hurt you or the child."

Devon let her arms fall and pushed herself upright. She

pulled her bodice up to cover her nakedness as she looked at Hunter. In the blue depths of his eyes she saw his fear and knew she had to reassure him. "Hunter, I've never been pregnant before, but I don't think you will hurt me or the babe with your lovemaking. Women have been having babies since the beginning of time . . . and I seriously doubt they denied their husbands' attentions for the full term."

"I would take no chance with my babe's life just to ease my own desires," Hunter said, his voice firm with resolve, though his expression showed the strain of his decision.

"It would seem we've had this argument before, Hunter. And you seem to keep forgetting that the child I carry is also mine—and I wouldn't do anything that might jeopardize his life. I know you're concerned for our babe, but you are going to extremes. I am strong and healthy, so there is no need for this constant worry. Having a baby is natural," Devon said, feeling a twinge of jealousy over Hunter's concern for their child. She knew it was irrational to have such a feeling toward her own flesh and blood, but she couldn't stop herself. For once in her life she wished someone wanted her for herself alone.

Hunter raised a hand to caress Devon's cheek. His heart and body desperately wanted to believe what his wife said, but he had to be certain. "Perhaps you're right, but I've asked Dr. Langley to come out tomorrow to examine you. I want him to make sure everything is normal. You've looked pale for the past few days."

Though she yearned to act like a kitten and nuzzle his hand for a caress, Devon brushed his fingers away. "It's just the heat. England's summers don't get this hot; I fear I have as yet to adjust to Virginia's climate."

Hunter stood and proferred his hand to assist Devon to her feet. "My lady, I suspect my heir has a bit to do with the way you feel. Dr. Langley said I should not allow you to overexert yourself in this weather. It puts too much strain on the heart.'' Hunter grinned down at his wife before he dropped a light peck of a kiss upon the tip of her nose and turned her to do up her laces.

"Don't you think you should have asked me before you invited the doctor to Barclay Grove?" Devon said, her gray mood returning in force.

"I see no reason why. You carry my child, and I have the right to try to ensure that nothing untoward happens.''

Cecilia's painful reminder of where she stood in Hunter's life echoed in her mind. Devon's temper snapped. "I would think you could have at least had the courtesy to think of my feelings on the matter. It is my body as well as my child. But since you view me as only the vessel that gives life to your heir and satisfaction for your lust, I can understand your lack of concern for what I might think of Dr. Langley's visit.''

Hunter's brows knit over the bridge of his narrow nose as he frowned. He didn't know what he'd done to make Devon angry. Since learning he was to be a father, Hunter had found himself listening intently to the many stories of women who had died in childbirth, or succumbed to childbed fever, or whose child was stillborn. He wanted to take no chances with Devon's life.

"You are my wife, Devon. And should I feel you need a doctor, I will have him called.''

Devon's eyes flashed with fire. "Of late I had forgotten your Barclay arrogance, Hunter, but I won't again. And you and your doctor can go to blazes!''

"Devon, I insist you see Dr. Langley when he arrives. I won't allow your shrewish behavior to jeopardize our child's life,'' Hunter said, his own anger surfacing. He didn't know what had suddenly brought them to butt heads again, especially after the past week they'd spent together. However, at the moment he didn't truly care. In this decision Devon would obey him. It was in her best interests.

Devon turned and marched toward the bright sunlight

at the end of the trail. She felt Hunter's presence behind her, but never looked back. At this point in her life, she couldn't trust her own emotions where her husband was concerned. She'd give her soul to be able to turn round and throw herself into Hunter's arms, hear him reassure her that he loved only her and that their child was proof of the love that existed between them. But that was not to be. Her encounter with Cecilia had made that even more startlingly clear. Hunter still loved Elsbeth.

Devon entered the house and crossed the foyer to the stairs. She laid a hand upon the mahogany bannister to take the first step when Hunter's soft words stopped her. "Devon, I intended no insult."

Devon glanced over her shoulder at the man she loved and her heart melted at the bewildered look upon his handsome face. No matter how hard she tried, she couldn't stay angry with Hunter. She loved him too much. "I understand your feelings. I know you're concerned for the welfare of our child and I shouldn't have flown into such a snit. Blame it on the heat—or just my irascible temperament."

Hunter gave Devon a lopsided, boyish grin that could have charmed the devil himself. "We both have a tendency toward that extreme, my lady. And I pray my son doesn't inherit that trait from either of us, or I fear we'll have our hands full the first time he gets angry."

Devon couldn't resist his smile and returned the gesture warmly. "Perhaps our babe will be a she, sir. You keep saying your son, but you have an equal chance of having a daughter, my lord."

Hunter took a step closer and covered Devon's hand with his own. He looked into her forest green eyes and his voice grew husky with emotion. "It doesn't matter. If she has your eyes and hair, she will be as beautiful as her mother and I will be satisfied."

The breath stilled on Devon's lips as she looked into

Hunter's intense eyes. Her heart lodged in her throat at the heated emotion she saw in the blue depths. She desperately wanted to believe what she saw there was love, yet her mind, not her heart, ruled her head. Logic told her she was only imagining what she wanted to see. Hunter's concern was for his child and nothing more.

Devon withdrew her hand. Her tone was congenial, but it raised a barrier between them as surely as a bricked wall. "You might live to regret those words if our babe does inherit our tempers."

Wanting to drag Devon into his arms and kiss her into silence, but sensing her withdrawal, Hunter shook his head and glanced toward the second floor. "I doubt it. You must remember I already have experience in rearing a tempest. I have one upstairs right now."

Devon sobered as her gaze also traveled toward Cecilia's bedchamber door. "I haven't forgotten. Now if you will excuse me, I think I will go up and rest for a while."

The thick veins standing taut beneath the bronzed skin of the hand he rested upon the bannister, Hunter watched Devon ascend the stairs. His thick lashes narrowed as he wondered what had suddenly made her put the distance between them. He understood her anger and her passion, but he couldn't fathom her darker moments. They seemed to come so unexpectedly.

Hunter ran his fingers through his dark hair and turned toward his study. He doubted he'd ever understand either of the two women in his household. To be honest, the only woman he'd ever understood was Elsbeth: kind, uncomplicated Elsbeth. She was the same as the day he'd met her. There were no wild emotions brewing within her sweet soul. She'd never break the rules like Devon or Cecilia. She was a lady through and through. And though he loved her, Hunter was honest enough with himself to admit that Elsbeth would never make a man's blood run hot and fast like the two women of his household.

Hunter settled himself behind his desk and reached for the quill. He had to put the women in his life out of his mind and get down to business. If everything went as planned, tomorrow night he would have the maps to send to General Washington.

Chapter 13

Dr. Langley gently pressed down on the small mound of Devon's belly. Deep furrows etched a path across his forehead as he frowned and drew his lips into a thin line of concentration. Again he felt her belly and then drew in a deep breath before he stood back and looked down at Devon through a pair of square-rimmed spectacles that perched precariously on the tip of his nose.

"What is it, Dr. Langley?" Devon asked, her voice little more than an anxious whisper. The doctor's intense expression unnerved her.

Dr. Langley rolled down his sleeves and reached for the dark coat he'd draped over the back of the chair that sat beside the bed. He slipped it on and adjusted his cuffs before he said, "I'm not sure, and I seriously doubt it's anything to worry about, Lady Barclay."

Her throat and mouth parched with apprehension, Devon sat up and slid her feet to the floor. "I don't understand, Dr. Langley. Is there something amiss with my baby or not?"

The balding doctor reached over and patted Devon's hand gently. He gave her a reassuring smile that didn't vanquish the worried look in his gray eyes. "Of course you don't understand. This is your first child; this is all new to you. And an old fool like me should be kicked for making you worry when I'm not positive there is any reason to be concerned."

Devon's heart pounded against her ribs. The doctor's attempt to calm her had succeeded only in doing the opposite. "Doctor, please tell me what's wrong."

Dr. Langley released a long breath and nodded resolutely. "All right. It seems your womb is tilted to one side. At the present time I don't see that this is cause for alarm, but I do suggest that you moderate your activities to a certain degree until the babe is born."

Devon didn't relax. "Are you certain that my baby is all right?"

Dr. Langley smiled and gave her hand another reassuring pat. "Your babe is fine. Just don't overexert yourself." He stood and buckled the flap of his medical bag. "If you follow my advice, you'll give Hunter a fine, healthy heir in I'd say about five to six months."

"Dr. Langley, does this mean that I can't attend Colonel Braggert's dinner party tonight?"

"On the contrary. I do suggest that you leave the dancing to the single ladies for the next few months, but visiting friends won't cause any harm. I just don't want you out horseback riding or lifting anything too heavy. Nor should you be upset. Tension is not good for you or the baby."

Devon breathed a sigh of relief. She had feared Dr. Langley would forbid her going to Colonel Braggert's. Such an order would destroy her chance to be a part of Hunter's life outside the bedchamber. It was her only hope of proving that she could fit into his life and be more than just the woman who carried his heir. However, she wouldn't risk the health of her child for any reason, no matter how much she loved its father.

Hunter's knock came only a moment before he entered the bedchamber. The strange expression that flashed across his wife's face before she quickly looked away from him made Hunter's heart begin to thump uncomfortably against his ribs with anxiety. Nerves already stretched taut from his desire to bed his wife—and his fear of doing harm to her or the baby should he succumb to his needs—Hunter turned his attention to Dr. Langley. "Is everything all right, Doctor?"

"Everything is fine . . . as long as Lady Barclay heeds my orders."

Hunter arched a quizzical brow at Devon. "And pray tell, my lady? What exactly did the doctor order?"

Devon glanced down at the hands she had clasped in her lap. She sought an answer that would reassure Hunter that all his fears had been in vain, and also explain the reason for Dr. Langley's orders without alarming him even further.

However, before she had a chance to answer, the doctor interjected, "I was just telling Lady Barclay that there was nothing amiss with her pregnancy at the present moment. I just want her to take it easy and not allow herself to become overwrought or overexerted. It's just a precautionary measure. Nothing more."

"Exactly what does that mean, Doctor?" Hunter said as a lump of cold dread settled in the pit of his belly. Should the doctor deny him his wife's bed, he knew he would go mad before his child was born. He couldn't live under the same roof with Devon and never make love to her.

Sensing the direction of Hunter's train of thought, Dr. Langley grinned. Young men who had beautiful young wives never changed. As a matter of fact, old men with beautiful young wives didn't, either. Chuckling to himself, he gave Hunter a knowing look and winked. "Very little, really. She can continue her normal wifely activities without worry."

Relieved, Hunter crossed to his wife's side and draped a protective arm about her slender shoulders. "I can assure you, Dr. Langley, that I'll see that she follows your orders to the letter."

Dr. Langley, his wizened old face beaming with pride,

cast a smug glance at Devon and nodded his satisfaction. "I knew I could count on Hunter. Since the day I brought him into this world, he's never disappointed me. He takes care of those he loves." Dr. Langley glanced up at the tall, dark-haired man. "I don't necessarily agree with your present politics, but, like your father before you, you're your own man and it's your decision to make. As I've said, you have closer ties to England than most of us and it's a hard decision to go against your family. As a physician I don't like all this fighting and dying, but as a Virginian born and bred, it's in my blood to support the patriots until the last breath leaves me."

"I understand your feelings, and I appreciate the fact that you understand mine. Many of the people that I once considered my friends aren't as generous. Some have threatened to burn Barclay Grove to the ground and tar and feather me in the process."

"This war is not easy on any of us. I've seen wife turn against husband, and son against father," Dr. Langley said, shaking his head sadly. He glanced back at Devon. "Heed my advice, young lady. And don't hesitate to call on me should you have any questions or not feel well for any reason."

"Thank you, Doctor. I'll show you out," Devon said, coming to her feet.

"Nonsense. I've been paying visits to Barclay Grove since before either of you were born and I think by now I can find my own way out." He glanced about the bed-chamber and smiled. "As I recall, this is the very room in which I brought Hunter into this world."

Without another word, the doctor made his way to the door. As it closed behind him, Hunter sank down on the side of the bed and pulled Devon onto his lap. His stern expression was unyielding as he tipped up her chin and looked into her forest green eyes. "You will obey the doctor's orders, won't you, Devon?"

"I have every intention of doing exactly as Dr. Langley bid," Devon said, uncertain of Hunter's mood.

"I'm glad to hear it," he said, and grinned that wicked grin that always made Devon's heart skip a beat. "And you're sure there is nothing wrong with you or the baby?"

"I'm sure," Devon whispered softly. The look in Hunter's eyes expressed his intentions far more than any words he could say. The doctor's assurances had freed him to surrender to the passion that sizzled through him like molten steel. Unable to wait a moment longer, Hunter lowered his mouth to hers . . . with an eagerness that took her breath away.

Devon yielded to the intoxicating kiss. The fever Hunter had started in the glade the previous day now burned white-hot as Devon wrapped her arms about her husband's neck and molded herself against his wide chest. She dug her fingers into the dark, gleaming curls, holding his head captive as she savored the sweet, thrusting tongue that teased her senses and made her shiver with anticipation.

Hunter moaned his pleasure against her lips as he maneuvered them onto the bed. His hands worked with such fervor that within moments they lay naked upon the satin counterpane. The afternoon sunlight bathed their bodies in warm gold as Hunter stretched his length out beside Devon and, propped on one elbow, proceeded to tantalize her with his hands. The muscles in his back rippled beneath his tanned flesh as he stroked her sensitive skin.

Devon's insides trembled as his warm, long fingers moved over her rounding belly to the dark glen at the apex of her thighs. She opened to him and arched her back as he delved into the dark, moist depths, stirring her senses until she lay reveling in the sensations his caresses created. Her gleaming hair fanned across the pillow in a wave of curling fire as she twisted and moved to the cadence he created in her blood.

The ancient rhythm throbbed and pounded through her,

making her body pulsate. She moaned her pleasure and bit down on her lower lip, fearing he would stop, yet knowing she would die if he didn't come into her soon. Unable to endure the torment, Devon stretched out her arms and wrapped them about Hunter's neck. Possessively she pulled him down to her. Aroused beyond the bounds of modesty, and driven by her need to have him, she captured his mouth as she pushed him onto his back and mounted him. She rubbed her swollen breasts sensuously against his chest, savoring the sensations like a cat, before her need to have Hunter's mouth upon her drove her to temptingly brush the coral-tipped mounds against his waiting lips. She gasped as he tasted a responsive peak. Her fingers bit into his thick-muscled shoulders as she moved to give him access to its twin. He suckled her as his fingers kneaded her soft buttocks and urged her to move against the phallus impaling her to him.

Devon moved instinctively, her tight young muscles capturing Hunter's flesh, caressing him until sweat beaded his brow and his body demanded release. The muscles in his corded neck swelled taut as he arched upward against Devon and spilled his seed.

Devon's climax exploded within her, shaking her from head to toe as she felt Hunter's throbbing release. She shivered as her head fell forward in submission to the ecstasy sweeping over her. A deep shudder reverberated in the very depths of her being and spread outward as she collapsed against him. Her hair spread in a silken mass across Hunter's chest as she lay breathing heavily, her heart pounding from the pure pleasure of their joining.

"God, you're wonderful," Hunter breathed, caressing the dark mahogany silk that covered them. "I don't know how I could have survived the next few months had Dr. Langley's orders included abstinence from lovemaking."

Devon chuckled as she rolled to his side and lay a graceful hand against his damp chest. She absently ran her finger along one rib as she said, ''I'm glad we don't have to find out, my lord.''

Hunter raised himself on his elbow and looked down at Devon. He lifted her hand to his lips and gently brushed a kiss against it. ''I didn't hurt you, did I?''

''No, Hunter. As Dr. Langley said, I can continue with my normal activities as long as I don't overexert myself.''

''Then perhaps you shouldn't go to Colonel Braggert's tonight . . . after this afternoon's exercise.''

''I feel fine, and a little exercise can be very beneficial for one's health,'' Devon said, and flashed Hunter an impish grin. ''Don't you agree, my lord?''

''I would have to be a fool not to agree, my lady. I feel far better now than an hour ago. Perhaps we'll have to try such sport again.''

Devon placed a restraining hand on Hunter's chest and wiggled away from him. She grabbed the sheet to cover her nakedness and shook her head. ''Nay, my lord. We have a dinner party to attend this eve and I must be at my best if we are to achieve our goals.''

A satisfied smile curved up Hunter's shapely lips as he lay back against the tousled pillows and watched his wife begin her preparations for their visit to Colonel Braggert's. He swelled with pride. He would never have dreamed when he'd first married Devon that he could feel anything for her beyond lust. But somehow, during the past days she'd begun to work her magic on him. The woman whose past had made him feel so smugly superior had vanished. In her place was Devon Barclay—a woman whose past didn't matter anymore. She was his wife and the mother of his child, and he felt fortunate to have her. By the day his respect for Devon and her strength of character grew by leaps and bounds.

The Barclay coach passed through the intricately wrought iron gates and rolled down the long drive that circled in front of Colonel Braggert's home, a brick, two-storied Georgian manor that he had confiscated after the signing of the Declaration of Independence.

Though he had not personally been confronted by any altercation, he justified his actions by declaring Williamsburg as a war zone. He told anyone who would listen about the dangerous position he commanded. He could very well be murdered in his bed by any of the city's residents at any time. Everyone knew that they were all in cahoots with the likes of Thomas Jefferson, Henry Lee, and George Washington, just to name a few of the radical Whigs. His feelings of eminent danger also justified his keeping guards posted at intervals around the eight-foot-high bricked walls that encompassed the property.

The colonel's residence reminded Devon of Newgate. She couldn't stop the involuntary shiver that passed over her as the coach swayed to a halt and the coachman opened the door and lowered the narrow wooden steps for Hunter. Hunter, his wide shoulders blocking the light, stepped down and turned to assist his wife. Instead, his sister took his hand and, seeing no need for courtesy toward the woman who had wrought so much misery in her life, left the coach with a toss of her lovely head and a flounce of her ruffled skirt. Eager to see Neal, Cecilia paid no heed to the rules of propriety as she allowed the footman to escort her up the flagged walk to the fanned steps. She didn't look back at her brother and sister-in-law as she entered Colonel Braggert's home alone.

Devon glanced at her husband's stormy face as he stood glowering in Cecilia's direction. ''She's young, Hunter. And she's still hurt by our marriage.''

Hunter, seeming to remember his wife and his manners at the same moment, turned to assist Devon from the coach. ''That is no excuse for her behavior. She's old enough to know how to act like a lady or I would never have allowed her to accompany us tonight.''

"Give her time, Hunter. She's never had to share you before."

Hunter smiled as his fingers cocooned Devon's hand warmly. "You sound like Elsbeth."

"Then perhaps Elsbeth and I have something else in common," Devon said, exiting the coach gracefully. Her tone was light, but the mention of her rival's name did little to ease the tension that had been mounting since leaving Barclay Grove. As in the old days in London, her nerves were making her stomach queasy with anticipation.

Devon drew in a deep, steadying breath as she took her husband's arm and walked at his side to the wide double doors that bore the colonel's coat of arms. She was grateful that her bouts of morning sickness had begun to lessen. She didn't know how she would have managed to make it through the evening with her pregnancy and her nerves adding to her stomach's restive disposition.

"Lord and Lady Barclay. I'm so glad you were able to come tonight. I've told our guests all about you and your recent marriage," Colonel Braggert said as Devon and Hunter paused upon the threshold to the drawing room, where Cecilia already held court with several uniformed officers.

"It is our pleasure, Colonel Braggert," Hunter said, exuding the charm that had saved him from the scorn many other loyalists had suffered at the hands of their neighbors. Proud of the fact that many considered Virginia the hotbed that had bred the revolution, its citizens didn't look with favor upon anyone who opposed their views on independence and supported the British. "May I present my wife, Lady Devon Barclay."

Colonel Braggert bowed graciously and accepted the hand Devon extended. He politely touched his lips against her skin and said, "A pleasure, my lady. I'm so sorry that my invitation intruded upon your honeymoon, but I'm grateful that you so generously saw fit to join us tonight.

Now please allow me to introduce you to our guest of honor.'' He proferred his arm to Devon after receiving a consenting nod from her husband, and led her toward the group of officers surrounding Cecilia. ''Colonel Sumner, may I present Lord and Lady Barclay.''

Anxious to make Hunter's acquaintance, Neal turned to Hunter—with only a polite glance toward the woman who paled visibly at Colonel Braggert's side. Wives didn't interest him unless he felt giving them his attention could be of some benefit to himself. At the present moment, it would be more advantageous to acquire Hunter Barclay's goodwill. His friendship was a necessary ingredient for Neal's plans for his future with the lovely Cecilia and her uncle. ''Good evening, my lord. I'm pleased to finally meet you. I've heard much of you from several of your friends in England. And I've been told by many that you possess a great deal of influence in this colony.''

Hunter's hair rose at the nape of his neck as he shook the hand Neal proffered. Every instinct he possessed warned Hunter to be wary of Colonel Sumner. He didn't recognize the man's name, but he knew he had seen the man somewhere in the past. However Hunter couldn't pinpoint the place or time. He didn't press the memory. Sooner or later it would come. It always did.

A wry grin curling up the corners of his full lips, Hunter said, ''At the present time I seriously doubt you'd find many of my neighbors who would agree with you, Colonel. Most Virginians believe in the cause of liberty, and I'm considered the thing created by the devil himself—a loyalist.''

Neal's soft laughter pierced Devon to her soul, shattering all the peace and security she had found in Hunter's world. She was looking at the man who had sworn to see her executed for her crimes against him.

Cold, icy dread careened down her spine and made her knees suddenly turn to jelly. The blood drained from her face, leaving her skin ashen. A white line of tension edged her pale lips. She gripped Colonel Braggert's arm for support. "Colonel, I feel slightly faint. Do you think I might rest a short while?"

"Of course, my lady. Would you like to go upstairs, or would you prefer the quiet of my study? The windows have been opened to let in the cool evening air."

"Your study, please. I'm sure I'll feel much better after a few breaths of cool air."

Colonel Braggert patted her hand. "I'll tell your husband that you are unwell."

"No," Devon said, shaking her head. "He's talking with Colonel Sumner and I would hate to disturb them. Please, just escort me to your study and then I should be just fine."

Colonel Braggert cast an anxious glance at Hunter before he did as Devon bid. He showed her to the chamber, paneled in dark, gleaming walnut, and quietly left her seated upon a Queen Anne settee near the open windows overlooking the river.

Devon lay her head back and closed her eyes. She had planned to pretend she felt ill to gain entrance to Colonel Braggert's study, but the sight of Neal Sumner had made it all too real. Neal Sumner's arrival in Virginia made her sick at heart. Should he remember her, he could destroy her world as Hunter's wife, her world filled with the man she loved.

Devon covered her face with her hands and pressed her fingers down against her skull as if to eradicate Neal from her thoughts. If she could succeed in putting him from her mind, hopefully he wouldn't exist in reality. And when she returned to the drawing room—with Colonel Braggert's papers securely hidden beneath her gown—Neal Sumner would have disappeared like the bad dream that he was.

"Please, let it be so," Devon murmured, and let her

hands fall to her lap. She took in her surroundings for the first time. She had to concentrate on the reason they had accepted Colonel Braggert's invitation tonight. Hunter needed the maps of the British troop movements, as well as any documents that might help the patriots to turn the war in their favor.

Drawing in a deep breath, Devon squared her shoulders and came to her feet. She resolutely crossed to the large desk scattered with papers. Neal Sumner might destroy her, but until he did, she'd do everything within her power to help Hunter.

She loved her husband with every fiber of her being, yet during the past weeks she had also come to admire and respect Hunter for his beliefs. He didn't have to risk his life to help gain independence for the colonies. He had enough wealth and family connections to turn his back upon them and accept his place in the House of Lords when his uncle died. But Hunter hadn't chosen the easy path. He was a man who wouldn't dance to King George's fiddle. He loved Virginia, the land of his birth, the land that would also nurture his children. And like herself, Hunter wanted them to be free to live life as they saw fit, to seek their own happiness, to choose their own future.

Devon flipped through the stack of Colonel Braggert's correspondence that lay on the desk. Finding nothing of interest, she began a thorough search of the desk drawers. Moments later she stood chewing thoughtfully at her lower lip, fingers tapping out a tattoo against the shining dark wooden desktop. Her green gaze roved over the room, searching every nook and cranny for any place that could be used to hide valuable documents. Spying a large painting that looked curiously out of kilter hanging over the mantel, Devon smiled brightly. Colonel Braggert was clever, but not quite clever enough to fool the Shadow.

Within moments Devon had the documents secured at the waist of her chemise. She dropped her gown back into place, straightened the painting so no one would suspect anything amiss, and then patted the slight bulge in front of her. For a brief moment she felt the same rush of excitement that she'd experienced during her robberies as the Shadow. The thrill passed over her and made her want to laugh aloud.

Recalling herself back to her surroundings, Devon quietly left the study and made her way back to the drawing room. She paused upon the threshold and searched the room until she saw Hunter. He stood talking with Neal Sumner. There stood the two men who had had the most influence upon her adult life. Her enemy and her lover. Both men were handsome and powerful, and both men had it within their power to destroy her in very different ways. However she didn't fear Hunter. He wasn't cruel or evil. He might not love her, but he'd never harm her for the sheer pleasure of watching her suffer. Neal Sumner would. He'd extract his revenge in any manner, just to prove his power.

The thought did little to bolster Devon's courage. It took every ounce of her willpower to suppress the urge to turn and flee Colonel Braggert's before Neal recognized her. She sought to reassure herself with the fact that as Hunter's wife, she would be protected.

"Well, dear sister-in-law, I see you've decided to rejoin us," Cecilia said, pausing at Devon's side. She fanned herself coquettishly with an exquisite fan made of tortoise-shell and satin. Her gaze roved over Colonel Braggert's guests as she spoke. "I had hoped you'd see fit to hide yourself away all evening since you obviously don't belong here with the rest of us."

Devon stiffened. Tonight of all nights she didn't need Cecilia's cattiness. She had enough to deal with knowing her greatest enemy stood only a few feet away—talking with her husband as if they were long, lost friends. Devon's tone reflected her mounting annoyance with the younger woman as she bit out between clenched teeth, ''I would think you'd have more to entertain you tonight than taking snips at me. Surely some of the young men here interest you? If you'd put as much work into being charming to them as you do in being mean to me, you'd have them all falling at your feet.''

Cecilia's narrowed gaze moved over the room until she found the blond head of Neal Sumner. She smiled smugly at her sister-in-law. ''I don't need to make myself charming to the boys Colonel Braggert invited tonight. I already have the man I want, dear, stupid, Devon.''

Cecilia snapped her fan closed, turned her nose up haughtily in the air, and left Devon staring after her in bewilderment. Devon watched her disappear through the glass doors that led out into the garden before turning her attention upon the group of men who had caught Cecilia's eye. Only two men in the group were young enough to interest a girl Cecilia's age, and one of those was Cecilia's own brother. That left only Neal Sumner.

A foreboding chill tingled a warning down Devon's spine and settled as a frigid lump in the pit of her belly. She tried to deny the implication of Cecilia's hint. The girl couldn't be involved with Neal Sumner! But logic won out over incredulity as reality settled heavily upon Devon's slender shoulders and made them droop with the burden of her knowledge. Somehow her sister-in-law had become acquainted with the British colonel and thought herself in love with him.

Devon glanced once more toward the doors and felt her heart go out to Cecilia. No matter what the girl had said and done to spite Devon, she didn't deserve to be used. Like so many others, herself included, poor Cecilia thought Neal Sumner was in love with her . . . when he intended only to toy with her affections to gain his own ends.

Devon clenched her fists at her sides as her sparkling

green gaze came once more to rest on Neal Sumner. Cecilia might despise her, but she was now Devon's family, and Devon would protect her as fiercely as she would Hunter. She wouldn't allow Neal, a man who knew exactly how to manipulate young women's hearts, to take advantage of a naive girl who was young and inexperienced and ripe for the picking.

Devon drew in a steadying breath and crossed the room to her husband's side. She had to warn Hunter of the danger Neal represented. He was a threat to the entire Barclay family. Devon touched Hunter's arm, attempting to draw his attention without attracting Neal's.

Hunter glanced down at Devon. She stood quietly, her beautiful young face pale.

Before he could say a word, Colonel Braggert broke in congenially, "My lady. I do hope you're feeling well now."

A frown passed over Hunter's face, quickly followed by a look of understanding. He patted the hand on his sleeve before he smiled broadly at Colonel Braggert. "Sir, I'd like you to be the first to know I'm to be a father."

Disconcerted and mentally calculating the days since Hunter's marriage, it took a moment for Colonel Braggert to recover his aplomb enough to fake a wide, congratulatory grin. "I'm honored. Now I understand Lady Barclay's earlier malaise. Let us drink to your future heir."

Colonel Braggert called for his private stock of champagne to be served, but Devon paid no heed to the activity Hunter's announcement created about her. She stood frozen in place by Neal Sumner's dark stare of recognition.

Her fingernails bit into Hunter's arm through the fabric of his sleeve and he felt his heart still at the look of terror that flickered across his wife's face. He followed Devon's stare and immediately recalled where he'd seen Neal Sumner before—on the witness stand at Devon's trial. Hunter protectively covered his wife's hand with his own. He had to get them away from Colonel Braggert's before Neal re-

vealed Devon's identity, or he throttled the man for being
such a bastard. He didn't know which he wanted the most.

"Colonel, I ask your forgiveness, but I fear Devon and
I can't stay to enjoy your generosity. She's suddenly taken
ill again and Dr. Langley was precise about his orders.
She's not to exert herself or become overwrought." Hunter
spoke to Colonel Braggert, but his eyes held a silent warning for Neal Sumner to keep his distance.

"I'm sorry to hear it," Colonel Braggert said, feeling
slightly put out by Hunter's leaving. He'd just ordered one
of his finest bottles of champagne uncorked and the man
had the audacity to refuse to stay and drink it—just because of some doctor's advice. Civilians! Braggert fumed
silently. They thought to do exactly as they pleased. However, his tone was conciliatory when he spoke. "And I do
understand. You must see that Lady Barclay adheres to the
doctor's orders. I would hate to see anything happen to
your heir."

"My sentiments exactly," Hunter said. "Now if you
will excuse us, we will find Cecilia and then be on our
way. Thank you for a lovely evening, Colonel. Soon you
must come to Barclay Grove and allow us to return the
courtesy."

"I pray your lady has a speedy recovery," Neal interjected as Hunter turned to escort Devon away.

Hunter glanced back at him, his own dark blue eyes
glacial. "I'm sure she'll be fine once we're back at Barclay
Grove. And as the doctor advised, I intend to see that
nothing upsets her in the future."

Threat taken and eyes glittering ebony malice, Neal
watched Hunter and Devon disappear through the doors
that led to the garden. He'd seen Cecilia's escape in that
direction a short while earlier and had meant to follow her
when Hunter Barclay's wife had seen fit to reappear.

Looking at Devon Barclay for the first time had made
his heart stand still. It had taken him but a moment to

realize he was staring at the little bitch who had injured him. Oblivious to those around him, he had mentally relived the horrific moment the burning coals had eaten away his flesh; deforming his hand into a useless club. For months he had wished that Devon Mackinsey still lived so that he could make her suffer as he had suffered. His wish had come true.

A cold, hard smile spread Neal's shapely mouth. He would have his revenge, and no one would stand in his way this time. No court, or influential husband, or even his hopes of marrying Cecilia would keep him from punishing Devon Mackinsey Barclay. And before he was through with her, she'd know ten times the pain he'd endured.

"I don't know why we have to leave because Devon doesn't feel well. You could have just sent her back home, Hunter," Cecilia said peevishly. She'd had about all she could take of Hunter's concern for the little slut he'd married. It was ruining her life. She'd had only a few words with Neal before Colonel Braggert had introduced him to her brother. Hoping that Neal would settle his business with Hunter, she'd gone into the garden to wait for Neal when Hunter had come for her. With the way things were going, Neal would never get the opportunity to conclude his business with Hunter so that he could openly call upon her at Barclay Grove.

"Cecilia, I've had just about all I'm going to take of your rudeness to me and to my wife. Since the day you learned of my intentions to marry Devon, you've acted like a spoiled brat. I've put up with it instead of tanning your bottom like you deserve. I thought that after a while you'd come to accept my marriage, but I see that you're determined not to even make the effort."

"At least I'm honest about my feelings. That's more than I can say about you, big brother. You act the perfect husband—when I know you only married her because she's pregnant, not because you have any real feelings for her.''

Devon felt the bile rise in her throat. She didn't want to listen. She knew all too well how Hunter felt and it sickened her to her soul to have it thrown into his face.

"My feelings are my own concern, young lady. And from now on you will keep your barbed remarks to yourself. What is done, is done. I've made my decision and you will accept it. Devon is my wife and the mother of my child.''

Cecilia flounced back against the seat and turned away from Hunter. Lips pouting, she stared out the coach window at the dark scenery and pointedly ignored her companions.

Hunter leaned back against the velvet seat and released a long, slow breath. The night had been a disaster. He took Devon's hand within his own and held it comfortingly against his thigh. He glanced at his wife to find her staring blankly at the opposite side of the coach, her lower lip held pensively between her teeth, her brow furrowed with worry. His own brow creased with concern. Dr. Langley had been adamant about Devon not becoming overwrought. But how could she not when she had come face-to-face with the man who helped sentence her to death?

"Everything's going to be all right, Devon. I promise you. I'll not allow anything to jeopardize our child,'' Hunter said softly.

Devon glanced at her husband and nodded. She was grateful for his understanding and the comfort he offered. And she wanted to believe him. However, she knew from the look on Neal Sumner's face when he recognized her tonight that Hunter was wrong. Everything was not going to be all right. Sumner was going to do everything within his power to destroy her, and he would do the same for anyone who got in his way.

Hunter put his arm about Devon and drew her close.

She rested her head against his shoulder and tried to ignore the angry glances she received from Cecilia. For tonight she was with her husband and she wouldn't allow anything to ruin their moments together, not even her sister-in-law's vindictive looks.

When the coach drew to a halt in front of Barclay Grove, Cecilia didn't wait for the coachman to assist her down. She threw open the door and was into the house in a blink of an eye. She sped up the stairs and slammed her bedroom door loudly behind her.

Paying no heed to his sister's angry departure, Hunter lifted Devon into his arms and carried her into the house and up the stairs to their bedchamber. He lay her down upon the bed and began to slowly undress her.

Devon didn't protest. She couldn't. His tender ministrations soothed the demons tearing at her soul and made her world safe. She reached up and gently laid her hand against his swarthy cheek, looking into his intense blue eyes. Hunter was her guardian angel. He had saved her life once before and he would do it again. There was nothing for her to fear from Neal Sumner as long as she had Hunter to defend her. He would protect her and their child from harm.

As Hunter unlaced her gown and slid it down over her hips, the crackle of paper broke through Devon's languid reverie. Reminded of their mission and the documents she'd taken from Colonel Braggert's study, a sagacious little smile tugged the corners of her lips as she sat up and retrieved the papers from their hiding place at her waist. She handed them to Hunter proudly. "I believe these were the reason for our visit tonight."

Amazed, Hunter unfolded the documents that showed the movements of the British forces. He stared down at them, slightly bewildered. So much had happened during the last hours that he'd forgotten the reason he'd accepted Colonel Braggert's invitation in the first place. Hunter looked back to Devon. "How did you manage this after the shock of seeing Colonel Sumner again?"

"I had help from Colonel Braggert," Devon said, and with a smile explained what had transpired while he talked with Neal Sumner.

"There are some advantages to having a burglar as a wife," Hunter said, and threw back his head and roared with laughter. Tears glistened in his eyes, then his laughter began to ebb and he looked at Devon with new-found respect. A crooked smile played about his lips as he relaxed. The laughter had relieved the tension wrought by the last hours and he felt once more in charge of the situation. Devon was his wife and he'd not let anyone harm her. Hunter tipped up Devon's chin and brushed his lips against hers. "My lady, I would stay the night at your side, but I fear you have made that impossible. Due to your cleverness, I have work to do. I must see that these papers get to General Washington as soon as possible. Mordecai will have to leave immediately." Giving Devon no time to answer, Hunter brushed her lips with his own once more and then left her.

Devon slipped beneath the sheet and lay back against the pillows. She curled on her side and hugged the pillow close, wishing it was her husband. She smiled contentedly, despite the shadow Neal Sumner had cast on her future horizon. Tonight she had seen a look of respect in Hunter's eyes and her hope of winning his heart surged anew within her breast. Someday, if given the time, Hunter might come to love her as she loved him.

Devon's eyes slowly closed and she slept, too exhausted to allow anything to intrude upon her slumber.

Chapter 14

Neal looked at Colonel Braggert as if he'd suddenly grown two heads. "What did you say?"

Colonel Braggert swallowed uneasily and cleared his throat. He made a helpless gesture toward the mantle, where the painting hung askew. "The maps and orders for Cornwallis are gone."

Neal's face flushed a dull angry red. "You're telling me that the orders I brought from England have been stolen?"

Colonel Braggert wiped his brow and sank down in the chair behind his desk. He nodded bleakly. "I'm afraid so. They were here last night before dinner, but when I went to get them this morning, they were gone."

"Damn it, Braggert!" Neal swore and slammed his fist down on the desk so hard that papers scattered in all directions. "How could you let this happen? You know how important those orders were. They transferred the power from the Northern colonies of New York and Pennsylvania so our troops could focus on Virginia and the rest of the South. The loss of those papers could very well jeopardize our position here in the colonies."

"I know," Braggert said gloomily, his shoulders drooping.

"Who could have taken them? Who has entrance to your private quarters?" Neal asked as he began to pace Braggert's study. A muscle worked in his jaw and he held his damaged hand tightly against his side as he absently rubbed it.

"I haven't the slightest idea. No one is permitted on the compound who could be suspect. And my servants are loyal as well. They would die for me."

Neal flashed Braggert a look that clearly revealed his doubts about anyone's loyalty to such an incompetent. "Surely there is someone who might be suspect? You can't believe everyone who comes here is loyal to the crown?"

Braggert shook his head and stated confidently, "I don't allow traitors in my home. I'm sure of every man, woman, and child before they cross my threshold. It's too dangerous otherwise. The savages in these colonies don't think twice before slitting a man's throat for their beliefs."

"Did any of your guests come in here last night?" Neal probed, eyeing the man he considered a fool. Neal didn't doubt for a moment that a Whig spy had infiltrated the buffoon's household and stolen the documents. All that was left was to retrace each guest's steps throughout the evening. Then they would have their traitor.

Colonel Braggert's face screwed up in a thoughtful frown before he shifted uneasily in his chair. He shuffled the papers in front of him and cleared his throat before he looked once more at Neal. "Ah . . . there was one that I know was in here."

"Who?" Neal demanded.

Colonel Braggert shifted restively in his chair and answered, "Lady Barclay. But I'm sure she could have nothing to do with the missing documents. She's the wife of one of England's most loyal subjects."

Neal's words came hissing through his clenched teeth as he turned on Colonel Braggert. "You damned fool! The woman is a convicted thief and you allowed her in the same room with information that could well win or lose the war for us? Damn you, Braggert. Have you no sense at all?"

Insulted, Colonel Braggert came to his feet, his own face flushing under Neal's censure. "How dare you speak to me in such a manner! And in my own house! I have done nothing wrong. Lady Barclay is the wife of Hunter Barclay, and even you are aware of his position here—as well as his connections in England. He is the one man whose loyalty I would never doubt."

"Then you're an even bigger fool than I first thought. Your Hunter Barclay is in this up to his traitorous eyes. He married a convicted felon, one who I personally had arrested and helped get sentenced to hang."

"You must be mistaken. Lady Barclay couldn't be the same woman," Colonel Braggert said, shaking his head in denial.

Neal raised his damaged hand and slowly unwound the white bandage from the scarred, deformed appendage. He held it up in front of Colonel Braggert's face and growled, "Do you think I could ever forget the woman who did this to me?"

Colonel Braggert's eyes rounded and he slowly shook his head. His shoulders slumped in defeat.

Neal jerked the white linen back around his clubbed hand. "Now get me a company of men to go with me to Barclay Grove. You may be fool enough to believe Hunter Barclay is an innocent bystander in all of this, but I know differently. In her thieving days, Devon didn't go after important military documents. She liked gold and jewels. The theft last night was planned by someone who knew the orders had been left in your care. And that someone wasn't Lady Barclay, but her husband—the spy."

"I still can't believe it of Hunter. He's never given me the slightest inkling that he supported the rebels."

"No one said Hunter Barclay was stupid," Neal ground out. "But he did make a mistake when he married Devon Mackinsey. Had he let her hang as she deserved, he probably could have kept making you and everyone else look like fools while he spied for the rebels.''

Resigned to the fact that he had severely misjudged Hunter Barclay, Colonel Braggert rang for the corporal and gave orders for a squad of men to accompany Colonel Sumner. They would go to Barclay Grove . . . to arrest Hunter Barclay and his wife as traitors to the crown.

Unaware of what woke her, Devon stretched her arms over her head and yawned widely before throwing back the covers and sliding her feet to the floor. A dull, crampy feeling settled in her lower abdomen, but still bemused by sleep, she paid no heed to the minor discomfort. She slipped on the lovely blue satin robe Hunter had purchased for her when he'd visited Williamsburg the previous week and padded over to the dressing table. Hiding another yawn, she settled herself on the stool. She ran her fingers through her tousled hair as she eyed her image in the mirror. Dark circles shadowed her eyes and her pale skin held none of the healthy glow that usually tinted her cheeks.

Devon lifted the brush and ran it through her tangled hair. She didn't wonder at her wan complexion after last night's encounter. Seeing Neal Sumner again had been enough of a shock to her system to make her pallid. She'd just have to take it easy for a few days and give herself time to recover. Hunter had assured her that everything would be all right and she'd not allow herself to doubt him.

A moment later, Devon forgot Hunter's assurances when Cecilia burst into the room, her eyes wide with shock. ''They've come to take Hunter away.''

Talons of icy fear settled at the nape of Devon's neck as she stared at her sister-in-law. She didn't want to believe what the girl said. Yet she knew in her heart that somehow the British had learned of Hunter's connection to the patriots. Devon's voice broke as she asked, ''Who's come to take Hunter away?''

Ignoring Devon's question, Cecilia narrowed her eyes accusingly upon her sister-in-law. "This is all your fault, isn't it? You're the one responsible for taking the documents from Colonel Braggert's last night and Hunter is taking all the blame to protect you."

Devon didn't wait to hear any more accusations; she sped past her sister-in-law and down the stairs to where Neal Sumner and several men held Hunter bound. Devon froze at the sight. Her knees went weak and she gripped the mahogany bannister for support. She didn't—couldn't—look at her husband as she addressed Neal. "What is the meaning of this, Colonel Sumner?"

A cruel little smile tugged up the corners of Neal's shapely lips. "I think you already know, madam. You and your husband are to be arrested for spying for the rebels." His smile deepened. "It seems I can't arrest you again for the crimes you were convicted of in England, but I can get you for this new one."

Devon's nails bit into the gleaming wooden rail. "My husband is innocent."

"Hush, Devon. I've already admitted that I'm responsible, but you knew nothing of what I planned, nor did you act as my accomplice."

Devon's horrified gaze shot to Hunter. How could he admit to treason? And how could he accept all the blame when it was her idea to steal the documents from Colonel Braggert?

"I don't understand," she said, her eyes silently pleading with her husband to tell her what he wanted her to do.

Accurately reading her look, Hunter said, "I've explained that I would never allow you to be involved in such a scheme in your present condition. My heir means more to me than anything else."

Devon glanced once more at Neal Sumner. He understood Hunter's meaning as well as she and was vexed at the impasse that it presented. He wanted to hang both of them, but there was little he could do to involve her if Hunter continued to confess to the crime. Like Neal, she knew Hunter's reasoning. He would admit to any crime to protect his child.

Neal's scathing gaze raked over Devon. Her pregnancy was very evident beneath the sheer night rail and robe that she wore. A muscle worked in his cheek. He was wise enough to know that even staunch loyalists wouldn't approve of him taking a pregnant woman into custody after her husband had already confessed to the crime and denied her involvement. Neal leveled his gaze once more upon Hunter Barclay. "You think you are clever, but you'll not think so when you're on one of our prison ships. From what I'm told they are floating hellholes that make Newgate look like a palace." He nodded to the guards. "Get him and the women out of here and then torch this place. It'll never harbor any more rebels."

Cecilia came flying down the stairs, her face stricken. "Neal, surely you don't mean to burn Barclay Grove? This is my home."

Neal's cool gaze raked heartlessly over the young woman. "I'm sorry, my dear. I have no choice. Had your brother not turned traitor, then perhaps things between us could have come to a better end than this. I'm duty-bound to dispose of traitors and their property in the name of His Sovereign Majesty, King George."

"Duty! I thought you cared for me," Cecilia said, heartbroken. She was stunned by Neal's cruelty.

"Don't be foolish. We could have gotten along well as husband and wife, but as for caring for you, my dear, that is silly. You were a means to an end and now you are of no use at all. Your brother's treasonous actions have destroyed your usefulness to me. I seriously doubt your uncle will even recognize any of his American relatives after he's made aware of this episode."

"You bastard!" Cecilia cried, launching herself at Neal

like one of the Furies. Claws bared, she raked his face before two soldiers managed to drag her away and imprison her arms behind her back. She still struggled against them as they led her, none too gently, out of the house and down the front steps.

"I'll deal with you later, bitch," Neal growled, glaring after Cecilia as he dabbed at his stinging face. No one marked him and got away with it—as he was soon going to prove to Devon Barclay.

Struggling against the ropes that cut into the flesh about his wrists, Hunter lunged toward the man who threatened his family, but the guards stopped him. He swore violently at Neal, calling up his canine heritage as well as the vermin side of his family tree. A stout blow from his guard sent him to his knees. He shook his head to clear it and muttered another oath. A nod from his colonel, and the guard clubbed Hunter across the back of the head, sending him into the black void of unconsciousness. He hung limply between the two men as they dragged him from the house and tossed him across the back of a horse. They hog-tied him, hands and feet, to the saddle.

Braced against the wall, Devon stood frozen in place, unable to move to help her husband or sister-in-law. Her insides felt as if a great fist were driving itself downward in an effort to push everything within her outside. She wrapped her arms protectively about her rounding middle and squeezed her eyes closed as she sent a silent prayer to heaven. A merciful God would not take her child and his father from her on the same day.

Devon found no merciful God. Bile rose in her throat as an unbearable pain clamped down on her. She gasped and her eyes opened wide to look into the dark, menacing gaze of her enemy. Neal Sumner stood smiling at her, enjoying her agony.

"Help me," Devon begged, her hand sliding over the smooth paneling at her side to keep from falling.

Neal laughed softly and sent the rest of his men outside before he closed the space separating them. His breath was hellishly hot against Devon's face as he said, "Help you, bitch? Nay. I'll not help you. You nearly destroyed me, and now I will have my revenge."

Breathing heavily, Devon moistened her dry lips. "Do what you will to me, but don't make Hunter and Cecilia pay for my crimes against you. They are innocent. Hunter was only trying to protect his child."

"Perhaps, but that doesn't change anything. He's confessed to treason and he'll hang for it, just as surely as you'll die here at Barclay Grove."

Devon sagged beneath a new wave of agony. It ripped through her abdomen and she felt hot moisture dampen her thighs. Tears of grief for the child she knew she was losing trembled on her lashes and then cascaded down her ashen cheeks in crystal rivulets of mourning. She slowly sank to the floor at Neal's feet. Her words were little more than an anguished whisper: "I'm losing my baby."

Neal stood over the woman that he hated with every fiber of his existence and felt no remorse for the small life he'd help extinguish. "It's just as well. And you can take heart, for you'll not live long enough to grieve for your little bastard."

Neal knelt on one knee in front of Devon and took her chin in his hand. He raised her face so that she had to look him directly in the eye. He smiled cruelly. "You managed to avoid the gallows at Tyburn, but you'll not cheat death a second time." He brushed his lips bruisingly against hers in farewell. "And when the house crumbles in flames about you, remember they are just a taste of what awaits you in hell, bitch."

Like an abused rag doll, he tossed Devon from him with such force that she couldn't keep her balance. Her temple banged against the edge of the stair and stars exploded before her eyes a moment before merciful darkness swept her up into its comforting embrace.

Neal stood triumphantly over the prone figure of his enemy. She lay at his feet, her gown and robe bathed scarlet with her blood. He turned triumphantly and strode from the house. He mounted his horse and ordered Barclay Grove burned to the ground. The soldiers lit torches and carried them inside. The fire began on the second floor.

Cecilia screamed and twisted against her guards. ''No, you can't. Devon's still in there.'' Getting no response from the man she'd so foolishly given her heart, Cecilia began to call for her sister-in-law. She received no answer. After several more attempts, Cecilia's cries finally ceased and she sat with head bowed, weeping quietly.

When smoke began to plume from the windows and doors of Barclay Grove, Neal smiled his satisfaction of a job well done. He had captured a traitor to the crown and had his revenge upon the woman who had scarred him to his soul. He glanced at the young girl he'd also taken prisoner. He had no more use for her. There was no evidence that the stupid chit had been involved in her brother's scheme. She'd be questioned once they reached Colonel Braggert's, but then she'd be released to go as she pleased.

Her brother was another matter. From Norfolk, Hunter Barclay would be sent North to a prison ship to await trial after the war was concluded.

Neal led the squad back down the drive and turned east toward Norfolk. He didn't look back at the funeral pyre he'd created. For him, Devon Mackinsey Barclay was now a part of his past. He'd had his revenge, and now it was time to look toward the future.

Mordecai smelled the smoke before he saw the dark cloud rising over the tops of the trees. Cold fear tore through him as he realized that Barclay Grove was on fire. Spurring his mount into a gallop, he raced toward the flames he could see through the trees. He'd come back across the woods separating Whitman Place from Barclay Grove. After delivering Hunter's message to Seth, he'd stopped in to have breakfast with Elsbeth. Never dreaming there could be trouble at Barclay Grove he'd taken his time, enjoying the morning with the woman he loved.

Mordecai reined his mount to a skittering halt and leapt to the ground before the animal came to a full stop. He rushed toward the servants who stood wringing their hands as flames licked greedily out of the windows on the second floor.

"Did everyone get out all right? Where's Hunter? Where's Devon? Cecilia? How did this happen?" Mordecai asked, grabbing one of the serving girls by the shoulder and swinging her about to face him.

She shook her head sadly, her large dark eyes brimming with grief. "The soldiers come and set the house afire. They took Mr. Barclay and his sister, but we haven't seen Lady Barclay."

"You mean to say you're all standing around out here when Devon could be inside? My God, you all need to be whipped to an inch of your lives for the cowards you are!" Mordecai swore as he jerked off his jacket and ran toward the watering trough. He plunged the coat beneath the water and then wrapped the soaking garment about his head. He made his way up the steps, but found the heat unendurable.

The sound of glass shattering overhead as the fire exploded the windows sent him to his knees. Sadly he acknowledged if anyone were still inside the inferno they were no longer alive. Mordecai started to turn away when he glimpsed the blue of Devon's robe near the foot of the stairs.

"Devon!" he shouted over the crackling fury, but received no answer. Not knowing whether she lived, but unable to just leave her to burn, Mordecai drew the jacket firmly over his head and began to crawl across the hot heart of pine flooring. Ignoring the blisters that rose on his palms, he raced the flames that crept steadily down the stairs toward Devon. Gritting his teeth against the searing heat that scorched him through his clothing, he dragged Devon into his arms and stumbled to his feet. He staggered out of the house and didn't pause as the timbers of the ceiling came crashing down behind him. The roof of the veranda trembled and sparks soared toward the blue sky as it also collapsed a moment later.

Unable to go further, Mordecai stumbled to his knees with his unconscious burden. His face burned red, he fought for breath, his singed lungs threatening to capitulate to the abuse they'd endured. Mordecai gasped and struggled for life as he collapsed into the dust beside Devon. In his throes to survive, he didn't hear the sound of horses' hooves and wagon wheels coming down the drive from Whitman Place. He was vaguely aware of Elsbeth's gentle voice as he was lifted into the back of a wagon, cushioned by straw and blankets. When the wagon was set into motion Mordecai lost consciousness as Elsbeth held his head in her lap and urged him not to surrender to the black-robed figure of death that hovered so near, just waiting to claim his trophy from the devil's handiwork.

From the deck of the *Black Angel* Roarke watched the unkempt girl wander aimlessly along the waterfront. Even from the distance there was something vaguely familiar about her. As she neared the docks, the image of a tiny girl he'd met only once before floated into his mind. The girl possessed an uncanny resemblance to his cousin Cecilia Barclay. So much so that he could swear it was her.

Roarke discounted the idea before it fully formed. Cecilia Barclay would not be on the docks in Norfolk, looking much like a lady of the evening garbed in the stained, rumpled gown that had seen far better days in the past.

Unaware of the strange looks she received from the few

seamen who passed by, Cecilia strolled along the waterfront, unable to decide what to do or where to go. She felt an urgency to get far away from this place, but for the life of her she couldn't seem to remember the reason that lay behind her feelings.

In a state of shock from weeks of incarceration and interrogation, Cecilia had managed to blank out the past hours.

Cecilia raised a smudged hand to brush a stray strand of windswept hair out of her eyes. She frowned at the red, rusty stains beneath her nails and wondered what she'd done to get so dirty. The same color splashed her gown across the bodice. Cecilia shook her head, unable to remember anything beyond her imprisonment at the British compound near Norfolk. Colonel Braggert had turned her over to Neal Sumner after he'd assured himself that she was innocent of treason. Her memory ended there.

The thought of Neal Sumner sent a foreboding chill down Cecilia's spine. He was the man who had shattered the safe, secure world that Hunter had always provided for her. It had come crumbling down about her like an avalanche, making her confront the war that she'd naively thought didn't concern her. Like an eastern gale it had stormed into her life and swept away everything and everyone she had loved.

Cecilia's lips trembled as she drew in a shaky breath and cast a frantic look about. Even Devon, the woman she had thought she abhorred, was now gone from her life, as was Hunter. He had been shipped out two weeks ago with several other men whom Braggert considered traitors because of their belief in freedom. Paying no heed to the direction she traveled, Cecilia continued to make her way along the pier and, suddenly, found herself confronted by a tall, rakishly handsome man who wore a gold earring in his left ear. Bemused, she stared up into the oddly familiar face and wondered where she'd seen him before.

"It is Cousin Cecilia, is it not?" Roarke O'Connor asked. He took in the soiled gown and the spots of what looked like dried blood that speckled the front of her gown and stained her hands and sleeves.

Cecilia's brow puckered in consternation as she tried to recall ever having met the man before. "I am Cecilia Barclay, but I fear I don't know you, sir."

Surprise made Roarke hesitate and he searched for the right words. The girl looked a fright, but she seemed not to notice. He cleared his throat and said congenially, "I doubt you'd remember our one and only meeting. You were little more than a child when I came to pay a visit on your brother at Barclay Grove. Even then you showed signs of the beauty you've become. Hunter should be proud of you. By the way, how is my dear cousin? Have he and Elsbeth married yet?"

Cecilia's eyes brimmed with tears and her lower lip began to tremble uncontrollably as she stuttered, "I—they—Hunter has been arrested and they've burned Barclay Grove. Devon is dead." A white line edged Cecilia's pale lips and the color slowly drained from her skin, leaving her ashen as the impact of everything that had transpired during the past weeks took its toll upon her. Her knees buckled and her eyes rolled back as she sank in a dead faint to the wood planking at Roarke's feet.

Taken aback, Roarke stood frowning down at the prone figure of his young cousin, unable to decide what to do with her. His first reaction was to walk away and leave her where she lay. However, he finally bent and lifted her into his arms. Face darkening with frustration, he glanced from side to side, as if to find a place to deposit his unwelcome burden, but seeing none, he gave a shrug and strode up the gangplank to his ship, the *Black Angel*. He couldn't just leave Cecilia lying on the docks, no matter how he felt about her brother. She was his flesh and blood even if the lordly Barclay clan didn't claim any kinship with him. And from the looks of her she was in trouble.

Roarke's expression hardened with the thought as he took the small flight of stairs that led down to the captain's cabin. He lay his unconscious burden down on the bunk he'd had constructed especially to suit his needs. Covered with a thick velvet counterpane, it was unlike most ships' bunks. The same width and length of a regular four-poster bed, it was strung with rope springs, and layered with feather mattresses. It served all the captain's needs for a bed, whether it be for sleep or sport.

Roarke covered Cecilia with a blanket before he turned to the cabinet where he kept his supply of spirits. Made of black chinoiserie and inlaid with mother-of-pearl, it had been a gift from China's emperor for favors rendered. Taking out a decanter of brandy, he poured the amber liquid into a cut-crystal goblet and slowly sipped the fiery brew as he considered the girl's outburst before her faint. If anything she said was true, then his dear cousin had for once found himself on the wrong side of the fence. It didn't matter about Hunter's guilt. They would soon teach him what it was like to be a man with no one to come to his defense. He would learn how it felt to be without the power of his family name and the fortune of the Barclay holdings at his command. Roarke didn't envy him the lesson though he, himself, had learned it at an early age from those who called him a bastard and his mother a whore.

Grimly Roarke tossed the last of the brandy down his throat and welcomed the burning sensation as he turned to the door. He needed the sunshine to banish the shadows from his mind.

He glanced back at Cecilia before he closed the door behind him. There was also the mystery of why his lovely cousin had been wandering around on the waterfront. When she revived from her faint, he would have his answers and then he'd take her wherever she wanted to go—

just as long as it was away from him. The Barclays, be they male or female, made him remember things he wanted to forget, things he had worked to put completely out of his mind, things that made the bile rise in his throat when he had to look into his past.

To Roarke's annoyance Cecilia didn't wake until the following morning. Exhausted from her ordeal, she slept the night through in the center of his down mattress while he had to make do with a woolen blanket and a makeshift hammock strung in the corner. Unused to giving up his comfort for any woman, Roarke's mood was already black when Cecilia opened her eyes and stared at him in horror.

"Who are you and how did I get here?" she asked, panic-stricken.

"Damn! I'm in no mood to mollycoddle you, cousin. I'm Roarke O'Connor, the black sheep of your illustrious family. And I brought you here because I couldn't easily have left you on the docks when you fainted at my feet yesterday. Now if that answers all of your questions, I suggest you get yourself up from my bed and make yourself ready to be taken home."

Cecilia frowned as she recalled their meeting the previous day, yet she couldn't remember any reason that she should have been on the docks in Norfolk. However, she did remember the flames that had swept through her home when she and Hunter had been taken by the British. Her voice trembled as she said, "I have no home. The British soldiers burned Barclay Grove last week."

"Then what you said before you fainted is true? Hunter has been arrested?"

Cecilia nodded, suddenly realizing she had no place to go when she left his ship. She said as much to him.

Roarke ran his fingers through his sleep-tousled hair, exasperated for allowing himself to become involved with the girl's situation. He shrugged one wide shoulder. "I don't know any more than you. But I do know you can't stay here. I set sail at the end of the week. Perhaps Elsbeth will allow you to stay at Whitman Place for a while.''

"Yes," Cecilia said, latching on to the first ray of light to pierce the darkness that had shrouded her life since Hunter's arrest. "That's where I'll go. Elsbeth and Mordecai will know what to do to help Hunter.''

"I hate to be the bearer of sad tidings, but if what you say is true, I doubt anyone can help your brother now. Few men survive the British prison ships. If lack of food or the guards don't kill them, then disease will.''

Cecilia clamped her hands over her ears and vehemently shook her head. "I won't hear it. Hunter will not die, no matter what you say. He can't. He has to live to make Neal Sumner pay for killing Devon and their babe.''

Roarke shrugged. He'd not argue with the girl. She was near hysteria, and he'd not point out that Hunter would probably prefer death to what he would suffer on board one of the five prison ships the British had anchored in the Long Island Sound.

He'd heard that men fought like dogs to get the few unsavory morsels of food their captors tossed to them. Vermin and lice infested the prisoners and dysentery was so rampant that they had to lie in the bloody filth because there were no adequate toilets. He had personally witnessed the disposal of the dead from the prison ship *Jersey*. The bodies had been callously heaved overboard at high tide. Unfortunately when the tide went out the gruesome, crab-gnawed evidence lay exposed in the mud banks.

No, he couldn't tell Cecilia what her brother faced. It might break the slender thread she seemed to have upon her sanity. All he could do was to get her to Whitman Place as soon as possible. Then he could wash his hands of the entire affair, just as the Barclays had washed their hands of him and his mother so long ago. He had far more important things to do in his life than to get involved.

"Then it's settled. I'll go rent a coach to take you to

Whitman Place while you make ready. I'll have Cook send up something for you to eat and some hot water to wash.''

"I'm grateful for your help," Cecilia answered honestly. There were no more little-girl games left within her to be played. She had grown up during the past week. The war had made it necessary.

A short while later Roarke stood absently stroking the muscular neck of the bay mare that the livery had harnessed to the buggy he'd rented for Cecilia. However, he made no move to leave the stable. He stood eavesdroping upon the conversation going on in the stable yard beyond the wide stable doors.

"Have they found the girl yet?" the young private asked the sergeant as he bent to cinch the saddle of his commander's mount.

"Nary a sign of her. It looks as if she just up and disappeared into thin air after stabbing Colonel Sumner. We've searched the waterfront and had the roads watched for any attempt she might make to get back to her friends on the other side of the James."

"Sarge, I know it's none of me business, but what was the colonel doing with the girl locked up in his rooms? Colonel Braggert had already made sure she wasn't a rebel."

"That's a stupid question. And you'd know it, too, if you'd ever laid eyes on the chit. She was a real little beauty. And she came from good stock, too. I hear her uncle, Lord Barclay, has the king's ear."

The younger soldier chuckled as he tightened the cinch and flipped the stirrup back into place. "If I was the king, I'd not take too kindly to someone who had me ear."

The sergeant shook his head. "Why in hell I even talk to the likes of you, I'll never know. Ye don't have an ounce of sense in that thing you call a head. Now let's get going. Colonel Braggert is chewing nails because of Colonel Sumner's sudden demise."

"They were good friends?" the private asked, swinging himself into the saddle of his own mount.

"Naw. Colonel Braggert's just worried about his own position. It don't look good to have one of your commanders killed in his own bed, especially after losing such important papers."

"I see yer point, Sarge."

The two soldiers kicked their mounts in the side and rode away, leading Colonel Braggert's prized mare. A frown marring his handsome face, Roarke watched them go. He now had his answer about why Cecilia Barclay had been wandering the waterfront. She had killed the man that she'd said was responsible for her sister-in-law's death. Roarke's frown deepened with puzzlement. The girl didn't act as if she even remembered her crime.

Roarke ran a hand across the back of his neck and shook his head as he turned back into the stable to return the mare and buggy to the livery. He no longer needed a means of travel on land. He couldn't risk allowing Cecilia to leave the *Black Angel* until he had all the facts. Should she be caught now, she'd be hanged outright with no thought to a fair trial.

"Damn," Roarke muttered as he strode back toward the docks where his lovely young cousin awaited. Should she be found on board the *Black Angel* he, too, could be arrested as her accomplice. Deciding it was not in his best interest to have that happen at this juncture in his life, Roarke walked up the gangplank and began to give orders to set sail immediately. For now he would take Cecilia to where she would be safe. When he learned the truth of her guilt or innocence, he'd decide what to do with her. And damn it, no matter what he said, she was his flesh and blood and he'd protect her because she was a Barclay.

Chapter 15

Empty of all emotion, Devon sat watching the thick, gray fog roll in from the James River. Its misty tendrils obscured the landscape, wrapping the live oaks and magnolias in a caul that seemed to void the land of life. Drops of moisture beaded on the slate roof and ran like tears over the eaves to splash noiselessly upon the flagged stone walk that led up to the wide porch surrounding the manor house on all sides.

A grim little smile flitted across Devon's lips as she watched the droplets shatter against the stone. Like herself they still existed, but now they were merely fragments, tiny remnants of what had once been. Devon drew in a long breath and looked once more at the shroud that now cloaked the landscape. She recognized it for what it truly was: a death robe.

Devon accepted her fate, no longer possessing the will to fight. All of her life she had struggled to keep death at bay. She had stolen food as a child, then money and jewels as an adult to thwart it. She had cheated the dark angel when Hunter rescued her from the gallows at Tyburn Hill, but death would not be denied once more. Death had proven his strength over her when he'd taken first her child and then Hunter. Now he crept stealthily closer and she welcomed him.

Devon lay her hand against her flat belly and drew in another shuddering breath. It had now been six long, anguish-filled weeks since death had claimed the small life she had carried beneath her heart. Tears welled in her eyes. Tears that she could no longer stay. Tears from her past, tears that she had held inside throughout the years of hardship, tears she'd refused to shed. They now came in relentless torrents, brimming and spilling over in her grief.

Devon swallowed hard against the ever present misery that clogged her throat and made it difficult for her to catch her breath. She had lost Hunter's child, and now there was nothing left to bond her to the man she loved.

Devon closed her eyes against the memories that rose to assault her already wasted spirit. She didn't want to think of Hunter. He, too, was now lost to her. There had been no word of him since he'd been sent North to the prison ship and, in her heart, she knew he, too, was dead to her though Mordecai did his best to reassure her that Hunter was still alive. However the anxious expression in his pale blue eyes belied his assurances. She knew, as well as he and Elsbeth did, the reputation of the British prison ships. And though they had never voiced their worries, each feared the worst.

A trickle of tears slowly seeped from beneath Devon's lashes and ran unheeded down her pale cheeks. No. She wouldn't fight death. She longed to be gone from this earth where she'd known little since birth but pain. She wanted to be with those she loved. She had no one left in this life.

Absorbed in her morose musings, Devon didn't hear Elsbeth come out onto the porch. Nor did she glance in the other woman's direction when she realized she was no longer alone. She sat staring out past the damp, green lawns, awaiting the dark angel that hid in the cold, gray fog.

Her brow puckering with concern, Elsbeth stood quietly watching Devon for a long moment. She tried to think of some way to bring Devon back to life. She lived, but her spirit was gone. Physically she had healed from her miscarriage. Her heart beat and she drew breath, but that was all Elsbeth could say to confirm life in Devon since learning of Hunter's arrest and the loss of their child. She'd sat here on the porch all day long, every day, taking only a few bites of food when a tray was brought to her. In truth, Elsbeth feared Devon was set upon grieving herself to death. The sad part was that there wasn't anything Elsbeth could do to stop her. Devon's depression seemed to worsen by the day.

Elsbeth quietly crossed to where Devon sat and seated herself in a high-backed rocking chair. A floorboard squeaked as she slowly began to rock back and forth. When Devon made no sign that she even knew of her presence, Elsbeth looked at the despondent young woman and felt her heart twist. Dull-eyed and motionless, she little resembled the vibrant young woman Hunter had married. "Devon, would you like for me to bring your lunch out here?"

Ignoring Elsbeth's question, Devon didn't look at her as she asked quietly, "How can you be so generous to me after all that I've done? I know how much you loved Hunter and, were it not for me, you'd now be married and he would still be alive."

Elsbeth continued to rock slowly, her own gaze traveling over the lonely, gray landscape, her thoughts going to the man who now searched for any information that might lead him to find a way to free Hunter if he still lived. How she loved Mordecai and his loyalty to those he loved. She'd not change anything in her past if it meant she'd not find Mordecai's love. A flicker of guilt passed over Elsbeth. How could she be so uncaring when Hunter's very life was at stake?

"You're right, I've loved Hunter since we were children, but I hold no animosity toward you for what transpired.

And I believe everything always works out for the best, no matter how we feel about them at the time."

Incredulous, Devon looked at Elsbeth for the first time. Her pale, taut features reflected her disbelief as well as the strain of her grief. "How can you say that things always work out for the best? My child is gone and Hunter is dead because of me. Had he never saved my life, he would now be alive and Cecilia would be getting ready for her coming-out ball as a girl of her age should. Instead, she's being hunted for murder and will hang should they find her."

"Devon, you can't blame yourself for what has happened to Hunter or Cecilia. It wasn't your fault that Cecilia stabbed Neal Sumner. And it was Hunter's decision to help the patriots long before he met you. He knew the chances he was taking when he began spying. But like so many others who have given everything, even their lives, he was willing to take the risk to see Virginia free of British rule."

"But I'm responsible for his arrest. Had Neal Sumner not recognized me, Hunter would never have come under suspicion."

"Perhaps, but we knew from the beginning that it would be only a matter of time before someone began to question Hunter's loyalty. It surprised me that he wasn't suspected sooner. He moved too freely among both camps to keep suspicion at bay. Others who have continued to be loyal to the crown have been tarred and feathered by the Whigs, while Hunter managed to escape such a fate as well as keep Barclay Grove prosperous during a time when few loyalists could even sell their crops. Had Colonel Braggert not been such a fool, he'd have guessed long ago that he had a spy in his midst."

Elsbeth paused and drew in a long breath to ease the tightness that formed in her own throat as the thought of never seeing Hunter again crossed her mind. "And you have to remember, we have no proof that Hunter is dead.

You have to try to believe that he is alive somewhere, Devon. And that he will come back to you. We also have to believe Cecilia is also safe . . . wherever she might be.''

Devon's eyes again misted with tears and she turned her face away. She prayed Elsbeth was right and that Hunter was alive, though she knew Elsbeth was mistaken about him returning to her. Devon's fingers curled against her empty, flat abdomen. There was nothing now to keep Hunter bound to her, and she'd not ask it of him. She loved him too much to keep him away from the woman he truly loved: Elsbeth. He was Devon's soul, and should God ask it of her, she'd willingly give her own life in exchange for Hunter's.

God, let Hunter come back to those who love him and I vow I'll never darken his life again, Devon prayed silently—even as a figure rode out of the mist toward them. Catching only a glimpse of dark hair and chiseled features, Devon sprang to her feet and was running down the steps before Elsbeth could stop her. Hunter's name trembled upon her lips as the misty tendrils swirled about the rider, momentarily obscuring him from view. She came to an abrupt halt as the mounted figure burst out of the gray caul only a few feet from where she stood.

Recognizing Hunter's wife, a look of relieved surprise flickered across his handsome features. A roguish smile curled his shapely lips as he easily reined his mount to a halt. The gold earring he wore sparkled against his swarthy skin as he gave a graceful half bow from the saddle and doffed his tricorne hat and said, ''My lady, it is nice to see you are not dead as I had been told.''

Heart frozen and feeling far from alive, Devon looked up at the man she'd mistaken as her husband. Anger shot through her with the welling of disappointment and her voice filled with icy accusation. ''You're not Hunter.''

Roarke O'Connor gave a graceful nod. ''How astute,

my lady. But I've come to speak with you about Hunter and his sister, Cecilia.''

''You're not Hunter,'' Devon again said accusingly, grief descending once more in a tidal wave of anguish. She suddenly felt as if she'd lost Hunter a second time. She swayed unsteadily upon her feet, unable to endure the agony that ripped through the fragments of her tattered heart.

A man as adept on horseback as on the quarterdeck of the *Black Angel*, Roarke swung himself agilely to the ground and caught Devon before she collapsed to the ground. He lifted her easily into his arms. She didn't move, but stared blindly past the man who so resembled her husband.

''Take her inside. She's been very ill and doesn't need to get chilled,'' Elsbeth ordered, leading the way into the house and up the stairs to Devon's bedchamber.

Roarke gently deposited Devon upon the wide double bed and stood aside as Elsbeth covered her with a blanket. She tested Devon's brow for fever. Satisfied that she'd not had a relapse, Elsbeth murmured, ''Rest now, Devon. You'll soon feel better.''

Elsbeth, knowing nothing else to do for the despondent woman, turned her attention to the handsome sea captain. A gentle smile of welcome relaxed the harsh lines of worry about her mouth. She led him into the hallway and eased the door closed behind them. She was unaware that the door didn't close completely behind her as she looked up at Roarke O'Connor.

She had always liked Hunter's cousin, even when they were children and he did everything within his power to try to prove that he didn't need anyone or anything. Even at such a young age she had felt that he shouldn't be judged for the things in his past that he couldn't control and, when others had shunned him, she had tried to give him her friendship. It hadn't always been easy, especially in the last few years when his reputation was growing by leaps and bounds. But she tried to remember that the man whom many considered a pirate had once been a small, lost little boy who had stuck out his chin and taken the knocks—and had said be damned to the world when his heart was breaking. That had helped her overlook many of his actions. "It seems you do deserve your reputation with the ladies, Captain O'Connor. You do make women swoon at your feet."

Roarke shrugged and lifted one dark brow negligently, accepting the statement as his due. He knew his effect upon the opposite sex without being told. Elsbeth's smile deepened as she shook her head in amusement. "It's good to see you again, Roarke, though you're still the rogue you've always been."

Roarke affectionately embraced Elsbeth and his lips curled in a rakish grin. "Will you never change, Elsbeth? Here you are, taking care of the woman who stole the man you loved."

"I fear we're too much alike, Roarke. Neither of us will ever change."

Roarke chuckled as he looked down into Elsbeth's plump features. "Fortunately that news is only half bad. The world needs more angels like you, but could well do without devils like me."

"Rogue perhaps, but devil? I think not. You're not as bad as you'd like people to believe."

Roarke raised his hands in the air as if to ward off her compliments and lowered his voice to a husky whisper. "Please, you're trying to ruin my reputation." He cast a wry glance about the hallway as if to assure himself that they could not be overheard. "I pray you don't plan to spread such nonsense around. What would my ladyfriends say? It'd spoil all of their fun. It seems they enjoy trying to tame the wild beast in me."

"All right. I'll say no more. I'll keep my opinions of

you to myself," Elsbeth said, the banter leaving her. "All jesting aside, what brings you to Whitman Place?"

"I've come to speak with you about Cecilia," Roarke said, sobering.

Elsbeth looked up, surprised. "Then you know where she is?"

Roarke nodded. "Aye."

"She's all right?"

Another nod. "Aye. She's in a safe place."

"Thank God!" Elsbeth breathed a sigh of relief. "We've been worried to death. Mordecai managed to learn that Hunter had been taken North, but until the soldiers came here last week searching for Cecilia, we'd had no word of her. Is she well?"

"As well as can be expected after everything she's been through."

"Then you know about Hunter's arrest and the accusations against Cecilia?" Elsbeth asked.

"Cecilia has told me some of what transpired at Barclay Grove and about her incarceration at the British compound."

Elsbeth's heart stilled expectantly. "Did she tell you that she killed a British officer?"

Roarke shook his dark head. "No. She's spoken of nothing that happened after leaving Colonel Braggert's. From the way she acts, I don't believe she even remembers killing Sumner."

Elsbeth's heart went out to Cecilia. "Perhaps that is for the best. Were I in Cecilia's place, I wouldn't want to remember taking another human's life."

His male mind failing to understand Elsbeth's reasoning, for he had always savored his revenge upon his enemies, Roarke said, "From what I've learned of Colonel Sumner, he deserved killing. He did his damnedest to destroy Hunter and his family—as well as everything he possessed. The man even had the Barclay shipyards burned, as well as the vessels still in port. There's little left now of my illustrious cousin's empire.'' Ire flickered in his dark blue eyes. ''And as for what motivated Cecilia's actions, I seriously doubt that the colonel had further interrogation in mind when he took the girl back to his quarters. But until she remembers what happened, we can't prove that he attacked her. All we can do is keep her out of British hands.''

''Will you keep her safe?''

''For as long as I can. You know I've taken no sides in this war and it would do me little good to be found hiding a girl wanted for the murder of a British officer. That could very well put a noose about my own neck and no one is worth that, especially a Barclay.''

''Can't you end your war with Hunter? The past is dead. Let it rest.''

''The past is never completely dead, Elsbeth. As long as I live, I'm the skeleton in the Barclays' closet. Just as my mother was when she was alive. But that's nothing to concern you. That's between me and Hunter.'' Roarke glanced toward Devon's door. ''Is she going to be all right?''

It was Elsbeth's time to shrug and shake her head sadly. ''I pray she will. Since the loss of her child and Hunter's arrest, she seems to have lost all will to live. Hopefully Hunter will be freed after his trial and he can come home.''

''Hunter's been sent to the *Jersey*, Elsbeth. It's a death ship. There isn't much chance that he'll ever make it to trial.''

''For Devon's sake, and Cecilia's as well, we can't lose hope, Roarke. It's all we have at the moment. Mordecai feels the same as you about Hunter's chances of surviving. He intends to go North himself and help Hunter escape.'' Elsbeth's voice reflected her concern. ''Without the Barclay ships, he'll have to travel over land which only increases his chances of falling into British hands." Elsbeth paused and drew in a weary breath. "I don't know how I would manage if something should also happen to him."

Roarke placed a comforting hand on Elsbeth's shoulder. "You would manage, Elsbeth, as you always have. And no matter how you hurt you'd be here to give comfort to Hunter's wife and Cecilia without ever considering your own needs."

Elsbeth's face brightened with an idea. "It would be far safer and quicker for Mordecai to travel by ship. Roarke, you could help. You have a ship."

"Are you out of your mind? I have no intention of getting myself involved any further in Hunter's troubles. I've taken his sister to safety and that is enough. I'll do no more."

"Don't you understand that I'm not asking it for Hunter, but for me, Roarke?" Elsbeth said. "You've always known how I felt about Hunter. He is my family, as he is yours." She didn't add that she would also lose the man she loved should Mordecai die.

"Damn it, Elsbeth. Can you not realize that I haven't ever been a member of the high-and-mighty Barclay family? I'm Roarke O'Connor, bastard. And I owe the Barclays nothing."

"Please, Roarke. Forget that Hunter is your cousin. Just think of him as any other man who you've been paid to help. You'll never regret your decision. You'll find yourself much richer."

Roarke considered Elsbeth's offer and then nodded. "All right. Tell Mordecai to meet me at the *Black Angel* tomorrow night. We set sail as soon as he's on board. I'll take him North but, Elsbeth, I won't risk my men or my ship if it comes down to it. Hunter isn't worth that to me."

"I can ask no more of you, Roarke. Someday I pray that you and Hunter can become friends. I know he'll be grateful for all the help you have given him and Cecilia. I am.''

''As I said earlier, you've always been an angel, Elsbeth. You're truly the only good woman I've ever met.'' Roarke smiled at the blush that touched Elsbeth's cheeks at his compliment.

Unaware that the open door allowed Devon to overhear their conversation, Elsbeth and Roarke continued talking of their plans for Hunter's rescue. Devon squeezed her lids tightly shut at the rush of excitement that passed over her. It took every ounce of willpower she possessed to remain quiet and still. She knew Elsbeth, in her own way, was trying to protect her by keeping her ignorant of Mordecai's plans—because of the very thing Devon was feeling at the moment. She wanted to rush North as fast as possible and rescue Hunter.

The thought rekindled Devon's spirit, buoying it from the depths of the depressive quagmire it had been in since the death of her child. Renewed life surged through her limbs and her heart raced. When Mordecai sailed North on the *Black Angel*, she would also be on board. Devon was determined to give Hunter back the life he had given her at Tyburn. It would be her last act of love for him before she left his life.

Dressed once more as the Shadow, Devon crept up the gangplank and stealthily made her way across the *Black Angel*'s deck to the hatch leading down to the deck below. Using the instincts her days as the Shadow had honed to a keen edge, she crept along the passage until she found a cabin where she could hide until they were out to sea. Once under sail, the captain wouldn't turn the *Black Angel* back to port because of a stowaway.

Devon crawled beneath the narrow bunk and pulled the woolen blanket over the edge to hide her whereabouts should anyone enter the cabin before they set sail. The gentle rocking of the ship, the stillness of the cabin, and the lateness of the hour all served to make Devon sleepy. She strained to keep her eyes open and stay alert, but after several hours, her eyelids slowly closed and she slept, deep and sound. She didn't hear Roarke's orders to up anchor and set sail. Nor was she aware of the first mate who entered the cabin, glad at last to get some rest after his shift at the wheel in the wee hours of the morning.

The sun rode high in the sky when the seaman's eyes snapped open and his brows lowered as he strained to hear the strange sound that had awakened him. For a moment he had thought it came from beneath his bunk. Frowning, he ran a hand over his face and yawned widely. It must have been a rumble of distant thunder that had awakened him. He nodded and yawned again, ready to get a few more hours of rest before he had to go on duty. His eyes had just slipped closed when the sound came again. He rolled onto his side and slowly edged back the blanket to view beneath his bunk. His eyes widened at the sight of the figure dressed in black breeches and coat—with the glorious mass of mahogany hair fanning about her!

"All right," the first mate ground out as he grabbed Devon by the arm and pulled her from beneath the bunk, "who in hell are you . . . and what in hell are you doing in my cabin?" He didn't give Devon time to speak. He jerked her to her feet and toward the door. "I'm taking you directly to Captain O'Connor. I'm not getting blamed for smuggling a woman on board dressed like a man. I'm not getting keel hauled for something I didn't do."

Devon had just managed to collect her wits and dig her heels in as the door to the captain's cabin opened to reveal Mordecai Bradley. He stared first at Devon and then at the first mate. "What in the hell. . . ?"

"That's what I'd like to know. I found this girl hiding under my bunk. And I didn't put her there."

Roarke came to the door upon hearing the commotion.

Like Mordecai, he looked at Devon and then the first mate. His face darkened with fury as he glanced back to Mordecai. "What is she doing here?"

"Damned if I know," Mordecai muttered, his bushy brows lowering over his angry blue eyes. "But I'm damned well going to find out, and then we can set her ashore."

Devon raised her chin obstinately and jerked her arm free of the first mate's iron grip. "I'm not going anywhere, Mordecai—except with you to free Hunter."

Mordecai rapidly shook his head. "You're going back to Whitman Place, where you belong. I'll not have your life on my hands. I'm going to rescue Hunter, not get myself murdered by him for letting something happen to you."

"I'm going with or without you, Mordecai. That's up to you," Devon said evenly. She'd not back down, no matter what either man said. She would go with them—even if she had to threaten them with exposure.

"I said you're not going, Devon, and I meant it. It's far too risky. As soon as we round the cape we're going to set you off at the nearest settlement. This isn't going to be like taking the papers from a fool like Colonel Braggert. The games are over. This is now life and death."

"You can demand and threaten all you like, but I'm not changing my mind. Hunter is my husband and I will go with you."

"Damn! Don't I have any say in this matter? If you both have forgotten, I'm risking my ship and crew to help a man who despises me."

One pair of pale blue eyes and the other of forest green turned upon Roarke, waiting for his decision.

He lifted one shoulder and gave Devon a wry grin, amused that this woman thought she had the gumption to face British bullets for the life of a man who didn't love her. It would be interesting to see how long she lasted . . . before she crumpled like all the rest in the face of reality.

It was a nice thought, but things altered drastically when your life was put to the test. "I say let her come. She can remain on board the *Black Angel* while you get Hunter out. It might even be best that she is here if he's in bad shape. He'll need care, and who better to do it than his wife?"

"Have you lost your mind? She could be hurt or worse," Mordecai said, outraged at Roarke's suggestion.

Roarke flashed Devon a conspiratorial smile. "From what I gather, you have only two choices. You can allow her to come with us to keep an eye on her, or you can let her go off on her own, where she's likely to get herself killed." He raised his hands flippantly in the air. "The decision is yours, Mordecai."

"Damn stubborn woman," Mordecai muttered to himself as he nodded his agreement, then looked Devon squarely in the eyes and warned, "If your foolishness costs Hunter his life, your own won't be worth a farthing."

"Thank you," Devon said sarcastically. "I appreciate your support."

Another wry grin touched Roarke's shapely lips. "I hope you know what you're doing, my lady. For if you don't, then you could well be risking all of our lives—and I've not agreed to forfeit mine for my cousin's."

Devon looked at Hunter's cousin with disgust. "I know why you've come, Captain. And you will be well paid for your services."

"Aye, I'll be well paid, but gold can't buy life," Roarke said, sobering at the memory of his agreement with Elsbeth. Let the girl think what she would. The final arrangements had been between him and Elsbeth alone, and no one would ever know the truth about them. He certainly wouldn't tell Hunter's wife that Elsbeth could talk a saint into sinning or a man into giving his services for nothing. No, he'd never let that be known.

"Have you no loyalty?"

"My loyalty is to who pays my price, my lady."

"You're disgusting. Your own flesh and blood is imprisoned by the enemy and you have to be paid to help him."

"As you already know, there's no love lost between my cousin and myself. Your opinions are your own, but I suggest you keep them to yourself in the future or you'll find yourself in the hole like anyone else who insults the captain of the *Black Angel*," Roarke said, annoyed.

Mordecai held his breath, praying Devon would say something to fire up Roarke's temper and he'd set her ashore. The girl had been through enough without having to face what they might find when they reached the *Jersey*. The last he'd heard, Hunter was alive, but that information had been weeks old. Their entire plan might be for naught. Hunter could already be dead.

Devon disappointed Mordecai by tempering herself. She nodded her agreement. "I will keep that in mind, Captain. I will do nothing to jeopardize your helping Hunter. I owe Hunter a life, and I plan to see the debt discharged once and for all. Then everything will be settled between us."

The night was as black as a tomb. Overcast, the clouds hid the quarter moon and the multitude of stars that bedecked the sky. The sound of the waves lapping against the *Black Angel*'s hull seemed overtly loud as the small boat was lowered over the side. The rope ladder came next, thumping against the wood and sending chills down the backs of the seamen who feared the sound would carry to shore.

"If all goes well, the *Black Angel* will await you near Sandy Hook. You have four days to make your way across the island to our destination. And should you not be there as planned, we sail with the tide."

"We'll be there," Mordecai said as he swung himself over the rail to the rope ladder. A moment later he was in the small boat, ready to take up the oars. He pushed away

from the *Black Angel* and began to row in earnest. When
the frigate was no longer a black smudge against an even
blacker sky, he eased his pace. He mustn't overtire himself; he still had a half league to go before he reached the
Jersey.

Mordecai jumped with a start when the tarpaulin in the
end of the boat began to move. He squinted into the darkness, tense and ready to do battle. Hand gripping the hilt
of the knife at his waist, he watched as a small figure
emerged from beneath the canvas covering. It took less
than a moment to recognize his stowaway's identity. "Blast
it, woman. What in hell do you think you're doing now?"

Devon seated herself on the opposite plank seat. Her
voice was low and determined. "I'm going to help you
rescue my husband."

"Devon," Mordecai said, making one last attempt to
talk some sense into her, "you're risking Hunter's life. I
thought you cared for the man."

"I do, Mordecai. More than anyone will ever know.
Now row. I heard what Captain O'Connor said and we
don't have all night."

Mordecai's breath whistled through his teeth in exasperation as he again lifted the oars. He felt like tossing Devon
over the side, but he didn't have time to argue with her,
much less do battle. Every second counted if his plan was
to succeed. He had to reach the prison ship and be on
board just after the guards checked their prisoners for the
last time that night. Then he had to get Hunter and be off
the *Jersey* within the hour if he wanted to make the rendezvous with Roarke at Sandy Hook in four days' time.

He eyed Devon grimly. Thank God Elsbeth was nothing
like the tempest Hunter had married. A woman like that
could age a man by years in only a few hours' time, or
make a murderer out of him. But he also had to admire
her courage. Few women would have survived the ordeal
at Barclay Grove much less taken it into their heads to

rescue their husbands from an enemy prison ship. She and Hunter were made for each other.

The oars sliced through the choppy waters, taking the small boat toward the *Jersey*. Mordecai maneuvered the dinghy alongside the prison ship, avoiding the lantern light that spilled through the portholes from the officers' quarters and dappled the ebony water with golden flecks of liquid confetti.

He bent close to Devon and ordered in a hoarse whisper, "Stay here and guard the boat. I'll find Hunter."

Devon nodded mutely. She had come to help rescue Hunter, but she recognized the flaw in her own plans. It would do neither her husband nor Mordecai any good should she be foolish enough to board the *Jersey* without knowing anything about the placement of the guards or the whereabout of the prisoners. Remembering her own intricate plans when she and Winkler planned her robberies in London, she knew she would be useless and could only alert the guards of the escape.

Mordecai turned toward the rope ladder that had been carelessly left dangling over the side of the *Jersey*. His contempt was expressed on his craggy features as he set his foot in the first rung. The British were so confident that they were crushing the revolt they didn't worry about an escape attempt from the outside. Tomorrow they would regret their arrogance.

"God be with you and bring you and Hunter back," Devon whispered as Mordecai disappeared in the darkness overhead.

The breeze picked up and turned chilly. It lifted the waves and splashed sea spray over Devon as she struggled to keep the dinghy from bumping against the side of the *Jersey*'s hull and alerting the guards of her presence. Hours seemed to pass. Her shoulders ached from the strain of her efforts and her muscles cramped from the tension. The salty mist soaked her coat and breeches and she sat shivering from cold and dread. Fighting to summon enough strength to wrestle with the dinghy, another sound alerted Devon to the presence descending the rope ladder. He carried a large burden over his shoulder; the small boat tipped dangerously from side to side at his weight and Hunter's.

"Row, woman!" Mordecai ordered, glancing anxiously up at the deck. He'd left two guards unconscious and one— Mordecai gave a mental shrug—dead. This was war.

Even in the dark, Devon recognized her husband. Relieved, she picked up the oars and began to row with all her might. She wanted nothing more than to reach out and touch him, to assure herself that he still lived, yet she obeyed Mordecai's order. She wondered at the source of her new vitality when only moments before she'd believed she could fight no longer. Now, looking at the dark form slumped against Mordecai, she felt she could conquer the world. Hunter lived. Her love lived. God had finally seen fit to show her mercy.

Chapter 16

Devon crouched near the edge of the field. She absently swiped a hand across her face to rid it of the droplets of moisture that the morning mist had left upon her skin. In the distance, the weathered farmhouse looked deserted in the dull gray of the midday gloom.

Devon searched the surrounding area for any sign of life, but found none. Secure that they would be able to sneak into the barn unseen, she signaled Mordecai with a wave. A moment later he came staggering from the forest with Hunter draped over his shoulders. Concern etched a path across Devon's brow as she glanced up at her husband and then back to the man who held him on his feet. "I don't see anyone, but it doesn't matter any longer. We have to get Hunter out of this weather or he'll die."

"Yer not wrong there. Fever and rain don't make a healthy mix," Mordecai said as he gazed toward the barn. "We'll hide in the hayloft until I can find out if the farmers be friend or foe. In times like these, it's hard to tell the enemy . . . when they might even be your neighbors."

"I wish to God this war was over," Devon muttered as she lifted the sack that held the last few morsels of food they possessed. Mordecai had planned well, but he'd not taken into account the weather turning foul, nor that his contacts would be arrested by the British two days before he helped Hunter escape from the *Jersey*.

Since leaving the prison ship, things had not gone well

for them. The storm had come up soon after, tossing the small boat off-course by several miles. When they had finally reached shore, Hunter had been too sick to walk under his own power and Mordecai had had to carry him. His fever hadn't abated, but had grown steadily worse, and now, three days after his escape, he slipped in and out of delirium, muttering about General Washington and Cornwallis.

"I'll go up to the farmhouse while you go to the barn," Devon said, slinging the sack over her shoulder.

"Have you gone mad? You can't let anyone know we're here until I know for certain how things stand. If they're loyalists they'll turn us over to the redcoats. That would mean Hunter's death for sure."

"And if I don't get some medicine and warm food for Hunter, he'll die. Either way, I'll lose him," Devon said, undeterred by Mordecai's objections. She couldn't stand by and just watch her husband die without making an effort to save him, even if it cost her own freedom.

Mordecai glanced into the fever-flushed face of his friend and released a resigned sigh. He nodded solemnly. Devon was right. Hunter needed help or he'd die. He labored now to draw in a few ragged breaths.

Devon left Hunter and Mordecai at the edge of the farmyard and made her way along the fence to the weather-browned, board-and-batten house. She stepped upon the porch and was greeted by a chorus of roosting chickens. They squawked at her from beneath the eaves, where they'd flown to get out of the elements. They clucked and resettled themselves comfortably as Devon knocked on the rough-hewn wooden door. From the inside came the sound of scraping chair legs and then, a moment later, the door opened to reveal a young rosy-cheeked woman. She awkwardly touched her hair, patting a stray strand back into place. She eyed Devon curiously, marveling at her visitor's dress. She was unused to seeing a woman garbed out in men's clothing. After what seemed an eternity to Devon, she finally found her voice and said, "Ye must forgive me fer staring, but we don't get many visitors out this way. Won't ye come in out of the weather and have something to warm yer bones?"

"Who is it who's come to visit, Mavis?" a deep male voice asked from the interior of the house.

"It be a lady, Latham, but she's dressed like a man," Mavis said as she stepped back to allow Devon entrance. Her cheeks flushed a deeper hue and she flashed Devon an embarrassed look as she realized she might have offended her guest. "Forgive me, mistress. Me mouth oft gets me in trouble for I have a tendency to say what's on me mind."

Devon smiled. The woman's directness was a refreshing change after months and years of secrets. It touched the part of Devon that was tired of hiding her feelings, tired of pretending that she could accept living with only the crumbs of life. The loss of her child had forced her to face the fact that she didn't want to always live in someone else's shadow. She wanted and deserved to come first in another person's heart—without forcing them to accept her, as her grandmother and Hunter had had to do. She was now a woman, a woman who had lost much in life, and now it was time for her to put the past behind her and go on. Since the day she'd learned of Mordecai's plans, she had begun to see that by releasing Hunter, she would also be releasing herself from the bonds that had shackled her since childhood.

"Mistress," Latham repeated for the second time, "yer welcome to our home."

Jerking her thoughts back to the present, Devon smiled at the bewhiskered man who had risen from his chair near the fire. "Thank you for your kindness. But I must tell you that I have two friends who are in need of help. One is sick with fever."

Latham thoughtfully bit down on his long-stemmed clay pipe and drew in a puff of smoke as he looked at his young wife. Seeing the softening in her eyes, he nodded. Mavis was ever the one to take in stray animals or birds with broken wings. She'd no more let him turn this woman and her friends away than she'd let him kill the woodchuck that had been eating the vegetables in her garden. He glanced back to Devon. "Where be your friends?"

"I left them in your barn. I hope you can find it in your heart to allow them to stay there until the rain stops."

"Mavis can help ye with the fever. She's ever collecting herbs. Says they have healing in 'em."

"And they do," Mavis said confidently, already turning to the cabinet where she kept her basket of herbs. She'd learned the art of healing from mother who had learned it from hers. Healing was a gift that had been in her family for generations.

"How can I ever thank you for your generosity?" Devon asked.

Latham chuckled as he settled himself once more in front of the blazing fire. "Ye don't have any reason to thank me. It's Mavis who'll be doing the healing. I'm only saving me hide by not objecting. She'd skin my head of what little hair I have left should I turn you away," Latham said as he picked up the battered leather-bound book he'd laid aside earlier and began to read the scripture. "Do unto others as ye would have them do unto you," he said quietly without ever glancing up at his guest.

Guilt rose its weary head and nudged Devon's honesty. "Sir, I would also have you know that we are patriots."

Latham took his pipe from his mouth and nodded sagely. "I suspected as much or you'd have gone on into town where the British are camped."

As if nothing had been said, Mavis took several blankets from the cupboard and handed them to Devon. "Ye'll need these to ward off the chill in the barn. Ye go along now and I'll be along shortly. I need to brew a nice hot tea for yer friend. It'll help reduce the fever and give him strength.''

Holding the blankets close to her heart, Devon felt tears of gratitude well in her eyes. She gave Mavis a wobbly smile and again said, "Thank you," before she fled to find Hunter and Mordecai in the barn.

She couldn't believe their good luck in finding people such as Latham and his wife, Mavis. Even after she covered Hunter with the blanket and tucked one about herself while her clothes dried, she didn't let down her guard until she heard Mavis killing a chicken for their dinner. She knew then they were safe. No Tory would willingly feed a rebel—unless it was to the sharks.

The fourth day passed with Hunter still delirious from his fever. Mavis worked diligently to bring it down. She forced herbed tea and chicken broth down his throat while Devon bathed his heated skin. The *Black Angel* sailed south as Hunter began to respond to Mavis's medicine.

On the sixth day after his escape, he opened his eyes for the first time. Hollow-cheeked and beard-stubbled, he stared in confusion at his surroundings. He sought to remember where he was and how he'd gotten here as he turned his head and found Devon asleep on the hay at his side. Starved for the sight of his wife, he devoured her with his eyes, taking in her lovely features before allowing his gaze to move slowly downward to the sweet swell of her breasts pressed against the material of her shirt, and then further down to the smooth curve of her hips. He frowned as he took in the man's shirt and breeches, wondering why his wife was once more decked out as the Shadow. Puzzled, his gaze slid over her once more, passing down her flat belly to the long, shapely legs encased in the black breeches. Hunter's frown deepened as he realized something was amiss. His heart seemed to freeze as his gaze rested once more upon the lacings that held the cloth closed across her belly—her flat belly—the belly that should now be swollen with his child.

"My God!" he murmured aloud, his raspy voice reflecting the sorrow and sympathy for the woman at his side.

The sound of his voice awoke Devon from her light sleep. Immediately she came alert, raising herself on her elbow; she placed a hand against his brow to test it for fever. A wobbly little smile touched her lips and her eyes brimmed with tears of relief when she found it cool.

"Your fever has broken," she whispered, hardly able to believe her prayers had been answered.

Still weak, Hunter captured Devon's hand within his own. "Aye, my fever is gone, but what about you, Devon?"

"I'm fine. You are the one who has been ill," Devon said, ignoring the question in his eyes. She couldn't talk about their baby. Not now.

"The babe?" was all Hunter said.

Devon looked away and felt a renewed sense of emptiness where once her child had been. Her voice was husky with emotion as she quietly said, "I lost the babe the day you were arrested."

"I'm sorry, Devon," Hunter said, his heart going out to her. He wanted to tell her that they could have more children in the future, but the words died on his lips as she pulled her hand free and sat up. Now was not the time to speak of other children. The loss was still too new to be assuaged by anything he could say.

"You've been very ill, Hunter," Devon said, resolutely drawing the blanket up and tucking it in around him. She forced herself to brighten. "Do you think you feel up to eating anything? Mavis has made a wonderful chicken stew today. It will help you regain your strength."

Hunter frowned and made an effort to sit up, but the abrupt motion made the barn spin dizzily before his eyes.

He sank back against the pile of hay. Breathing heavily, and with heart pounding wildly against his ribs from the exertion, he fully comprehended how weak his fever and his imprisonment had left him. He looked up at Devon. "Who is Mavis and how did you get me off the *Jersey*? And where are we now? The last thing I remember clearly is thinking I would never see the sunshine again . . . because I'd never leave the bowels of the prison ship alive."

"Let Devon get your stew and I'll answer yer questions," Mordecai said as he clambered into the hayloft and settled himself comfortably on a pile of hay. "There's much that has happened since you were taken from Barclay Grove."

Hunter's gaze moved once more over his wife's slender form and he nodded sagaciously. Sadly he was already aware that much had happened to his family since his arrest. "I also have information that must reach General Washington. The folks spoke freely on the *Jersey* of their plans and troop movements. They never imagined any of their prisoners would live to tell what they heard."

"Then I'll let you two talk while I go and fix Hunter a dish of Mavis's stew," Devon said, already moving toward the ladder. She was happy that Hunter had regained consciousness and that his fever had left him; however, she needed time to collect herself. She hadn't realized how hard it would be to talk about the loss of her babe until he had asked her. Now she had to find the strength to speak about it as well as to find a way to tell Hunter that he would be free of her as soon as he was well. She feared both would break her heart.

Two days later Hunter sat sipping a strong cup of Mavis's herbed tea. Freshly shaved and feeling like his old self, he watched Devon and Mavis picking green beans in the small vegetable patch beyond the farmhouse. Fenced in to protect it from the cows and horses that were allowed to roam free, the small garden plot provided Mavis and Latham with fresh vegetables in season as well as enough to store in the root cellar for the cold months of winter. Unaware that they were being observed, the two women laughed and chatted companionably together.

Sensing a presence at his side, Hunter looked up to find Mordecai had paused to watch the women, too. After a few moments he glanced down at Hunter. "Have you told Devon that you intend to meet with Washington instead of going back to Virginia?"

"I intend to tell her this afternoon. Latham has gone into town to try to buy a mount for me. If he succeeds, I'll be leaving in the morning."

"Devon's not going to like you traipsing off when you're not fully recovered."

"I'm well, and it's imperative that I see General Washington. It's as we suspected from the information we stole from Braggert. The Continentals must move south and block Cornwallis's efforts to take the Southern colonies. Now is the time to move if Washington means to win this war." Hunter glanced once more toward his wife. "I want you to take Devon and return to Whitman Place. She'll be safe with Elsbeth until I return."

"I'll do as you ask," Mordecai said, himself ready to return to Whitman Place and its lovely mistress.

The evening was cool. A full moon crept over the trees and bathed the night in silver. Hunter and Devon sat quietly together on the bench outside the barn door, enjoying the serenity surrounding them. Mavis and Latham had already said their good nights and Mordecai had discreetly left them to themselves, feigning a wide yawn and proclaiming his need of sleep before finding his bed of hay in the barn.

Hunter draped a strong arm about Devon's shoulders and pulled her close. She lay her head against his chest and wrapped an arm about his hard waist as she savored the steady drum of his heart and the peace she found within his arms.

"Devon," Hunter said quietly. He didn't want to break the spell of enchantment the night had woven about them, but knew he had to tell Devon of his plans. "I'm leaving in the morning to go and see General Washington. I have information he needs and it can't wait. I've asked Mordecai to take you back to Whitman Place until I return. Then we can decide what we want to do about our future."

Devon didn't move. Relief and heartbreak mingled as one. His decision had opened the door for her own departure without having to confront him with her plans. And when he returned to Whitman Place, he would return to the woman he loved without being burdened by a marriage he didn't want. Devon squeezed her eyes closed. God! How it hurt to think of never seeing Hunter again. But she wouldn't change her mind, no matter how much pain it caused her. She had nearly cost Hunter his life, and she loved him far too much to continue to make him suffer because of her. He was a good man, a man who deserved to be happy.

Devon looked up at Hunter. The silver light of the moon bathed her face and revealed all the emotions she'd tried to keep hidden. Her love for Hunter glistened like diamonds in the pools of her forest green eyes.

"Then love me tonight to say good-bye," Devon whispered as she reached up and captured the back of Hunter's head to draw his mouth down to hers. Hungrily she opened her lips to his questing tongue and moaned her surrender as she molded herself as close to him as possible.

Hunter pulled his mouth from hers. Breathing heavily, his heart thudding with desire, he looked anxiously down at his wife. "God, how I want you, but I'm afraid I might hurt you so soon after the baby. Are you sure you're all right now?"

"I need your love to heal me completely," Devon whispered, pushing aside the grief that seemed to be a constant thing in her life since the loss of her child. She wanted Hunter to love her, needed him to love her, needed him to give her back her life.

Hunter required no further encouragement. He stood and pulled Devon into his arms, capturing her mouth in a searing kiss that sent their senses reeling. He swung her off her feet and strode toward the shadows at the forest's edge. He took the path that led to the spring where Latham had built Mavis a springhouse to keep her butter and milk cool. There, in the small moon-drenched glade, he set Devon down and stripped off his own clothing to make a bed for them.

Glorying in the beauty of his wife, he slowly disrobed her. He savored each inch of the luscious body he unveiled, caressing, kissing, and tasting his fill. She stood proudly before him, captivating his senses until he could control his desire for her no longer. His body throbbed, his muscles bunched expectantly as he lay her down and spread her legs to receive him. He gasped with pleasure as he sank his turgid flesh into her warmth.

Exultant, Devon moved with Hunter, taking him deeper within her with each thrust. She ran her hands down the back that was now marked from the British whip and cupped his firm buttocks, drawing him even closer. The friction created by the hair of his chest and legs against her skin only heightened the sensations flooding through her body. She reveled in them . . . and stored the memory away for the years when Hunter would no longer be part of her life.

Together they tumbled into the black velvet universe where only the hot, coursing currents of sensation existed. Their bodies throbbed, burned, and then exploded into the white light of euphoric bliss. Their cries of fulfillment mingled as one before Hunter recaptured Devon's lips with his own, once more branding her as his forever.

Devon lay in her husband's arms, her flesh still joined with his. She felt the sting of tears and fought to stay them. She failed. They coursed down her cheeks as she pressed her cheek against Hunter's bare chest and clung to him.

Hunter felt her shudder and raised himself above her. Concern etched a path across his brow as he looked down at her. "Damn, I knew it was too soon. I knew I would hurt you, but I was too selfish to stop."

Devon brushed at her eyes and gave Hunter a wobbly smile. "You didn't hurt me."

Hunter's frown didn't ease. "Then why are you crying?"

Devon's lower lip quivered and she swallowed with difficulty. She couldn't tell him her tears were for the years ahead, when she would no longer be in his life. Nor could she tell him they were also for the times in the past that she should have savored. But now it was too late to tell him any of it. At dawn she would watch him ride out of her life.

"For a woman who has always prided herself on not being a weepy female, I seem to cry a great deal lately."

Hunter bent and brushed his lips against her brow. "You have a right to cry, love. You've been through hell of late. There are few women I know who could have endured the loss of a child and then set out to free their husbands from prison as you did."

If they loved their husbands as much as I do, they would, Devon thought as she looked up into Hunter's moon-shadowed face. But all she said was, "How could I not try to help you? I owed you a life. If you will recall, you once saved mine."

"You owed me nothing, Devon. Only God can owe or collect on a life saved, not man. What I did, I felt I had to do. You shouldn't have been sentenced to hang because you were trying to keep your grandmother from starving."

Devon's eyes widened. "Then you knew why I stole?"

"Aye. Winkler had a tendency to talk when he was plied with strong spirits," Hunter said, and smiled at the look of longing that crossed Devon's face. He knew from how she spoke of Higgins and Winkler that she missed them dearly, considered them her family. And that was why he'd sent for them two weeks after their marriage. They should arrive in Virginia within the next two months if everything went well. But he'd not tell Devon now. He wanted it to be a surprise. Hopefully he would have Barclay Grove well on its way to being rebuilt by that time and she could have her family about her once more.

"I don't know if I ever thanked you," Devon said.

"In many ways, love, but you can do it again if you want to," Hunter said, giving her a roguish smile and wriggling his hips against her. His tumescent flesh pressed hot and pulsing against her moist warmth and she opened to him without hesitation. He plunged deep within her, burying his length in her satiny sheath. It pulsed, caressing him until every sinewy muscle in his body tensed with the need of release. Spirals of pleasure circled out from his belly, rippling, moving sensations that made his heart feel as if it would pound out of his chest. He gasped for air, drawing it deep into lungs that felt constricted by his desire. Unable to hold back the intense pleasure any longer, he began to move his hips to the music of passion flowing through his veins. Faster and faster came the tempo, until he exploded, spilling his seed deep into Devon's womb.

"Good-bye love," he whispered as he collapsed over Devon's soft body, cushioning his weight on his elbows and his head against her full breasts.

Devon held him to her. "Good-bye love," she echoed. But only she knew hers wasn't a momentary farewell. She had just given her last gift of love to the man who possessed her heart and soul. And now she would leave him.

Chapter 17

God! How good it felt to be back home, Hunter thought as he reined his mount to a halt in front of Whitman Place and gazed about the well-kept grounds of his friend's home. After delivering his news to General Washington, he'd set out immediately for home, though, due to Neal Sumner, he no longer possessed Barclay Grove. However, he still had his family and friends. Tragedy had visited them, taking his child and home, but he and Devon could have more children and the house and shipyards could be rebuilt. In his present mood, the future looked bright. The war had begun to turn in favor of the Continentals and he looked forward to the challenge of rebuilding what the war had destroyed of his holdings. It wouldn't be easy, but he would succeed. With Devon at his side, he couldn't fail.

Hunter dismounted, wondering at the lack of welcome. The front door opened to reveal Elsbeth and Cecilia as he stepped upon the porch. He glanced about for Devon as he opened his arms to his sister. She rushed into them and burst into tears. Gently he cradled her against him, stroking her dark hair and murmuring the words of comfort he'd used since she was a child, though his puzzled gaze never left Elsbeth. Her tense expression told him something was not right.

"Hush now, pet," Hunter said, setting Cecilia away from him. "There's no reason to cry. I'm home safe and sound. And I'm glad to see you are. I worried that O'Connor wouldn't be so generous as to bring you home.''

"Oh, Hunter," Cecilia said, weeping. "Roarke brought me back to Elsbeth, but he took Devon away.''

Hunter's expression went stony. His gaze snapped to Elsbeth. "What is she talking about?''

Elsbeth's shoulders drooped wearily. "Perhaps we should talk inside.''

"To hell with inside. I want to know where my wife is." Hunter's voice was a low, angry growl. Every inch of his tall frame seemed to exude menace.

"It's as Cecilia said. Devon left with Roarke.''

"I'll kill that bloody bastard!" Hunter swore viciously. "I knew when Mordecai told me he'd helped Cecilia that it was too good to be true. He helped my sister so he could steal my wife!''

"No. It's not as you think," Elsbeth said quickly. Closing the space between them, she placed a restraining hand on Hunter's arm. "Roarke didn't want to take her, but she insisted. And he felt it better for us to know where she was instead of allowing her to just up and disappear. He's sent word back that he left Devon in Charleston.''

His skin mottling with fury, his fists clenched at his sides, his face granite-hard, Hunter turned and marched down the steps to where his mount was tethered. Without a word he climbed into the saddle and turned the horse toward Barclay Grove.

"Hunter, wait," Cecilia cried, and made to go after him, but Elsbeth held her back.

Elsbeth shook her head. "No, let him go. He's lost his child, his wife, and his home. He needs time to think, to mourn and to be angry.''

As if driven by the furies, Hunter rode wildly up the drive to the charred ruins of his home. He reined the lathered horse to a halt and swung himself to the ground. He let the reins fall loose as he turned to look at the legacy bequeathed him by the man who wanted to revenge himself upon Devon. Charred black timbers stood at odd angles to the sky while the melted glass glistened in the afternoon sun. This had been where he was born, where he'd wanted his children born, where his child had died.

A muscle worked in Hunter's cheek as he gazed at the ruins through narrowed lashes. This had all happened because of one woman: Devon Mackinsey. God how he hated that name, how he hated her. Hunter gave a sad shake of his head and his shoulders sagged.

No. Even now he didn't hate Devon. Even now when he felt as if he'd lost everything, he couldn't hate her. Even now, with his world turned upside down and as dark as the burned-out timbers of his home, she still held some part of him.

Hunter drew in a ragged breath and felt hot moisture sting his eyes. His world had darkened when he'd been arrested and his home had been destroyed. Again his world had dimmed when he'd learned of the loss of his child. But through it all there had been a bright light that had kept him going: Devon. Devon—his little thief who had feigned the cockney accent and talked him into setting her free for a price of a kiss. Devon—the beautiful, regal young lady who had proudly claimed she was a thief, but not a whore. Devon—his innocent lover whose passion had seared him to his very soul. Devon—the woman he'd forced to marry him. Devon—the mother of his child. Devon—his partner against oppression. And Devon—the only woman he had ever loved.

Defeat far blacker than the ashes of Barclay Grove welled inside Hunter. Devon had been his life, but he would finally accept the inevitable. He could not force her to stay with him—any more than he could make her love him. The time for coercion was past. She had left him of her own free will and, no matter how it hurt, he'd let her go. She had suffered enough at his hand. She deserved some happiness from life. She'd had little enough of it in the past.

The night settled in over Barclay Grove and the man mired in despair. Elsbeth found Hunter sitting beneath one of the tall magnolias, staring vacantly at the dim outline of what had been his home. Sensing he didn't need the sympathy that her heart urged her to give, she braced herself to challenge Hunter and his love for his wife. "Are you just going to sit here all night or are you going to come back to Whitman Place and have dinner with us?"

Hunter didn't look at Elsbeth. "I'm going to do exactly what I damned well want to."

"Just as you've always done. Will that bring Devon back?"

Hunter's head snapped around and he eyed Elsbeth hostilely. "Elsbeth, we've always been friends, but stay out of this. It is none of your business what I do or don't do where my wife is concerned."

"Then sit here and mope, but don't expect any sympathy from me. If you love your wife the way I think you do, you should go after her."

Hunter came to his feet, towering over Elsbeth. "What does love have to do with it? She left me. She doesn't give a damn about me. I had to force her to marry me in the first place. And when she saw her chance to be free of me, she took it." He looked at Elsbeth with pain-filled eyes. "Don't talk to me about love."

"Did you ever talk to Devon about love, Hunter?"

Hunter stilled, searching his memory. He had called Devon his love, but he had never actually said he loved her . . . because until today he hadn't truly realized it himself. Shamefaced, he shook his head.

"Then you intend to let her go without ever telling her how you feel?"

"From where I stand, I don't have much choice. She's already gone."

"You could go after her."

"It's too late, Elsbeth. She's made her choice."

"It's never too late unless you're dead. And from where I stand, it looks as if Devon loves you."

"She has a funny way of showing it," Hunter barked sarcastically.

"She risked her life for you. If she'd wanted just her freedom she could have waited until you died on that prison ship or were hanged for spying. Instead, she went with Mordecai to help rescue you. She grieved for the loss of your child, but until she found out you were alive, Devon wasn't alive herself."

"Since we were children, you've always had a way of talking me into doing things I don't really want to do."

Elsbeth smiled. "I think you really want to go after Devon. I think you were just sitting here tonight trying to find a way to appease your male pride and also follow your heart."

Hunter smiled. "I think you are right, as usual. You know, Mordecai is one lucky devil."

"I'm glad you approve," Elsbeth said as Hunter walked her back to her horse.

The boat docked in Charleston in the late evening. Hunter, anxious to be on his way, stood by the rail waiting for the gangplank to be lowered to the dock. It had taken him longer to reach Charleston than he'd first surmised when he'd taken passage on the small frigate. The captain had wisely outmaneuvered several British vessels guarding the coastline by hiding in the inland waterways until the enemy sailed away. The entire voyage had been tension-filled, which had done little to help Hunter's own apprehensions about finding his wife.

Roarke had left directions to Devon's whereabouts, but that had been weeks ago. She could now be hundreds of miles away . . . or something far worse could have happened to her. A woman alone in a place torn by war could easily find herself in jeopardy. Colonel Neal Sumner was a prime example of the dangers lurking at every corner for any unsuspecting female.

"Sir, the plank's down," the seaman said to Hunter, drawing his thoughts to the present.

"Tell your captain I debarked. If everything goes as planned I should be back here before dawn, ready to set sail."

"I'll give him your message," the young seaman said, smiling broadly. He knew who Hunter Barclay was. The man owned several ships that made the international trade routes. That was his dream. That was what *real* sailors did, and he'd be extra nice to the man who might remember him sometime in the future when he applied for a berth on one of his vessels.

"Good man," Hunter said, already moving down the gangplank. From Roarke's directions, Devon had taken a position as a serving maid in one of the waterfront taverns. Hunter ground his teeth together at the thought of his wife serving other men. His blood had boiled when Mordecai first told him what his wife was doing. Now his blood only simmered at the thought.

The full moon shimmered across the indigo waters, illuminating the many taverns erected along the quay to garner every pence they could from the seamen who came into port to quench their thirsts for both the throat and body. Music and laughter drifted out into the beautiful night, marring its perfection and reminding Hunter that some man might even now be putting his hands on Devon. Again Hunter clamped his teeth down. A muscle worked in his jaw and his eyes narrowed as he spied the swinging sign identifying the Sandlapper Tavern.

Squaring his wide shoulders, Hunter checked the loaded pistol beneath his coat as well as the knife sheathed at his side. He'd come to find his wife, and if necessary fight his way out with her. And whether she liked it or not, he was going to tell her of his feelings come hell or high water or British redcoats to her rescue.

Arm in arm, two drunks stumbled out of the tavern, laughing in high humor at something one of them had said. Hunter watched them until they weaved out of sight, then he entered the Sandlapper. His dark blue gaze swept over the occupants of the tavern, quickly assessing the type of clientele it catered to. His first glance told him that the Sandlapper was frequented by ships' captains, colonial planters, and merchants.

Relieved that he'd not have to fight bilge rats, his gaze sought out his wife's mahogany head. His muscles tensed across his flat belly at the sight of Devon serving flagons of ale to several men. Again his eyes narrowed, their blue depths sparkling with annoyance. He didn't glance from right to left, but made a straight line to his wife. She glanced up as his shadow fell over her and her eyes widened in shock. She swallowed uneasily and cast a fearful glance toward the beefy-faced owner.

"What are you doing here?" she finally managed.

"What in hell do you think I'm doing here? I've come to talk to my wife."

"We have nothing to say to each other, Hunter. Now please leave before Mr. Garrett gets angry. He doesn't like for his maids to talk too long to the customers."

"Devon, I don't give a damn about what makes Mr. Garrett angry. I'm not leaving here without you. Do you come peacefully with me or do I have to carry you out of here? One way or the other, you're going with me. And my pistol will back me up." Hunter opened his coat to reveal the shining weapon holstered against his side.

"Let me explain to Mr. Garrett and then I'll go," Devon said, knowing full well Hunter would use the weapon should anyone try to stop him from taking her away. She wanted no more blood shed because of her.

Hunter's hand wrapped around her upper arm. "If you tell him anything, tell him you won't be back. No matter what you say or how you feel after we've talked, I'll not allow you to come back here. You deserve better, Devon. And I'll see you have it."

Devon, her heart beating with excitement, glanced once at the tavern owner and then walked out of the Sandlapper with her husband. She had hated every moment she'd spent in the place, but it had been the only work she could find after leaving the *Black Angel*. She had gone each day, hoping to find better employment, but with the state of uncertainty that existed in Charleston at the moment, she'd had no other option but to stay at the Sandlapper if she wanted to continue to eat.

Hunter didn't speak as he led her down the cobbled street to the sandy thoroughfare that wound its way along the shoreline. The waters, dappled with silver moonlight, lapped at the white beach. The beauty of the night took Devon's breath away and reminded her of another beach, and another night, that she'd spent in Hunter's arms. It had been the night her child had been conceived. She was certain that had been the time because of the feelings she'd experienced, as well as the knowledge that afterward, Hunter hadn't touched her again until they were married. Devon paused, unable to go on with the memories of that night assaulting her senses. She looked up at Hunter with eyes strained with the emotions that she'd tried to ignore, emotions that had kept her wrapped in webs of confusion and heartache.

Hunter looked down into her wan features, noticing the strain for the first time. His voice was soft and filled with pent-up emotions as he said, "Devon, I didn't come here to force you to come back with me. I came here for only one reason."

Devon remained mute, silently fighting her own need to throw herself in Hunter's arms and say be damned to all her decisions. During the past weeks she'd thought that she couldn't love him as much as she'd thought while at Barclay Grove, but now she knew that she loved him even more. And it was tearing her apart.

Hunter moistened his suddenly dry lips. Apprehension filled him. He swallowed and cleared his throat. "Devon, I couldn't let you leave my life without first telling you that I love you." Saying the words made it easier and he opened his heart. "I didn't realize it, but I've loved you since the first night I set eyes on you in London. I had had an inkling of it several times before Elsbeth made me face the truth, but I was too stubborn and too big a fool to accept what my own heart was telling me. And I pray you can forgive me for all the tragedy and pain I've caused you."

Devon felt the world tremble beneath her feet. The man who held her heart and soul was telling her that he also loved her. It took a moment for her to react. She gaped up at Hunter, tears brimming in her wide, wonder-filled eyes. "You love me?" was all she could say.

"More than you'll ever know."

"But what about Elsbeth? She is the woman you have always loved. She's the woman you would have married had I not conceived your child. And she loves you deeply. She's told me so."

Hunter smiled tenderly down at Devon and placed both hands on her shoulders. His dark blue gaze met her forest green eyes, silently confirming the words he spoke. "Elsbeth is like a sister to me. And as far as her feelings for me are concerned, you don't have to worry. It seems while we were getting ourselves married, Elsbeth and Mordecai were also discovering love. They will marry in the spring."

His fingers tightened on Devon's shoulders and he gave her a light shake. "Woman, can't you understand what I'm saying? It's you I love and no other. I want you as my wife. I want you to come back to Virginia and help me rebuild Barclay Grove for our children.''

''Hunter, I'm afraid to believe what my heart has wanted to hear for so many months,'' Devon said, her voice breaking. ''I can't be second choice. I have to know that you love me and only me.''

Hunter released an exasperated breath as he drew Devon against him. His mouth claimed hers, showing her rather than telling her of his feelings. He knew no other way to make her understand that there could never be another woman to fill his heart and soul like she had done. She was a part of him, a part that he treasured beyond anything he owned. Battles still waged across the land, but the woman in his arms had given him the freedom to love and in return *be* loved. She had shown him that life was neither black nor white. It was created out of a mixture of textures and colors, like a vibrant tapestry woven of the same strong, silken threads that had bound his heart to Devon's and made him a whole man, not just a shadow.

Hunter's silent demand for her love and then his husky, whispered plea of, ''Love me, Devon. I need you to love me,'' left Devon unable to fight any longer. She wrapped her arms about his strong, corded neck and surrendered her heart. Together, they would build a new Barclay Grove and help build a new America for their children.

They sank to the moon-drenched sand. Tonight they would begin to build a new family. . . . A short time later, they lay in each other's arms, sated—and content that they had accomplished what they had set out to do. And fully aware if they hadn't, they had years together to work on it.

A personal note from the author:

Dear Reader,
  Thank you for reading my books. I hope I have given you a few hours of adventure and pleasure with my work. I, myself, love to read as well as write. I find so much pleasure in reading that I can't abide the thought of anyone not being able to experience the same joy that I have found through the years with books. And I would ask each of you to do our country a favor. If you know people who can't read or need help to improve their reading, please encourage them to attend one of the many programs available to help them learn to read.

          Best Wishes and Happy Reading,

          Cordia Byers

                    Cordia Byers